The Worl
Stars

Edited by Chris Butler

Published by Deborah Jay, 2015.

The World and the Stars

Edited by Chris Butler

First published 2015

Cover art by Deirdre Counihan

This book is dedicated to

Peter T. Garratt

Table of Contents

Acknowledgements

"Foreword: Turning the Cards" is published here for the first time. Copyright Mike Ashley 2015.

"Introduction" is published here for the first time. Copyright Chris Butler 2015.

"Mitochondrial Mom" is published here for the first time. Copyright John Frizell 2015.

"Ondralume" first published in *The Magazine of Fantasy & Science Fiction*, August 1992. Copyright Tanith Lee 1992.

"Substitutes" first published in *Daily Science Fiction*, February 2013. Copyright Colin P. Davies 2013.

"Glittering Spires" first published in *Scheherazade #9*, 1994. Copyright Elizabeth Counihan 1994.

"From the Point of View of the Dog" first published in *Scheherazade #27*, January 2004. Copyright Daniel Kaysen 2004.

"MS Found in a Kangian Wintercamp" is published here for the first time. Copyright Sue Thomason 2015.

"The Battery Caverns" first published as "Under the Overlight" in *Interzone #165*, March 2001. Copyright Nigel Brown 2001.

"Dusking" first published in *Lady Churchill's Rosebud Wristlet #24* (Small Beer Press), August 2009. Copyright Liz Williams 2009.

"Golty's Burrow" is published here for the first time. Copyright Paul Laville 2015.

Foreword: Turning the Cards

Mike Ashley

There's an art to compiling an anthology. Maybe a bit of science, but it's mostly art. Because it requires imagination, understanding and, above all, an ability to know what works.

Does that sound like an art?

Anyway, the point is that putting together an anthology is not simply a case of bundling up a bunch of stories and handing them over like a trolley load of shopping. It's like a painting, or a building, or a sumptuously cooked meal. It has to look right, feel right and, yes, taste right. Everything has to be in the right place, which doesn't necessarily mean in the right order. Things can be deliberately out of place because that makes them memorable...

In fact, all the stories have to be memorable but in such a way that they don't clash with one another. If the book is put together with the right degree of imagination and vision and panache then the whole is always bigger than the sum of the parts.

And for that you need (here comes the 'bleeding obvious') good stories, good writers and (a little less obvious) diversity.

Diversity is difficult. Some stories may need to contrast with others, or complement others or quite simply surprise the reader, make them laugh, cry or open their eyes with wonder.

I say all of this, not just because this book has been compiled with all the right loving care, attention and imagination — that goes without saying — but because of to whom this book is dedicated: Peter T. Garratt.

Peter died in 2004 at the age of 54. It's long enough ago that some may not remember him or know of his work. He was, by profession, a clinical psychologist, but by vocation he was a wordsmith, a storyteller, an ideasmith and a maker of worlds. His profession helped him understand the workings of the human mind but his vocation allowed him to develop this into intriguing tales of human interaction and achievement. He sold some thirty or so stories — one is included in this volume — and what is most noticeable about them is their diversity. He had a fascination for ancient legends, particularly those of King Arthur, and that was how I first encountered him, when he contributed to one of the Arthurian anthologies I was compiling. That's how I got to know him, and it grew into a friendship.

One of the pleasures of compiling an anthology is working with the contributors. There were many occasions, when I was planning a new volume, that Peter and I would knock ideas around to see if a story might develop. And it did not matter what was the subject of the anthology, Peter usually had the knowledge and imagination to create a suitable story, whether it was an Arthurian legend, an impossible crime, a tale of the Napoleonic Wars or, and this one proved to be my favourite of all his creations, an insight into the Charge of the Light Brigade.

Now there's diversity for you, and I knew I could count on Peter producing a story for any of my anthologies that would be original, distinctive, entertaining and often educational.

Peter started and used to run the Montpelier Writers' Group in Brighton, and many of the members of that group, past and present, have contributed to this anthology. So, I like to think that in addition to their writing talent, imagination and individuality, there is also a little bit of Peter — that part of Peter from which I benefited in our phone calls, creating ideas and then reworking them into something unusual, appealing and above all different.

It may seem hard to believe that there can be so many stories in the world, thousands upon thousands, and yet each can be either subtly or radically different, like so many millions of snowflakes. How can the human imagination create so much diversity?

That, of course, is the skill of the master storyteller, and the wonder of it is that that skill can be passed on, through the ability to share thoughts either through the story itself — we've all read stories that have inspired us — or through forums like a Writers' Group or Workshop. It is through such sharing that diversity emerges.

That sounds like a paradox, but it isn't. Because the ability of the human imagination is limitless, just like the World and the Stars.

And to harness that imagination, and bring it together in a volume such as this is definitely an art. Isn't it?

Introduction

Ask any number of writers what they most enjoy about the writing process, and you will get a different answer from each one. One will say they love the rush of the first draft. Another will say they love the editing process, or researching, or creating characters, or structure. They might love to entertain, seek to understand the world around them, or even find in writing a kind of therapy. Perhaps there are as many different answers as there are stars in the sky.

The point is, there is always something that drives a writer on, that makes the enterprise not simply worthwhile but essential to their life. For me, the most satisfying thing is the end result. Until the story is completely written it is a problem of sorts. How can something that is incomplete be considered otherwise? It requires work. It requires modification. It requires me to sit in front of a computer at the end of a long day and work on it when it would be so much easier to do... almost anything else.

But when it's done! Then I can enjoy a certain satisfaction. It did not exist before but now it does. I imagine architects or builders or painters must feel similarly. Perhaps anyone who ever transformed a garden or decorated a room will recognise the feeling.

And in turning my hand to editing this anthology, I discovered I enjoyed it in entirely the same way. It is the end result that is satisfying, the fact that the book exists where it did not before, and now the world would not seem right without it. Along the way there were problems to solve. Technical headaches such as applying a consistent copyedit to the stories across the whole book, without messing with an individual story too much. Checking with a writer on nitty-gritty details: Did you really mean to say *this* on page six?

For the purposes of this anthology, the distinction between science fiction and fantasy did not interest me greatly. The imagination of the author is paramount, their purpose in telling the story, and the craft with which they execute their idea. One thing I felt compelled to contribute was a paragraph to introduce each story, to set the tone for the reader before they launch in. In a book as diverse as this one, I think it is helpful for the reader to know there is a guiding hand at work, to feel a sense of purpose in the way the stories have been arranged and that the journey is one for which there was indeed a map and a plan.

To do this required the editor to know the stories very well, to have read each one many times, and to have visualised how each story builds on the one before, or is an antidote to it, or otherwise satisfies in the way any good journey does.

The title, *The World and the Stars,* was deliberately chosen to allow for almost any kind of science fiction or fantasy story, and I wanted the book to be a showcase for the infinite places genre stories can go. So we have alternate Earths, distant worlds, dystopian futures, historical fantasy, and more.

Hopefully the reader will experience that sense of wonder as they travel from each "world" to the next. Forwards and back through time, to worlds near or far away, and to worlds where life is strange, and unexpected.

John Frizell's story takes us to the future, a security checkpoint, and the compound beyond. Tanith Lee's story contrasts the vast grandeur of the universe against the smallness of those who inhabit it. And in Colin P. Davies' dark SF tale, mysterious doppelgangers pursue a father and daughter, but to what end?

Elizabeth Counihan takes us to a distant world and on a fabulous science fantasy romp. Daniel Kaysen brings us back to an alternate Earth, one with a different history of moon landings, and an unusual perspective on the life of an astronaut. And Sue Thomason takes us to a mysterious and disorienting world, and its Kangian settlement.

From Nigel Brown we have mystery of a different kind, at the edges of a world even its inhabitants do not fully comprehend. Liz Williams takes us back in time, and sideways, to a reality of dark magical forces. And from Paul Laville we have a mad journey through the wreckage of an engineered world.

Deborah Jay takes us on a worldship where the engineered population are lost and searching for a new world to settle. Gareth Caradoc Owens' battleground is at the border of the mortal world and the land of the dead. And Sarah Singleton leads us into an alternate history from which we might never escape.

In Carmelo Rafala's story we have a world of pirate seas and ancient alien technology. Leigh Kennedy gives us a dark futuristic glimpse into a craft filled with sick and dying refugees. And Stephen Gaskell shows us how emerging artificial intelligence might begin to change our world.

Jenny Davies shows us the danger of refusing to see the world as it really is. Alex Robinson reveals a dark chapter of our own history. And Deirdre Counihan takes us deep underground, beneath the kingdom of Avalaam.

In Peter T. Garratt's story we witness an alternative journey of Odysseus. Cherith Baldry takes us to a fragile fantasy world, barely held together in a dying universe. And for Matt Colborn's story we travel to the planet Mars.

Heather Lindsley's story reveals a very different kind of family living amongst us on Earth. My own story takes us to the war-torn planet of Minoru. And to end we have Rebecca J. Payne's world of fabulous flying ships.

My thanks to Mike Ashley for contributing the foreword to this book. Mike is unnecessarily modest about his own work as an anthologist, preferring to call himself a "writer and researcher". Mike's multi-volume *History of the Science Fiction Magazines* is published by Liverpool University Press. As I write this he is currently working on Volume 4, covering the years 1981–1990, and Volume 5 covering 1991–2001.

I once wrote a story in which I described an alien landscape as being plain and unremarkable. The story was submitted for comment from my "crit group". Then, as now, the Montpelier group was populated by writers with varying levels of experience. This was quite early on in my development as a writer, but others were more established. I recall Peter T. Garratt pointed out to me that it would have been much better if my alien landscape could have been fabulous and memorable. It is perhaps the single best piece of writing advice I ever received. It applies to every aspect of writing. And it applies to this book too. I hope you find it fabulous, memorable, and a whole lot more.

Onwards, then. For the world and the stars await...

— Chris Butler, 2015

Mitochondrial Mom

John Frizell

John Frizell was trained in biochemistry and works in ocean conservation for Greenpeace; his science fiction short stories have appeared in Odyssey *and* Nature. *He writes historical fiction as well, which has been published in* The Mammoth Book of Men O'War, *and he has recently finished a novel set on sea and land during the Napoleonic Wars. In his spare time he walks, builds robots and sings.*

In the story that follows, John takes us to a future where giving birth is forbidden, if you're only a Striver. And yet, a security checkpoint, and the facilities beyond, might provide a path to fulfilment for a suitable candidate...

The security guard was watching closely but she didn't exude the cold contempt Siggy was used to and treated Siggy as a guest, not as a potential intruder. There was no queue and although the checks to enter the Chang compound were even more intense than to get into a tube station they went quickly.

"You're good to go," said the guard; she was taller than Siggy, which was unusual. "You'll get your stuff back when you leave."

"But my helper is in there," Siggy said, pointing at the transparent box holding her clothes and shoes.

She looked apprehensively at the sunlit paths winding between the buildings scattered over the landscaped grounds beyond the security point. Blank eyeless buildings surrounded the grounds. The Changs owned all the buildings around the oasis they had carved out of the city and they did not care to be overlooked.

"I can't go outside without it. It's illegal."

"Don't worry. The law doesn't apply within the compound. Take this."

The guard hung a badge around Siggy's neck.

"You go over there," she said, pointing. "If you go the wrong way the badge will flash red."

Siggy had no doubt that the room she arrived at was clean to the point of sterility but it smelled of flowers, not disinfectant. There was so much space. She could walk between things without turning sideways. The man who welcomed her didn't need the white lab coat he wore to mark him out as a doctor.

Dr Vaux called her Sigrid and spoke with professional warmth, working through three generations of her family history, asking questions that Siggy had already answered online. He watched a voice stress analyser as she answered. Once when Siggy was unsure of her answer and once when she didn't know, Dr Vaux probed more deeply until he was satisfied that Siggy was telling him all the truth she knew. There was a pelvic exam, blood tests and ultrasound imaging of her ovaries.

"Let's get you on the treadmill," he said, just as she thought it was over. "You'll be glad your street clothes are with security."

Siggy ran harder, and for all she knew further, than she had ever run before. Her borrowed clothes were soaked with sweat.

"Arm please," said Dr Vaux. "Blood sample."

A drop of something numbed her skin. The expertly applied needle did not hurt at all. Even the antiseptic wipe was fragrant.

"Why a second blood sample?"

"It's a bit hard to explain. Do you know what mitochondria are?"

"Powerhouse of the eukaryotic cell. Originated from bacterial symbiots about two billion years ago."

He looked at Siggy as if seeing her for the first time.

"I wanted to do medicine," explained Siggy.

When she had failed to get into medical school she had told only her best friends. That dream was dead and there was no point in regrets. This was the first time in five years she had spoken of it.

"That's too bad," said Dr Vaux, his warm voice sounding a touch condescending. "It's hard to get the marks isn't it?"

"I had over 95% in everything. I had 100% in biology and 99% in chemistry."

Dr Vaux shifted, suddenly uncomfortable. His eyes questioned.

"It's not just marks," said Siggy. "You need relevant life experience like volunteering in a clinic."

Her parents both worked but they could barely afford to keep her in school. Supporting her through six months of unpaid work, away from home, had not been an option.

"Would you like something to drink?"

The liquid Dr Vaux poured was a deep cloudy orange and it came from a glass jug. The tumbler was real glass. Siggy reached for it slowly. It went against the habits of a lifetime to drink anything without waving her helper over it to check for toxins, accidental or deliberate.

Siggy forced herself to drink, trying to look relaxed. It was wonderful. It was a symphony of flavours, not the single note of the synthetic drinks she had had all her life. It was like the dimly remembered taste of fresh fruit.

As Dr Vaux typed on his keyboard, Siggy poured herself another glass, turning so she could see the screen. He was entering something in the last cell of a long row near the bottom of the page. Her name was in the first cell and above her row were filled rows to the top of the page. It was not the first page. She turned away.

Showered, dried with real cotton towels and dressed in her own clothes again she made her way quickly toward the nearest subway, eyes down so as not to make contact with anyone but constantly glancing around to watch for threats.

As a little girl Siggy had loved holding babies and caring for them. She had wanted to be a mother ever since she'd been old enough to understand what being female meant, but there was no way she could save up enough for the birth tax.

She glanced around. There was probably a pregnancy sniffer in the crowded, seatless Strivers subway carriage taking her home and if it detected anyone the ubiquitous cameras, with their face recognition programs, would tag every woman onboard and track them all. She probably passed a thousand cameras and fifty pregnancy sniffers a day; the exact numbers were secret.

Selling an egg was her only real chance at motherhood. She would never see her baby, never hold it. But she would be creating someone out of herself and projecting a person into the future. And it would be a better future than she could provide. She could still taste the vivid flavours of the juice and feel the fluffy towels. Her life had taught her not to hope but she did anyway, hoping that she had met the criteria, whatever they might be.

"Go, go, go."

The chanting and party spirit enveloped her as she stepped through the door of her flat. Her roommates were clustered around the screen watching the semi finals of Striver to Thriver, cheering on their favourites. The air was full of sweet, illegal smoke.

"Enjoy," said Faisal, an ex-boyfriend, holding out a plastic bottle of real vodka.

"Not drinking."

He raised his eyebrows and dug in a pocket for a brightly coloured little baggie.

"I'm on a one month detox. Remember?"

She didn't like to lie but telling the truth would have broken the nondisclosure agreement she had signed to get into the program.

His shoulders drooped a bit. He wanted Siggy back.

Two days later she got a message giving her an appointment

to return.

"Nice to see you again," said the tall guard. "Many are called but few are chosen."

She reached out to shake hands and handed Siggy a card with her name, Lisa Helgadottir.

"I live out there, just like you, and I know how tough it can be."

She slid Siggy's helper over a plate on her desk.

"My number's in there now. Call me if you have problems."

Siggy looked at the woman's rippling muscles and the smoothly controlled way she moved. It reminded her of a karate master she had once met. Siggy had always been good at sports, she could keep going after others quit, but she was wiry, not muscular. She smiled back at Lisa.

Dr Vaux was warm and professionally friendly, just like last time.

"We need to get you started on hormones," he said. "We have to synchronise your menstrual cycle with the cycle of the egg recipient to ensure it will implant properly. Then we shut down your egg production till the time is right."

Siggy had read up on all this stuff but she listened politely. It clearly made Dr Vaux happy to instruct.

"You will need to come in every day for these," said Dr Vaux as he finished the injection.

"I could inject myself," Siggy said, regretting the words as soon as she said them.

He looked at her, assessing her.

"I believe you could. But do you really want to go out on the street carrying syringes? We could deliver them to you but do you really want them in a flat shared with five other people? And what about their boyfriends, girlfriends and visitors?"

"I'm sure you are right," said Siggy, bowing her head as if to superior wisdom.

The visits became a daily routine — little bursts of luxury, bright windows in a life of endless same.

When she arrived at the checkpoint she just looked into the retinal camera so it could log her in, Lisa nodded her through security and that was it. She couldn't deviate from the path to explore the grounds but she could walk slowly and enjoy the illusion of belonging, waving at people she saw in the distance. There were cool breezes from concealed vents and the sun, filtered through an unseen membrane high above, played over the landscape like shafts of warm gold.

The follicle stimulating hormones made her giddy but Dr Vaux said all was well.

"We should be able to collect soon," he said.

She felt a chill settle through her. She would have to return to an ordinary life that was too ordinary now. But her genes would stay, even if she could not.

He injected her with chorionic gonadotropin to mature the eggs and set a time to collect them. Her motherhood was about to begin.

Siggy was running a full hour ahead of time on egg collection day. She had got into the habit of arriving early and chatting with Lisa over tea in the guard station, out of the burning sun, polluted air and random threats of the London streets, waiting until the appointed time. One of her peripheral scans noted a man heading directly toward her. She watched him without making eye contact. The nearest emergency help point was a hundred metres behind her. She put a hand on her helper, ready to squeeze for an emergency call, wondering what the police response time was like today and how much she would have to pay for calling them.

The man stopped three paces away and looked directly at her. He was in his early forties, plump and comfortable, not threatening. His clothes fit well and his hair was in the latest style.

"I'm Barry Cotton," he said. "I'm a journalist."

He was holding a helper in his hand. It was not flashing, as it would be if it were touching anyone but its registered owner. She pinged it with hers. He was who he claimed to be. He was as harmless as he looked.

"I'm an investigative reporter and I have an interesting offer for you."

He led her toward a Thriver's bar a minute away. She heard the clink of chipping hammers and smelled fresh paint among the other odours; he took her arm to lead her around a work gang. By accident she made eye contact with some defeated looking seventeen-year-old in paint splattered orange coveralls. Dirty red hair straggled out from under a plastic hardhat. Last month the girl had probably been in school before failing one exam too many and now she was scraping, priming and painting a set of railings, watched over by bored guards armed with microwave pain throwers and stun grenades. Siggy extracted her arm the moment they were past the guards.

The bar's doormen nodded to Cotton and one escorted them around the security queue. They strolled through the detector arch with their shoes on and their pockets full. Siggy heard a brief bleep of alarms before the operator silenced them and waved them through. They were swept past another queue and shown to a table and when Cotton waved at a waiter he actually came over.

"You are in a unique position," said Cotton. "Your access to the Chang compound gives you a chance to blow open the whole story."

"What story?"

"The truth behind how the rich oppress us and use us, just like they are using you."

"The Changs aren't using me, they are paying and I'm glad to help."

"Help," chuckled Cotton. "That's an interesting way to put it. I'm no prude but..."

The waiter arrived with a bottle of wine that would have cost Siggy two or three days' wages. Cotton poured a glass, waved his helper over it and showed Siggy the reading. It was the sort of thing close friends do instead of scanning each glass from a shared bottle but it felt wrong, like calling someone you have just met by their nickname without being asked.

"This is very nice and generous of you, Mr Cotton," she said, putting her hand over her glass, "but I'm off alcohol right now."

"Right now? So you normally drink? Perhaps this is some kind of medical thing?"

"I can't say."

It was dawning on her that he thought she was a sex worker.

"Why don't you tell me what you want," she said, putting her elbows on the table and looking directly at him.

"Well, 95% of the population are Strivers, 5% are Thrivers and the rich 0.1% own 98% of the wealth. Everyone is working flat out but if the wealth were spread evenly we could all work two days a week and have all that we have now."

Siggy listened with half an ear. This wasn't news; everyone knew. And it wasn't going to change. The politicians all depended on funding from the rich to be elected. She had almost been thrown out of school at age sixteen for writing an essay saying that and more. After the first and final warning from the head teacher her favourite teacher, Mr Finwood, had asked her to stay behind at change of class.

He had yelled at her, quoting the warning, in a harsh voice that was completely unlike him, moving forward, crowding her until she finally backed into a corner. His hands were in front of him at waist height and she felt rising panic. What was he going to do? His fingers twitched.

"Sigrid."

He was finger spelling. She had got good marks in signing too.

"You are perfectly correct in what you say but very unwise to say it. Learn to keep your head down."

With his back to the classroom cameras no one could see what he was doing.

She had followed his advice ever since.

"I don't know much about that," she said when Cotton finally ran down into silence.

"It could be worth your while."

He named a sum equal to a year's pay for her and then fumbled in a pocket, coming out with a plastic bag containing a large pill. He put it on the table between them. To anyone watching it would look like a minor drug deal.

"Just swallow it. Come back here afterwards and tell door security you are with me. We'll take you to a four star hotel and you can enjoy unlimited room service while we wait for it to, ah, emerge, so we can download its memory. Your name will never appear in any article."

There was real enthusiasm in his voice now, unlike when he had been making his pitch for social justice. And the big budget and expensive wine didn't fit her idea of a social crusader. She excused herself and went to the toilet where she scraped her elbows on the walls squeezing into a cramped cubical to use her helper in private. Mr Cotton was an investigative reporter in name only. He was a gossip columnist making a good living prying into the lives of the rich and famous. But he was offering a lot of money.

Back at the table she scooped up the pill and slipped it into a pocket.

"I'll think about it."

"This is your golden opportunity. It's a lot of money."

"I have to go. I don't want to be late."

"Take it just before you arrive. It only has a one hour lifetime. Do it before you turn the last corner so you are out of camera range."

She walked briskly down the street, constructing a decision matrix in her mind.

Doing this bit of spying was unlikely to endanger the baby. She was contractually obligated to deliver the eggs. If she were somehow detected they would just collect the eggs anyway and cite contractual violations as a reason not to pay her. And she wouldn't get the fee from the journalist either. No money at all.

If she took the risk and succeeded she would get both payments.

The turn to the Chang compound was coming up. She should swallow the thing now. All she had to do was walk in and Lisa would wave her through the checkpoint.

Lisa. Lisa trusted her. Lisa had offered her help and protection.

Siggy was as capable of lies and cheating as anyone else but she had a rule, learned from her father. "Don't be first." It's a bad idea to lie to someone who has been honest with you.

She eased the pill out of its bag, wondering what was in it. Password sniffers? Counter security mapper? Or did it have active devices? Virus casters? A zombie worm? She raised a hand to her mouth, thinking about the money, and just before she turned the corner flicked the thing away. She didn't look back to see where it landed.

"Special scan today," said Lisa, her eyes cold. She walked Siggy over to a transparent tube a meter wide and a bit over two metres high and opened a door. Siggy stepped in. She felt nothing but she knew that electromagnetic fields were probing her body, inside and out.

Lisa watched, unsmiling. A man Siggy had never seen before operated banks of controls. Images built up on screens. There was one of her naked, another in which her body had gone transparent and her digestive tract was being carefully examined.

"She's clean," said the technician. The door popped open. Lisa's face warmed.

"Why didn't you call me as soon as you left that scumbag?"

"I was thinking about his offer," said Siggy, blurting out the truth.

Lisa hugged her. Her arms felt like velvet over steel.

"Temptation is a bugger isn't it? But you did the right

thing. You're good to go."

She hung Siggy's badge around her neck like someone awarding a medal.

Up on the table in Dr Vaux's operating theatre, Siggy was relaxed, blissed out on the sedative. The hissing from the flexible tube running into her vagina and the soft professional exchange of words between Dr Vaux and the ultrasound operator guiding him as the gentle suction deep inside her plucked the ripe eggs like fruit from her ovaries was just background chatter to her; she was dreaming about her babies. She could see them in cradles, helpless but alert, she could see them in summer dresses, blond and lanky, playing in a garden where they didn't need masks or sun block. They all looked like her.

"That's fifteen," said the ultrasound operator. "That's all we are going to get."

They put her in a recovery room, still dreaming of her babies.

Two hours later she was dressed, clear headed and ready to go. She would be back at work tomorrow. She looked at Dr Vaux, judging the time, then took the plunge.

"When the baby is born, can I see a picture? You could send it on Amnesiagram — it will only last ten seconds and can't be copied. I just want to see the face. Just once."

You can see the adult in a day old baby if you have the right eyes.

Dr Vaux's face hardened, the way Lisa's had done.

"You know I can't do that. If you had said this three hours ago I'd have had to cancel your contract, but given where we are now I'm prepared to overlook it."

His face softened a bit and he put a hand on her shoulder in what he probably thought was a reassuring way.

"Anyway you'd see nothing. These eggs will have their nuclei removed before they go to the recipient."

The room seemed to evaporate around her, vanishing like a dream at the moment of awakening. Nothing of her would remain, no genes for hair colour, face shape, build, intelligence, nothing of what made her herself. Her dream of second hand motherhood had been just a fantasy.

She should have realised. Rich people don't want your genes, they want theirs and they believe that only the genes of the most successful should be propagated. Tears streamed down her face. Dr Vaux looked embarrassed.

"There will still be a bit of you. Your mitochondrial genes will remain."

Great. Little loops of bacterial DNA. Forty genes out of twenty thousand. She would be 0.2% a mother. She tried to stop crying but she couldn't.

"It is not my job to point this out to you Sigrid but I am not forbidden from doing it. You have extraordinarily high mitochondrial function. We tested hundreds of women and none of them came close to you. Donor regulations allow you to provide eggs four more times. I am sure that other Families would wish to purchase from you."

The tears were still coming but they were thinning out as Siggy started to weigh her options. Five times this fee was a lot of money, enough to make the jump from Striver to Thriver. She tingled as she realised that with the right partner real motherhood would be possible. The tingle changed to pure joy, the dreams of her babies surged back and the tears came again.

And the subtext of Dr Vaux's words was starting to become clear. If her mitochondria were so good then she could charge more for her eggs. She could become a mitochondrial mother to half the Families of London. She took a tissue and dried her eyes, reflecting that her mitochondria would give the offspring of the rich more endurance so they could work even harder to the detriment of the poor. But she doubted that it would make anything worse.

Lisa looked uneasy as she took the badge from Siggy. It didn't fit well on someone so confident and decisive.

"Look," she said, hesitating. "I'd like to see you again."

Lisa. Lisa would make a fabulous partner. Siggy could get all the sperm she would need for the price of a drink. She would probably get the drink bought for her.

“I’d love to,” she said.

Ondralume

Tanith Lee

Tanith Lee is one of the world's most acclaimed writers of Fantasy and Science Fiction, and she was awarded the 2013 World Fantasy Award for Lifetime Achievement. She is a prolific author of over 90 novels. Many are available in new e-editions along with newer books such as Cruel Pink *(Immanion Press, 2013) and* Turquoiselle *(Immanion Press, 2014). A new ghost story collection in two volumes —* Ghosteria *— is now available from Immanion, as is the story collection* Colder Greyer Stones *(NewCon Press, 2013).*

In Ondralume, two sisters, Ondain and Unniet, plead with the gods to bring rain to their parched and dying land. But can their sacrifice save their people? The answer might come from another world, or from the stars...

And now we dance the salamander's dance
Surrounded by the fire....

So the poet Vult had written in his stone tower seven kirts to the east. And many more kirts away, another poet in another land had written in his marble house these words: *Cinder-eyed, we children of the unkind, turn upon our pyre.*

Ondain raised her statue's face to the sky. Beneath her veil, her pale golden hair shone at the sun's terror. As with all her people, all people of all the lands of Ondralume, her eyes were silver, not cinders, yet like cinders they felt; she, too, was the salamander. She raised her golden arms, her hands in the gesture of prayer. "Give us this day the rain, we entreat you. Give us this day our life."

The sky had been a soft turquoise-green, so she still remembered it. Now it was brown, and pinkish with great swathes of dust. The sun was a ball of pain. It hurt to think of the sun. From everything the long, hot shadows cut like wounds.

The hills were only hardenings of the sky, darker, redder. On the sides of the hills lay the whitening bones of things that had died when the grass withered and the streams shrank to cracks of steam.

In the stone village, many had gone to their houses, shut the doors and windows, and not come out. The dry fountains on the oblong plazas stood in attitudes of thirst. Whole villages died in this way in all the lands.

To the north, in the mountains, bones lay thick as the snow that no longer gathered there. The drought had lasted one entire lumin, and the seasons of the lumin had not changed it, but had been changed. The cold time was a heat. A yearlong heat without pity, without a breeze, without one single bead of rain.

At Ondain's back the temple showed its pure façade, its tall apertures opening to the ground, the walls and floors of marble no longer cool, burning white and pink like the world.

The other priestesses waited in their soft robes, their arms upraised and hands in the gesture of prayer. They sang the hymn to the rain, composed by the poet Vult ninety lumins ago, when rain yet fell, a thankful hymn born after the Time of the Fear.

Ondain sang every fifth line alone, her sweet voice lifting as her hands did, to the sky.

The gods would hear her. The gods must hear. Why this punishment? What had they done amiss?

Send us your mantle of water, sang the priestesses, and the crowds below in the valley, catching the words clearly from the great amphitheatre of the temple, wept their burned-out tears. So many tears and not one tear of rain. How was it possible? There had been the Ceremony of Weeping held as never before in Ondain's lifetime. Her sister, Unniet, had been chosen to lead it. Unniet was perfect in her beauty, only fifteen lumins in age. She had begun the Weeping, and she and her fellows had Wept all through the dark. They had spoken of their miseries and the agony of the people; they had remembered the Time of the Fear when the sun vanished and the stars went out. How they had Wept, in confusion and fright.

But dawn broke like rock. The dust rose from the bowls of the valleys, and copper shade was on the hills. In the villages a hundred more went in and shut their doors.

The Ceremony of Weeping had not ended the drought, as the sacrifice of the last horned cattle had not ended it.

The hymn finished. The High Priest on his eminence turned and gazed upon the priestesses, and the people in the valley. Above his robe, his head was masked by the skull of one of the great fire eagles. The eagles still survived the drought, still circled sharply above the plains, searching for carrion the sun had not picked clean. Long since, all other birds had fallen songless from the scorched skies. The eagle mask was the sign of strength, and through its eyelets the silver eyes of the High Priest stared from another country that lay between the world and the heaven of the gods.

"Go now to your homes," said the High Priest, his voice borne like the eagle to the edges of the valley. "Fast there, and drink only a little of your wine though your thirst be great. Scourge yourselves if you can bear it. During every lur, kneel often and offer penitence to the gods. They must be appeased. Go now to your homes."

With a dreadful faint sighing, the people began to disperse along the straight roads between the marble posts. All across the lands, such priests prayed and gave such instructions. It would be easy to fast: there was little to eat, and bellies had shrunk, and mouths were dry as dust that wine did not slake — and anyway, the wine ran low in the jar, as the last river had run before it vanished like a worm into the earth. And they were easy, too, prayer and chastisement, for the heart churned always with horror and grief. There would be eighty burials, paraphrase of thousands elsewhere, this lur, most of them children. They would go into the little neat graves beside the graveyards of the sacred pets, the slim cats and birds and snakes who had already perished. And in the places of adult death, also, the white markers rose like new flowers that grew despite the drought.

The priestesses moved in a mild white wind under the arches of the temple. The High Priest beckoned to Ondain.

"Father?"

"Maiden, something more must be done."

"I know it," she said. And a circlet of fire enclosed her waist, pressing on her.

"Our last resort. Our last display to heaven that we acknowledge our guilt and will expiate our guilt in the final extremity of blood."

Ondain bowed her head. In her cinder silver eyes, the tears that were not the rain gathered, but did not fall.

"You yourself are among the comeliest and best, and your sister, Unniet. You two will be among those sent to stand beneath the selecting light."

"I bow before your judgment."

"Whichever is chosen," the eagle mask said to her, its strange eyes remote, compassionless, and holy, approaching the eyes of gods; "whichever the light selects will in three lurs lie here before the people to die, that heaven may be satisfied."

"To this I consent, Father."

"You have no fear."

"Fear again is all about, as once before. What is my little fear to that?"

"So then he told me he was going to visit his sister at Palm Springs, and I *believed* him. I really did. I believed that son of a bitch."

Terri-Louise pulled on strands of her blonde hair viciously, some ancient Latin genetic urge to rip them out, perhaps.

"Well, I said to you, Louie, didn't I?"

"You sure did. And I sure never did listen. Why was I

such a dumb fool? Tell me that?"

Too wise to attempt this feat, Terri-Louise's caller said gently, "Oh, — you're not, honey. He'd have fooled anyone. He's a real syrupy bastard, that one."

"I work for the guy," said Terri-Louise, self-condemnatory; "I should have *known*. The way he treated all the others. I thought I was different. Just vanity, I guess. He's used me, and now he's gotten someone he likes better. So he wants to keep me hanging on? He can *forget* it."

"Yeah, you bet, Louie."

"I'll tell you what I'm going to do," said Terri-Louise, idly glaring down the six-hundred-floor glacier of the office building on Wideway Nine. "I'm going to take off out of here for an early weekend myself. Assistant be darned. He's just used me like any old secretary; that's all I am. Maid of all work. And bed warmer if there's nothing cuter. You care for cocktails at The Rose? I'll use my darned expense account."

"You *bet*, Louie."

"O.K. I'll meet you there at" — Terri-Louise consulted the elaborate timepiece fastened on the wall, which was otherwise a massive representation of a cream-white ammonite, coiling in and in forever, until it hit the clock — "say, sixteen sharp."

"To the second, Louie. Oh, what'll I wear?"

"That's another thing. I'd better go now and have my manicure done. I saw a real nice gold polish. They can tint your hair up to match. Better get going."

"See you there, Louie. Bye."

"Bye."

With some satisfaction, Terri-Louise slammed down the OFF switch of the phone cube, releasing the image and voice of her friend in need. Although she was raw, the idea of the afternoon spent in pleasures, and the office of her hated lover left abandoned, reassured her. There was a whole list of stuff he had left her to do. She glanced about at it all, and at the towering room with its emerald chairs and sea-blue divan like a bed — and it might just as well have been — scene of her seduction and befoolment by that *shrork*. The place was full of his executive toys. She had already started to pay him out, having heard of his infidelity this morning. Things were left unwound, things unmaintained, the plants unwatered and wilting in the fake air of these glass heights. "Oh Ms Baume, I'm so sorry but I have to go. I have a virus. Yes, there are so many bugs now, aren't there? I just can barely see, you know. No, there's nothing to do up here."

She rose with a swing of her firm and unappreciated, carefully dieted, and carelessly manhandled hips. Just let that *shrork* find out what he'd lost. Let him come in Monday and see how things swung without her ministrations. It was the weekend tomorrow. Three days of negligence.

"Yeah, and I'm not even going to feed that." She glided from the office in a hail of scent, and went down in the gunshot smoothness of the elevator, humming the *Marseillaise*.

Twenty priestesses stood in the high chamber of the marble temple on Ondralume. At their centre was the great low altar, recently laved with a scant wash of wine. Incense smouldered, the smoke hurtful to arid throats. The priestesses trembled, or did not tremble. And the light rose from the altar, a globe like a bubble of the harsh sun itself. It lit the room fiercely, showing up the faces, all beautiful, all like statues. In the living silver eyes was tragedy or resignation, dread or ecstasy. Only Ondain's eyes were blank, a statue's eyes.

And then the light wheeled down and came to rest — upon the forehead of her sister, Unniet.

Despite all her training, Unniet cried out in terror.

It was Ondain who spoke the word: "No."

"The Truth is here," said the High Priest from the shadow. "Let none dispute it."

Unniet wept with fear.

No longer a statue, Ondain showed an awful and overwhelming concern. She went to her sister and took her hands.

"Hush now; be brave. The life of the world rests on you."

Unniet quieted in a second terror, feeling the power and onus of her fate.

"He had all these things," said Terri-Louise, as lemon liquor stole independently up its straw toward her lips, at the minutely air-controlled Rose. "He has a timepiece made by *Arbour*."

"My!"

"And a fossil wall, like in the da Vichi mansion."

"Really?"

"And all these African plants." She sucked the liquor. "Yum. They'll die; I didn't mist them."

"Oh Louie!"

"Now, don't 'Oh Louie' me. You said he's a bastard. And what a waste of all that money anyhow. I swear there are things in that office of his could keep a family of social dependents for a year."

"Yeah."

"Why, the rat's even gotten a whirlie."

"My God."

"You see?"

"You didn't—"

"Yes; I *didn't*."

"But what didn't you, Louie?"

"Didn't feed the darn old thing. Not this morning. Not tonight. Soon as I found out, I stopped being his devoted slave. Why should I run around misting his Africans and feeding his whirlie, when he's at Palm Springs, cooking some other pie? It's too hot for remorse."

"It's always too hot now."

Unniet went down into the cavern beneath the temple. Ondain went with her, as her sister, to undergo the purification at her side.

They stood in the basin of fluid, alike as two golden stems. They were washed with perfume, not with water. The cavern, once icy even in the heat, was warm, smelling of old bones and the grindings of rocks to dust. Now and then Unniet wept, but she did not protest; neither did Ondain say again, No. But Ondain thought: *She is fifteen lumins. She is afraid.* And again the words of poets came to her. *The salamander's dance surrounded by the fire. We children...*

Ondain thought of all the lands, and her brain could not hold them, their mountains and plains, the blackened sands where once had bloomed their fields and flowers, the empty dishes of their lakes. She thought of the dead in the delicate graveyards, the dainty skeletons of animals and children. But again the image of Unniet weeping beside her drove these images away.

She should not die. She fears it.

Ondain considered the Time of the Fear. The wisest sages had not fathomed what had occurred. The greatest poets, such as Vult, had written of it, but offered no theory beyond the anger of the gods. But after the anger, heaven had forgiven men — for otherwise, how else should mankind have survived? It was true: many had been lost in the quaking of the earth, and some had died of pure fear, so well the time was named, as the inexplicable darkness, sunless, starless, covered the earth. It had lasted many lurs. And then, as abruptly as at its going, the sun came back over the hills and mountains, shone down upon the waters that then had graced Ondralume, reflecting like a lovely face — how they had loved the sun then, now their enemy. And by night the stars had occupied their proper places. Perhaps not so brightly arrayed; there was some debate upon this. And certain astrologers had averred that not every star was in its section. Some had vanished forever. Yet there were stars enough to light the nights of Ondralume. And over the giant fissures in the earth, the flowers grew, and in the waters, the fish played. And the children walked solemnly up and down the straight roads, leading their sacred long-legged birds and slender, sleek cats, or with the snakes curled about their throats like precious necklaces. If the gods had raged, surely the gods had set rage aside.

Yet, in the time of second chance, this now befell them.

A tear, hot, scalded Ondain's hand from the cheek of her sister. They stood alone, robed, below the basin, while a priestess spoke to them of the duty and the right to die to console the gods and to save the people, all the peoples of Ondralume, with their goldenness and their silver eyes.

Clyde Braxi, Jr, known to his assistant and former lover, Terri-Louise, as the *shrork*, lay in the palm of Palm Springs, a little prone to flooding now, yet still a great place, with a lush young woman from the computer terrace.

He had impressed her with many matters, not least, he assumed, his exercise-trim and safe-and-healthy Indoor Sun-tanned body and its wonders.

"And you must see my office, Sue-Ann. One wall is the da Vichi Ammonite."

"Yes?"

"And a timepiece by Arbour."

"Swell," said Sue-Ann, who was thinking about dinner and whether to wear the black or the red.

"But the best thing of all, I managed to get a whirlie."

"What the heck is a whirlie?"

"My God — you don't know?"

"I'm telling you, aren't I?"

"Well, it's a misnomer, really."

"Ms who."

"I mean, it doesn't whirl; it spins. So fast you can't see it. Just like us."

"Are we spinning?" Sue-Ann girded herself to give further assurances to Mr Braxi about his sexual athletics. But it transpired that this was not what he meant.

"They found them — out there." He waved at the window misleadingly. "A group of several hundreds. They were proved to be sentient, but nobody quite knows how. And then they die if you touch or move them. Or they used to. And you couldn't get one — you just could not — money no object.

And then they found some safe way of capturing and transporting them, inside a kind of dome..."

"Honey, what are you talking about?" asked Sue-Ann, who had come to feel that overpretense of admiration might at this point only cause complications.

"About the whirlie, for God's sake."

"Oh."

"And I had Simes get me one. It was real difficult. But Simes is a good guy. Beautiful little thing."

He must mean the whirlie?

"Matches the decor of the office. I just hope" — a vague niggle, like the first intimation of indigestion, nibbled at the edges of Clyde Braxi, Jr's awareness — "I just hope that dumbella I have working for me remembers to feed the goddamn thing. They tell you. Don't miss a meal, on any account. You have to put the food in through this really complicated lock arrangement—"

Sue-Ann fell to wondering if Clyde Braxi, Jr, was likely to want her again before dinner, and if it would be O.K. to go and shower now.

Three Lurs passed like one. The sky was changeless brown and pink, the red hills quivered in heat haze, and the sun poured down its venom. Seventeen children died. They were the last in the villages of that temple. There were no more children. And in the wombs were only the dead, like stones, that would not be born.

No rain fell on the land about the temple, or in any of the lands of Ondralume, or in the bone-white mountains. No rain. Not a tear of it.

But Unniet wept.

She said nothing. She did not eat the provisions, the best of all that they had, that were brought to her and to Ondain. Even the sweets of honey she would not taste.

Unniet wept.

Ondain entered the inner room of the High Priest, and there, like a last eagle, he perched upon a chair of basalt, and turned his skull toward her.

How she had gone in awe of him all her days as a priestess, and as a daughter of the villages, she had been frightened of him. But now she knew him suddenly for a man, standing between her and the gods, a guardian with a vital and fearsome labour, but only mortal. And the death's-head seemed too heavy for his fragile face. She spoke swiftly and clearly.

"Father, Unniet is afraid to die. The gods will not accept unwilling sacrifice. It may bring worse wrath on us. The very sun may fall from the sky."

"So it may. What odds? Better perhaps than this slow torture."

Then she knew her strength, hearing the dregs of his in this terrible speech.

"Father," she said, "as Unniet's sister, I have been purified beside her; I have eaten the sacred bread and tasted the honey. Let me die in her stead. I am not afraid. I am glad to give my life for rain. I *ache* for it."

"Yes, so you do." The High Priest rose and touched her forehead as the light of selection had touched Unniet. "For this, you were prepared beside her; for this, you also were deemed worthy. Be it as you say."

In her lonely bed, Terri-Louise, slightly drunk, shed tears at her lost lover and no longer called him the *shrork*, but: *Clyde, Clyde, how could you treat me that way?*

And then she thought of the wilting Africans she had neglected, and the whirlie she had not fed, and she wept for them, too, and because she might lose her job.

The sun was stamped like a blazing nail above the hills.

In the valley the people had gathered, as in every place they would gather, where there had been time for word to reach them of the fate of the priestess, from which hung the destiny of Ondralume.

Was she beautiful and unique, enough to compensate, to entice the gods to forgive?

Ondain came out among the other priestesses, and in the valley they saw her, and that she was.

Unveiled, her head crowned with flowers of parchment, naked without shame, clad in her glamour for the eye of heaven.

The heat beat upon her body, golden as the honey of death. Behind lay the white temple where her sister wept, for Ondain now. Before her was the old fire eagle raising his arms, saluting the malign sun.

She lifted her head and prayed in her soul for her death to salve the anger of the gods. She prayed for rain, and in that moment felt a breeze upon her breasts, her lips, but it was an illusion. From her mind, she put the shadow despair. Firmly, she went forward to the block of stone where she must lie. And lying down, she let them anoint her with wine and perfume under the pink-powdered brown vault that had been the sky. And Ondain thought of nothing but the words of Vult — *salamander's dance, salamander's dance* — and of the scorpion that stung itself to death surrounded by the flames. She knew; she knew it was too late.

Clyde Braxi, Jr, pelted into his towering office on Saturday, having spoken with Ms Baume over the phone. She had talked about floods for three minutes, then told him.

He heard the timepiece groaning as he entered, for its nine-year crystal had been left uncharged on Friday. He saw the African plants lying in a heap like cabbage; he saw the toys throbbing and bobbing to the wrong tempi, and the moving picture stuck on a singularly stupid frame. But it was at the whirlie that he hurled himself.

"Oh Jesus," said Clyde Braxi, Jr.

The whirlie had changed colour. It had been an exquisite pale turquoise-green, with faintly gauzy driftings over its surface, the mimicry of clouds, as if it truly had been a tiny world — he was wrong in the origin and spelling of the word *whirlie*, which was actually *worlie*. Now it was not green or blue or gauzy. It was a ghastly orangey reddish fawn, a disgusting, nauseous tint that showed at once it had been starved, for the manual had warned him.

With shaking hands, Clyde Braxi, Jr, took out the feeder and measured a double dose into the tiny airlock contraption attached to the worlie's vacuum-sealed container-dome. He watched the food go in, disseminate, and seem never to have been. He measured out another dose, and put that in, too.

"Bitch," said Clyde Braxi, Jr. "Bitch, bitch."

Probably he had overloaded the system now. An enraged look had come onto the surface of the flawless round of the worlie. Like a boil about to erupt.

They had found them out in space, hundreds of them, these tiny things like worlds, with tiny dots of brightness like miniature suns swirling before them. Too small for life, of course, though apparently vaguely sentient. Perhaps too intelligent, for to touch or move them caused death. Then a method of minimum disturbance was devised. They were captured and quickly sealed into a soup of their own atmosphere, their "suns" reconstituted, their "stars" relit, or as near in facsimile as possible.

Not all survived, but many did, and — providing that the computer-processed nutrients were fed into them thereafter, providing that they were not moved about, they bloomed. Beautiful little things. Colourful and glowing. Friendly.

"She killed it, that bitch," said Clyde Braxi, Jr, staring at the ominous boil.

Then he turned his back on the worlie and made tigerish Monday plans for the infinitely fireable Terri-Louise.

As the golden blade descended, Ondain felt tears creep from the corners of her eyes. In vain.

And then there came from out of the enraged and ghastly sky a presaging gout of thunder. The herald of the Deluge.

And Clyde Braxi, Jr, waiting for the fireable Terri-Louise, who was going to be, after all, too sensible to come in on Monday, fell to thinking of Mars and Mercury, those deserts, and Venus awash with waters. And later, oddly, of the hole in the ozone layer.

Substitutes

Colin P. Davies

Colin P. Davies is a Building Surveyor from Liverpool, England, and has been writing fiction since last century. His stories have appeared in Asimov's Science Fiction Magazine, Abyss & Apex, Daily Science Fiction, Paradox *and elsewhere. His story "The Defenders" was in* The Year's Best SF #22, *edited by Gardner Dozois. Colin's first collection of short stories,* Tall Tales on the Iron Horse, *was published by Bewildering Press in 2008. A second collection,* Voices, *was published by Immersion Press in 2014. Colin is currently working on a comic fantasy trilogy for Young Adults based upon his short story "Clifford and the Bookmole". For more information visit* www.colinpdavies.com.

In Colin's story "Substitutes", offworlders have come to Earth, and Melinda and her Dad are on the run. She sees patterns everywhere, in the stars or in the bubbling water of a stream — but what does this signify, and where will it lead...?

Sometime after sunset on a blustery evening in late summer, with the offworlders' orbital station a small bright misshapen moon over the choppy water of the river and the glittering barges of the loyal rich fighting at their moorings, a slim girl came skipping over Westminster Bridge like a leaf carried on the wind. She danced down Belvedere Road, her pale face bobbing through the crowds, and ducked into the alley beside the bookies.

In a ground floor apartment, Melinda watched her Dad, Brian Johnson, former cop, rush from monitor to monitor, press a button here, enter a code there, as he followed the girl from street to street. “She thinks she’s won,” he said. “If she thinks at all.”

Melinda willed her wheelchair across the thin carpet to get a better look at the street scenes. Hard shapes of light and dark; sweeping strings and spots of significance. There was a language in the lines and Melinda could almost hear it. She smelled purpose and saw promise.

Dad saw only threats.

“Mel...” Dad said with an unsteady voice. The back of his blue T-shirt was dark with sweat. “Could you get me a drink? Water.”

“Sure.”

“With ice... if there’s any left.”

Melinda wheeled into the kitchen and crashed the footplate of her chair into the fridge — the top door swung open. She reached in for the ice and cupped cubes in her hand. A glass. She needed a glass... should have got it first. Attempts to anticipate only caused confusion. Trial and error. She’d get there eventually, if Dad had the patience.

She knew he had the patience.

She found a glass and added the ice and then the water. Her hand was shaking and ripples patterned the surface of the liquid. She tried to read them. Out there. *Out there!* The girl was coming. What girl? She was certain that Dad had told her. Not to worry. No substitute for... She dried her hand on her jeans. For what?

As she trundled back into the parlour she heard Dad say, “They always find us.” He was slumped at a table, tired but not defeated.

Dad would never be defeated.

Melinda had not always been confused. There had been a time when she could gaze at the stars and see only beauty, not patterns — a time before she forgot how to walk. Now patterns *were* beauty, and they spoke to her. The TV said it was a gift from the offworlders, given to only a few; the ability to hear the language of the universe, if not to understand it. But Dad said it was an alien disease, seeded by stealth.

Three years ago they had been living in the far north, away from cities, away from the alien overseers, in a white cottage that smelled of roses in the summer and paraffin oil in the winter. Out front, a long garden stretched up to the passing lane and, to the rear, the vegetable garden ended in a stream and then the woods. As Melinda started to change, the bubbling water provided hours of stimulation for her pattern-seeking brain. She never found a pattern, but she did notice the movement in the trees beyond the stream, when the man first found them.

"Hello, Melinda," he said, with a voice so deep that she almost laughed. "Don't be scared."

The black-clad figure stepped with spindly legs over the narrow strip of water to stand upon dry grass.

"You know my name," Melinda said.

"I know lots about you. You're thirteen years old, left-handed, your eyes are grey, you have a doll named Lucy... and you like ice cream."

Melinda gasped. "How do you know?"

"All girls like ice cream."

"I mean..."

He raised a hand. "I know what you mean." The pale, hooded face smiled, then he started up the narrow path between the cabbages and runner beans towards the cottage.

She would have called Dad, but it didn't seem important. Besides, he was cooking and Melinda liked his cooking. By the time it did seem important, the man was in the kitchen.

Through the open doorway, she watched the visitor flick a finger to draw a picture in the air — a sheet of paper.

Dad peered out into the garden. "Mel... get back in the house!" But she remained standing in the garden, paralysed with curiosity.

"Get out of here!" Dad told the man. "I'll never let you take her."

"Read the certificate. I have the authority."

"You'll need more than that. Are the police outside?"

The man shook his head. "We don't want a scene, just compliance. Why not comply? The offworlders are not unreasonable. In fact, they view themselves as a highly moral race."

"Their notion of morality is inhuman."

"Hardly surprising, but they are trying to do the right thing." He waved a hand and the certificate vanished.

"Right for them." Dad stabbed a finger towards the official's face. "Mel stays with me."

"Maybe you should let her speak for herself."

"She's... confused." Dad glanced at Melinda. "She can't know what she wants. They did that to her."

"They will also make you wealthy. One of the loyal rich."

"I don't need to be rich."

"And, of course, you'll receive a replacement."

Dad waved a steaming kettle like a weapon. "You just don't get it..."

"You need to understand that you don't have a choice. None of us have a choice."

Dad poured the scalding water over the intruder's legs.

The man shrieked and careered out of the kitchen and away across the garden.

Dad stood, empty kettle clutched in his hand, with a look on his aged face that Melinda had not seen since the day her mother walked out.

"You got the floor wet," Melinda told him, and she went to fetch a mop.

"I've lost her." Dad threw himself back in his seat and spun away from the screens. "Too many people. I just can't see the girl." He turned back to search again.

"Can I go to my bedroom?" Melinda asked as she drove her chair towards the hallway.

"What do you want? I can get it for you."

"I don't know." Music started up in the apartment

upstairs. Melinda tapped her fingers to the thud of bass. "To sing."

"I'd like to hear that. Could you sing for me now."

Melinda circled back towards Dad. Did she know how to sing? "No, I don't think so."

After a moment, Dad said, "We've got to be ready."

"Ready, steady... what game are we playing?" Melinda parked her wheelchair in the open doorway to the kitchen. She thought she could smell hot biscuits in the thick warm air. Odd how a thought could bake a scent. She giggled.

Dad turned to smile at her. "What game do you want to play?"

"The stars." Melinda noticed beads of water on her Dad's hairless head.

"We can't go out there just now," he said.

"Is it daylight?"

"No." A movement on a monitor caught Dad's eye. A girl dressed in a rust-coloured suit, and with long black hair just like Melinda's, dashed below a street lamp. "Okay, it seems that we can play." Dad opened a drawer and took out a heavy handgun. He checked it and stuffed it into his belt. "There may be some noise."

The morning after the kettle incident, Melinda was surprised to see packed suitcases in the hallway. Dad's cheeks were red in a way that worried her. He had a set to his jaw like toothache. Yet still he smiled. "Good morning, Mel."

"Are we going somewhere?" She stumbled across to him; sometimes she found it hard to put one foot before the other. He steadied her.

"I was wrong about this place," he said.

"I don't think you're wrong."

"I imagined we had more time." He moved the suitcases closer to the door.

"Let me help."

"You can help by watching."

"Watching what... the woods?"

He put a heavy hand on her shoulder. “No. Don’t go near the woods. Watch for the taxi.”

“I promise I won’t go into the woods. I won’t get lost.”

“No.” He brushed strands of dark hair from her forehead. “If I lose you, I lose everything.”

When the taxi arrived — a dusty black three-wheeled Hansom with dark windows and white-wall tyres — Dad hauled out the cases and waited by the passenger door. The driver came around the car to help. Melinda was surprised to see it was a young girl, about her own size, in a smart maroon suit and with her hair tucked under a red cap. Dad dropped a case and it burst, sending clothes across the dry dirt.

“Let me help, Mr Johnson.” The driver stooped to gather the clothes.

Dad yanked the cap from her head and long black tresses fell. The girl smiled.

“Dad,” said Melinda. “She looks just like me.”

“Dad,” said the driver. “She looks just like me.”

Dad lifted Melinda into the back of the taxi, bundled the cases and loose clothes in after her, and turned to face her copy. “Stay away from us!”

“I didn’t mean to alarm you, Mr Johnson, only to show that I can be your daughter in every way. Thoughts, memories, emotions...”

“Mel stays with me.”

Inside the taxi, Melinda pressed her nose to the glass.

“But she has a destiny,” said the driver. “Few can navigate the stars in special space. She’s needed.”

“You’d never understand. You’re too different.”

“I’m not that different. Ask me anything. A childhood memory, a favourite game. Your wife gave us everything. I was made to be your daughter. I *am* your daughter.”

“I don’t know *what* you are, but you’re not Melinda!”

“I’m flesh and blood. I think. I speak. I feel pain.”

“You’re a commodity... cheap technology. A salve for an alien conscience. A *substitute!*”

"Substitutes are people too."

"Are they?" Dad glared at the girl and Melinda wondered why he was shouting at her. Then she saw two black-clad men emerge from the trees at the side of the road and hurry towards the taxi.

"Just keep away from us!" Dad yelled. He jumped into the driver's seat and threw the vehicle forward.

Melinda looked out of the rear window and saw the girl still standing there in a cloud of sunlit dust. Then Dad braked hard.

"Dad?" said Melinda. "Is she my sister?"

He put the taxi into reverse and accelerated backwards faster and faster until there was a heavy thump at the rear. "No," he told her. "She's not your sister." The taxi jerked forward again and they sped off down the lane between the hawthorn hedgerows. After several sharp and sudden bends that tumbled the cases and clothes all over Melinda, Dad glanced around and saw she was laughing. "No, Mel... she's not even human."

"I've killed three of them so far, and I'll kill more."

Was Dad talking to her? Melinda was concerned at his agitation. He seemed upset. She drove her wheelchair closer.

"I know how to hide," he said. "How to disappear. Yet they still find us and keep on coming. The offworlders aren't going to give up." He was staring at a street monitor where the girl was flitting from shadow to shadow.

Melinda touched his arm. "Why is this happening? You won't explain."

"I have explained, Mel, but you get mixed up. You don't remember."

"I remember that you said it was about me. I was important."

"Of course you're important." He took her hand. "You're my daughter."

"I meant, important to them... the offworlders."

"They infect all children, Mel, with something like a

disease. They're trying to trigger a change. It works on a few and the rest are unaffected. It's hit and miss. A game of numbers... and yours came up." He squeezed her hand a little tighter. "They think I should be satisfied with a substitute, a fake you, while they take you off to guide them across the galaxy."

Melinda recalled nights of looking up at the stars. The beauty and, later, the patterns. "I think I might like that."

Dad winced as though wounded.

There was a knock on the door to the apartment.

Dad leapt up and rushed into the hallway. "Go through to the kitchen and keep the door shut," he told Melinda. "And be ready to leave in a hurry. We may have to go out the back way."

Melinda did as she was told and parked her chair on the aged and broken tiles. The blinds were drawn and a water heater hissed quietly. Above her head, the bass thudded like the excited heartbeat of the building. She listened for sounds from the hall, but could hear nothing. She spied the biscuit tin. Dad would never let her have a biscuit now, so near to dinner. She bumped the chair into the cabinet and grabbed the tin, prising the lid off, delighting in the sweet scent. So tempting, but his rules were strict. He said they had to be.

There was a gentle knock at the back door that led into the yard. She replaced the tin and wheeled over to the door. Again the knock, and a voice. "Melinda... open up. We have to go quickly."

"Dad?" She turned the key, then reversed as the door eased open.

Dad stepped inside. "Come on. If we're quick, she won't even know we've gone."

Confusion whirled. Had Dad changed his clothes? Did it even matter? "Can I take some biscuits?"

"Why not?"

She drove out into the yard and followed him through the rear gateway. They rustled through windblown litter up the dark alleyway towards the street and the crowds. As the high walls moved past, Melinda nibbled at a biscuit and gazed upwards, out of a black canyon toward an expanse of sky. “I can see the Milky Way.”

“Can you see the patterns?”

“*Yes!*” They were beautiful, incoherent and yet somehow she knew she would learn to read them.

Some distance away, a shot rang out, but she hardly noticed.

Melinda saw only stars.

Glittering Spires

Elizabeth Counihan

Elizabeth Counihan comes from a writing family. Her grandfather, Douglas Newton, was a successful novelist and her father a BBC journalist. She has had stories published in numerous magazines including Asimov's, Interzone *and* Nature Futures *as well as in various anthologies. Her novella* Forests of Eden *is available from PS Publishing. Elizabeth spent many years working as a family doctor in Sussex. With her sister Deirdre she edited the British fantasy magazine* Scheherazade. *She is currently writing a science fantasy novel.*

In the story that follows, Elizabeth merges Science Fantasy and Austen sensibilities to playful effect. A young princess might well have to navigate not just the mores of her society, but also the wild, fabulous rogues and creatures that inhabit her world...

"In ancient times it was believed that each world was formed in the shape of a fabulous animal. This one was said to be a Hedgehog curled in a ball. We are only the mites living on the tips of its spikes. Who knows what fleas live down there?"

He pointed downwards, over the edge of the stone balcony. But Miranda gazed into the distance, as if her eyes could penetrate the jagged mountains that blocked the view of her destiny; mountains which had encircled her for the whole of her life. To her they were a jewelled ring of shining colours which she was soon to break. She turned to him smiling.

"Please don't lecture me any more, Dr Danser; I am aware of the legend, you know." She plucked a flower from her hair — the white camellia, reserved for the daughters of royalty — and tossed it over the edge. She watched it floating down, drifting through a gap in the mist, bouncing upward again on an eddy, becoming a speck in the distance.

"Convection currents..." he faltered. She was delighted to see a pink flush appear just below his glasses. "It's still my job, Madam."

"Only for a few more days, Dr Danser — Conrad. Don't be so serious! And please, it's 'Miranda' not 'Madam'." She touched his sleeve. "It's my turn now. I'm going to teach you the Swirl, so you can live up to your name. Put the player on."

He hesitated a moment and then crossed the stone floor and put a hand just inside the archway that led to the study. There was a faint click followed by the sounds of flutes, harps and tambourines. Two long legged steps took him back to the parapet. He grasped it with both hands and leaned over, craning his neck to watch the falling weights.

"I don't care how the mechanism works, so don't bother telling me. Let's dance. I've only a few more weeks of freedom," she pleaded.

He straightened up and shook his hair back. It was blond and floppy.

They went into the study and began to dance. He knew how to do the Swirl.

"It was all the rage when I was an undergraduate," he said.

"But that must have been ages ago! It's supposed to be the latest thing."

"Perhaps you are a bit behind the times here. Or perhaps it wasn't all that long ago."

When he smiled there was a little gap between his front teeth.

Miranda was aware that her full red skirt swirled very effectively. She pulled him out onto the balcony again. The music came to an end and was replaced by the soft cooing of a dove as one of the Royal Pigeon Express flew above them on its way to the dovecote.

Their hands met on the parapet just as she had intended.

"I think we should stop now," Conrad said. He wasn't out of breath, but his eyes were bright.

"No one is going to throw you down the mountain. Not nowadays. It's quite safe." Just as she was getting somewhere too.

"It isn't proper."

There was a knock at the study door.

She released his hand and turned once more to look at the crags and spires all around them, their colours slowly changing in the oblique light. The shadow of the Netherworld crept up the western mountainsides like a talon stretching out to grasp her, to take her from the world of light, as one day it would take all people, even princesses. She watched the sun's rim touch the spear point of the highest peak.

"Excuse me, Madam. The fitters are here."

It was Elaine, Miranda's lady-in-waiting. She had entered silently and stood framed in the arch like an angel in a picture. She was a little older than Miranda, but not as tall. Miranda envied her delicate appearance.

Conrad bowed politely as they left, but she was certain that he turned immediately to watch the sunlight slant through the distant peaks. Tomorrow he would be sure to give her a lecture on the chemicals that shattered each beam into a different rainbow.

Miranda's wedding dress was fitted in the room known as the Crystal Hall. The couturier was Madame Zweitz, arrived that day from Mont Pierre. She was attended by the dwarfs John and Marie O'Brien. Madame explained the significance of the various features of the dress, predominantly blue to symbolise Miranda's future husband, Carol Decyel, but merging into green at the hem and sleeves to represent her father's house.

"You should wear your hair long, Madam. It is the fashion at Castel Decyel especially if the hair is dark."

"Have you been there?" Miranda asked.

"I've seen the Prince," said John, speaking for the first time.

Miranda looked at him. There was something sinister about his deep voice and black beard with that childish body. She imagined him with a dagger in his mouth.

"I have his picture," said Miranda, "but can you trust the images in this room?"

John watched the Prince, full-size, walk towards them on the other side of the crystal wall.

"It's a good likeness," John said. "He is an excellent fellow so they say and the family is powerful. Your father has chosen well."

The lady-in-waiting uttered a shocked exclamation. Marie laughed.

"You must forgive us, Madam. It is a tradition that the O'Briens speak their minds no matter what the company."

The picture dissolved, to be replaced by a beautiful young woman with long black hair, wearing a dress that matched her eyes. Miranda was surprised and delighted to recognise herself.

That night she and Elaine spoke of their futures.

They sat in the Princess's bedchamber, warm candlelight flickered on their faces — it was one of Miranda's luxuries to use expensive beeswax rather than cheap electricity.

"I wish that you were to stay with me at Decyel. It is so far from here and I will be among strangers," Miranda said.

"But Madam, I shall rejoin you just as soon as my Juniper can get a transfer. Speak to the Doge again. He must hear you this time."

They exchanged tragic glances. In spite of all entreaties Elaine's fiancé had, because of his junior rank, been denied the command of the Princess's Escort for the hazardous flight over the mountains, and must remain at Monte Verde as part of the Doge's personal guard.

"And we shall be together for the journey and my wedding. What an adventure! I shall miss my brother and my father and yet I can't wait to fly up in the air like a sky singer and look at the Hedgehog's spiky back from up there. And I want to see the Castel on the Cobalt Spire and meet Decyel."

Her voice was firm now. She could visualise the horizon and see herself looking over the unknown eastern slopes of the Green Range and into the pits of the Netherworld. Mysterious lights winked. She drifted down.

Someone screamed. "Miranda! Oh wake up Madam!"

It was Elaine. Miranda, eager to go on dreaming, pushed her away.

"There's something crawling outside the window!" Elaine whispered, her terrified fingers digging into Miranda's arm.

They heard a stealthy hiss, something being dragged over glass. Miranda leaped out of bed, doused the light and ran to the window.

Elaine dithered, knowing she should not let her mistress go near the source of danger, but too timid to protest.

Miranda waved an impatient hand at her.

"Fetch the Guard! Quick!" she snapped.

She was aware of Elaine's stumbling egress behind her, but by now her nose was pressed against the heavy glass. It was pitch-dark — no moons tonight — she could see nothing and the rustling had stopped.

When the Guard thundered in, their captain bowed and led the Princess into the antechamber.

The lady-in-waiting threw a silk wrap around the royal shoulders and gazed adoringly at the Captain, who Miranda now recognised as Juniper, Elaine's beloved and the owner of the handsomest legs on Monte Verde. He was issuing terse instructions now.

A man stood guard by the window. The rest were ordered to search the ramparts. They wouldn't find anything of course. They never did.

"It was a Netherling... oh I'm sure of it. Creeping into windows to suck the blood of babies..."

"And virgins, Elaine, don't forget the virgins," said Miranda scornfully. "It was probably a bat or perhaps an owl." She felt her skin prickle. They both knew that owls and bats didn't scratch windows like that.

But the Guard did find something.

Wantonly and apparently without motive four men had been murdered, their throats cut as they took a late drink together on the battlements. One had been the Doge's personal valet, one the castle's Second Chef and the third the Doge's senior Balloon Master and most shocking of all, the fourth had been a Deacon of the Chapel Royal.

After that night the Doge ordered flyers around the castle during the hours of darkness as well as the usual sentries. Miranda and Elaine became used to seeing criss-cross beams of light outside the bedroom window and the occasional flashing eye of one of the flittercats ridden by the daring Captain and his patrolmen.

Dark rumours spread from the flag tower to the deepest prison. Was there a scheme from one of the neighbouring dukedoms to undermine morale at Monte Verde?

Or perhaps the dreadful Dame of the Glass Mountain, gazing at the reflection of the widowed Doge in her frozen spyglass was plotting to destroy him by her secret arts.

Were the local reavers, under their new leader, probing the Doge's defences before massing for an aerial attack?

But the most popular theory was that the assassin had been a Netherling, one of those legendary creatures who were supposed to live in the Depths where no human had ever set foot, but who were said to climb up to the Heights in search of human blood when the fancy took them. After all, who but a creature of the Dark would commit sacrilege as well as murder by killing a man of God?

But gradually the talk died down. No further killings

occurred near the castle. The Doge's Guard arrested a man who stabbed his employer in a tavern brawl on one of the lower peaks, but that was a common enough event.

Miranda became the focus of attention as the day of her departure drew near.

She spent more time with her father than she had done for years. They looked out from the battlements together on many a morning, blinking as the sun broke its light on the distant mountain spires, or watching the swaying cables bringing merchandise and tribute from the petty lords of the smaller peaks that surrounded their little kingdom.

Some of the lords, arriving by flittercat or cable-drawn gondola, presented their wedding gifts in person.

Miranda received them graciously and listened to their barely concealed chagrin, ("Such a pity that the Doge found it necessary to marry his daughter away from her own people") or ambition, ("How is Her Highness's brother? He must be nearly ten years old now; very near in age to my little Arlene.").

The Doge smiled quietly and ignored them.

The bride's trousseau was complete and Madame Zweitz had returned to her own mountain, but the O'Briens begged to accompany the Princess on her voyage, and the Doge, to Miranda's surprise, had agreed.

The various members of Miranda's entourage were now gathering in preparation for the journey. An envoy, in the blue and silver livery of Decyel, had arrived to escort the party. She was a tall, middle-aged woman wearing the tabard of a career diplomat. She removed her white fur hat and a stiff flag of auburn hair fell forward as she bowed, male fashion, to the Princess.

"Chatte Blanche, at your service Madam," she said.

And of course there was the replacement Balloon Master and his crew; as well as the Guard of Honour, hand picked by the Doge himself, and to be led by Captain Boito, who was small, bowlegged and Juniper's senior in rank by two years.

Elaine sulked, but Miranda smiled and chattered all day.

At night she sometimes wept quietly while Elaine snored, and then scolded herself, remembering that she had agreed to this adventure from the beginning, assuring her father that it was what she wanted.

There were no more lessons now, and when Conrad Danser requested an audience Miranda thought that the time had come for her to say goodbye to another friend.

"What will you do now, Dr Danser? Do you have another ignorant princess to instruct?"

"No Madam, er... Miranda. I'm going back to the University. I've always wanted to you know..."

"Oh... those glittering spires! Won't you miss me at all, Conrad?"

He pushed his hair back. She always managed to fluster him these days.

"I thought... if you would permit me. The northern part of the route, it's on the way..."

She saw her smile reflected in his glasses. When he strode out, head high, shoulders square, it occurred to Miranda that Captain Juniper could well have a rival in the best-looking legs contest.

When scholarly individuals like Conrad, poring over antique texts, read of "rosy fingered dawn", they were perplexed by what they took to be the colour-blindness of the ancients.

Dawn, as the moderns perceived it, was a violent, unladylike affair; a sudden, blinding light that quenched the stars and moons and slammed against the jagged peaks with such force that it shattered into a spectrum.

Dawn was a blast of trumpets; a signal to advance.

It was the traditional time to start on long journeys.

In that glittering light, eyes shone with anticipation (Miranda and Conrad) or with tears of disappointment (Elaine). The tall Balloon Master already scanned the route ahead, his eyes guarded from the fierce light by brows like thunder clouds, his black beard shading the face of Captain Boito beside him.

Green and blue pennants fluttered from the royal gondola suspended from its silken balloon, a globe of blue shot with green, held in a golden net. Every battlement, balcony, parapet and embrasure was crowded with people waving ribbons and handkerchiefs. Every peak within viewing distance had its crown of daredevil climbers eager to watch a unique spectacle.

The gondola already contained Elaine, Conrad and the O'Briens (Marie would act as maid to Miranda and Elaine, John's function was unclear), ten guardsmen (two of whom were from Decyel) and the vessel's crew of six.

Only the trio of well fed military flittercats, tethered to the craft, were oblivious to the excitement. They slept in midair, held up by the inflated gas bladders in their portly bellies.

The onlookers turned towards the royal balcony as the sound of a trumpet announced the presence of the Doge. He was wearing his ceremonial green robe. His right hand was resting on his young son's shoulder. On his left was Miranda. The crowd could not hear what they said to each other, but she curtseyed and kissed his ring of office before he embraced her for the last time. She bent again to kiss her little brother and then, preceded by the Prince's envoy, walked down the narrow floating bridge to the gondola which was to be her home for the next few weeks. Captain Boito and the Balloon Master followed.

A huge cheer from the multitude was interrupted by a series of deafening reports, rapidly becoming a continuous roar of echoes, as the Great Gun of Monte Verde fired the royal salute.

This was the signal to cast off.

The *Green Princess* answered with a gout of flame from the firing chamber. Freed of the guys, the ship rose gently and started north.

Miranda, gazing downward, could see the spines of their curled hedgehog world — a gaily coloured hedgehog, with a green stripe marking the range which included her beloved Monte Verde.

Conrad spent his time peering down through a spyglass as if he could learn the secrets of the Netherworld by looking at it for long enough; but no telescope could penetrate those sunless depths. Sometimes he mounted the rigging and helped the crew.

Miranda wanted to climb the inspection ladders and reach the balloon itself, but Captain Boito opined that it was too dangerous, and on this occasion Elaine agreed with him. Miranda watched enviously as Chatte Blanche and the Captain perched side by side on one of the high platforms, took careful aim at the Great Turns that followed the *Green Princess* snapping for food scraps. Both were excellent shots with a harpoon gun, and the birds made a welcome addition to the pot.

She pleaded with Boito. “I won’t get another chance like this. I’m probably going to spend the rest of my life at Decyel. At least let me ride one of the cats!”

The Captain was still a little unused to her frank manner, but he shook his head so vigorously that his splendid moustache took a while to catch up and was still bouncing as he spoke.

“I can’t risk it, Madam. Please don’t forget that we cannot take St. Bernards on such a long journey. A Fall would be the end of you.”

And of your bright new career, she thought crossly.

By night the royal party sat around the glow of the balloon’s fire chamber after the evening meal, listening to descriptions of Decyel from Chatte Blanche (whose real name was Annie McIver) or shivering at stories of the Dame of the Glass Mountain from Marie O’Brien.

When Captain Boito got up to sing in that rich tenor voice of his, Elaine sulked and Miranda wished he would be quiet so that she could listen to Conrad’s guitar accompaniment. Irritated, she raised her eyes to the balloon and then started violently as she saw the dwarf John O’Brien hanging like a spider from the rigging. He grinned reassuringly — impudently, she thought. Why had her father allowed him to come on this trip?

The next day they ran into a swarm of transparent parajellies. The lookout failed to see them, and before the Balloon Master had time to shout "Get Below!" a cloud of floating shapes descended waving deadly tendrils.

Boito and several of the guards drew their pistols.

"No!" cried Chatte Blanche. "If you scatter the venom you could blind us! Cover your faces!" She pulled her ornate tabard over her head and flung it over Miranda.

There was a terrible scream from high up near the balloon and a man plummeted from the observation post. As he hurtled by them he appeared, to the horrified onlookers, to have a shimmering mist enclosing his body. Within a second this had become suffused with feathers of scarlet until the whole jelly was visible, outlined in its victim's blood. Clinging together, predator and prey fell towards the dark, but just before the human component Fell into the Netherworld the keener sighted could just perceive a red dot detach itself and float away.

But at that time all those on deck were too busy saving their own lives to comment on such horrors.

"Free the flittercats!" Boito shouted.

There was a ferocious caterwauling followed by the sound a balloon makes when it deflates rapidly. The cats were using biological jet propulsion to chase their dinner.

The Balloon Master called again for everyone to take cover. By that time the ladies, even Chatte Blanche were safely in their sleeping quarters. Miranda, freed from the tabard, looked around and counted heads and then stared through the porthole. A wide-eyed cat flew past grinning; its teeth dripped jelly. There was a hoarse scream outside. Elaine joined in. Marie looked anxious.

The door burst open and Conrad stumbled in, followed by John.

"Um... do any of you ladies have a... handkerchief?"

Conrad asked shakily. “Oh thank you, Miss O’Brien.”

He took his glasses off and wiped them. “First time I’ve found an advantage to wearing the things,” he added.

“The schoolmaster said he *wanted to take a closer look*! You, Sir, are an idiot!” It was difficult to tell if John was smiling or snarling through that beard.

Miranda looked down at him with the hauteur of generations, but before she could speak there was a knock at the door and Marie opened it to admit Captain Boito and the Master.

“I can inform Your Highness that the attack has been repulsed,” Boito said, “but, alas, at the cost of another life — one of your men, Madam.” He glanced towards Chatte Blanche.

“I can only say that such a thing should have been impossible. We had assurances that our route would be free from dangerous native species.” This time he looked back at the Balloon Master. The Master mumbled something about freak air currents, but nobody quite heard what he said — he had a strangely soft and muffled voice for so large a man.

That night, when prayers had been said for the two dead men and order had been restored, Miranda and Elaine were alone in the royal stateroom. Elaine went to the door and opening it, looked into the antechamber (which served as Marie’s cabin). When she returned she spoke in a whisper.

“Miranda. I’m afraid.”

Miranda frowned impatiently.

“Madam I... I think someone was trying to kill me. Someone tried to push me out of the gondola during the parajelly attack.”

“Who was it?”

“I couldn’t see. I was covering my eyes like we were told. Please take me seriously, Madam! Think of that thing outside the castle window.”

Miranda felt an unpleasant hollow feeling in her chest.

“Why should anyone want to kill you? I’m a more likely target, surely.”

“There’s something queer happening, Madam; two deaths on our voyage already.”

Miranda suddenly recalled that mental image of John O’Brien with a knife in his teeth. Why had the outlandish dwarf and his sister come on the journey? Elaine spoke again.

“And I’d certainly be dead if it wasn’t for John O’Brien,”

Miranda started. “The dwarf? Why?”

“He held on to me — stopped me going over. He must be incredibly strong. But I think I know who the traitor is.”

“Who?”

“Captain Boito,” whispered the Lady-in-waiting.

They had been travelling for a week now; gliding northwards at first following the eastern side of the Green Range, but then towards the east and the Distant Range, which lay between them and their destination. The craft’s shadow, which they had watched trickling over the tops of the green mountains, was swallowed by the utter black of the Abysmal Gorge that now lay below. At night when the glinting kaleidoscope of the mountains had been snuffed out, a novel and eerie array of lights spread below them as the Netherworld came into its own. Miranda could see fire pits like red eyes, golden streaks, which Conrad had told her were almost certainly molten rivers and very occasionally, flashes of lightning far below, always followed a few seconds later by a low rumbling noise.

Marie, standing beside her, muttered the old children’s rhyme:

“People great
And people small
All are born
And all will Fall.”

As they approached the Distant Range the Master ordered some of the ballast to be jettisoned and the balloon rose until it glided above a blanket of cloud. Ahead, a break in the highest columns of the range faced them like giant panpipes.

Conrad became agitated. He turned to the Master.

"You're making for the Pipe Pass aren't you? I understood I was to be put down at Hautlac Eyrie. You will have to stop there for fresh water and provisions surely? If we go this way we will miss it entirely."

The Master's bearded chin jutted obstinately; his burly neck was red.

"Change of plans, Schoolmaster. We don't have time to stop."

"Why not? And my name is Doctor Danser, if you please."

"Likelihood of foul weather — sixty percent chance, I reckon, at this time of year. Can't afford the delay. And I'm Master on this ship, Doctor."

Conrad turned away angrily and spent the next hour attacking John O'Brien with the practice foil. O'Brien usually ran rings around him, but not today.

"It's completely illogical," he complained later to Chatte Blanche, who had also defended herself unsuccessfully against his swordplay. By this time most of the ship's company was on deck watching the fencing.

"The Pipe Pass is miles out of our way," he continued.

"I've heard of that route being used," she said. "The winds can be very treacherous up by the lake when the volcanoes are active. I think our Balloon Master knows his job. You may have to delay your trip to the University." Her thin lips twitched slightly. "Who knows, perhaps your Princess will invite you to her wedding."

But Conrad was already looking up at the sky, to be followed by the rest of the company. They heard a high-pitched keening coming from high above them.

"Stormvultures! Perhaps old Blackbeard is right," John O'Brien said.

Two shabby, black shapes with red-tipped wings sailed past the gondola. The flittercats set up a yowling and almost immediately the clouds boiled up from below to engulf them all in a dense fog, which changed rapidly to an avalanche of rain.

The balloon was beaten like a kettledrum. The gondola swayed violently flinging two guardsmen to the deck.

"All passengers and peaks men to quarters!" shouted the Master in his high, muffled voice.

In the space of a minute it had become almost pitch dark.

"This way Miranda," called Elaine.

Miranda couldn't see anything. There was another lurch and she fell over and began to slide down very slowly. The deck had become a hill. She had never before felt so much terror at the prospect of an imminent Fall.

A sheet of lightning scorched the sky and that instant of illumination was enough for her to orientate herself and see that she was within reach of the guardrail.

There was an almighty crash of thunder as she snatched one of the coiled emergency ropes which were firmly attached to it at regular intervals.

"Madam, come towards me. I'm holding the door open." It was Conrad's voice.

The eerie light of the next flash revealed the position of everyone on deck caught at one instant like frozen ghosts.

Elaine was clinging to one of the safety straps attached to the door of the living quarters. Conrad, fighting the gradient, pushed against the door itself and at his feet was a dark figure, its right hand stretched out to reach for his ankle. Something gleamed in the other hand. Elaine cried out in the split second before the thunder roared again.

With another lurch the gondola righted itself.

The deck was now only a few degrees off the horizontal allowing the Princess to scurry uphill towards her companions. She was aware of a struggle, a man's cry of pain and another shouting, "Got him!" She put her hand out, groping wildly until she clutched a handful of Elaine's dress. She felt for the doorframe with her free hand, held onto it and tugged with all her strength. The two young women fell into the room together. The light came on automatically. Elaine scrambled to her feet and backed away from the door.

A dripping swordsman had crossed the threshold.

"I got him," repeated Conrad. "Don't know who it was, but there's a hole in him somewhere." He shut the door.

Miranda got up and went into her room, directing the other two to follow.

"Well, it certainly wasn't a dwarf," Conrad said a few minutes later when Miranda had explained her uneasiness about the O'Briens.

He and the lady-in-waiting were standing in front of the seated Princess. All three dripped uncomfortably.

"He had a knife! I couldn't see his face, but I'm sure it was Boito!" said Elaine. "Oh I wish Juniper was here!" Her tears added to the puddle of rainwater on the floor.

Miranda told her to pull herself together.

"The question is not just who, but why," said Conrad frowning thoughtfully.

"Something crawling outside your window at the castle..."

"A Netherling..."

"Nonsense, Elaine!" This from the Princess.

Conrad continued, waving a finger in schoolmasterly fashion.

"Murders at the castle... an apparent attack on Elaine and then on me." He took a few paces around the tiny stateroom, ducking his head to avoid the ceiling.

"Madam, you must send an express courier to His Highness the Doge. I believe you are in great danger." He indicated the basket containing the Princess's pigeons.

"If only we could use the wireless rays of the Ancients..."

"Well we can't, so it is pointless to wail about it," Miranda said. A picture flashed across her memory. "I think the assassin is left handed."

"Boito is right handed," said Conrad.

Thanks to heroic efforts from the Balloon Master and his men the *Green Princess* survived the storm. With the passengers and guards ("damned peak-clingers") confined to quarters, he and his crew were able to repair the rent in the balloon and reinflate it, but they had lost a great deal of height and were hovering perilously close to the zone a few hundred feet above the Netherworld, where air currents were utterly unpredictable. Only John O'Brien, whose prowess on the rigging proclaimed him a true balloonist, was allowed on deck.

The gallant flittercats had acted as tugs in helping to keep the craft steady during the turmoil. The planet had designed them, like the parajellies, to survive the excesses of its climate. But the troubles besetting the voyage of the *Green Princess* were not yet over.

With the repairs scarcely complete, and the vessel not yet underway, the cry of "Reavers! Reavers!" floated down from the lookout post.

Captain Boito and his men thundered on deck. The more foolhardy passengers left their cabins in spite of indignant orders from both the Master and the Captain. Everyone hurried to the forward end of the gondola.

A dozen winged shapes could be seen descending from the direction of the Pipe Pass. As they approached it was possible to see that each gigantic bird carried two heavily armed men.

"Rocs! Real live rocs! Amazing!" cried Conrad. "I thought they were extinct." He snatched Captain Boito's telescope and jammed it to his right eye.

"I'll have that instrument if you please, Doctor," snarled the Captain. He whirled around to face the Balloon Master and the assembled company, his moustachios flapping wildly.

"Action stations, men!" he shouted. "I'm taking command now. Rodrigo, guard Her Highness! Master, have the cats hauled in! Sergeant, issue ammunition to all male personnel. Yes, passengers too."

Two of the ship's crew reeled in the three flying steeds and two of them were immediately mounted by members of the Royal Guard.

The sergeant returned white-faced from his trip to the armoury and, bending, whispered something to his commanding officer. The Captain looked aghast.

"We will do our best, Sergeant. Issue everything available," he said quietly, and then raising his voice. "There is a... temporary shortage of laser packs: Men! Use your harpoon guns when I give the order." As he vaulted onto his cat he hissed, "There is treachery aboard!"

At that moment the door to the Princess's quarters opened and the four women passengers made their appearance on deck followed by a protesting Guardsman Rodrigo.

Miranda, looking pale and determined, stood there every inch a princess.

On her right was Chatte Blanche wearing a sheathed rapier at her belt and carrying a crossbow. To her left was Elaine, wide eyed and clutching a sharp pair of scissors. Bringing up the rear, Marie held a vicious-looking curved knife in each hand.

John O'Brien ran to the guardrail and trained a telescope on the leading roc.

"So that's their new leader," he muttered as the grinning pirate chief came into focus. "Black Jamie Jonah himself."

"That's odd," said Elaine, who had overheard him. Marie looked up at her.

"I mean it is a bit of a coincidence although I suppose it's a fairly common name..."

But the rest of her words were drowned by a terrifying ululation. The enemy was upon them.

The wings of the great birds almost brushed the sides of the gondola, which rocked in the wind of their passage. Black Jonah, a burly man with a shock of black hair, balanced upright on the broad saddle of his mount. He brandished a laser pistol in his right hand. With alarming precision, the second rider on each roc aimed his weapon at the Princess.

"Nobody move or the Princess dies!" roared a red headed man next to the chief.

With death defying skill Jonah leaped from the saddle

directly onto the deck of the *Green Princess*. His men, equally acrobatic, followed screeching horribly. Chatte Blanche pushed Miranda to the deck and, kneeling in front of her, took careful aim with her crossbow.

"Fire!" yelled Boito from his flittercat and fired his harpoon gun.

Chatte Blanche loosed a bolt at the red headed pirate who had threatened the Princess and he dropped to the deck before he could bring his laser to bear.

Conrad adjusted his glasses and drew his rapier slowly as he gazed at the pirate chief. Something was nagging at the back of his mind. He leaped to defend the Envoy as she fitted another bolt.

The pounding of heavy boots rocked the ship and then there was a whoop of delight from Miranda's troops as a shot from Boito's weapon felled one of the great birds; it spiralled shrieking into the abyss, dragging its rider to his doom.

But retribution was swift. Rapiers, arrows and even harpoon guns could not win against lasers, and when Boito gave a sudden cry and slumped in his seat the royal party lost heart. In the end the reavers forced the remnant of their opponents to retreat to the centre of the deck until they were all huddled against the balloon's fire chamber. The fight was over.

One of the ruffians pulled the Princess to her feet. Black Jonah swaggered up, grinning ferociously.

"Thanks for your help Brother!" he said, waving at the prisoners.

"Brother?" said Miranda, looking around puzzled.

But before she had time to speculate further, a small shape with a knife in its teeth plunged from the rigging and hurled Jonah to the deck. Everyone had forgotten the dwarf.

The chieftain's smile was erased as he felt O'Brien's knife shave the stubble on his throat.

"I have a warrant for your arrest, Black Jonah! Anything you say will be used to incriminate you if I have anything to do with it and you had better get your men to release the prisoners or I'll cut your throat before showing you the warrant card," said John through his teeth.

The pirates stood looking at their fallen leader, waiting for instruction. John twanged his knife against the Chief's Adam's apple.

"Do as he says!" croaked Jonah.

With a gesture of disdain Miranda shrugged off the hairy hand that grasped her upper arm. The other members of her party raised their heads and looked more hopeful.

"Move away towards the stern rail all of you!" grated John, twisting the knife again.

The invaders backed away until there was a gap of several feet between them and the ship's company.

"Throw your weapons overboard. Now!"

All of the prisoners turned to watch the pirates who slowly, and with great reluctance began to jettison their pistols and sabres.

That was the ideal moment for the traitor to show his hand. As John O'Brien watched for any false move from the pirates, a figure leaped forward from Miranda's group and fell upon the dwarf from the rear, wrenching the knife from his hand.

The pirates roared victoriously and surged back from the rail, the remainder of their weapons gleaming. Black Jonah rose rubbing his neck.

"Thanks again Brother," he said to the Balloon Master, who held John at arm's length in his strong left hand.

"I knew he reminded me of someone obnoxious," said Conrad. "Without the beard they would be identical."

"We are identical!" said the Master.

"I did try to tell you," said Elaine. "Think of the Master's name. It's Jonah!"

"I'm Walt. He's Jamie — identical twins."

"Except that he is left handed and has a beard." They laughed in unison.

"Same silly squeaky voice too," gasped John struggling in midair.

"And now for the little policeman! Hold him still Walt," Jamie said slowly, raising his laser pistol and taking aim at the dwarf.

There was a shot.

John continued wriggling.

It was the pirate chief who looked down in disbelief at the red stain spreading over his chest. He groaned and collapsed to his knees.

John squirmed free and snatched up the pistol which he promptly turned on the traitor.

"Oh, well done Madam!" he cried.

Everyone turned towards the Princess who was to be seen tucking a smoking pistol into her garter, her haughty demeanour utterly dismissing the slightest hint of impropriety.

But all was not yet over.

The remaining twin lashed out with furious speed knocking John off balance.

The pirates turned on the royal party and a furious melee ensued. This time the fight was more evenly matched. The pirates had lost many of their weapons and their Chief lay dead in a pool of blood. They still had the advantage of numbers, but Miranda and her followers, knowing that their cause was just, fought with ferocious bravery.

John brought down three scoundrels with Jonah's pistol, one of them a roc-rider (he had retrieved the weapon after Walt, the Balloon Master, knocked him down).

A bolt from Chatte Blanche's crossbow disabled another of the riders, who dropped his firearm into the chasm and was thus rendered useless. She was immediately assailed by a huge ruffian with a sabre, but Marie, a knife in each hand, hamstrung him from behind and he crashed to the deck to be dragged to the side by two of his comrades.

Miranda's troops cheered. The reavers were now in full retreat.

But the traitor was still armed and dangerous. Pursued by one of the loyal balloonists, he turned, dispatched him with a laser shot and leaped for the rigging. Then, clinging onto the ropes with one hand, he peered between them and took careful aim.

"Look out Miranda!" shouted Elaine.

She and the Princess threw themselves down beside the wounded guardsman they had been tending. But a blue and silver figure had already dived in front of Miranda into the path of the deadly beam. Chatte Blanche crumpled to the deck without a sound.

The athletic Balloon Master tried to leap onto one of the remaining rocs, but his path was blocked by a knot of loyalists, one of whom succeeded in knocking the pistol from his hand, but was unable to hold onto him.

Walt jumped again, and swarmed upwards towards the balloon, climbing ever more quickly in the knowledge that he was hotly pursued. At last he turned at bay and faced his enemy. Seeing who it was, he laughed.

"So you are curious to see the Netherworld, Schoolmaster. I'll grant you your wish. I still have this!" He flourished his sabre left-handed.

Conrad, too, had drawn his sword, but he appeared afraid. Walt, nimble and barefoot as a monkey, continued to taunt the scholar. Conrad retreated clumsily on shod feet, clinging to the ropes with his left hand and flailing ineffectually with the rapier held in his right.

The two climbed ever higher. The balloon's shadow loomed over them, its bulk blotting out the sun. Conrad glanced around, and then retreated again, parrying desperately.

From far below, the onlookers heard the clash of steel and saw the Doctor move around until he could be seen with his back to a patch of bright sky between the edge of the balloon and the top of the mountain peaks to the west. The setting sun, until then eclipsed by the balloon, now blazed forth as an eye-splitting crescent at the balloon's lower margin. Conrad seemed to slip and Walt advanced, slashing at his opponent's head.

Conrad ducked and the sun shone full in Walt's face.

As the traitor attempted to shield his eyes Conrad lunged, and followed the hit with a high kick to the midriff.

And so, with a strangled cry of, "Damned peak-clingers..." Walt Fell.

Miranda and Conrad sat watching another sunset. Three days had passed since the rout of the pirates. But victory had not been without loss. The reavers had lost two of their birds and ten of their men but in their retreat had holed the balloon and towed away two of the flittercats. The *Green Princess* had drifted downwards, the last cat guiding it onto one of the lower peaks of the Distant Range, where the crew anchored the gondola to one of the projecting spires. The deflated balloon drooped over the edge.

Worse than the loss of the balloon, four more guardsmen and two balloonists had died in the fighting; and Annie McIver, the Chatte Blanche, who had been pierced through the heart saving Miranda's life. Wearing her tabard of office, she was cast into the abyss by the remaining guardsman from Decyel.

Boito had survived in spite of a serious shoulder wound. It was his bravery that had prevented the capture of their last flittercat, fighting off an attack from one of the roc-riders with the deadly accuracy of his marksmanship. He lay now in the cabin quarters of the gondola tended by a repentant Elaine.

The sun performed its usual pyrotechnics, shimmering behind the rose and coral of the westward spires before it winked out.

Lights appeared in the balloon-silk tents of the guards.

They were getting short of food now, but at least there was water. They could hear it splashing down the mountainside a few feet from where they sat and see it sparkle in the reflected starlight.

"How much longer, do you think?" asked the Princess.

"Two days there as the cat flies… three days back with

turbo-balloons say... Pity we can't communicate better. I believe this is the only recorded planet where it is impossible to use wireless waves, you know."

"Yes, I do know. You've lectured me on it. Remember? We'll have to make do with Marie and John. They amaze me. A whole family of international detectives."

She laughed, recollecting their last conversation. John had bowed formally.

"Farewell, Madam. My wife and I offer our sincere good wishes for your future happiness."

"Your wife? I do apologise, Marie. I thought you were John's sister."

Marie had smiled. "I am, Madam. The O'Briens keep themselves to themselves."

They heard a faint scuttling sound.

Conrad moved a little closer.

"Yes, the O'Briens! Hired by the Doge to protect you because they had intelligence of a kidnap plot. And all the time, the traitor..." He stopped suddenly and rose very quietly to his feet.

"Look!" he whispered.

Miranda followed the direction of his pointing finger still faintly visible in the twilight. Something small and black, little more than a shadow, was climbing out of the depths of the gorge. It turned burning golden eyes towards them. Miranda gasped and drew back, but Conrad lowered his hand and held it palm up towards the creature. It hesitated, and then rose to stand on its hind legs. Did it, too, raise a hand in half salute, before scuttling down into the utter blackness of the pit?

"A Netherling! They do exist. I knew it!" He sat down again.

"They will have to believe me. When I get back to the University I will raise an expedition. I'll get the money somehow; it may take years, but I'll do it! A new native species... probably intelligent... Homo profundus danseri..."

He laughed and suddenly Miranda felt his arms around

her. The faint light from the newly risen Lunette caught his glasses so that his eyes seemed to glow.

"When God made the worlds he thought it would be fun to make each one like an animal. Our world is like a spiky Hedgehog curled in a ball. We live on the tips of the spikes."

Miranda smiled at her children. Little Carol laughed with delight. He loved animals. Five-year-old Cordelia was more serious.

"Does anyone live down at the bottom of the spikes?"

"No one knows for sure. Down there is a world of mystery."

Cordelia pushed her hair out of her eyes. "When I grow up I'm going to find out," she said.

"Yes," her mother said. "I think perhaps you will."

When Cordelia smiled she had a little gap between her front teeth.

From the Point of View of the Dog

Daniel Kaysen

Daniel Kaysen's short fiction has appeared in a range of venues including Strange Horizons, Interzone, *and* Black Static. *His stories have been reprinted in* Best Horror of the Year, *edited by Ellen Datlow, and* Science Fiction: The Year's Best, *edited by Rich Horton.*

Daniel is a master of subtle strangeness. The story that follows is strange not only in terms of the story being told, but also in the manner of its telling. What do we think of when we look up at the moon? What does it mean to us, and to those who share their lives with us? And what should we think of a man who goes out into the empty vastness of space, and chooses to come back home...?

As we walk down the street I think: *This is exactly why he came here.*

It's early morning, and we're going to fetch the morning paper. The streets are quiet compared to the fear and hurry of the company town. Just a few people here, just a few cars. Just the right number.

Back there, in the company town, there was too much of everything. And none of it leaving him in peace, even when the news was good. When the news was good cars would honk their horns and people would come up to him, clasp his elbow, slap his back, shout syllables at him. Hey. Man. Great. I would watch him responding, trying not to slide away, trying to smile back, trying to be upbeat, but a second or two behind their emotions. Like a child in church, trying to catch up with the hymn, under the pastor's enthusiastic glare.

It was bad enough when the news was good.

And then he went away, and when he came back the news was bad, and even his closest friends hesitated when they saw him. Fixed their faces, the best they could manage. Took deep breaths and rehearsed their casual greetings. They walked in clouds of sudden fear at the sight of him, those people, those friends. The fear took away their friendship but they didn't know it.

And the enemies — which was everyone else, really — walked in clouds of anger. Damped anger mostly, though a couple of men once threw punches. My master put an arm above his head to ward them off. And after that his cower smell was stronger, each day we stayed in the company town.

So now we are here. The cower smell grows fainter by the day. Still there, cower smells never disappear, but there are other smells now, other sounds, around him. He whistles sometimes, when he is pottering at home. Once or twice I've even seen him looking at the guitar. One day he'll play again, cursing softly when he goes wrong in the picking, as he always did in the company town. Maybe his picking will go better now.

Of course, some people here still vaguely recognise him in the street. He was a face in the newspapers back a times, when he went, when he came back. But there are so many faces in the newspapers. And there are so many words. The faces and words detach after a while. I'm sure most of the people here have forgotten that he wasn't a hero, that the trip wasn't a success. To them he's just a guy who went and came back.

There's always something more important, here. Simple things. Falling in love. Falling out of love. Births and deaths and marriages and church bells. Faces in newspapers are ghosts, here. Thin people. Respected but not central.

He buys his morning paper and we walk to the diner and outside the diner he looks at me.

And I sit on the sidewalk, in my spot, no need of a leash.

We're good like that. We smile at each other. See, I say to him, I know the routine. I'll sit here while you go drink your coffee. And see, he says to me, I know the routine. I'll sit in the diner while you watch the world go by.

Go sit I tell him. I'm fine.

So he goes into the diner, and I watch through the window, like I do every day.

She's there. The waitress, and she smiles the smile she's taken to smiling when he comes in, and he smiles his shy smile back.

When he comes out again I will smell his happiness on him, I know. Happiness and attraction. I will smell her happiness on him too, her happiness and attraction.

Through the window their mouths move, but I cannot hear their song. Knowing him it is a song of small things, a piano song. He doesn't talk like orchestras or operas, he doesn't talk like loud noises or surprises. And watching the waitress I guess that she doesn't either. I think she's always lived here, but this time of her life, this time of her self, is like moving here from a company town.

A machine to clean streets goes past, and I turn to watch it. Its brushes hustle the kerb. Smells from it, many smells, a carnival of smells.

A dog barks in the distance. Yap-dog. Barking at cars.

You wouldn't last long in the company town, o yap-dog.

And then I turn round once and I see it in the sky. The silver moon, pinned and empty in the blue of the morning.

Worse than the yap-dog, the silver moon.

And then I lie down, put my head on my paws, watch him smiling, her taking longer than she should to talk to him.

One of them will ask the other soon, in a week or a month: dinner? a movie? and the other will smile and nod and say yes, that would be nice. And it will be nice, I think. They will hold hands one day. I will get to smell her, say hello, be on my best behaviour. Be there when wanted, and wander round the yard when they want to be alone, sit on the porch under the swing when master wants me, him scratching my head, as he tells her of his orchestral past.

He'll cough and look up at the sky, perhaps the silver yap-dog moon will be there and he'll narrow his eyes a little.

What is it? she'll say.

And he'll tell her. I went, he'll say.

To where, she'll say, gentle.

To the moon, he'll say. And they'll be quiet.

And then he'll tell her. Before he went he was a hero in the company town, the town of the company that built the rockets. Chosen from all the country to be the man to go to the moon, and so he went, on his own.

The men a while before him had gone with others. But when they sent men together, however many or however few, they were up there too long and bad things happened. The metallic walls started closing in. The stars were pinprick eyeholes, watching them, whispering bad thoughts to them about their companions. Accidents happened. There were funerals, under flags, when they came back again.

So they tried sending a man on his own, but he didn't land and he came back and they said he had space dementia. Then another. Same thing, so they searched all the country for a man to go, one final test. A quiet man. Someone who could stand aloneness. And he was that man they found, a quiet man in the company town. He was the final test. Could a man go to the moon alone? Could a man live on the moon alone?

Much rested on this. Everything rested on this.

If he could survive then they could scatter quiet men to the moon, like silent fireworks, and they could all go there in their separate pods, men building all day and sleeping all night, in their separate sectors, preparing for the moon villages to come, the moon towns, the moon cities. One day the moon would all be concrete and trees, if only they could seed it with scattered men, men who could handle the journey alone and working alone.

He'll fall silent then. Perhaps she'll take his other hand. He'll scratch my head and offer her coffee, but she'll want the end of the story, under the stars.

The thing of it was, I was a hero, he'll say, with a small sad laugh. The man chosen from all the country. I didn't believe it, he'll say quietly, that I was a hero, and she'll squeeze his hand.

He'll say: I went and on the way I spoke to the President on the radio. Strange the things that happen in weightlessness.

And then orbiting the moon, once, twice, checking the landing site, watching the mountain shadows dancing like ghosts and sundials. Watching the mountains. The most beautiful mountains, he'll say.

She'll nod.

This is a mountain town we are in. Mountains in sight of the porch. That's why he came here.

And you know what I thought? he'll say. I thought: life's too short. I miss my home and my friends and my dog. What in hell excuse me am I doing the way up here, orbiting the moon? It was the mountains that made me think that. They're very beautiful up there, and beautiful things remind me of life and how it's very short.

So I came back. Didn't even land on the moon.

The President didn't call on my way home.

I told the reporters what I'd seen, what I'd thought. They could have jailed me for that, it wasn't what I'd agreed to say. But life is too short to lie.

And that was the end of the plan. No more moon of concrete and trees. I was mad, they said, like the others, they all agreed it. Space dementia syndrome. Space dementia of the pseudo-nostalgic variety. Everyone said I was mad. But they hated me too. Thought I had done it on purpose, lost them their jobs.

And I found my home wasn't my home any more, and my friends weren't my friends any more. Only my dog was my dog, so we packed up a trailer and drove till we came to the mountains. And here we are.

Good, she will say.

And I will get up and go and sit down next to her, and she will scratch my head, I think, and that will be that. Marriage one day. Births one day. Funerals one day.

Until those days the moon will circle and the mountains will be still and their shadows will move like sundials and ghosts and every morning he will fetch the paper and she will take a minute too long to talk to him and I will sit outside, smelling the smells, watching the mountains. Thinking of life being short and good.

When the wind is in the right direction I can hear the traffic, from the highway many miles away. Like a billion bees, trapped under glass, buzzing buzzing for more concrete.

When the air's too cold I can feel the stiffness beginning in my legs. It didn't used to be like that.

And when I am sitting outside watching them in the diner, strangers stop to say hello to me, talk to me, scratch me behind the ear, and I am on best behaviour. I say hello, and I remember their smells for when they come back.

Word gets around in a town like this. Good words get around quicker than bad.

So when people notice they're dating, the new man in town and Cathy from the diner, Maggie's daughter, people will say: what do we know of him? And they'll say: wasn't there something to do with the moon? And they'll frown, trying to remember if the ghost face belonged to a good story or a bad story, or a good story that turned bad or a bad story that turned good.

The world will stop as they try to remember. The shadows will still and the moon will halt.

And in that pause — while they're reaching about in the land of the ghostfaces, in the land of the dead — someone will say: that's his dog. You know the one? Sits outside the diner in the mornings, good as gold.

Lovely dog, they'll say.

Best behaviour.

And that will be it and they will smile: about time a

decent man found Cathy.

He does seem nice, that man, another will say.

Lovely dog, they'll say, with a nod. You can judge a man by the company he keeps. I've always said that. Haven't I always said that?

And the moon will return to its circling and the mountain shadows lengthen and the world will shift and move on.

MS Found in a Kangian Wintercamp

Sue Thomason

Sue Thomason lives in North Yorkshire with a GP and four cats. She has had a handful of short stories published in magazines and original anthologies, has completed NaNoWriMo four times, and is now working on a Proper Novel. She is Chair of Milford SF Writers Workshop (www.milfordsf.co.uk) and sometime book reviewer for VECTOR, *the critical journal of the British Science Fiction Association (www.bsfa.co.uk) and* FOUNDATION, *the international review of science fiction published by the Science Fiction Foundation (www.sf-foundation.org). Her other interests include cats, running, back-country backpacking, mathematical knitting, playing the flute in various musical genres and omnivorous reading.*

There is a tradition of "MS Found in a..." stories, which interested readers might like to investigate, perhaps starting with one Edgar Allen Poe. Here, Sue presents an intriguing science fictional take on the theme. The narrator of the story initially seems to know their purpose in carrying out fieldwork study of the Kangia, but after a "standard mindwipe" is anything known for certain...?

Day 1

Dropped off by airboat just outside the settlement line of a Kangian summercamp. I'm carrying a standard field support pack, and I've had a standard mindwipe. The Kangia are a friendly and hospitable neo-Inuit people inhabiting the shoreline of New Ellesmere. And that's all I know about them. Everything more specific has gone; everything! I've triggered every node in my memory store, and there's nothing there. Welcome to the joy of third-year fieldwork! It's a bit eerie, actually. I keep pulling data cascades that just aren't there. It's such a weird feeling, not to know. This must be how the early explorers felt.

I've gone through the standard greeting routine, which worked fine, and set up my tent where they showed me to. I'm cooking supper on my own dinky little stove. Feels like playing house. I'm all self-sufficient and cosy. The Kangia seem cute. And at least I don't have to start from scratch with the language. I mean, fieldwork's only a hundred and twenty days; with no translat I'd still be pointing and grunting, never mind plotting my integrated social profiles. Which I've started on, by the way, with an informant called Mikak. One look at the visuals should show you why — who could resist a grin like that!

I did hear of someone who cheated on her fieldwork, once. Didn't get a proper wipe. No, what happened was, she did a lot of untagged learning from physical media; watching visuals and reading books. Taking notes, I bet she did that too. It has to be cheating. They guarantee that everything we need for a good degree is on the linefeed. Learning offline, all that stuff in random storage, unwipeable... what an unfair advantage to take into fieldwork, right?

Day 3, I think

I had no idea how hard it would be to keep track of time without a watch in permanent daylight! I'm not sure how long I've been here... three days maybe? There are times when most people are inactive/asleep, and times when most people are active/awake, but some people definitely have longer or shorter "days" than others.

The summercamp routine is to hunt and gather, then render nearly all of the food into concentrate, which is kept in standard weather-sealed brick-packs. The food is shared between the Kangia and the *kirrik*. My translat says "dogs", but I don't remember that normal dogs hibernate? They must be gene-tweaks of some sort; maybe mods of marmots or something like that? I think they're very small, for dogs.

I know I should be talking up my journal every night, but I'm too tired; I've been picking berries all "day"! And the "day" before that, I walked for some very long time or distance up the river with Mikak to check out the slug traps. No; I can't think of something I'm probably going to have to eat as "slugs". I'll leave them as *oklo*. I hope I didn't show too much disgust! It's a Standard Fieldwork Problem, after all; eating the stuff that your study subjects eat. I remember something from the linefeed about an alternate where they'd artificially enriched the ocean until it was basically plankton soup. And that was their staple; a meal was basically seabroth, with maybe a dish of shellfish and a couple of growing-trays of sallet on the side. This was a formal diplomatic meal, and some outworld guest was making polite small talk to the person on her left, and he asked her how different this was from her meals at home. And she described her breakfast, using the impersonal nonspecific, which was their extremely polite conversational mode... And this man just stared at her, and said, "You put *dead things* in your *mouth*?"

So you have to remember, other cultures find us just as gross. Which is really hard to realise, I mean to feel personally, not just to know as a fact, which is one reason why we do fieldwork, right? I mean you have to respect the Kangia for choosing to live in a marginal environment, and their lifestyle works for them. And I can maybe see some of the attraction; there's some beautiful vegetation here...

But it's so quiet. I must say I'm missing my audio feed. My only sound input here is ambient. You know, environmental; like a meditation channel or something. I never realised that the Great Outdoors was so quiet. There are water sounds, and the sound of the wind against the tent. Sometimes a kirrik will whistle. Yesterday I heard a bird; a raven, Mikak said. And that is *it*. And, I'm embarrassed by this, but I should record it — I feel that my voice is too loud. The other people here, they don't talk much. And their voices seem to melt into the earth. Half a dozen paces away, I can't hear what they're saying. But I guess they can hear me talking up my journal right now, even though I'm trying to keep it quiet.

What I'm saying is, I don't feel like talking so much. It's a valid adaptation to local conditions.

It's... when I talk, it makes the silence stronger. I can feel it pressing against the walls of my tent.

It's like my talking is annoying the silence somehow. That's a really great insight into the animistic worldview, right?

Anyway. I'm going to bed now.

Day... not sure

I am now making "sinew". It's a step towards becoming a Useful Member of Society. I can't do the really good, threadlike stuff, but any size between string and rope I can manage. I have also been cutting greenstuff for the kirrik, and picking over the drying berries — a very boring job. This area is just about collected out, and we're preparing to move to another summercamp. (The word for "tent", by the way, translates as "summerhouse".) We are going "the kirrik way", which apparently means easy travel. I must admit I can't see why the Kangia keep kirrik. They don't eat them, or hunt with them; they're no use as sled-dog equivalents because they spend the winter asleep. The explanations I've had make no sense so far. "We help the kirrik; they help us." "The kirrik guide us; we do for them what we can." This last with a shrug and a smile from Simerak, watching a fox eat a dead kirrik. Ugh.

They're very calm and cheerful, the Kangia. I've never heard a voice raised in anger, or seen a child in tears. They're very patient. A job takes as long as it takes. They smile a lot, and there's the little laugh, "Aha!", which is pretty much an actual Kangian word. They take bad news with the shrug-smile, and say "Ah, well," and then add one of a small number of very old joke tag-lines, none of which strike me as remotely funny. I mean, what's funny about "a person could build a winterhouse out of those stones"? That one's a classic; it will always elicit "Aha!" and the wonderful grin. Maybe if I knew the whole joke... but there seems to be a prohibition on telling them. That's old jokes; there is also "after-meal foolery", an informal contest of capping one-liners, which gets very bawdy and inventive. But even the wittiest and funniest after-meal lines are never repeated the next day.

Some days later
Jinak is pregnant! Congratulations all round, nobody can stop grinning. This is a great opportunity to check out Kangian kinship webs; also naming customs. There's a big camp-wide discussion/argument about whose name Jinak's unborn should eventually receive. There are apparently three stages to becoming a person; the ceremony of Welcome (which we're holding tomorrow before breaking camp); the ceremony of Seeing the Light (apparently the actual birth process, also called "going out the door of the winterhouse"), and the naming ceremony. These are commonly (but by no means always) staged in that order. A person who has thus "opened three doors" is *tikerak* (a person or visitor or guest), and lives in This World. Other persons, such as the unborn and the dead, are *takornatak*, strangers, outsiders, and live in That World. People from other settlements or bands are takornatak until they have been formally welcomed into Our Camp over the settlement line; if you see such people while you're out hunting or gathering (highly unlikely), you should simply turn away without saying anything.

The fieldwork is going well, I think, but I swing between fascination and boredom with the Kangia. I was bored this "morning", daydreaming about pick-up, and I couldn't remember exactly when or where that was supposed to happen. I know I'm supposed to travel with this group. My pick-up will find me, I guess. Worrying, but I do remember being warned that this might happen. You get the mind-wipe, and then you get plunged into a new environment, intensive learning, attention focused on the unfamiliar. The vivid new stuff can overwrite anything that isn't directly relevant to the current situation. Short-term memory is enhanced, but familiar long-term memories tend to degrade. It all gets sorted out after fieldwork, of course; I do remember that.

Three sleeps later
What a dreadful journey! If that counts as "easy travel", I give up!

We had the Welcome for Jinak's unborn, which boiled down to a lot of chanting in "net language" (untranslatable garbage), on a three-note tune that had me grinding my teeth after the first few dozen repetitions. Then we formally erased the settlement line, and let the kirrik loose. And can those little bastards *run*! Everything had been packed up into one or two-person loads. The two-person load is slung on shoulder-poles — where do they get the wood from? The poles are obviously cut from something that grows eight or ten feet high, and I've seen absolutely nothing above low-bush height. A surprising amount of gear was simply abandoned; Mikak just smiled and shrugged and said, "We can make more."

So we jogged on... and on... and on! I got hungry, and ate a couple of munchy bars I had in my pocket. Then we went on and on some more. Eventually, the kirrik slowed down and we slept — in the open (you only put tents up inside a settlement line), and I got bug-bitten and stiff. And when the kirrik woke up, the whole damn thing over again, until they finally hunkered down in some different, special way, and Simerak led the elders in setting up the new settlement line. Apparently kirrik will sometimes run for a week. I never want to see it, that's all I can say!

And all the time, it's smile smile smile. Someone drops a pole-load in the middle of the coldest bloody river in the cosmos, and it's "Aha!" The kirrik run into a tussock-bog, and we're wading around in gloop, and it's "Aha!" "Aha!"

The boy Sevu goes off to track one of the kirrik that's left the main group, and he sets off a stone-slide; "Aha; one could build a winterhouse with those stones!" And finally, I am so bloody tired I can hardly see where I'm going, and totally accidentally I step on a kirrik and the damn thing gives me a savage bite on the ankle, and it's "Aha, aha!", and I have to go down on my knees and apologise to the kirrik. That's right; I have to apologise to the *kirrik* before I can dress my ankle. If I died of rabies, that would probably be really funny too. Not that I'm going to; I don't think they have rabies here.

I could have cried. I did cry, actually, yesterday afternoon. I have blisters and bug bites and I'm *filthy*, my hair is a *mess*. Everyone else has gone out smiling, to pick berries, and I'm playing hookey and I don't give a damn.

After another sleep

Much better for a day off, a few good meals and some sleep. I... really, I behaved very badly yesterday by these people's standards. But it's as if it never happened. They're still friendly, still smiling. Jinak showed me the gene template for her unborn girl; I'm no expert, but I have to say it looks a really neat design.

Simerak dropped by to tease Jinak; "I'm sure you're after my name for that unborn of yours!"

"Aha; where could I find a better name?"

"I don't know. It's my gift to you, then, when I go to Tortannetok."

"You're going this winter? Soon?"

"I think so, yes."

"That's good." And Jinak smiles, and turns away.

Later, I said to Mikak, "You're so calm and cheerful all the time. You know, I really admire you for that."

"And I admire your generosity. You shared the last of your winterfood with the children, and everything you've gathered, you added to the common store." And she smiled at me, and walked away.

So there you are. If you want to be loved, hand out sweets to the kids.

Last summercamp of the year, apparently
These people, they all know something I don't, something important. I'm missing something. This feeling is probably just the result of repeated not-quite-conscious attempts to trigger a blocked memory cascade. I did have a really creepy idea, a few days ago, that maybe they had, you know, *wiped something else* before I came here, and I'm not really who I think I am at all. This is stupid, of course. The Kangia host fieldworkers every year. I was lucky to get the slot. This kind of paranoid fantasy is simply one of the more annoying side-effects of the wipe.

I just can't help wondering...

It's great that we now have days and nights again. I missed the nights. Things are getting cooler, although we've been moving south. The vegetation is turning. The sun's not up for all that long, actually. Dawn and dusk are beautiful...

Frost overnight. Snow soon.

How long was I supposed to be here?

Later
We reached the stony rise outside the *tornat* (wintercamp) at about midday. Most of the band went straight in while I stood and shivered outside the settlement line. It looked like a good kirrik hibernation ground, with a line of dens dug into the sunward slope.

Mikak came back for me and led me in over the settlement line, holding my hand up in the grip of friendship, and grinning. The band was in a very good mood, having found the walls of the winterhouses standing firm, and last year's food caches intact and undisturbed. The Foxes' Cache had been dug up and scattered, of course, and people just walked right over the bones and gravegoods as if they were stones and dirt. To the band, of course, these things are no longer in This World; they belong now to That World, along with the unborn and the dead, "and everything else that does not carry a name", according to Mikak. "The names that can be named, they are in This World. All the rest, the names that cannot be named, and all the nameless, they are in That World." And that's about the most coherent explanation of Kangian religion that I'm ever going to get.

Later

The band held a ceremony to determine whose household I would live in over the winter. The usual: chants in "net language" (nonsense words, endlessly repeated with minor variations to one of three very simple, monotonous tunes; the chants are used as a form of self-hypnosis), drum dances, conspicuous consumption of fresh and dried food, and a formal contest of boasting songs. Mikak won.

Other things I must talk up: laying down next year's caches, kirrik hibernation ritual.

Winter is the time for visiting. Jinak's family are off to visit another wintercamp near Big Lake, a journey of several days over an arm of the Ice. I asked to accompany them, but apparently winter visiting invokes a very complex web of reciprocal kinship obligations. Simerak suggested that perhaps later in the winter, I could make a visit to Tortannetok, which seems to translate as "another winter village", or "the other winter village", which doesn't sound like a unique proper name to me. But Kangian placenames are curiously non-specific. I've noted three Big Lakes, two Not As Big Lakes, a dozen Good Landings, an area simply called Berries, four places called Oklo Trap... and of course, the place we're currently staying, wherever that is, is referred to as Our Camp; you only refer to a camp by its place-name when you're not actually camping there. And a lot of places have summernames and winternames; I suppose everything does look very different when it's frozen or covered in snow. It's been snowing for days now; I should have said. Short days; the sun's scarcely up. Long hours of predawn and dusk, and the dark between them growing, growing...

Later, in the dark

Why, why did I let them mess with my mind? I must have trusted them. Who was I? Who am I? I can think of a number of reasons to interfere with someone's memory in a major way, none of them pleasant. Maybe I was a criminal. Or insane. Maybe I was kidnapped and wiped of all incriminating memories and dumped here, in a "safe" location, while ransom demands were made. Maybe it's political; maybe I was a dissident, an objector to something. They all add up to a person who didn't fit in. A person that society wanted to remodel, or sideline somewhere safe. Maybe I really am a student on fieldwork. It just doesn't seem very likely at the moment.

I don't think I like myself very much. Not that cheerful inane person who started fieldwork here. I fall back into being her regularly, whenever I get really scared. But if I'm not really her, who am I? Why replace whoever I really was with *that*? Why did I let them? Did I try to stop them? And why is it wearing off now? Why am I so paranoid?

I wonder sometimes if I'm ever going to get back home. Wherever home is. This place feels timeless. It feels like a hard place to leave. Like a place that will absorb me without trace.

(untitled)
I'm going to *write* this, write out the whole thing. I took Literacy as an optional module, one time. I did it on impulse and off-campus, it might not have got onto my record. And I don't trust them any more.

The Kangians are fakes. I mean, the people are real enough, and genuinely pleasant, I think. But their society is a fake. It's too small, there's no conflict; surely people never really lived like this! I don't believe an isolated group of fifty people could ever form a modern-viable society. They spend so much time getting food, they don't have time to develop the complex of interlocking skills and professions that are the minimal requirement for any contemporary culture. They don't keep *records*. Records are dangerous, they say; locking down the life of the story. They're *actors*, playing at living the simple life. *Why?* Who are they working for? What's really going on here?

I'm frightened that I've been sent here to die.

And these people don't do fear. They don't acknowledge it; it doesn't exist for them. They push it away, ignore it, pretend it doesn't exist. The Big Lie: we are all cheerful all of the time. Happy happy natives; never bored, never frightened, that doesn't happen. Disaster is met with smiles and shrugs. Any negative stuff at all, is met with denial, with an immediate turning-away of the attention. Do these people have no empathy, no compassion? Do they never suffer? Do they never die?

Why am I here? Why, *why*?

I suspect I'm never going to know. Fieldwork, yeah, to do my fieldwork. To play my role, perform my allotted task. In other words, to live my life.

I've stopped worrying about being a mindwiped criminal. Maybe I've been looking at this the wrong way. Maybe this isn't a punishment, but a privilege. A learning opportunity, an experience to be treasured.

So, what is special about it? Not the Kangians. They are the most *ordinary* people I've ever met. They seem to concentrate all their attention on common, mundane tasks: gathering, mending, walking, fetching water...

The landscape is very unspoiled. Of course, that's what you'd expect on a fairly new colony planet. If that's what this is.

Maybe the special thing was the time without night. I remember, I think I remember, that there is, or was, a major religious group whose Afterlife was eternal light. No; it was a dualist Afterlife, with some enjoying eternal light, and others suffering eternal darkness. My experience of "day", not days, feels timeless, changeless. I was stuck in an eternal present. Endless night is even weirder. Past and future are becoming ever harder for me to imagine clearly. And so is being-here-now. This isn't even the present; it's outside time.

We are inactive, waiting, waiting...

I'm trying to remember something. Anything. I have thoughts, or memories, or feelings, that I think are static, changeless, but they're not. Nothing is permanent. I remember meeting a friend, twenty years ago maybe; a warm memory, but a much-eroded one, there's only a nubbin of it left. He won't look like that any more, if he ever really did. I can't really remember what he looked like. I can't remember his name. I've visited that node again and again. Was that person really important to me, or was it the warmth, my feeling of warmth, the memory of warmth kept alive by revisiting it again and again. I'm cold nearly all the time now...

Twenty years ago — *how old am I?* There are no mirrors here...

Who was he?

Who am I?

Deep snow and darkness. The storms have stopped. The changeless stars wheel above us, over the changeless, impermanent landscape of snow and ice. The snow looks almost luminous under the stars. Two of the elders have asked if I want to go with them on a visit to Tortannetok, the Winterhome of the Wise, out on the Ice. I remember a story about an ice palace, and a story about how hunters make dome-shelters out of ice blocks. I started talking about that, and Simerak nodded, "Aha!". The Elders live in Tortannetok. They must be wise to live there, to survive. People go out to visit them, to gain wisdom, to learn the winter stories. I'm honoured that I've been asked to go along on this trip out onto the Ice.

The stars are amazing.

Salik is pregnant. She's going to name her baby after me.

The Battery Caverns

Nigel Brown

Nigel Brown has had fiction published in the UK, USA, Italy and Japan, including a story selected for The Year's Best SF 9, *edited by Hartwell/Cramer. He was born in Portsmouth, England, and now lives near London with his family.*

"The Battery Caverns" was originally written for a John Christopher tribute issue of Interzone *magazine, Christopher having been a major favourite of his, "up there with Heinlein, Asimov and Clarke."*

In Nigel's story, Jak is a member of a clan living within the labyrinthine tunnels of his 'world'. Conditions are worsening, and fearsome raiding parties from other clans are scavenging for the precious battery pods. To survive, Jak must learn the true nature of his environment, and the cause of the seismic tremors that threaten to tear it apart...

The translucent tunnel shook. Jak kept his balance, bracing himself against the coarse cellulose wall. At first he thought it was another quake, but he was wrong. It was a raid.

This far out, near the limit of the world, the vascular tunnels were only partially lignified; thin enough to shake under the pounding of metal-shod feet. Copper Clan raiders were close by, perhaps just around the next bend in the passageway.

Jak raised his cuff-mike to his lips. "Uncle," he called. "Tell the Warden the raids have started again!"

Static answered him. Uncle Aden was out of range, maybe already with the Warden — the one person who could keep the peace. Jak was on his own.

He could run back towards the Battery Caverns, but they

would see him — catch him. The tunnel behind ran for miles, with few side chambers. Nowhere to hide.

The underlight, as always in the lower levels of the periphery, shone up through the semi-opaque floor; it only revealed the faint shadows of the vessels that hung beneath the tunnel he was in. He considered cutting down, to reach them, but there were no cracks in the tough floor fibres where he could break through. And how could he be sure there was air in them?

Once, at the very bottom of the world, his friend Daren had breached the lowest tunnel's floor. Jak had been further up, at a junction of arteries, safe in a ventilating draught. A spray of poisonous gas had erupted from the widening hole, surrounding Daren, burning his lungs, choking him as he scrambled towards Jak. Jak had pulled him to safety, glimpsing blurred patches of white, green, blue through the dazzling bright rupture before the wound's edges had leaked enough hardening fluids to seal it.

The raiders were closer. Soon they would see him.

Jak peered upwards into the gloom above his head and spotted a darker shadow, a split in the lignin fibres that parted to form a hollow in the ceiling — too small for a man to hide in, it was just big enough for a boy, and Jak was underweight for his age.

The clacking of the raiders' footfalls echoed around him.

Jak scrabbled at the rough fibrous wall, feeling for handholds. A splinter stabbed into his palm. Ignoring the pain, he grabbed at the hanging fibres and used them like ropes to haul himself up the wall, out of sight, finding easy footholds on the cellulose strands. Squeezing his thin body into the hollow, he wedged his pouch, with the precious battery pod, into a notch in the tunnel roof and lifted his feet clear just as the first raiders came into view.

They had come from the Dark Heartlands, marching far out into the limit of the world to bypass the deeper, more-travelled passages. They probably planned to tramp back through the network of branching vessels and surprise villages like his, under the Battery Caverns — they dared to break the Warden's Peace.

The raiders passed beneath him. He glimpsed staffs, shockguns and nets of vines. Thirty men in all. The last he recognised: the shaved head tattooed with jagged lines, the white cloak patterned the same, rimmed with silver thread — Timon, Chief Ortha's advisor.

They were heading up the tunnel, away from his village.

Had they been successful? Their wheeled cart held field provisions: mushroom fruits, jars of threadjuice — but no stolen battery pods! If the village patrols had beaten them off, surely some of the men would have been injured in the fight. Uncle Aden had warned him the raiders had become more desperate of late; even ate the flesh of those killed in battle rather than leave them to waste on the battlefield.

After a few minutes the tunnel ceased to shake; the rumble of the cart's wheels, the murmur of the men's guttural conversation died away. Jak pulled himself out of the hollow and climbed down.

He continued back along the main artery towards the village. This was meant to be his triumphant return from his first battery hunt. His cousins Cruf and Geg should be waiting for him to stroll with pride into the village store, to ceremoniously deposit his prize into the village coffers to mark his passage to adulthood — but now Jak dreaded what he would find back home.

He tried the radio again. Would his uncle be safe? They had parted company only hours ago; Jak to undertake the rite of the initiation hunt, Aden to meet with the Warden of the Battery Caverns.

"Jak!" The voice was faint and tinny, but welcome. "Have you won your first pod?"

"Yes."

"Well done! Head straight back home. Don't wait for me." Aden's voice grew fainter as Jak descended along the tunnel. "The Warden hasn't arrived yet. I don't know how long I'll be."

"There's been a raid," Jak said. "The nearest Copper Clan to us — Ortha's Clan. One of the raiders was Timon."

Aden was quiet for a moment, then: "Are you certain it was Timon himself?"

"Yes. I saw him when he came to the village — that time when Ortha demanded tribute to stop the raids."

"Get back to the village as quick as you can. I'll tell the Warden. He'll put a stop to this."

Jak continued downwards. His ears popped as the air grew denser. Drawing his tunic closer around himself, he shivered in the cooler air of the lower tunnels.

Outgrowths of fibrous material began to obstruct the passageway. Not the soft pliable epidermis they tore off in strips to use as raw materials for the village factories, but older bark, almost as hard as metal. Deeper in, where his village was, the underlight had gone, replaced by patches of luminous fungi which coated the walls. Jak saw lines scoured through the fungi overhead, where the raiders' staffs had scraped along the top of the tunnel. The pungent smell of bruised fungi made the back of his throat raw; he blinked back tears.

As he approached his village, the tunnel walls became rougher and thickened with lignin. Here was that curious twist in the tunnel, like the inside of a braid, there was that gnarled corner, perhaps made by a collision of debris from a quake.

He turned a corner. The way was blocked completely. He faced solid wood. The tunnel had fractured. It continued, but above, or below or to one side, not here, and he had no way of cutting through the dense sclerenchyma, even if he knew which way to go.

This was why the raiding party had turned back!

He recalled that while he had been creeping amongst the forest of root columns in the Battery Caverns, hunting for his pod, the whole world had lurched beneath his feet. And this was the result — his route home was sealed off.

He couldn't try to find another route around the obstruction because the quake had rendered his geographical knowledge redundant. It would be quicker to ascend again, cross through the peripheral levels, then reach the village through a major artery from another direction. No doubt that was what the raiders were planning. Yet he could spend ages trying to find his way through the unknown paths above his head.

There was one hope — the Warden. He could give him guidance through the maze at the top of the world.

Aden had mentioned that the Warden lived above the Battery Caverns. His uncle had parted company from Jak at their entrance. It was a good place to start.

Wearily he set off up the slope of the tunnel. The battery pod was beginning to weigh heavily in his pouch, its nodes rubbing against his waist, but he would not leave it. Not after bringing it so far.

As he followed the raiding party, Jak found evidence of their passing. His sandals crunched on the discarded rinds of mushroom fruits. Every now and then he came across an empty threadjuice jar, littering the passageway.

Then another quake hit. Jak heard a distant, deep rumble. The wood groaned and cracked, protesting under an immense strain, and the tunnel floor shook, tilted suddenly downwards, flinging Jak onto his back. He lay there, trembling, waiting for the tunnel to drop further. Eventually the rumbling died. Silence returned to the passageway. He stood up warily, but the tunnel seemed stable.

Jak set off again, but more cautiously, holding on wherever he could until, climbing up inside the network of ever-diminishing tubes, he approached the top levels of the world.

In the deeper regions, out in the periphery, a pearly glow lit up the lower tunnels through their translucent floors. As he climbed, this gave way to the toplight. Now, as Jak strode up a steep incline and turned a corner, a whiter, brighter light blazed into his eyes. As he stumbled forward, dazzled by the sudden glare, he knew he had arrived at the Battery Caverns.

The entrance was an opening that had been widened by previous generations who had carved ornate swirling patterns and jagged lines — the ancient symbol for electricity — around its rim.

Jak stepped inside, the muggy air smothering him in warmth after the cooler drafts in the tunnels, onto a narrow ledge set above the floor of the first cavern. He gazed along it, looking for raiders. He saw the dark clumps of battery pods, each the size of his fist, that hung beneath the bright ceiling; the thick roots of the battery plants plunging from the ceiling down into the floor, that seemed to fill the cavern space with an almost impassable tangle of fibres and woody columns; the waist-high undergrowth that housed the battery rat burrows, with their treasury of fully-charged pods.

He could see where the raiders had passed, where the weaker roots had been forced apart so they could squeeze through the maze.

Then he spotted the body of a man, sprawled below in a pool of blood.

Jak climbed down quickly, his horror growing, his heart pounding. This was nobody he recognised. He was too old to be a raider; his face and forearms were tanned a rich bronze colour, not bleached with the sallow complexion of one from the Dark Heartlands.

He felt the old man's cheek, clean shaven beneath white bushy eyebrows. The skin was cool. This must be the Warden...

How had this happened? Jak was devastated — his world was tearing apart. The Warden had always been here, regulating the battery harvest between the Clans, keeping the peace by his threats to withhold supplies. Only he had the mysterious power to discharge the pods if they left the Caverns without his approval, leaving them unenergised and worthless. Jak gazed at the slight body with reverence, trying to match it with the all-powerful image he'd held in his head since childhood.

And where was Uncle Aden?

Then he heard a whoosh of air, but twisted around too late. A netvine shot over him; it pinned him to the ground. Figures emerged from the darkness under the ledge.

Timon and two men.

Jak struggled, but the net held him fast to the ground. One of the men raised his sword, holding the point over Jak's head.

"Stop moving!" he shouted. "Stop! Be still!"

Jak lay quiet. They had him. His heart thumped so hard he felt dizzy, but he knew he must stay alert. Look for any opportunity to escape.

Rough hands unwrapped the vine from where it curled around his legs and trunk. He stood up, clumsily.

"He was Mathias. My father," Timon said, looking at the body of the Warden. His voice was thin, like the whistle of air through the world's narrow arterioles.

Up close, Jak could see Timon was hollow-cheeked, his eyes sunken, his limbs like sticks — he looked starved, yet he was close to Chief Orthas; he should have had the pick of their meagre food supplies.

"I last saw him when I was a boy, your age," Timon continued. His dour face tried to smile, but sank back into a bleak expression. "I celebrate his life!"

Timon drew a knife from his belt, grabbed a fistful of the old man's hair, and slashed it free with one stroke. Placing the hair in a pouch, he bowed his head for a moment, muttered some words in a strange and guttural language, then turned to one of the men.

"You! Give me your sword!" The man's face was pale. He trembled as he handed Timon the bloody copper blade, hilt first.

"This fool struck my father down. Killed him before I knew of his actions. What would you do, boy?"

Jak shook his head, unable to speak.

"He was doing his duty," Timon mused bitterly. "I cannot

punish him for that." He returned the sword.

"And you," Timon said. "Are you following orders? You are a collector of batteries for your village? A skilled climber of these roots?"

Jak realised that Timon was unaware of the harvesting process; how the rats climbed the roots, gnawed ripe, fully charged pods from the clusters, and took them back to their nests to store them as energy supplements. His Clan harvested them from there, always leaving some for the rats.

Now the Warden was dead, the raiders would take all the batteries, the rats would die, and fresh batteries would become unattainable.

"Yes," Jak replied. "I collect the batteries."

"They send children to do this work?" Timon wondered. "We must learn this, too." He scanned the tangled forest of roots. "I see that makes sense." He pointed to the twisted and crushed roots in front of them — the hole leading into the darkness. "It took hours to force that way open. My men are scouting out this space. Orthas has plans for this region, where food grows so well in the toplight, and power batteries are ripe for the plucking."

Jak felt sickened when he heard Timon's words. The raids had become more frequent — so this was preparation for a full scale invasion of the Battery Clan's territory! He had to warn the village — Uncle Aden and the others. But how?

Timon continued: "I see that children would find it easier to pass through, to squeeze between, to climb above. You can help me, my friend. Don't let me hinder you in your duty! Collect some pods! Teach us!"

Jak could see he had no choice. He pointed at the gap between the roots.

"You first, sir."

Timon laughed. "Oh no! You'll do your work between us."

They entered the tunnel through the roots together. Inside,

Jak kept alert for the sound of Timon's other men ahead. There was no sign of them. Away from the cavern wall the root density thinned. The men had made good progress cutting the tunnel out — it disappeared into the quiet gloom. Jak guessed that they had already reached the opposite cavern wall by now. They were probably exploring the further caverns, equally full of roots. And rats.

There was a rustling to the sides. Invisible movements in the undergrowth around them.

Timon and his men ignored them, unaware of the danger.

"Do you climb to the ceiling and cut the pods down?" Timon asked.

"Yes," Jak lied. "I'm looking for a gap in the root system, where I can climb through."

Timon glanced up. "Here," he said. "Here's a space." A clump of battery pods were visible from where he stood. They clustered around the top of the root column, dark globes against the bright glare of the cavern's ceiling. "Typical of you people, to make such an issue of collecting these."

They watched Jak prepare to climb the root. His mind raced. Touching the rubbery column this low down was safe, but he knew that the insulating outer skin of the root was thinner, then nonexistent near the cavern ceiling. Electrocution — death — waited for him at the top.

The surface of the root was rough enough to afford ample handholds. Jak hauled himself up. His pouch, containing his battery pod, knocked against him. It gave him an idea.

He dropped back to the ground.

One of the men lifted his sword menacingly, but Timon placed a restraining hand on his sword arm.

"Haven't you learned your lesson yet?" He turned to Jak. Do your job, collector."

"I will," Jak said. "But here..." he reached into his pouch and pulled out the battery pod.

A flash of delight crossed Timon's stern face. He snatched it from Jak's hand.

"Thank you!" He glanced at the swordsman. "See, violence is not the only answer! You're a quick learner, boy. Up you go, then!"

Jak turned and resumed his slow progress upward. When he was above their heads, he looked back down and said: "That battery you've got. Is it charged?"

Timon examined it, turned it around in his hands, pressed the two nodes which protruded from its ends. They glowed slightly, indicating that the battery was full.

No rat could resist the surge in the local electric field.

Dark shapes darted out from the undergrowth, claws extended. Timon started, then screamed as the battery rats clawed at his legs, scraping weals across the skin, drawing blood, scrabbling to possess the battery. The swordsmen waved their weapons, but the space was too narrow to swing them. They hesitated to stab at the whirling bodies of man and rats.

Then the rats were gone, back into the undergrowth with their prize.

Timon was lying on the ground, a red stain of blood spreading through his cloak. His men stood over him, aghast.

Jak jumped down and sprinted away, back along the tunnel. He heard cries behind him, then the thudding of feet as the men pursued.

There was a rat battery nest near the tunnel entrance. It was his only hope of concealment. He squeezed between the columns and waded into the thick undergrowth. The tangle of fibres slowed him. He tripped and fell onto the brush. There was a deafening screech, then a small body wriggled from underneath his chest. The rat, stunned by the impact, shook its head, baring sharp fangs.

Thwip! A vine whip cracked the air by his face.

"Got yer!" The voice was triumphant.

Jak rolled to one side, then scrambled behind the nearest root column. The cavern floor was softer here, where the root plunged through it to draw nourishment from below.

"Watch out!" The other man cried. "Another one!" His

shockgun buzzed. “Got it!”

Jak glanced back. The rat was frozen in death at their feet, its claws still extended. They raised their guns again and advanced towards him.

Jak had no choice. He squeezed between two columns, trying to conceal himself in the gloom. It was no good. They would be able to pick him off, even if he was out of their reach.

He stepped backwards; stopped when he felt the column. The ground dipped a little, sloping down towards the edge of the root. He was aware of a hissing sound. Another rat nest? Stumbling, he felt the ground give way. The hiss grew louder. It was under his feet. He grabbed at the undergrowth, but it only held his weight for a moment, tearing, ripping, leaving him clutching fistfuls of cellulose. The men fired at him, but missed as he disappeared downwards. The root grazed his back as he slipped down beside it, still falling. The cold rush, the drenching of liquid... he tasted it — retched the foul stuff out. The light was a dim circle above him, but the strong current pulled him down, under the torrent. He blacked out.

Jak opened his eyes. He was lying on a bunk. He sat up, feeling dazed and weary. Bright light flooded this place, dazzling him. Gradually, he saw he was in a room unlike any other he had seen. It was filled with the glare of the upper tunnels, but the light came from the walls as well as the ceiling. The room was a framework of wood, over which an opaque membrane quivered and shook like a live thing.

Two others were in the room, at the far end.

“Hello, boy.” It was Timon.

The shock flushed through Jak, jerking him wide awake. He gasped and stood up, ready to run. Then he saw the other man more clearly: the crimson headband, the drooping moustache, the smiling eyes.

“Uncle Aden!” he exclaimed. He sat back on his bunk, confused. Was Aden caught, or was Timon a prisoner?

His uncle grinned. "We pulled you from the nutrient flow, Jak. Timon knew where you went down. The rest was plumbing. Lucky for you we've got a map."

Aden pointed to a large panel of metal, set against one wall. It displayed patterns of lines and figures, similar to the inscriptions at the entrance to the Battery Caverns. Yet here they flowed across the shiny surface, changing shape as Jak watched them — hairs stood up on the back of his neck.

"This display tells us much of what goes on, Jak. Welcome to the Warden's home."

"Where are we?" Jak asked.

"Directly above one of the Battery Caverns," Aden replied. "Think of it as a bubble set in the roof of the world, the highest place you can go. The Warden can survey his domain from here."

Jak stared at Timon. "What's he doing here?"

His uncle laughed. "This is my older brother, Jak. Another uncle for you."

Timon said: "I did not know who you were until you came here, and Aden told me. I regret that — it would have saved us all a lot of trouble." He glanced down at his bandaged legs.

"The Warden was our father," Aden said. "And your grandfather. His name was Mathias Electa. He was waiting to meet me in the Battery Caverns when he was killed by Timon's man."

"Not my man!" Timon exclaimed. "Ortha's! I understood too late that Father was killed on the Chief's instructions. Orthas has lost patience with the Warden's Peace." His eyes filled with tears. "Didn't he realise the danger from the Copper Clans? They owed him no allegiance. He rationed the battery supply to them by his authority alone."

Aden's expression clouded. "That was his responsibility."

"I accept that!" Timon said. "But you can't expect me to rejoice in my people's suffering." He sighed. "Brother, we'll mourn Mathias later, but more pressing matters must be attended to first."

"Yes, Timon," Aden agreed. He turned to Jak. "When Timon was a boy, he was sent to live with the nearest Copper Clan to our village. It was Mathias's way of finding out what was going on in the Dark Heartlands."

"I supplied him with plenty of information," Timon said. "My reward was to live under the impassable dark roof of the deepest Heartlands, to eat thin fungi gruel and watch my companions suffer as their batteries ran out, and were replaced with less than their fair share."

"But we're all in danger now," Aden said. "That was the message I got from Father." He turned to Jak. "Mathias summoned both of us. Timon arranged to travel from the Dark as part of a raiding party. He intended to leave them before they reached our village, but the quake altered his plan."

"So why did you want the batteries, then?" Jak asked.

"They are a crucial resource for the people I live with, Jak. Can you imagine what it's like to live in the dark? The cold? The Dark Heartlands have no toplight at all; even the underlight is dim — in places we must feel our way with our staffs, like the blind. I couldn't ignore the opportunity to gather fresh batteries."

"So you're still our enemy!"

Timon looked sad. "Ignorant villagers pampered by the warmth and light of this region think that, boy. I admit I know little myself of the ways of your Battery Clans." He sighed, and for an instant looked very old; Jak saw the family resemblance to the Warden — the same deep eye sockets and bushy eyebrows.

"You're too young to remember, boy," Timon continued. "Time was when our peoples were brothers, as I am to Aden. We traded copper, even tin, gold, iron in those days, which we brought from the deeper Heartlands; we exchanged them for batteries. Metals for energy, and around us wood grew for all, free for the shaping."

"Nothing comes free," Jak said. "The Copper Clans would take all the batteries until there were none left. You should understand that — your father did."

"My loyalty is to the Dark Heartlands, boy. It has not diminished, despite our blood-ties."

Aden placed a reassuring hand on his shoulder. "You've had the hardest task, brother."

"The people I've lived with for so long are called 'cannibals' by some," Timon continued, in a voice almost dropped to a whisper. "I know that! But we live further into the darkness, where the food supplies have begun to fail. Who amongst your people would not do as they have done, when that desperate, that starving?"

Jak was silent, shocked by Timon's words. He had no easy reply.

"The boy's not responsible for the plight of the Dark Heartlands, Timon," Aden admonished. "He's got a lot to learn yet."

Aden helped Jak off the bunk and led him to a wall, lifted a flap in it. A further membrane lay beyond it, but it was transparent.

"Look, Jak, your grandfather could survey this region from his home up here..."

At first, Jak was dazzled by the glare and he could see nothing at all. Like the difference between passing from the lower tunnels into the higher Battery Caverns, this was another step up in brightness.

Aden was patient. He waited until their eyes had adjusted, and Jak could make out some details.

"It's a cavern!" Jak exclaimed. "So bright! So big!" His gaze followed the wooden floor stretched out before them, searching for an opposite wall — it must be very far away.

"No, Jak," Aden said. "What you see is a vast wooden platform — the top surface, the outside, of our world."

Jak tried to make sense of the scene. Failed.

"But those plants..." he pointed to the surface, translucent in patches, mottled with greenery which spread out into the distance.

"Those are the tops of the Battery Caverns — the battery plants seen from the outside."

Closer to, he could see broad leaves, threaded with tendrils which fastened them flat and tight to the... roof?

"The leaves collect the solar rays and store their energy in the pods further down the stalks, under the roof," Aden explained.

Deep jagged cracks ran away from the translucent areas. They increased in number until they reached the platform's edge, ending in... nothing. Beyond this surface lay tiers of white, green and blue which seemed to go on forever. He'd last seen them when his friend Daren had nearly died.

"But what is this place?" Jak asked.

"We're standing on the roof of the world you've known, Jak. This is where the toplight comes from," said Aden. "Our family knows this, even your father did. Those layers you see past the roof are clouds."

Timon joined them at the window. He continued: "This world we all live in is a vast platform which floats over a sea of gas, boy, amongst those clouds. It's shaped like the top of a giant mushroom, but a hundred miles across. We live inside the edge of it. The Battery Caverns, the regions you're familiar with, lie on the upper side.

"This bubble, the Warden's home we're standing in, is probably only one of many around the rim, near the edge."

Jak's mind spun. "You mean there are other Battery Caverns? Other Wardens?"

"We don't know that," Aden admitted. "We only know our own small regions."

"But why should our place be different to anywhere else along the perimeter?" Timon argued. Jak noticed that his face became animated, slightly flushed. Thoughts of the regions beyond their own interested him deeply; perhaps they relieved Timon's mind from dwelling on his own people's plight.

"What's beyond the platform?" Jak asked him.

"The sea of gas the platform floats on is nothing more

than a giant globe, floating itself in a greater emptiness. The ancient name for it is Uranus."

Jak frowned.

"You don't have to worry about that, Jak," Aden said. "I want you to know, however, that our world was built by men, long ago, for us to all live in — an enormous biological habitat. We don't know where our ancestors came from originally. Perhaps down there," he pointed at the gassy sea, "I doubt that, though." He tapped on the membrane. "We can't breathe the air outside, Jak. It's poison to us. The Warden was one of those who have carried this knowledge, preserved it, since the earliest time."

"Look!" Timon cried. A vast crack had appeared near the edge. It linked up with some of the other cracks, ran parallel to the edge, and widened as he watched.

Even at this distance, the ground trembled beneath them again.

Aden ran to the display panel, but Jak stood there with Timon, both of them transfixed by the sight.

As the crack opened, he saw the structure within; a thick layer of wood, then hollows and holes — even at this distance he could see that they were the broken ends of tunnels and caves. Then the segment beyond the crack dropped away, and out of their sight.

The edge of the world was closer now.

"We're rising," Aden said. They turned from the window. The display panel flickered with writing that Jak struggled to follow. He failed, but Timon stared at the figures as they scrolled across.

"I see!" Timon said. "The weight loss — losing that peripheral section has enabled the platform to float higher in the atmosphere."

Aden looked at him, amazed. "Those must have been the quakes... the beginnings of fractures. Father must have seen the danger from up here, wanted to warn us."

Timon turned to Jak. "This is why we were summoned here, boy. To witness this event." He held his hand in front of him. “This is the platform we live in. It takes material from the gas around it to provide us with food and air, but as it does so, it increases in weight. It sinks.” He lowered his hand. “Then it gets too deep into the atmosphere.” Jak looked puzzled. “The gas which surrounds it,” Timon explained. “It must lose its edges periodically to restore equilibrium!” He raised his hand again.

“But that means that part of the world has gone forever!” Jak said.

“That was an empty part,” Aden replied. “The far peripheral areas were abandoned when the tunnels crumbled and lost breathable air.” He gazed at Timon. “But this hasn’t happened before, to my knowledge.”

“No,” Timon agreed. He pulled at his lip with anxiety. “Do you think this is part of what’s happening elsewhere? The failure of my Clan’s fungi crops?”

Aden shrugged. “The platform is more dynamic than we ever thought. I must return home at once. The Battery Clans must be alerted to the danger in the periphery.” He glanced out at the many cracks that were still visible across the surface of the roof, near its edge. “The outer caverns must be evacuated, their food stores saved. You must stay here, Timon, and monitor the cracking; you can use the radio to warn me of the danger areas.”

“No,” Timon said. “I cannot stay. My people must be warned to avoid the periphery too, lest they inhabit it and fall to their deaths. Orthas has plans to escape the Dark Heartlands — I must counsel him otherwise. This is no safe region for the Copper Clans to migrate to.” He eyed Jak. “Would you help us, boy? I’ll understand if you have reservations.”

“You want me to stay here, by myself?” Jak asked. The idea excited him, yet he hesitated. “Why should I help your Clan?”

“Because they are people, Jak. No different from you. More desperate to survive, perhaps.”

Jak recalled Timon’s words as he looked into his uncle’s

sunken eyes: the darkness, the cold, the failing crops... a deep sympathy stirred within him.

"I'll do it," he agreed.

He looked out of the window at the battery plants that basked under the toplight. Below them were the Battery Caverns, and underneath, miles of tunnels, caves, all he had known before...

Then his eyes lifted — he gazed at the clouds that floated beyond the edge of the world.

Dusking

Liz Williams

Liz Williams is a science fiction and fantasy writer living in Glastonbury, England, where she is co-director of a witchcraft supply business. She has been published by Bantam Spectra (US) and Tor Macmillan (UK), also by Night Shade Press and Prime Books, and in magazines such as Realms of Fantasy, *and* Asimov's Science Fiction. *She is the secretary of the Milford SF Writers' Workshop, and also teaches creative writing and the history of Science Fiction.*

She has published fourteen novels and two short story collections, and has been nominated multiple times for the Philip K Dick Memorial Award, and for the Arthur C Clarke Award.

In Liz's story "Dusking", a young girl, Emily, longs to escape the watchful gaze of her aunt. But if she goes out into the woodland at night, to see what can be captured there, she might find something darker and more primal than she bargained for...

You don't go dusking when the moon is dark, everyone knows that. Too many things waiting in the shadows, coming to cling to your little light, coming to bite and snap. But when the moon is full or new, that's the time to go dusking, and that's when you find all the young couples out in the parks and on the downs, dressed in their Sunday best, carrying candles in a globe of glass, chasing spirits under the oaks.

We didn't have such practices in Greenwich. It was too close to the river, but when my parents died and I was sent to live with my aunt in Blackheath, it was all the rage. One could buy trapping globes in the local market, in a variety of pleasing colours. I remember that in the year of my arrival at my aunt's, blue was very popular, but then, it was during the summer and as the winter months drew on, the blue globes were put away and red ones took their place.

I was too young to go dusking, my aunt said. I begged and pleaded, but she refused, and took to locking me into my bedchamber early in the evening, with a supply of improving literature. My aunt was devout, fervently so, and she disapproved of dusking; it encouraged the Others, she said, and that would never do. Perhaps if I had been a boy, she might have relented.

Of course, the more she disapproved, the wilder I was to do it. I used to lean out of my bedchamber window with a jam jar with a candle in it, but I never attracted anything larger than moths. Only on one evening, close to the autumn equinox, did something else come close to the flame. I saw it briefly, because it veered away into the eaves as soon as it saw my face reflected in the light: it was a small, pinched thing, the colour of dead leaves, with little sharp hands. I often wonder what would have happened if I had caught it. You're supposed to let them go before sun up, but plenty of people forget and find a leaf in the bottom of the globe in the morning, or a bundle of twigs.

This was not the only restriction placed upon me by my aunt. Education was frowned upon for girls, particularly any interest in the developing sciences. I was not to go to school, although she instructed me in Bible study at home. I was to learn needlework, and the basics of the culinary arts, and household management. I grew increasingly frustrated and resentful as the years went by. I remembered what I had learned in my mother's house, but I could do nothing with it: I had no books here, nor access to them.

We only spoke of it once. I'd burned a saucepan, again. My aunt had not been pleased.

"If you would just apply yourself to the *rudiments*, Emily..."

I drew myself up. She was a short woman, and I was no

taller, but I pretended. "I," I said, "have *Skills*."

My aunt looked me straight in the eye. "I," she replied, "am well aware of *that*."

Clearly, they were yet another thing of which she Disapproved.

And so I began to plan. I despised the necessity; I found it tedious. But until I had reached my majority, this sort of thing had to be done.

Then, when I was sixteen and some way along with the planning, a young man asked me to go dusking. Chaperoned, of course, by a friend of my aunt's — the young man's mother, in fact. Tristan was eminently suitable, my aunt considered, and I think she was hoping that he might offer for my hand and thus relieve her of the responsibility of myself. I was young, true, but better marry me off as soon as possible and find a more appropriate channel for those skills I'd mentioned... There was a belief in those days that marriage, and all that it involved, could tame all those wild and latent powers that occasionally afflict young ladies.

It wasn't a view to which I subscribed. But I thought I should like to go dusking, all the same.

Green globes were very fashionable that year. When Tristan asked me to go dusking with him, autumn was sliding into winter; it was the end of October, and London had been touched by the edge of the great storms that had swept so much of the north and west. Wild nights, with the trees lashing against the windowpane, a thundering rain whipping even the sluggish Thames into a froth. I loved this weather, but it was clear that Tristan was deeply concerned about my health, that I might catch a chill.

"You are so *pale*, Emily. Perhaps it's just that your hair is so very fair. But I worry that this weather will be too much for you."

I could have told him not to fuss. I'd never had a day's sickness in my life — not a genuine one, anyway. Instead I lowered my eyelashes and murmured that it was so kind of him to worry. I could feel my aunt watching me as I did so;

it's sad not to be trusted by your closest relatives. My plans took a little hop forward.

"But I have a thick velvet cloak, Tristan, proof against even the harshest winter chill. And I think I — I should like to venture out. If you're quite sure it's safe, of course."

Thoughts of the woods, of bone and blood and the wet black earth, the wind ripping through the trees... I didn't know where these thoughts came from, but they were occupying more and more of my attention. I felt my aunt's gaze sharpen like an icicle, as though she could see into those thoughts. I lowered my head still further and gave a little *I-must-be-brave* sigh. Tristan put out a hand, as if to reassure me, but the icicle stare drove it back.

"I shall be quite sure to protect you, Emily. I — I'd do anything." He must have realised that he'd said enough after that, because he grew pink and flustered. I gazed at him admiringly, all the same, and the pinkness increased.

"I should be pleased to see you settled, Emily," my aunt said, stiffly, after Tristan had made a blushing farewell. I'd learned by now not to argue: it was pointless. Instead, I nodded.

"I should like a home of my own, aunty." It was quite true; I didn't have to say what sort of a home, after all.

"Perhaps I have misjudged you," my aunt said, but not as if she believed it. "I suppose you can't help your ancestry, after all. Your poor mother—"

I dabbed my eyes with a lace handkerchief and I think that helped, too.

Upstairs, in my own chamber, I looked out at the weather hissing across the heath, the gaslights blurring the city beyond.

Her mother disappeared, you know.

It broke her father's heart. He didn't live long after that.

I'd heard the whole story by now, delivered in whispers behind the parlour door. My aunt had never liked my mother, I think, but I didn't know why. To my knowledge, mama had never actually *done* anything; she was always so meek and mild, at least until she'd vanished. Run off with another man, my aunt had said, still whispering. But I didn't think that was true. And she'd looked so much like me: the same fair hair, almost white, the green eyes that in some lights took on an odd chestnut tinge, nearly red... My mother had been considered a beauty.

It is my opinion that my aunt thought that I had not shown enough proper mourning at my father's death. Children are frequently stupid; I should have made a better job of it.

It rained solidly for a week, which meant that there could be no dusking anyway. The Others won't come out when it pours, although I've seen them at the edges of storms, flashing in the darkness like snatches of lightning. On the Friday night, however, the sky cleared over and a thin new moon rose over the heath. Tristan, still flustered, presented himself and his mother on the doorstep at six thirty in the evening. I waited modestly on the stairs, clutching my new globe, a stout jade-green affair with a night-light smouldering in it.

"Emily? I thought, if you wish — ah, I see you are ready. It is quite chilly, we must make sure you wrap up warmly."

My cloak was green, as well: the colour of forests, with an enveloping hood. I liked the hood, it hid my expression at convenient moments. And I liked the greenness, which matched my eyes.

Watched like a hawk by my aunt, and with Tristan's mother promising to have me safely back by nine, I took his arm demurely and we stepped out onto the heath.

The lights of London blazed beyond and I felt a small strange pull, not to the lights themselves, I thought, but to what they represented: the freedom. If I had my way, I'd run across the heath and down towards the river, and then through the streets and beyond to the northern moors, and — I blinked.

"Are you quite well, Emily?"

"I think so, Tristan. You're right, it *is* a little chilly."

We weren't the only ones dusking. There were a number of other young couples out with globes, and on the other side of the heath a girl was chasing a little light with a series of squeaks, like an excited mouse. I sighed. I supposed I'd have to behave in a similar fashion.

Tristan's mother parked herself on a nearby seat in a complacent manner. I was slightly surprised by this: I would not have thought that I was all that marvellous a catch, but then there was that rather large inheritance to consider... My aunt might not have seen fit to point out my shortcomings, hoping as she was to be rid of me.

Tristan showed me how to hold my globe up to the new moon, how to weave it to and fro in order to attract anything that might be passing. I allowed myself to be shown; it was possible, I found, to treat it as a game.

"And don't be frightened if anything comes close," he instructed me. "They're just — just like butterflies, or moths."

Moths with sharp teeth, I thought, and pointed fingers, but I giggled in a vacuous manner and this seemed to please Tristan. I held up my globe, moving it clumsily from side to side, and permitted Tristan to show me once more how it was done. He looked at me as my gloved hands were enclosed fleetingly within his own, but I affected not to notice. Over on the bench, his mother coughed, and he dropped his hands. I saw the new moon through the green wall of the globe, distorted, like a smile on its side.

And then something huge and bee-like was humming and buzzing around me.

"Look!" Tristan cried, very excited. "You've nearly got one!"

Of course I had. I'd known that I would, without knowing how I knew. Earth and roots and something whistling up into the darkness — the thing that was hissing around the globe sheared away, towards shadow.

"Nearly!" Tristan was still marvelling. "I don't think I've

ever seen one so close before."

I'd taken careful note, of the long wings, as lacy as a dragonfly's, the pinched countenance, human-like, but only as far as mockery, the sharp nails, black as thorns.

"There's another one!" Together, briefly united in purpose, we ran across the heath, ignoring the sudden agitation of shuffling from Tristan's mother on the bench. Scarves fluttering, my cloak billowing out behind me, our flying feet — but we could not catch it. The little light, dim as blue gas, danced and tumbled ahead of us, heading for the fringe of woodland that lay at the far end of the heath. It disappeared within and Tristan caught my arm as I was about to go after it.

"Better not go in there, please, Emily," he said. I pretended to be breathless.

"Why, I hardly knew where I was," I told him. It was almost true.

"I must not tire you out. Perhaps we should go back..."

I did not want to go back. I wanted to go on, into the black shadowed woods, into the city and slip along the riverside in the light of the smiling moon. But instead, I nodded, feigning exhaustion, and let myself droop. We walked slowly back, with Tristan talking — I think — about his studies, and parted company on the doorstep.

Later that night, I woke. I thought at first that something was tapping on the windowpane, a branch in the rising wind, but then I saw the flickering light. I got out of bed and went to the window. It was perhaps the length of my hand, scratching its nails down the glass. The moon was just visible behind it, low above the city and almost swallowed by a bank of cloud.

I did not hesitate for more than a moment. I was too curious. I opened the window and let it in.

Like moths... it fluttered around the room, now high, now low, until it came to hover near my face. I did not like having it so close to me. Its eyes were a dim burning gold; I looked for a sign of reason, but found none, or at least, not as we would know the word. Its mouth opened and I saw pointed teeth. It did not speak. Instead, its hand shot out. Too late, I stumbled back, but I felt the minute tear of its nail across my eye. There was a blinding pain, which lasted for a second: I think I cried out and then pressed my hand to my mouth. I did not want my aunt bursting into the room, demanding explanations.

And I could *see*, as if a little rent had been torn in the fabric of the world. The moon, again sailing through cloud but this time, not coming out again, fading to a circlet of dark above the garden of the house: I knew it was my aunt's garden, because I could see the back wall, the long skeins of ivy. Someone was standing underneath the ivy, statue-still, looking out, as if carved from a block of night.

I knew I had to go to this person. Not now, but when the moon was dark, when you are not supposed to go dusking, when you might meet something you cannot catch. Nor was I to meet it here, but in the patch of woodland on the edge of Blackheath. I bowed my head. Something hot and wet ran down my cheek, like a tear.

The rent closed and the window banged in the wind. I was left with a stinging eye and a memory of a shape in the night, and the knowledge of what it wanted.

I feigned illness, sent word to Tristan that I had caught a cold on the heath, was not feeling my best. My aunt watched me, not believing at first, but I let myself droop and drift and grow even paler, and I think she finally allowed herself to acknowledge that there was something wrong with me. It might even have been true. I stayed huddled beneath the covers, listening to the rain on the window and the wind in the trees, dreaming of forests and the endless moor, the stars above me and the world below. I did not know where these dreams came from, only that they were a part of me, and in all of them, I saw those flickering lights.

When I rose, I sat staring out of the window, at the thin sliver of an old moon. It did not look as though it was smiling now.

Next day, I told my aunt that I felt better. I also allowed myself to appear despondent, saying that Tristan must think me terribly foolish. I moped so successfully that my aunt eventually offered to allow me to convey a message to him, via his mother.

I asked him to meet me in the parlour. He came several minutes early; I kept him waiting.

When I went downstairs I apologised as prettily as I could. This time, his mother had not accompanied him: it seemed that she, too, was suffering from a chill.

"I'm afraid I have a dreadfully weak constitution," I murmured.

"I don't think girls should be too robust," Tristan declared. "All those women wanting to be nurses, for example — it's not ladylike."

I put a hand to my throat. "I should hate to be a nurse," I said. Well, that was true enough. "But I do feel much stronger. I was wondering if—?"

"Perhaps just a stroll?" Tristan suggested. "It is not the time for dusking, you see."

He paused expectantly, perhaps anticipating an argument, but I meekly agreed.

"If you wrap up well..." His tone was solicitous, but there was the faintest note of hectoring beneath it and I repressed a smile. So with all marriages, I thought. And surely that was why my mother had run.

My aunt told us that she would be watching from the parlour window. She would be watching, but would she be able to see? The sky was clear now, so a glance through a gap in the curtains told me, but I could smell the rain in the air, seeping under the door and through the cracks in the windowpane, overpowering the musty potpourri scent of the parlour.

"I should not want to be too late," I faltered.

And that was true, too.

So we walked out onto the heath, Tristan and I, just as we

had done a little while before, but this time I held no globe in my hand. The stars were a burning river across the city sky that mirrored the river below, but of course there was no moon.

I took Tristan's arm, shyly, and pretended to let him guide me across the heath, but it was I who was guiding him: exclaiming over a moth, feigning interest in a dropped glove. Soon we were near the grove of trees that lay at the edge of the heath.

I could feel it waiting. It was very strong and the smell of iron surrounded it. At that moment, I understood why the Others are said to hate iron: it is a blasphemy to them, for it mimics the scent of blood and yet is metal, a made-thing.

A gust of wind scoured across the grass, stirring the trees. Tristan glanced away and at that moment, I snatched at my hat and threw it beyond the bushes.

"Oh!" I clutched my hair. "My hat! The wind caught it, how silly!"

And letting go of his arm, I dashed into the woodland.

"Emily! Come back!"

But I did not. I ran on. I could hear him crashing through the undergrowth behind me.

"I can't find my hat!" I cried over my shoulder.

"Emily, you must come back!"

It was ahead of me. I could feel it, waiting. And then it was as though the hidden moon sailed out and I could see again.

Someone was standing in the glade. It was huge, hunched, a mass of shoulder and neck. I saw the antlers rearing up from its brow and the glitter of a golden eye. It stood upright, much taller than a man, and it wore a cloak of leaves. The iron smell was very strong and the ground was moist beneath my feet.

I began to speak.

"I have brought what you asked for."

But the voice wasn't mine. It drowned mine out. Very slowly, I looked around. Tristan stood behind me, holding out a green glass globe. And from the corner of my bewildered eye, I saw the horned thing step forward.

I do not know what they plan to do with me, only that they are pleased. My mother escaped, they explained to me, ran from both the human world and the Other, and that sort of thing will never do. So they have the next best, instead; they have me, her daughter.

I should have remembered that shy girls and stammering boys might, sometimes, be motivated by the same things.

It's comfortable enough here. There is a velvet couch, a small table, rugs. Food is delivered three times a day and it is always the same, sugary, and satisfying for a short while. But when I glance at my surroundings, from the corner of my eye, I see that the velvet couch is really a pile of rushes, and the rugs are leaves. The walls, however, are always the same: green glass, green as the grass upon the heath, or the leaves of the forest, or a watching eye.

Golty's Burrow

Paul Laville

Always ready to crack a 'hilarious' joke at the most inappropriate moment, Paul Laville continues to be astonished that his fiction turns out so grim. A big fan of dark thrillers, graphic novels, moody TV dramas, new technologies and big sci-fi concepts, Paul recently published his debut novel Awake In The Dark, *which he says is awesome and should be read by everybody.*

While Awake In The Dark *is a gripping murder mystery, "Golty's Burrow" showcases his crazed SF side. A world has been engineered and then suffered through a technology Armageddon. Races clash in the ruins, fighting for survival. An evolutionary stalemate needs to be broken if things are to change. But as Lorni and her twin, Prilly, discover, everything has a cost...*

It was you, or a remnant image of your face at least, that first pointed me here. It happened one morning when I was cornered, backed-up at the foot of a sheer mountain of ruins by a pack of dolls just minutes before dawn.

An entrance to Golty's Burrow was close; I could feel it vibrating but she wasn't letting me in. The dolls were running, leaping over the foothills of rubble, climbing across and down the ruins all crystalline talons, tails and teeth. They had me. I turned, dropped my sack of loot and whipped out my knives, ready to fight, to take them all on if I had to. But then the mountain shook. There was a hissing sound like escaping gas, and then both mountain and foothills came alive as whipping, thrashing shoots of metal grass exploded outwards. The metal grass went for the dolls, sliced them up, and in seconds I was covered in red spray.

I thought I was done for too, but the grass ignored me. I wiped fine blood from my eyes, bent slowly down to retrieve my sack of loot, and then, just as slowly, I walked away. A few steps on and the first flash of dawn slammed into my eyes, almost blinding me as it lit up the world for just a second.

Then it was dark again, and in that I moment I heard something behind me. Sounded as though the world was cracking.

I turned to look back at the mountain, my free hand hovering at my knife-belt. I tensed...

Another flood of light from the rising sun, and in that half a second I saw it.

The metal grass covering the mountain of ruins had arranged tiny bits of doll into something like your face.

Darkness again, and the image burned into my eyes. Had I really seen it?

Another flash of light, and the face was there. Huge. The mouth was jabbering like the image was trying to talk. It freaked me out and I'll be honest, I panicked. I turned away from the face and ran.

The grass reached out through alternating dark and light, pushing the face outwards as though it was chasing me. Every time I looked over my shoulder this thing was closer, larger.

Golty threw a door at a nearby ruined wall and without thinking I dived into her, safe at last.

So. You got my attention. Here I am: The survivor. Solo human. The Only Girl. Lorni the Last!

And there's the face I saw. Right in front of me now...

What? Oh... yeah. That was my twin. She's called Prilly and she lived with me in Golty's Burrow where she was made.

Before The End of Days, when I lived topside in some city somewhere, Brambel, the man I was staying with caught a doll and locked it away.

He was a J3. A soldier by then. I was in thrall to him only because he'd tried hacking my code. He'd botched the job and I didn't know who I was for a long time. Anyway he hid this doll in a specially-grown outhouse and it became his project instead of me.

But I digress.

Back in the Burrow, I told Prilly about being chased by the dolls and about them getting shredded by the metal grass. I didn't tell Prilly about the face. "Is that their blood on your face?" she asked.

"It'll come off, eventually." I backed away from her and ladled some flowerstuff into my breakfast bowl. I was so hungry.

"Why wasn't you spiked by the metal grass?" Prilly asked. "You said it burst out everywhere."

"I don't know," I told her. "It just... left me alone."

"Was they all dead then?" Prilly asked.

"Yup. Grass carved them up and carried the bits away."

"We could have eaten some."

Thought of that made me feel sick. She liked her animals, her meat and juices and blood. I'd stopped eating meat when she was born. Watching her tear at an animal I just felt...

"Golty says the dolls die easily outside," she said. "She says they're curious and stupid. They don't learn and they die easily."

"You could be right," I said. "They keep building them towers and then jumping off 'em."

She stared at me, her eyes burning like two hot stars in the glow from the orange spherical. "Golty's really upset for the dolls," she whispered. "She thinks they're all going to die if we stay."

"I don't care about the dolls!" I snapped. "I care about you and me down here. Scratching around for bugs and flower-clippings just so we can eat! Before you came along Golty used to provide. And now... now it's every night I've got to go up and risk my life topside just to keep the both of us alive."

"Pity you," Prilly said. Then: "Golty doesn't need to provide everything and you're an idiot if that's what you expect of her. You don't get anything without risk and if you were willing to push yourself out a little more..."

"What?"

She was crazy. Then she said, "What about the Credible Bargainer? You could get more stuff off him?"

"No."

"No?"

"You bargain with him, Prilly. See what you'd lose!"

She pushed her empty platter to one side and belched noisily. Flowerstuff always gave her bad wind.

"When you see him again," she said, "tell him we need some new modern atkinsons, or else we won't have any light." She smiled and then added, "Still, I won't have to look at your dumb face then will I?"

Bitch... I stood up and gathered the platters. The umbilical imprint was on the other side of her neck and it was larger than mine, being more recent, but otherwise her face was exactly the same as mine. It was her body that was slightly different. It had surprised me when she flopped out of Golty that there were these weird growths on her shoulder blades making her look hunchbacked. And she had no legs. For some reason Golty hadn't given her any. I thought something had gone wrong and maybe that had made her bitter and stupid.

She pushed off from the table, using her arms to move her trundler towards the grouchiebugs roasting on top of the orange spherical.

"I'm going topside again tonight," I said to her, trying to lift the mood. "We're in a good place. Seen a couple of really well-preserved houses buried deep, almost intact."

"Good for you." She put a gloveleaf over her hand, then dipped it into the fiery bowl to scoop up a handful of bugs. Her movements were ritualised, and with her mouth stuffed full of bugs she looked like an infested corpse.

I shuddered, wishing she'd never been made. I wished that Golty had said no when I'd asked her to make me a twin. But on the other hand I couldn't imagine life without her. Before Prilly I'd been lonely and I didn't want that again. The Ongoing War had made me a special kind of lonely that you only felt after you'd been to every city in the world and walked through the carnage of human meat spread about. When you walked through a place and could hear *nothing* but the sound of your own heartbeat, and your footsteps crunched over ruins now so far gone, so overgrown and so decayed, that there was nothing left to remind you what they might have resembled and when even the bones of all the dead people had gone, covered over or kicked or blown away, *that* was when you realised what it was really like to be truly alone in the world.

No more people.

Just me and Prilly.

And she's a twin. A copy.

No. I don't think the Credible Bargainer is a person as such. Didn't you see him land on the tower when he brought us?

In a box. Tattoos all over the outside of it. You must have seen it; I didn't imagine him. He brought us food and supplies. Always in return for something from my code. He's a collector, so he says. I'm surprised you've never seen him before, but I suppose he arrived after the War didn't he? From some other place.

That night, after sleep and supper, I went back out. Prilly sat by the dim, orange spherical, looking into its cooling depths. It'd be roasting flowerstuff and grouchiebugs for breakfast when I returned, and Prilly would tell me I was late. That was how it always used to be.

So my last night began as normal: I made sure my clothes were on tight, that my repellents were all working, that the blu-gel was packed deep down in my throat, and then I took our last modern atkinson and I left the Burrow.

If you were able to smash your way through the flesh of a topside house, using a big nullet like I used to, then you could find some fantastic rewards. In this swamp of a town alone I'd found something really special. I hadn't told Prilly, because I'd wanted to surprise her.

So, with the star-noise loud and the broken moon bright in the sky, I descended through the rubble and ruins, looking for the house I'd discovered the night before. It was deep down, hidden under some kind of dome, but even after all this time it still looked like a house.

In the middle of it, growing up through what used to be a bedroom, I'd found this tree full of samsons, which were Prilly's favourite sex-toys.

That wasn't the only surprise however...

Tonight I squeezed back into the house. It was still dead inside, and also serious dark; so I lit the modern atkinson, rubbing its tip with my finger and thumb. It sparked and spat red light for a second before bursting into a big, white flame.

It was an amazing house. Grown to a personal design and allowed to shape itself to the passions of its inhabitants. Whoever lived there years ago, they must have been happy and sensuous people I thought. It was full of suggestive holes and columns; open doorways like fat lips, and puckered skylights now sealed up and caked over. In its day the walls would have been soft to touch, with hidden features made from erectile material that only appeared when you stroked them. The floor would have been thick with soft fur.

I had to tread carefully. The columns holding up the ceiling were leaning, wilting. The furry floor was now a swamp and it made me sick with nerves to slosh through it.

A small cloud of snap-crackling fat-wasps followed me upstairs, heavy in the air as they buzzed my code, hooking their electrics into my cheeks. I ignored the symbols that flashed in my vision and I carried on moving, one step at a time.

Slowly.

There was a crust on the staircase. Like thin ice it covered a death trap, so I kept to the edges.

Shivering, teeth chattering and puffing smoky blue breath I swung the modern atkinson out to see what was up ahead. Nothing much but decay and rot. Everywhere I looked.

I crabbed over to the bedroom and walked carefully inside.

The bedroom was filled with green and blue light. It came from active cultures growing inside these two liquid beds in the middle of the room and it shone through the branches of the samson-tree weirdly. The liquid had started out as blu-gel, or something like it which allowed you to breathe, but now it was soaked with all the toxins in the air plus material from the two male sleepers, one in each bed, who had obviously died incumbent when Golty had killed just about everyone living topside at the time. Their bodies were still in there, bloated like human balloons kept all these years. Feeding the things that grew on them.

Never forget that sight.

Behind the tree, spare body parts hung from an exo-rail. They were protected by a sheet of translucent frosting that glittered when the modern atkinson hissed and spat across it. I smashed up the screen with the hard nullet Golty had made me and then I stepped in and made my way into the steam.

"Yes!" Deep inside I saw the real surprise, a pair of nice strong legs that I knew Prilly would appreciate. I was doing it for her, see? Golty could fix them on her. Maybe. It was worth a try.

I snapped the legs off the rail, checked to make sure that one was a right leg and the other was left, and both were female, and then I had another look around. There was all sorts in there: arms, feet, fingers and toes, you name it, all ready to be attached to either a woman or a man.

Seemed to me that the concept citizenry must have spent a lot of time swapping and replacing body parts.

Thunder broke out overhead. A sudden, deafening crash. Louder. Closer. I swore, leapt out of the wardrobe and ran for my life, clutching the legs.

Too late. The ceiling fell, great chunks of it knocking me down. My senses were reeling. All I could think of was that I had to keep hold of the legs, for Prilly's sake I had to keep hold of them as tightly as I could. But the deluge was too much.

The whole damn house just broke up and collapsed around me. The stagnant gel beds split, the samson-tree sheared apart, and everything tumbled down with me into the swampy foundations of the house.

Darkness...

And then...

Memories fired up, bursting like supernovae from the deep centres of my code. Happened every time I closed my eyes and I always saw, heard and smelled the same things. The same sequence. The same horror:

It was The End of Days.

There'd been a big fight in the city. Weapons firing all night. People shouting and screaming. Contrails curling in the sky. To stay out of the way I'd run into the outhouse where Brambel had kept the doll, and when I saw what he had done to it my instinct to care for the creature kicked in almost painfully.

Brambel had broken the doll's legs and he'd tied its hands to a bar grown across the ceiling. Its eyes had been destroyed and most of its head opened up. There was a gash across its belly and in the corner of the outhouse was a heap of what could only have been its insides — a pile of bloodied cylinders, coils and balls covered in blood and milk. I picked through them and I saw a tiny, lifeless folded-up thing wrapped in silver film.

Took a while for me to realise what it was but when I did...

I was crying as I pulled the dead doll down, and when it was free and the weight of it fell into my arms I saw that Brambel had grafted two hardened sails of brown skin onto its back. They'd crumpled, collapsed and shrivelled up, but they still looked like wings: a glimpse into Brambel's madness, the J3 Insanity I think it had come to be called, even by then.

Outside there were explosions. I could hear men and women screaming in the streets. It seemed everyone was killing each other and I didn't know why and probably nor did they.

I laid the doll down and scrambled to the wall. Dug my fingers in and ripped it open to risk a look outside.

Two moons in those days and both were moving quickly in the sky. Fires burned from gutted houses and animal mines screamed as they died. I saw it all, took everything in, mesmerised. I saw massive engines of destruction, ancient and scarred, slowly turning towards each other in the dark. I watched as silent, black spheres of death fell slowly, beautifully, blotting out the stars when they moved over them. Then a series of rapid, silent photoflashes lit up the city and I had to retreat into the outhouse, blinking spots out of my eyes, crashing through stuff almost blinded. I fell down and then scrambled around on my hands and knees. I crawled under a bench and pulled the doll in with me. Hugging the thing close I sang us both a lullaby, tracing with my fingertips the delicate swirls and spirals on the dead doll's skin as the world outside was pushed and pulled, beaten and broken.

It grew more difficult to keep singing, and eventually I stopped and just covered my ears.

Outside, people slaughtered each other using every means possible. I tried to remember a time when there was no war, when men from the cities weren't fighting men from the moons, and men from the sea weren't fighting men from the pods. When the J3s had just been gardeners and left people's eyes alone. Had there ever been a time when women were pregnant with children instead of chatter-bombs? When you could trust that your best friend wasn't going to explode in your house and cover you in acid or slow-burn? I might have remembered something of other days before then, but during that night with the doll, cowering under the bench in the outhouse, everything changed.

At The End of Days it was no longer about sides. Everything was being destroyed. Everything was fighting everything else and everything and everyone was a weapon.

Brambel burst in and saw me with the dead doll. "What have you done to it?" he screamed, then reached down and dragged me out by my hair. I had plenty of hair back then, long and silver, all braided up.

Brambel was stained and encrusted head to foot in gore. One of his arms was broken and he struggled to hold the nullet properly while he dragged me outside.

He ranted at me, kicked and punched me. He lifted my head back and spat obscenities into my face. Then he tried his usual thing, except that, because his arm was broken, he couldn't work his trousers whilst holding me down. I played dumb so he let go of me. He had to drop the nullet as well and that his was last mistake.

I rolled over, snatched up the nullet and jumped to my feet. Screaming out my first ever cry of sheer rage I smashed him across the side of his head and he never even raised his hand.

I'd never hurt anyone before then. But now I was going for it.

I was in pain. My code was angry. I could feel it burning, changing everything. Brambel staggered, looking confused even while the altered side of his head leaked blood. I went at him again and he couldn't stop me, couldn't react. I slammed the big hammer right into his guts with all my strength and he fell, making a sound I'd never heard before. Then I smashed the nullet into his spine and broke him utterly. He rolled and his eyes stared up at me. His mouth moved, blood and spit bubbling up from his stupid fat lips and I stood over him like an angel of fucking death.

It didn't end there. In my dreams I always wanted it to end there but it never did. I tried to call out to the blood-soaked little girl in the memories and tell her to stop, "It's over". But she never hears me and the scene plays out...

I stamped my heel down into his balls. I did it again, and again and again, and would have carried on all night, hard and fast as tears and spit and sweat flew from my face. I started laughing at what I could do, at the damage I could do to someone else and in that moment I thought maybe I understood the Ongoing War.

I wiped my face with the back of one hand, then I lifted the nullet up high.

Yes. I did it.

I made his head spray outwards over the ground, and bits of it hit the outhouse, I'd smashed it so hard.

Afterwards I went for a dazed wander through burning streets. I was covered in blood. My hair, my face, my clothes once all white were red with blood and gore. But I wasn't alone in that.

Corpses lay scattered. Armed soldiers and crazy people tussled as they smashed them up for parts. Others like me just sat and shivered, staring into space.

And then... then I saw it...

On the horizon a distant mushroom cloud reached high on its giant, crooked stalk. Ribbons of fire arced away from the destructive mass like slowly-falling flares. Behind it was another, and maybe another way off in the distance. The horizon grew brighter than day and the world seemed to split. A terrifying hurricane of noise and wind sprang up and quickly grew.

No way, I wasn't going to die!

Instead, I ran, stumbling through the carnage as fast as I could to the only place I knew that might keep me safe. I had to beg Golty to let me into her, because for a while it didn't seem like she would. But she recognised me at last and she opened up. Others tried to follow me as the nukes ripped through everything, but Golty pushed them away. Once I was inside her, she, in her madness and rage, unlocked her Terminal Code and destroyed just about everything that still lived topside. And what she unleashed made those nukes seem insignificant.

She did it in the blink of an eye.

Everyone.

Everything.

Dead.

That was The End of Days.

Like a woman rescued from drowning I sat up and gasped, raking at the air. First thought was: *I'm back in the Burrow.* But the light was blurry, the air was hot and misty and the shadows were all wrong.

Turned out I was in a Hive Tower. Where the dolls lived. I didn't know it right away. Bits of me didn't do what they used to and anyway I doubted the towers were meta-tagged.

I could breathe but not easily. My head was as fuggy as the atmosphere and I could feel it starting to choke me. The blu-gel was reduced to a few dried flakes I coughed out in panic. So that meant I'd been here about a day.

I was surrounded by dolls. There was a circle around me that was clear, but beyond that the dolls stood wall-to-wall, even right up the wall for some of them — hanging on by their talons. Mostly they were the silver ones, but some were blue and some were green or red and some were tiny, gripping the shoulders of the big ones with long, hooked fingers. Like children.

It freaked me out. I mean... Children? Dolls? Dolls having children? And I couldn't? Didn't seem right. But there they were, peeking out between the legs of the big ones and looking at me with their heads to one side.

I knew then that these dolls were not factory-made. They'd been born, right? Maybe it was me dying here, gasping for breath, but looking down through a glass floor I saw a room below, packed with these weird, steamy cells in which more dolls were crawling around and over each other pressing their faces up at the glass.

Threat assessment was in overdrive.

Then this massive golden doll came at me from above, hair

and clothes rippling behind it as it descended on its chains. I scrabbled away. It was a giant, like twice the size of the normal ones. Its skin was covered in patterns: swirls and gridlines and like I said it was wearing *clothes*. Actual *designed* clothes that flared out from its shoulders and waist. It wore jewellery: bracelets on its arms and ankles, and this crazy necklace with an oval pendant at its throat. Oh that was nasty. Right in the middle of the pendant there was this shrunken face of someone who looked a bit like Brambel. It screamed in silence. Tiny eyes squeezed shut and its mouth a grimace of sheer terror.

"What do you want?" I coughed.

I noticed three or four oval holes in a far wall, which looked right out into the bright sunlight pulsing outside. I wondered about making a run for it.

Could I do it? Yes. Golty's vibrations were everywhere. The tower was surrounded by doorways to the Burrow. She'd been looking for me.

Suddenly a terrific burst of pain damn near floored me. The shrunken face on Goldie's pendant opened its eyes and the mouth started moving like it was talking quickly.

Find him! a voice suddenly screamed from the shrunken thing in the pendant. *You're killing us!*

I made a dash for the nearest oval window. The pack of dolls all parted and the children screamed and shot out of my way. I leapt through the window and out into the sky, and that was when I realised exactly where I was.

Plummeting downwards I wanted to fly, and it seemed like the most natural thing in the world but it wasn't going to happen, right? I was falling head-down towards a field of metal grass. The landscape pulsed between light and dark as hungry knife-sharp blades reached up towards me.

"Golty!" I screamed. "Golty, you bitch!"

The ground rushed up towards me — No, I rushed towards it. Right?

Didn't really matter because at any rate I was going to hit it hard.

Then a gash opened in the earth and the grass was pushed away by a bubbling red mass that ballooned upwards from inside it.

I was laughing when I hit the mush and got sucked into the soft cushion of Golty's Burrow. She might have taken her time but she wasn't going to let me die. Wonderfully she folded herself over me in bloodwarm light and soothing liquid.

My baby-baby-baby. I'm so sorry-sorry-sorry...

I pushed into her, glad to be cuddled and warmed and hugged and be fussed over and I don't know how long I was in there for. An hour? A day? A year? However long it was it began to feel like I'd always been there, in the bubbling dark of her flesh, and I started to think that my life before this beautiful time had been a dream.

Something happened then: a sudden shift in perspective and then I was out. Shivering. Covered in slime.

Wobbling like a newborn I stood to my feet. Naked. Huddling the wall. I looked around, trying to figure out where I was.

I knew I was in the Burrow, but this was somewhere inside it I'd never been before. Or maybe Golty had changed things around again and I was only a few steps away from where Prilly and I lived. A light was coming from somewhere and I padded on bare feet towards it. I turned one corner and there she was: an ever-shifting, crystalline shape that stretched upward and throughout the cave at the centre of the Burrow.

Who was I kidding? To have done what she did at The End of Days, Golty had to have been as big as the world.

Overcome with emotion I lost myself in Communion, my thoughts shifting to the beat of her heart as she addressed my code and made it sing. I knelt as close to her as I could. Cried my eyes out with my face pressed right into her flesh. "Take me up again," I kept whispering as I shook like I couldn't control myself, all snot and tears. "Just take me in. I don't — I don't... I don't want to be like this any more..."

Yeah... I gave up there. After everything. The only time in my life I'd ever been that way, definitely since I killed Brambel. But maybe I just needed it that one time, to get through the shit in my head, to reach a decision.

My thrall didn't last. Something inside me had been broken a long time ago. Maybe Brambel really had screwed up my code, or maybe the damage had been done before that time. Whatever, no amount of crying or self-pity was going to change anything now. I was a survivor now, so I survived. That was all I had to do.

I rubbed the wet from my face and pushed myself up, stretching my shoulders, lifting my head high. I took a deep, deep breath, then started my walk through the heart of Golty. Deeper inside I heard strange, sickening howls. Unfinished things clung to her insides. I could see them trapped in the crystalline mass, unwanted. They all looked like me and Prilly. Really deep inside her now, where it was so hot I was dripping with sweat, I touched my fingertips to where bubbles of grey stone caked her shining crystal. They flaked away under my touch and there was more of it stretching away, eating up her natural light with darkened, crooked tumours. "You're dying," I whispered to her. "Shhhhh..."

Your face came again but this time it was Golty who planted the vision, right inside my head. With words spoken in my own voice.

Find him. Seek him out. Cross the world and call his name: Larmot Duran. Leave now. I'm so sorry...

No pain this time. I'd got the message.

"Where are we going?" Prilly asked me, rolling her trundler round in agitated circles.

I didn't answer. I just carried on stuffing my sacks full of the things we'd need for our journey.

"Lorni, tell me!" She was terrified. She'd never been topside in her life. So I looked at her and wondered how could this — this *thing* be so emotional? She was just a copy. Who said she had to have emotions? Or even pretend to have emotions? All she did for me lately was give me bad dreams.

"Golty's dying," I told her. "So we have to leave now."

"Dying?" she laughed. "That's ridiculous. I'd know if she was. You're just making it up to get rid of me. You're going to take me topside and feed me to the prowlers like you always said you would."

Prowlers! Based on what I made up for her she'd have thought topside was teeming with creatures. But there was no time for these things now.

"It's why she couldn't make you any legs," I snapped at her. "It's why she has no food for us. She's just... using everything that's left inside her to make more copies of me that'll never be born." Was that my fault? Had I given her some kind of instruction when I asked her to make Prilly that she couldn't break out of?

"It's not true!"

I didn't care what Prilly thought. It was true, I knew it. Golty had given everything to keep us — *me* — alive and now that was all she could do.

"I don't want to go," Prilly was crying. "Please, Lorni!"

She tried to fight me off as I tied a rope to her trundler and hauled her out. "We're not staying," I told her. While she screamed and ranted, I pulled her towards a door Golty had made for us. Outside in the night wind I thought back to the legs I'd found and lost which, if things had turned out different perhaps, could have given Prilly a new life.

So that was my last day in Golty's Burrow.

I pulled Prilly all the way to the beach where the air was better and mostly breathable even in daytime. It had taken me the whole night and now she was quiet and sullen. Once there I waited for the Credible Bargainer to show. Somehow he always knew when I needed him.

He came, flying towards me in his weird, tattooed box, spinning out of the storm clouds over the ocean like a ferocious shadow, huge and defiant of land and sea.

His impossible box stopped with a boom and hovered

over us, turning slowly. Prilly wasn't looking but I noticed that the bottom of the box was damaged. Bits of house clung to one corner and it was tilting to that side.

A flap opened and the Credible Bargainer's bald head poked out on the end of its long stick.

"Lorni," he said, sounding surprised. "What are you doing here? And what in the name of all that remains to shit on this world is that... *thing* you've brought with you?"

"I need something," I told him, shouting as loud as I could into the wind. "One last bargain."

He came down closer.

"I'm all ears," he purred. "What do you want?"

"I need to go somewhere."

"All right. Where?"

"To the city across the sea," I told him. "I want to find Larmot Duran."

The box lifted momentarily. Strafed to one side and around me. I turned with it.

"Duran?" he said. "Oh. Now. That's *interesting*. Something's changed, Lorni. Wait... You look different. You definitely sound different. Like you've had an... education." His head stabbed forward to look me in the eye and he frowned in suspicion. "What's going on?"

"Do you know him?"

He made a 'whatever' kind of face. "Duran? Yeah. Sure. I mean he's not the man he was..." Then he stared right at me, his eyes narrowed, dangerous. "He's just soup now," he growled, "but I'll take you to him if that's what you want." His box came to rest on the sands. Again I noticed the crumpled bottom corner. "There is a price, my dear."

"I know," I said. "And you can have it."

He was interested. "All of it?" he asked greedily.

"All of it."

Silently a black rectangle opened in the side of the box.

"Step inside!" he shouted, suddenly showman-like. Then the stick supporting his head angled down so that it was level with my face.

"Not me," I told him, eye to eye.

"What do you mean?" The head pulled up. "Don't try to trick me, bitch. A bargain is a bargain."

"I know. You can take her for your library." I pointed at Prilly whose face was a mask of dejection slowly changing into one of horror as she started to understand why I'd brought her here. "She's my twin," I told him. "She has my code. She was made from it."

The Credible Bargainer hissed and his stick rose up, carrying the head with it so he could see Prilly more clearly.

I turned on my heel and saw that the stupid bitch had started trundling away. Like that was going to do any good. She was using all the strength in her arms but the sand was making it hard for her and the growths on her shoulders stuck out hard as she worked them.

"*A twin?*" the Credible Bargainer screeched. "You never told me about this!"

I could hear Prilly blubbing and crying, whimpering as she struggled and fought to pull away. I didn't try to stop her. Fact was she'd never make it off the beach. Still, I had to give her credit for trying. I wouldn't have thought she had it in her.

"You say she has your code?" said the Bargainer. "All of it?"

"She has it all," I confirmed. "It's interpreted differently, and a lot of it is blocked off for now. But I can give you the cipher, the key to open it all up. You'll have my Ancestor Code for yourself then, the print of an entire race in your library."

"What about her mass?" he shrieked. "The code is nothing without the mass to give it shape."

"It's yours," I told him. "Reshape it however you want."

The head retracted and came back to me.

"You never told me you had a twin," he spat, his expression ferocious.

"And you never told me you crashed into that house I was in last night."

“An accident,” he said, smiling.

“So how did I end up in the Hive Tower with the dolls?”

His head bobbed and weaved, rising up. Smiling it faced me again. “All right. So the dolls made a bargain,” he explained, and now the head was so close I could smell his meat. “And you should see what they gave me in return for taking you to them. Did you know they’ve been trying to make contact with you for months?”

“And I’d thought they’d just been trying to kill me. They want me to find Duran,” I told him. “So does Golty. She thinks he can — Hell I don’t know what they think. But if I talk to him I can find out.”

“I took one of the dolls up in my box,” he said, like he wasn’t even listening to me. “The experience was too much for it, given what they were designed to do. It exploded under high velocity. Just like that! Bang!” He chuckled. “I expect you’re made of sterner stuff, in fact I know you are. So step inside why don’t you? And bring that... *copy* with you.”

I looked at the black rectangle on the side of the box and found that it was suddenly very difficult to breathe. I remembered the burst of joy I’d felt when Golty pushed Prilly out of her sac in front of me and I’d first looked upon her smiling, trusting face. Just like mine. For a second I rethought my plan. I could grab the Credible Bargainer’s head and snap it off its stick. I’d run to Prilly, grab the rope and pull her away, save her, save us both. Take us both away from here and we’d find somewhere else to live.

“A bargain’s a bargain,” he whispered, close to my ear as if he knew my thoughts. “And you’ve already pledged your price. I’ve accepted and that’s the end of it. For the code to your *twin* I’ll fly you to the ends of the planet and twice back round. Don’t worry, Lorni. *You’ll* be safe inside.”

I pushed all thoughts of escape away for good. Fact is we’d never find anywhere else to live if Golty died. And I had to survive.

Quickly the box heaved up into the air, turned and landed in front of Prilly with a boom. It looked like a wall, cutting off her escape route.

I walked up behind Prilly's trundler and ran her into the box.

She screamed when we went inside.

As we flew I asked the Credible Bargainer about you.

"You'll be disappointed, Lorni," he told me, his face floating in the darkness of the box, no longer attached to its stick. "Duran may be all that remains of the great world-builders and their Chancellery, certainly on this world, but right now he's little more than code-potential kept in a bubbling soup cauldron locked away in a rusty, old tank."

"The dolls think he's their maker," I said.

"Duran made a lot of things. It was his job, what he was paid to do."

"He can save them," I said. "Golty seems to think—"

"That's the last thing he needs to do."

I looked at him. "Am I missing something?"

The Credible Bargainer paused for a moment and then, in a slightly softer voice than I'd heard before, he asked me, "What did you see inside the Hive?"

Easy answer. "Dolls," I told him. "Thousands of them, all bunched up together."

"Critical mass," he said. "They need to get out of the towers but they can't do that without risking death. Were they all the same? Quickly now: think!"

"No," I answered. "There was a giant one. He was gold but the others were all different colours. Some were wearing clothes. And there were small ones. I thought of them as children."

"They *are* children," he said, "and your 'Golty' had nothing to do with *them*. And you presume to know what she thinks? I've been watching the creatures grow, develop. Twenty generations in now. They've learned fast and they've procreated fast — just as they were designed to do, about the only thing in their design that actually worked out. But now they're stuck."

"Stuck?"

"In their towers. Like a million crabs in a stagnant rock-pool," he said. "Do you know why?"

"No."

"Well you should. It's in your code, Lorni. Your Ancestor Code. This world, the Gul-T. It's all keyed-in to you, to your *type*. This world was made for you."

"For me...?"

"All right. A conceit. Not just you, but you and others like you. Wished for, designed and built by the concept citizenry as one of their many fancies. The dolls came afterwards, when the fighting started."

"I don't—"

"A world of angels and demons!" he said grandly. "That's what they wanted to build here, get it? It all started off well enough but then everything went to shit because what do angels and demons do?"

I shook my head.

"They fight. All through the ages, the eternal struggle between dark and light. And the concept citizenry, romantic idiots and dreamers lost in poetry and self-indulgence, never realised that their very souls would be the things that were fought over. The Chancellery took its fee and whatever was left here after the Ongoing War the Gul-T destroyed as a job gone bad. She kept you alive. She had to. It was her key instruction — to keep at least one of you alive for assessment. But the Chancellery isn't coming back. They've moved on. So you alone inherit the world, Lorni. Congrats, it'll be yours forever even while your 'Golty' sucks it dry and endures a prolonged death-agony for another thousand years."

The world spun. "Angels and demons... Which am I?" I asked.

"That's down to you I guess. And whatever you decide next."

"What do you mean? Decide?"

"Oh... You don't know?" He started laughing. "This is the

reason why the dolls and Golty want you to talk to Duran: The dolls live in their silos, which are complete ecosystems designed to nurture them to adulthood quickly. And like I said they're crammed full in there. They need to move out but they can't because the climate will kill them all."

"The world needs to change," I said.

"Now she gets it."

"Golty can change it...?"

"It'll be the last thing she ever does. It's a massive shift, Lorni, a total root and branch rewrite. It's a process you will not survive."

"You're lying to me. You don't know all this."

"Oh come on, Lorni. Don't act dumb. I've been around and I know stuff. I've sat on board meetings, looked at plans, advised and consulted on all kinds of things you wouldn't dream of. Fact is that unless you die — which you won't because the machine won't let you — the dolls can't move on. This world needs to change for them to thrive; all the crap your makers left behind needs to be swept clean away and that, my dear, includes you and your defence system."

"I have a 'defence system'?"

"The... the what do you call it? The metal grass," he explained, as if I was an idiot. "Designed as a countermeasure to attack dolls on sight. But Golty can't let you die because she's been instructed to keep you alive. It's a beautiful conflict. I don't know how long she's been struggling with it, or how the dolls came to reason it out. Golty made the original dolls so there might be some kind of communion there I guess."

"So... Kill the dolls or kill myself," I whispered. "Then where does Duran fit in? What can he do?"

"He can override the machine's core instruction and allow it to kill you, thus initiating the world-shaping process which will enable the dolls to break out and thrive," he told me. "Think about it. And while you do that, let me show you something."

Prilly appeared.

“What are you going to do with her?”

“I’m going to extract her code and show you what you are. Clearly, you don’t believe me and to be honest... I’m not sure I believe it myself. The myths of this place are totally outlandish, but it’s all been true so far... so we’ll see.”

Now he floated up to me. “The key,” he said, “if you please...”

I felt my code singing. The cipher was giving itself up to the stuff inside the box.

“Take it,” I whispered, symbols and numbers now flowing all around me. “But I want to know it all. I want to know everything.”

“I’m a Bargainer,” he said. “I’ll tell you what you want to know but in return... Actually no,” he said suddenly. And his face cracked into a hideous smile. “You’ve nothing left to give. So just this once, a parting gift if you like, it’s free of charge.”

The Credible Bargainer was ages old. He’d flown around this world for so long there wasn’t anything that wasn’t represented in his mnemonic library. So I learnt a lot during my journey.

I saw the horror at the heart of the deadly sun and the machines which made the animals. I delved into the J3 template and saw the corruption that had replicated itself within it. I experienced the memories of the concept citizens and looked in horror at some of their other fantastic creations, which they paid the likes of you to build worlds for.

When we landed here I was hardly out of the box when he applied the cipher to Prilly’s code and she changed. The box dissolved to leave her huddled, still without legs, on the roof of this tower.

For a second I thought the sequence had failed and we could go back to living together. I was so happy and I almost ran to hug Prilly and tell her how sorry I was.

I say almost...

Because then her head snapped up and she looked right at me in absolute, unmistakable hatred.

I fell back as she bared new teeth and hissed at me. Then she unfurled a pair of enormous black wings from her shoulders and took off with a thunderclap. An alien shriek rang out and soon Prilly was just a dark shape heading towards the stars on newborn wings that I'll never be able to grow.

That last sight of Prilly hurt me more than you can imagine and I...

Fuck you... when I set out on this I'd thought you were a god. But you're just one of many... what are you? Builders? Engineers? Goddamn *caretakers*? Whatever you *were*, when war broke out you turned your terraforming machines into weapons of mass destruction: I'm talking of Golty, designed to create life then changed at root level to manufacture weapons instead. And the dolls were that weapon. Except that something went wrong... yes? Something was botched with their code, similar error that made the J3s insane, and millions of them were churned out useless. Like me they couldn't even fly!

Anyway, here we are: One flightless, surviving demon or angel, and some semi-conscious soup in a tank with a picture of a face on the side, same face the metal grass, the dolls and Golty showed me, and it's nothing more than a — what did he call it? A fucking *brand logo*.

There's a whole new race at our feet and we're supposed to decide, you and me, whether they live or die.

Angel or Demon, I know exactly which I am now.

Perfect Fit

Deborah Jay

Deborah Jay originally trained as a scientist, specialising in genetics and embryo transfer, and had every intention of working in that field after graduation. Somewhere along the way she got distracted by her favourite sport, and ended up instead as a professional rider and trainer of dressage horses.

Alongside many magazine articles and two hardbacks on dressage training, she has also published two fantasy novels: The Prince's Man – a Five Kingdoms Novel *(Epic Fantasy) and* Desprite Measures – Caledonian Sprite #1 *(Urban Fantasy). The second in the Five Kingdoms series,* The Prince's Son *is nearing completion. For more information visit* www.deborahjayauthor.com.

In Deborah's story "Perfect Fit" a starship travels to a planet to colonise. But as time passes and resources dwindle, the promised world has not been found. The 'splicers' rely on genetech to keep the ship going, but for how long will the inhabitants of the ship tolerate their rule...?

"David's dead!"

The illicit words escaped into the sterile air of the culture chamber.

Roz's stomach clenched and she clapped a hand over her mouth, simultaneously squeezing her nostril flaps shut. Her eyes raked the splicing lab, visible through the transparent sheet wall. Had anybody heard?

More crucially, had she expelled any germs along with her words? Most pathogens had been eliminated from the closed environment before the worldship left Earth, but a small number had hitched a ride, and it was their presence that required Roz's specific genetic modification — the nostril flaps of the grey seal — which sealed her breath within her lungs for as long as she worked inside the chamber.

And now one startled exclamation might have brought ruin to the twenty fragile lives under her care. All she could do was hope that luck was on her side. So far it smiled upon her — no one had looked her way, her misdemeanour going unremarked.

If only she could be as fortunate with the microbes.

With trembling hands, she raised the dish of nutrient gel to eye level. The eight shrivelled cells that had once been a viable embryo were too small for her to see with her naked vision, but under the lens she used for stem cell harvesting, the evidence had been painfully clear; there was no coming back from that level of desiccation.

But why? Roz was certain she'd programmed the nutrient stream correctly. It wasn't as if this was the first time she'd prepared a source embryo for harvest; it was an integral part of her working life.

Cycling back through decon with the dish still in her hand seemed to take forever, and before she was through, someone noticed. By the time she stepped back into the lab proper, all the techs had gathered around, shock and sorrow dragging their faces down.

"Is that...?"

She nodded, a tear trickling down her cheek. "Yes, it's David. I've no idea why."

Her supervisor, Splicer Chao-xing, pushed through the crowd, anger pinching the small woman's delicate features. Roz cringed.

"You must have made a mistake," Chao-xing accused. "Did you check the nutrient levels?"

Roz's hands shook even harder, and someone gently removed the dish containing the dead embryo from her grasp before she could drop it. With stiff shoulders, Roz marched over to her workstation and pointed at the readouts.

"See? No mistake."

Chao-xing leaned in close to study the control panel, her jaw tightening when she found nothing to criticise. She moved to the next console where she made a deliberate show of inspecting the levels of the hormone mix being fed into the general water supply. The concoction, which kept the GM population of the worldship sterile, was on a completely separate system and could never have contaminated the embryos' discrete nutrient supply, but she checked it anyway.

"Hmph. There must be an explanation." She glared up at Roz, intimidating despite standing only as tall as Roz's shoulder. "Find it," she ordered, and stormed back to her work, the many slender tendrils she possessed in place of fingers knotting in a visible display of annoyance.

Roz shook her head and wondered, not for the first time, how someone so small could be so menacing.

When Roz had first entered the hallowed world of the gene splicers as a young tech assistant, she'd been wide-eyed with awe, and proud that she'd been designed to be a part of the worldship's elite and not one of its menials. Even better, she was part of the generation — gen 312 — that was destined to oversee the resurrection of the human race, just as soon as the worldship made landfall on the promised planet.

But now, despite a rapid climb in rank to senior lab tech, the highest position available to a non-splicer, that shiny new excitement had tarnished and turned to disillusionment when the predicted arrival date came and went with no sign of a habitable solar system. The journey continued with no end in sight. The pilots had no answer. Unknown variables must have affected the calculation, they said; no way to predict when they would arrive.

So the splicers continued creating GM humans to take the place of the increasing tech failures in apparatus made to last only as long as the planned voyage. Already the original four splicing labs had been forced to amalgamate, with only enough equipment left now to operate one. Without a way for the worldship to garner physical material for replacement parts, it relied increasingly on genetech.

"We'll have to inform all the male D's," a sorrowful voice intoned behind her, bringing Roz back to the immediate situation. David was dead, his line at an end. If the voyage continued it would be several gens before a D designation was used again.

Roz glanced towards the incubator housing her own progenitor, Rachel, as one of the techs stumbled forward.

"I'm a D," he choked out.

"Oh, Daniel, of course you are! We are all so sorry for your loss."

As the techs made plans for a memorial service, Roz turned her attention back to her readouts. Surely the answer *must* be there. Her nimble fingers raced across her control panel, trying everything she could think of, but in the end she could find no answer.

A shadow fell across her workstation and Roz glanced up. Chao-xing stood over her.

"We need to cultivate another embryo; you are authorised to enter Store N5 and withdraw a male DNA sample."

Roz blinked up at the woman; had the splicers no compassion? David was not yet disposed of, and they were ordering a replacement.

Chao-xing scowled.

"Now."

Compassion. What an alien concept to the splicers. They were scientists, creators of whatever GM individual the worldship's maintenance required. They were almost gods, in that respect. No one existed that they had not designed and created, splicing genes from whichever animal or plant species they deemed appropriate into the human DNA that was the raw material of their craft.

They didn't see the embryos as potential people, not as Roz did. Even knowing that those small bundles of cells were at too early a stage in their development to feel awareness or pain, still they were the building blocks of individual human beings. Deep down, Roz harboured the conviction that the endless forced replication of source embryos for harvesting was just plain wrong. Even if the creation of the GM workforce was essential to maintain the worldship, surely there should be a limit to the number of times an embryo could be split: there should be a point at which it was allowed to grow on and develop into the person it was destined to become, before it suffered the same fate as David.

Indignant and angry with Chao-xing's attitude, Roz rose to leave.

Perhaps the time to act had arrived.

Roz sidled in at the back of the crowded meeting hall and slid onto a chair in the hope that nobody would notice her arrival. The wooden seat creaked a protest as she perched on its front edge, and she drew a couple of deep breaths to settle her pounding heart. Accustomed to the sterile atmosphere in the lab, she almost choked on air thick with the smells of so many bodies.

She glanced from side to side to check who else was there and met a pair of beautiful velvet brown eyes, almond-shaped above sculpted cheek bones. Sam's lips curved up, and her stomach flip-flopped. She'd met him at her second meeting, and they'd made an instant connection, though under normal circumstances their paths would never have crossed. As a gardener, Sam's was not a profession normally found in the social circle of a lab tech, but these secretive gatherings defied the usual conventions, and for that, she was glad. Their relationship was blossoming fast, and even as Sam smiled at her, Roz's mind was darting ahead, imagining how his unique, fuzzy-tipped fingers might feel against her bare flesh. The tech side of her brain speculated what genes might have produced the specialised modification that allowed Sam to pollinate plants with just his fingertips.

Just then, Garth, the huge man responsible for instigating the budding revolution, rose to his feet at the front of the hall, towering over everyone else, even those still on their feet.

Roz's face snapped forward, severing the delicious promise in Sam's gaze. The assembly — several hundred, by Roz's reckoning — settled into reverent silence, overawed by the spectacle that was their leader. With the dense double muscling of his bovine GM bulging beneath his skin, Garth looked like he could take on the world and win. *Charolais genes, a mutation that had proven fortuitous for the beef industry*, supplied the tech side of Roz's mind. Sometimes she wished she could switch it off.

She'd seen countless modifications, but few as visually impressive as Garth's. Specially designed for heavy lifting, his super-manly physique had quite swept her off her feet when they'd first met, but things had not gone so well thereafter. She crossed her legs and squeezed her thighs together, recalling their embarrassing attempt at sex.

She'd heard all the jokes about 'size matters', but she didn't think that was quite what they meant.

"Friends," boomed Garth's deep voice. "Fellow slaves to the splicers, are we ready to carve out our own destinies?"

Masses of people lunged to their feet, roaring their support while Roz squirmed in her seat. No one on the worldship was really a slave, but once this group had named themselves so, they'd clasped the identity to their bosoms as a rallying cry for all GMs designed for menial labour.

Apart from the splicers, the lab techs, and the ship's skeleton crew, that meant pretty much all of the worldship's inhabitants. There were no pure humans on board; at least, not in human form. They existed solely as DNA, thousands upon thousands of minute samples, reverently preserved and stored in sealed containers throughout the ship, spread around to minimise the risk of any catastrophe short of the ship's total demise.

The seeds to restart life on a new world.

Roz dragged her wandering thoughts back into the packed meeting room. Garth was holding forth in the confident manner that had so impressed her when they'd first met, although she had her suspicions that such a chance meeting might not have been chance after all, nor Garth's attentions fully genuine. He had a plan, and Roz was his key component.

"We must tear the lab down and smash everything until no splicing can ever be done again. Human beings were not designed to do the tasks they make us for. Look around you, my friends — we are so accustomed to seeing our modifications that they seem normal. But that does not make it right! We come from pure stock, untainted human genomes, warped by the genes spliced into us to create monsters. Should we allow this to continue? I say no. What say you?"

More howls of approval almost drowned the few dissenters, but Garth noticed the doubters and held up a hand for silence. He was fair-minded, Roz couldn't fault him on that score; he was always willing to hear differing viewpoints.

"Rita, you don't agree?"

Roz craned her neck, peering through the crowd for a glimpse of her genetic sibling — another of Rachel's offspring — and was rewarded when Rita stood up. It was eerily akin to looking into a slightly distorted mirror. Rita's skin glowed with the same rich earthy brown complexion as Roz's. The broad brow, the tightly curling black hair, the round face and full lips; all the same. Only the nasal shape was different; no seal flaps for Rita, just a plain, straightforward human nose. Rita's GM was apparent only in the eteliolated slenderness of her physique, suited to fitting through narrow gaps and probably down pipes where no one else would be able to venture.

"What's the point?" Rita asked, her voice a reedy imitation of Roz's own. "Even if we were able to destroy the lab, what then? It's not as if we can change what we are."

Garth's face took on a patient mien. "No, we can't. But we can stop them from ever making others like us."

"But if the splicers don't produce any more children, who will run the ship?"

The question came from deep in the crowd, asking the very question to which Roz had the answer. Losing her inhibitions in her eagerness to reply, she surged to her feet.

"We don't *need* splicers to produce children — we only need to allow our progenitors to develop! For centuries they've provided the genetic material from which we are all formed; isn't it about time they were given the chance to grow on and become adults?"

Rita turned to face her. "I don't see how that will help. They'll only make one more generation, and we don't know how much longer this voyage will take — it's already over schedule, isn't it? Have they found the new world yet?

"You're missing the point," said Roz, getting into her stride. "Pure humans can procreate and produce future gens in the good old-fashioned way described in our archives."

"Really?" Rita sounded sceptical. "We can't. What makes you so certain it'll be different for them?"

Sidestepping the real answer — that the GM population would be able to reproduce just as readily as pure humans, if they didn't consume hormone suppressants every day of their lives — she offered the standard spin.

"Because there's nothing to stop them. They don't have the incompatible chromosomes, ribosomes or enzymes that we do; there's absolutely no reason why they shouldn't have offspring naturally."

Garth beamed his approval. This wasn't the reason Roz was crucial to his plans, but his appreciation of her backing radiated from his smile.

Silence fell in the wake of Roz's speech, and her heart began to thunder as she realised that everyone had turned to look at her. She swallowed, fighting the urge to flee the meeting and regain her anonymity.

Garth never gave her that chance.

"I hope that quells your doubts?" he asked, beckoning for Roz to come and join him on the platform at the front. On legs that suddenly seemed to resemble jelly, she tottered towards him as another voice raised the question she knew

Garth was about to answer with her help.

"But how can we get in there? We've been talking about this for generations, even before the labs amalgamated. Talk is easy, but without access it's all a pointless waste of breath."

"And that," began Garth, taking Roz's small hand in his huge fingers and drawing her up to stand beside him, "is why this lady is here. Allow me to introduce you all to Roz. She's a tech employed in the splicing lab."

For a moment the stunned crowd was silent. In that brief hush, Roz wondered if she'd made a terrible mistake. Perhaps they would satisfy themselves with tearing her to pieces, in lieu of the supposedly impregnable lab.

Next second, a barrage of noise slapped her squarely across the face. Cheers, jeers and questions all vied for dominance. Garth motioned for quiet as Roz sidled closer to his powerful form for protection.

"Why should we trust her?"

Garth heaved a deep sigh, making clear his disappointment. Roz could almost see the words: '*because I say so*' hovering on his lips, but he restrained himself.

"Because she wants change," he said instead. "Because she wants to see the embryos they harvest allowed to grow into the human beings they were destined to be. And because she wants the infants and children in the crèche right now to be the last monsters produced by the splicers."

"Chimeras, not monsters," muttered Roz, but the swell of approbation from the crowd drowned her out. Garth held up a hand again, and quiet descended. Heart pounding against her ribs, Roz forced herself to step forward.

"It's as Garth says. I'm sick of the splicer's callousness; I don't believe the architects of this mission ever meant for the embryos to be harvested for as long as they are now, and it's killing them. David died today and—"

Once more, Roz's voice was drowned out. She could feel the shockwaves of her announcement rebounding around the room, punctuated by wailing from those she guessed to be

David's offspring. Even Garth struggled to regain order in the wake of such news, and the mood of the gathering shifted perceptibly from discussion to militancy.

In that instant, Roz realised there was no going back; she'd made her choice when she'd decided to attend the meeting, and her words had sealed the pact. She was about to betray the splicers, the very people she'd been designed to assist and raised to work alongside. And all for the sake of a few tiny cells of living matter.

People, she reiterated inside her head. *Those microscopic cells have the potential to become real people — in fact, more real than we are.*

"When can we do it?"

Garth's face swam across her vision, and Roz realised she was crying, welling up with conflicting emotions. Relief, joy and terror all rolled together. She scrubbed a hand across her face, feeling the contours of her nasal flaps as she wiped away her tears.

She was doing the right thing, she was sure of it.

Burying any lingering concerns, she raised a fist and miraculously the room fell quite.

"Tomorrow," she declared. "Tomorrow we will destroy the last remaining splicing equipment and allow the embryos—"

The roar of approval cut off her final words, but Roz understood that her fellow revolutionaries were simply too excited to let her finish.

She turned to Garth, catching his sleeve as he moved away from her.

"Nobody's going to get hurt, right? And you will make sure the embryos are safe, won't you? Their environment is so fragile."

Tugging his sleeve from her grasp and turning away, Garth waved at a couple of his lieutenants and pointed at certain people in the crowd.

"Yes, yes. Of course," he threw over his shoulder as he stepped down from the platform. "We'll talk details later."

Left alone on the raised dais, Roz surveyed the heaving mob of menials as Garth waded through them, gathering his task force.

They're not details, she grumbled to herself, *they're* people.

Or they would be, after tomorrow. No matter how difficult things might become without a modified workforce, Roz was certain that they would find a way to cope. Human beings were resourceful. Hopefully more resourceful than their chimera offspring.

This is the right thing to do, she repeated inside her head, *it* is *the right thing to do*.

With absolute conviction that the word *traitor* was inked across her face for all to see, Roz kept her head down as she entered the lab and scuttled across to her workstation. She sucked air into her lungs as if she'd done a serious workout, and her hands shook so badly she struggled to work her console's delicate controls. Her mind flitted stubbornly from topic to topic, refusing to focus. She had no idea what she might say if Chao-xing showed up to find out why she hadn't yet begun cultivating a new DNA sample.

As her respiration started to settle and the world beyond her guilty feelings re-emerged, she became aware of a conversation behind her. Ice trickled down her spine as she identified the voices of two splicers.

"Did we make a mistake with gen 312, allocating them those extra few IQ points?"

"Maybe we did, but we were following the colonisation plan; how were we supposed to know they got the calculations wrong? It's not our fault."

"Well I, for one, am worried; I've heard rumours of secret meetings and a plot to take over the ship. Before now I'd have laughed it off, but this gen has the brains to do it."

Sweat trickled down Roz's back, and when a hand alighted on her shoulder, she almost leaped out of her chair.

"In a world of your own were you, Roz? Daydreams

make for mistakes, and we don't want any more of those, do we? Anyway, just a quick question: I believe you have friends amongst the menials — have you heard any rumours?"

Roz's insides clenched in panic, and she forced her face to blankness before looking up.

"Rumours?" She shook her head, running her fingers through her hair to disguise the tremors that ran down her arms. "Can't say I've heard anything of the sort. But then, when I'm with Sam, I'm kinda busy, if you know what I mean."

The younger of the two splicers nearly choked on his laughter, while his older companion's expression wavered between fascination and disgust, his tentacle digits writhing in indecision. Stuff of nightmares, those tentacles. Or the exact opposite, perhaps, depending on what, precisely, he did with his suckers behind closed doors. Roz had always wondered. A bit like she wondered how Sam's fingers would feel against her skin. Despite what she wanted her colleagues to believe, that was something she still hadn't had the pleasure of exploring.

"Time we were at work," said the tentacled splicer, and stomped away with stiff shoulders, trailed by his younger colleague, still shaking with mirth. The fact that a dalliance between a lab tech and a menial could be the cause of so much hilarity settled the knot of anxiety in Roz's stomach into a hard lump of righteousness; why was it so inconceivable that love might be found between folk outside of their normal social circles? It wasn't as if the worldship had a class system. Not really. Or if it did, it was the fault of the splicers, looking down on those they created as lesser individuals and as a result, somehow less human.

The splicers were chimeras too; they just liked to think they were superior.

Roz checked the time and, following a quick glance around her corner of the lab to ensure no one was watching, rose and hurried to the sealed outer door. She pressed her finger to the keypad and the door slid open. She stepped halfway through, standing firmly in place when the door tried to slide shut again. The corridor outside looked empty and for a heart-stopping moment she thought that Garth and his followers had changed their minds, and she would be found holding the door open without a plausible excuse.

Then her ears filled with the rustling sound of footsteps, and she pushed back, forcing the door wider as Garth approached at the head of a seething horde of wild-eyed menials. Adrenalin spikes shot through Roz's body: this was really happening!

She plucked at Garth's sleeve as he drew level.

"Remember what I told you: don't break the sterile seal on the culture chamber — it's back in the right hand corner of the lab and it's fragile..."

"I told them," said Garth, and moved on to join the conspirators. The trickle of bodies through the open door turned rapidly into a flood, and moved in a fraction of a second from silent to roaring anger, almost drowning out the cries of the lab techs and splicers, and the sound of smashing equipment.

Alarmed, Roz dashed back inside.

"Be careful!" she screeched, unheeded. "The embryos! Don't hurt them!"

But she was too late. In no time at all, the lab was trashed beyond repair, microscopes and lasers smashed underfoot, and the flimsy plastic sheets that formed the culture chamber hung in shreds from the ceiling, incubators overturned and tiny gobs of nutrient gel plastered across the floor with their precious cargos exposed to contaminated air. Roz dashed over and fell to her knees amidst the devastation, tears rolling down her cheeks to splash onto the fading remnants of the progenitor embryos.

Rachel, John, Chow, Tanu, Aziza, and all the others.

Gone.

And *she* was responsible.

A huge hand grasped her shoulder, pulling her up to her

feet. Garth's jubilant face swam past her blurred vision.

"We did it! We did it! We're free of them at last!" He shook Roz roughly, and whirled her in a jubilant circle. "We couldn't have done it without you!"

Bile shot up Roz's throat and she pulled away from Garth with a strength she did not know she possessed. She staggered a few steps and dropped to her knees, retching. He was right; they couldn't have done it without her. She was responsible for all this wanton destruction; for the deaths of the embryos.

A hand clasped her shoulder, pulling. Through her misery and shock she realised that it could not be Garth; the strength of the grip was far too weak, and when she turned her head she saw delicate fronds atop her uniform, undulating as though rippling in the gentle current of a calm sea.

When she glanced up, the eyes she met were anything but calm. Chao-xing's dainty features twisted with fury and despair. Blood ran from a cut on her forehead, dripping into the corner of one eye as she pinned Roz with her black gaze.

"Do you know what you've done? You've committed genocide. *You.* One of our trusted elite, yet you let those *animals* in here. They've destroyed *everything!* There's no way left to replicate workers. No workers, no way to keep the ship functional. I hope you're happy with yourself? Pity you didn't think through the consequences first."

And she staggered away, cowering as some of the menials spotted her and began jeering.

Dry gasps wracked Roz's already shuddering frame. She didn't think her shaking legs would hold her upright, but she *had* to move; she couldn't bear sitting in the wreckage of her life any longer. She stumbled to her feet and tottered to the place she knew best; her workstation, miraculously unscathed as yet, while the revolutionaries continued to wreak havoc inside the main lab. From habit, she scanned the now useless readouts, noting how the nutrient feeds were running at full capacity, emptying out into thin air, their delicate entrails torn until they bled out, like the blood vessels they were modelled upon.

The one piece of equipment left intact was the hormone feed, obliviously pumping its programmed concoction into the worldship's water supply, maintaining the illusion that the GM population was unable to reproduce.

But what if they could?

Chao-xing's words rang in her ears: '*No workers, no way to keep the ship functional.*'

But what if there was another way to produce workers? Okay, the outcome would be markedly more random, with no way of knowing how the spliced genes might be passed on, or how they would affect future generations. But that would make life more like it had been, back on old Earth, before genetech became such a feature of reproduction. It was worth the risk, wasn't it? They might still reach their destination, and with the fresh materials a new planet would provide, they could fabricate a new culture lab and use the stored DNA to rebuild a pure human race.

But not the splicing lab. That must never be rebuilt.

Roz reached out and shut off the hormone feed.

Ten Thousand Moons of Howling

Gareth Caradoc Owens

A cold war punk, Gareth Caradoc Owens writes fantasy influenced by moody Celtic backgrounds, rain soaked forests and unpredictable demi-mortals contrasted against a background of warring ancient gods. He has a honours degree from the University of London in Ancient Near Eastern Languages. His hard SF has been published in Nature, *as well as* Nature Physics. *Immersion Press launched their line with a collection of his short stories,* Fun With Rainbows. *He has twice been nominated for a British Science Fiction Association award and is currently a member of the Science Fiction Writers of America.*

In the story that follows, the Warchief Olambur stands with his army and priests at the border of the mortal world and the land of the dead, Nuji Giya. To repel the rising dead, Olambur is commanded to give up the Lord of Wits, Din Yirgish. Alliances are forged and battles fought, but in a war between gods and mortals there are bound to be casualties...

Olambur of Kess stood at the edge of the world looking into the invading realm of death. Behind him fruit laden Kiri trees and boundless fields of golden Shea grass, criss-crossed by silver veins of canals, stretched ordered and disciplined all the way back to the city called "The Gods' Gateway".

Warchief of Karadunia, Olambur stood with all that mortal proof of devotion to the Fifteen gods behind him, and at his feet, the realm of ripening and living green ended as if slashed across with an obsidian dagger.

A blanket of unnatural ash covered everything before him, seeping, dark, like old blood oozing from the netherworld. A choking blight across the living land. A tide of eerie substance consuming all it touched.

Olambur signalled to the old priest next to him, waving him to walk into the sulphur stinking ash field as if calling forward a unit of soldiers. The priest bowed, and head still low he began to shuffle towards the border between the two worlds. Prayer bells in his hand, burning incense tied into his hair, the wizened figure began to sing the ancient magics of lost Kinyir.

"At the command of the dragon spirit, living son of the eternal sun, the dead may not harm the living. The dust of Nuji Giya, land of no returning, may not blow under the Cover of the Four Corners."

Still chanting, the priest made three steps into the billowing dust, leaving footprints of flame, before the cinders rose up around him. Ash, brown like yesterday's clinker and studded with livid ruby embers, swirled in a whirlwind. Twisting, the wilful dust-devil grew, raging and becoming solid until towering over the man it pounced, layering itself around and clinging to his skin as if with hooks. It encased him, making him into a living statue.

Once he'd been cocooned like a spider's meal, the ash twister fell away. Silence, a dread-filled silence for a few heartbeats, even Olambur held his breath.

Fire exploded from the ash-man like bellows put to the forge. The imprisoned priest screamed, sudden and urgent, with a new understanding of the reality of agony, powerless to move, his soul consumed in unwilling sacrifice.

Olambur's hand tightened on the haft of his mace, but he stood as impassive as he could. The gods were always powerful enemies.

Controlled by the will of the spirit feeding from the flames, the man-filled dust furnace turned. Screaming, it faced warchief Olambur, his army and entourage of holy men.

Through the scream came words.

"Olambur, King of Strangers, render unto the dead that

which is their due. You harbour the running man, fugitive from death itself." The spirit's words, powered by shrieks as fire consumed the struggling priest, blasting his body and soul.

"Before Silver-Thirty closes his eye again, the Lord of Wits must cross the gateway of Burning Crown, or the dead will hold this land for ten thousand moons. So speaks the Bonded of the First Dragon."

The voice of the spirit ceased, but the screams of the priest did not.

In the distance, above the middle of the spreading cancer of ash, a ball of darkness formed, clouds of purple shrouding. Lightning made from the opposite of light, not mere darkness, not the mere absence of light, but the deepest concentration of light's ethereal counterbalance, sundered the day. Flowing like water from a cliff, the dark energy cascaded over the dead ash filling the world with night.

Where the black lightning struck began to rumble as if the Bull in the Earth had awoken and charged at the very pillars holding up the heavens. Olambur staggered as the world shook. The horses of the army stamped and whinnied, wild eyed they looked around, on the verge of bolting.

"Hold," Olambur commanded, taking back the step he'd lost. The soldiers held. Even the horses seemed to calm for a moment.

Then, surging up came a mountainous wave of ash. Nuji Giya pushed outwards as something old arose from the land of the dead. A lance in the side of the living Earth, the fabric of the four-corners pierced by the unwelcome nation.

Surging outwards, a great hissing wave of clinker, cinder, and choking dust came on. The horses on his right broke, rearing in their traces. They tried to get away, twisting and overturning their chariots, spilling driver and soldiers. The wave melted into the sea of ash already covering the land, and Olambur saw the rising of the lost city, the city stolen by the dead.

The tip of the highest temple, Burning Crown, broke

through into daylight and the walls thrust up from the underworld. Ramparts built by men but taken against an unpaid debt, arose from the invading soil of Nuji Giya.

For the first time in ten thousand moons the city of Uracha Deki broke the surface of mortal reality. Walls, once white and tall as distant mountains, now glowering embers of baked brown, dull as Greek coin, growing from the ground like teeth pushed from a bone. Defensive walls, older than memory and crewed by the blue glowing spectres of the inhabitants of the damned city.

The buildings seemed to shimmer for a moment before solidifying. Everything in Olambur called for the charge, to wave his army on towards the ramparts of the enemy, but no mortal foot could step across the ash, he had seen that for himself. He took a breath and let it out as a warcry of raw frustration. The army echoed it, greeting the returning city with their living fury. The cry died down, replaced by the regular beat of the soldiers chanting themselves into the world of battle.

The tall banded gate of Burning Crown shook off the store of dust on the hinges and swung open to let something out. The army grew quiet with the stillness of dread.

From the gateway a single figure swaggered. The grey shadow of something not a man, yet somehow manlike. A rolling gait like a fisherman familiar with the pitch of the deck beneath his feet.

The shade wore a cloak made from raven feathers and a large bag across its back, and with that swaggering rolling walk, it came forward across the ash until it stood grinning before the Warchief.

“Speak fiend. What do you want amongst the living?” Olambur’s voice as steady as anyone that ever addressed such an apparition.

Eyes, brown from edge to edge, set in grey blue skin looked up, and Olambur caught the flash of fury in them.

“Fiend is it?” The words were plain in Olambur’s ears but

the mouth of the creature made no show of talking. "I am Lord Good Earth. Your kind gave me name. I should have lived and died with the souls of my own people."

As he spoke, Lord Good Earth reached around and from the great bag strapped across his back he produced a skull. The dome of bleached white bone perfect and clean. The creature looked into the darkened holes where eyes had once been.

"I was an explorer, I followed the herds. I roamed alone with none but the beasts for company, until I came to the lands of your people."

Lord Good Earth leaned forward suddenly and placed the skull down into the ash, pushing and twisting so that only the top remained above the powdery surface. With one fluid movement he reached another from the bag, taking two steps before pushing that into the corrupted soil.

"The sons of a city blighted by a king too powerful, too mighty to be overthrown, found me." Another skull went into the ash. "They introduced me to the flesh of woman, they gave me beer and bread, then they shaved me, all for a joke."

Olambur watched without action. The spectre moved along the claimed territory of Nuji Giya as if behind a wall. The burning ash that consumed the priest now collapsed into nothing more than a shapeless mound, but the memory of his screams still fresh in Olambur's ears.

"And now I and the army of the risen dead demand restitution."

Olambur heard the shade speak, but the words blurred, he felt his fingers tighten on the haft of his mace. If the creature would just come within arm's reach, if he could just get the first swing in, the mortals might stand a chance.

"I know what you think Olambur, but you cannot kill the dead."

Olambur started at the sound of his name.

"I may not be able to kill you beast, but I will send you back whence you came." The army in earshot cheered at his words and the army further away cheered at the sound of their cheering.

Lord Good Earth sighed, barely perceptibly, Olambur saw it as only a pause before the creature continued to plant his line of skulls.

"Give us the Running Man, hand over Din Yirgish and we will leave these lands. None may be allowed to avoid death, not even the greatest of kings."

"How comes it," Olambur felt the question and it came straight to his mouth, "that death can call for a living man? Are not all our destinies written? What are you doing here?"

The shade of Lord Good Earth smiled, yet he did not pause as he planted another line of skulls behind the first.

"Your screaming priest was right, the dead may not harm the living, but when the living offend against the dead, once in ten thousand moons the Land of No Returning may raise an army and take what is owed to it." Another skull went into the ash. "Once before the soldiers of the dead rose up, and these walls," he indicated the city behind him with a jerk of his head. "And all the souls within, became indentured against the heart of their living king." Another skull. "Yet I still wait for Din Yirgish to arrive. I cannot leave this place, stuffed with the souls of man, and go to join the souls of my own kind. Not until that miserable Kullabite crosses the border of Nuji Giya".

Olambur shivered, as if aroused from daydream or woken from a holy trance. The shade of Lord Good Earth had planted a field of skulls that stretched all the way back to the walls of the risen city. While he talked he'd laid hundreds, perhaps thousands of the bleached bones into the otherworldly ash.

"Olambur." Lord Good Earth whispered in his ear like a mother waking a reluctant child. "Bring Din Yirgish here to Burning Crown."

The air shimmered and Olambur stood in a different place. He tried to understand the sudden change.

Without getting there, he stood at the top level of the

temple called “Look Up!” Below him, under the golden sun, spread the city of Kardunias, burnt dark and glazed in brilliant blue and yellow.

Vibrant and loud, the shouts of the markets, the zamzam music of the priests set to the pulsing beat of the tigi drums, the smells of roasting meat from the street sellers and the perfumes from the temple behind him. Olambur shut his eyes briefly.

“To be alive is to be assaulted by our five wits. I won’t give up the light.”

His mace already drawn and ready to strike, Olambur whirled around. For less than a heartbeat he saw a massive hand that covered and gripped his face, lifting him from his feet, his mace removed from his grasp as easily as a rattle taken from a fractious child.

“I take it you’re the current king of this place.”

The hand that held his face let go and pushed him back a couple of steps.

“You come and go so quick it’s hard to keep count.” The deep voice continued without any sign of exertion. “You don’t dress like the locals. Kardin Yira been invaded again?”

Olambur took another step trying to find fighting distance, but it was hard to get the measure of the man who now held his mace. The stranger hefted the weight of the enormous piece of greenstone as if it were a mere pebble.

“I’m Din Yirgish.”

The Bigman held out the mace, handle first, returning it to Olambur.

“The dead have risen in the fields,” his words stilted and oddly accented. “What they seek I cannot allow them to have.”

Olambur took the proffered mace with a petulant swipe.

“I have become aware of this,” he said returning his mace to his belt.

“My priests say that you were once a great king, the Lord of Wits. They still sing of your deeds, and always will, but this is a war between gods, can’t you take it somewhere else.

Don't mortals have enough weight to carry already?"

Din Yirgish looked down.

"The court of the gods has decreed the whole of my fate based on one third of my nature. I am neither mortal nor god, but I will not submit to their authority."

Olambur looked at the king who should be dead. Din Yirgish raised his eyes and Olambur met the gaze which had seen more years than any man had a right to. A fire burned, a rage, a furnace, lightning in the gale, and Olambur felt his hackles rise.

"I expect Lord Good Earth has given you his 'The dead shall hold this land for ten thousand moons' speech?"

Olambur nodded.

"Before Silver-Thirty crosses the sky. All of that is true, but what he never says is that if the Executed God is struck down by mortal hand then the city of the dead shall sink back into the sands of Nuji Giya."

Olambur screwed his face up.

"Executed god? What executed god. I'm a stranger, new to these gods and lands, but who executed a god?

"The other gods. There was a war and the First Dragon lost, killed in the fighting, but her husband was brought before the other gods and executed as proof of their power."

"So," Olambur spoke slowly. "This executed god became a god in the underworld?"

Din Yirgish shook his head, his face disappearing briefly behind a curtain of unbound hair.

"No one had ever seen the soul of a god before. He can find no place in the afterlife. That is why he chases me. He is neither one thing nor another, neither god nor shade, and me, I'm neither man nor immortal. He thinks that I am his balance, or the cause of the imbalance."

Olambur sat down on the edge of the temple steps.

"We endure wars, we suffer famines, pox, pestilence and plague, isn't that enough? Priests take our harvests, they tell us we were created to serve the gods, isn't that enough? We build mountains in our cities because the gods need to feel at home, we take the timbers of the barbarians because they need the scent of cedars, is all this not enough? Now we have to fight the dead because of some long forgotten war in heaven?"

"Why are you here, Olambur?" the question sudden as a jabbed fist.

"I must bring you to Flaming Crown to save the land of Karadunia."

"Yet you talk to me, you hear my words, you see my reason. I am the Lord of Wits. I will fight beside you Olambur, I will face my old friend Lord Good Earth, but you must meet Qin Gu the Executed God. Only a true man, born of woman can strike the blow that sends him back to Nuji Giya."

"Why don't I just kill you instead? Then I can drag your lifeless, overdue, corpse out to the monkey king and be done with it?" Olambur had a part of his soul with a direct connection to his mouth. Din Yirgish pouted.

"Well, you could have a go if you think you're hard enough, but what part of two-thirds god are you failing to comprehend. I could shove you under one arm and crush the life out of you, but then the dead will be free to roam these lands.

"Alright, if I can't beat you, merely the mortal offspring of fundamental forces shaping the heavens, how can I beat a proper god?"

"Qin Gu is only a dead god, mortal. Even the lowest living thing possesses a spark that he can never regain. No mortal made blade or spear can harm him nor the warriors in the army you are about to face, but I have touched the stone you carry, and it now carries an imprint of the power of the Fifteen. None of Nuji Giya can withstand its touch. As long as you keep swinging all will fall before you, Even Qin Gu himself."

Olambur drew his mace and looked at the carved greenstone ball. He had taken it from a great hall in the Sea Lands. The cedar haft came from the shores of the upper sea.

Edge to edge of his empire held in one hand. He could feel it squirm in his grip. It seemed to almost move as if it struggled to be free. The head of the mace, carved with foreign scenes and symbols of alien meaning, now glowed with a light blue effervescence he could only see when he looked away.

It buzzed in his hand calling for battle.

"You carry the imprint of the Fifteen Gods, under the protection of its power you can stride the ashes of Nuji Giya, you can destroy the warriors of the Land of No Returning, and you can smite the soul of a dead god. I will fight by your side. Your legend will be great, and your deeds will be sung as long as there are voices to sing them."

Olambur could feel a glow in his lungs. All the colour of vibrant life, raw and hungry. Calling for the passionate kill.

"I am ready."

"No, Olambur. We are ready."

Din Yirgish drew his axe made from star metal and slashed at the air. A purple rift opened before them as if a curtain had been slit with a knife. Beyond the glowing edges of the hole in the air Olambur could see the walls of Uracha Deki. The doorway jumped forwards and snatched them both, then in an instant disappeared.

Olambur looked around to see his generals and priests. But all stood still, really wrong still. The whole army seemed frozen. None made a move or reacted to his return.

The skulls Lord Good Earth had planted had grown from the ground and stood now as almost complete skeletons, like maggots struggling from split flesh. Olambur turned to Din Yirgish and caught a flash of faint blue. A smear of soul stretched from each man in his army to a corresponding skeleton.

"Soul frames." Din Yirgish answered the question Olambur had been unable to ask.

"It looks like the bones of a man, but the vines grow down into Nuji Giya and form a frame from the fabric of the netherworld. The souls of the dead wrap around them, it allows them to walk the living world, to touch and to move and to fight. But today they act like flytraps; they suck in the souls of the soldiers you brought to fight at your side. If we do not hurry we will have to cut our way through your own army to get to the city."

Din Yirgish took two strides into the ash and lopped off the head of the nearest skeleton. The stain of blue that Olambur could see, snapped back away from the fallen soul frame and one of the statue-still soldiers collapsed unconscious onto the ground, released from the dread attraction. Din Yirgish took another step and another skull flew.

Olambur looked at the ash, the collapsed mound of the incinerated priest still visible, then with a roar he ran at the nearest skeleton. The green stone came down through the curve of the skull. Two more steps and the mace came up smashing through the ribs of the next frame. Olambur looked down briefly and saw that he now stood up to his knees in ash. No time to fear it, he swung again and another trap released the soul of its victim. With each swing he and Din Yirgish smashed their way closer to the walls of Uracha Deki.

An arrow whistled through the air straight towards Olambur's face. He saw it come, but had no time to move. One of the soul frames near the wall had shaken itself free from the ash and stood with bone bow strung with sinew. The axe head of star metal flashed in front of Olambur's eyes and Din Yirgish cut the arrow from the air. Olambur glanced across at the Bigman, and a flash of movement caught the corner of his eye. A sword of bone, sliver sharp, long and wicked, cleaved the air where Olambur would have been. His left arm flashed around encircling the blade and grasping the cold wrist of the soul frame warrior he brought the mace down on the grinning death mask of a face.

The two mortal warriors moved through the wakening army, and every time they brought a soldier down, releasing his captured spirit, another rose behind to take its place. The ash became strewn with the broken bones of stolen souls.

Olambur experienced the rush as being in a crowd. The soul frames now moved, the blue stain enrobing them. As he lifted the greenstone to smash another skull Olambur saw that the blue mist took the form of the ghosts of his army wrapping the bones of the otherworld. With every swing his mace came down through the face of a friend or brother, shattering the netherbone beneath.

Olambur and Din Yirgish fought with cold fury. Each step forward taken from the army of the undead.

"Idu Weh!" Din Yirgish shouted up at the walls of the city. "Idu Weh! Open the gate, I wish to enter." At the crenulations a new face appeared, different to the ghosts that stood before them.

"Luwatu, open the gate." The figure disappeared.

Olambur turned his full attention to the fight. He felt a guilty start of intense pleasure as he brought the mace down through the face of his cook. Step by step the two kings fought on.

As one the ghost wrapped skeletons stopped, lowering their weapons and stepping away. The huge and ancient wood of the city gate swung open to reveal the main square, Lord Good Earth silhouetted, a shade against the shadow. He walked forwards and Din Yirgish stood waiting for him.

"Olambur, this is my fight. Go on, find Qin Gu."

"So Brother," Lord Good Earth ignored Olambur. "You have finally come. Sixteen hundred years I've waited for this moment. Sixteen hundred curse filled, dark and dusty years waiting for you. Today it ends, embrace me brother and set me free."

Olambur took one last look at the two as they began to circle each other, then he sprinted for the gate.

He ran across the threshold and up through the rotting wrecks of the market and began to climb the wide stairway to the temple. A line of the soul frames stood like soldiers to attention. They marked the way to the Flaming Crown. The dust of the darkness covered every surface. It flowed down the great staircase like a river. Olambur slowed as the skeletons made no move to hinder him. He loosened his shoulders and limbered his swinging arm, taking the opportunity to get his breath back.

The stairs wound in a curve up to the Kiyutu gate before the courtyard. Olambur entered like a wrestler expecting his opponent. To his right the broken bricks and burnt statues where all that was left of the Peak-House, the heart of the temple of the Flaming Crown.

Faces and arms of broken gods jutted from the rubble and wreckage, leaning at strange angles and pointing meaninglessly. The socket of the sacred pool before them empty like the eyes of the dead.

"So you have finally come, Din Yirgish." The voice disembodied like the screams of the ash covered priest. Olambur tightened his grasp on the mace. The ash in front of him began to move like the sea. Waves formed and began to break on the steps of the temple, and from the broken columns a figure began to coalesce.

Tall, and shaven like a civilised man, he wore a kilt made from lambs tails. Olambur saw the face grow from the clay, strong and handsome. Eyes sharp and sparkling like lapis lazuli and obsidian. The executed god materialised before Olambur's eyes. Growing more massive in stature with every passing heartbeat, Qin Gu stood, alive and full of the raw power of godhood.

Olambur felt a strange weakness, he looked briefly at his fingers and saw his hands tremble. Was this fear? Was this what it was like to be afraid?

Qin Gu took one step forward. He had become perfect, but still he carried on forming. A jagged wound appeared across his throat, and the god fell. The colour and vitality shining from the figure as it made itself, faded into the grey of wood ash.

With visible effort the god figure raised himself so that he stood on one knee. One hand went to his throat the other reached around and drew his thin metal staff from his back. He used the weapon to support himself as he stood once again.

Olambur had glimpsed the lost reality of the god briefly, but what stood before him now was the mere shade, the remnant of that living glory.

"Din Yirgish. Our life is mapped as star points of event and memory. The star of my brothers and children forcing my head down low to slit my throat like a praying animal, burns bright as Lady Pure Bird across the dawn sky." The god ghost held his staff before him, ready for battle. "But I have guided my course in these trackless underworlds by keeping my wits turned to the star of this meeting. I will end your stolen life and the balance between the worlds of living and dead will return to peace and darkness."

Olambur stood very still, the muscles across his shoulders tensed and balanced against the almost cramp in his calves. Cat with a mouse, waiting. Qin Gu looked in slightly the wrong direction when he spoke, almost as if he couldn't see Olambur properly.

"Why don't you speak, Din Yirgish?" Qin Gu swung a wide arc with his staff.

Olambur bent down and picked up a mosaic cone from the dust. With a flick he cast it across the courtyard. The living statue of the fallen god snapped across the space faster than any arrow Olambur had ever seen. Qin Gu's staff, sharp as a whip, broad as a tree trunk, smashed into the ground where the cone landed, making the city tremble beneath his feet.

"I know you're here Din Yirgish, I can sense the energy of the Fifteen on you. The essence of the living gods, plump with prayer and scented with offerings."

Olambur ran across the courtyard, years of stealth keeping his footfalls quiet as any assassin. One of the fallen columns of the temple lay at an angle and he slowed to keep his climb silent.

"Why don't you speak, Din Yirgish. Your fame is as Lord

of Wits."

Olambur reached a point on the column where he stood roughly the height of a man above the head of his opponent. He grabbed a pebble from the dusty surface and dropped it into the ash below. Qin Gu flashed across, and the great staff came down again like thunder from the mountains.

Olambur dropped from the column and as he did so he spoke.

"I am Olambur of Kess, demon, and you are unwelcome here."

The god ghost looked up at the words and his face met the downswing of the greenstone mace. Olambur's blow landed exactly on the line where chin meets throat. Qin Gu's head snapped back and the giant toppled like a stunned bull.

Olambur rolled to one side and stood up. The dead god lay still. Olambur saw the same blue glow that had wreathed the end of his mace now played around the head of the fallen giant.

The ground convulsed beneath Olambur's feet. The city trembled and dust came cascading down from the roofs of the temples. The whole world moved like the deck of a ship. Olambur took his mace and started back down the stairway to the gate of the city. He had won, he had bested a god.

The skeletons collapsed as he went past, the soul frames releasing each spirit back to the underworld. He crossed through the market between the rotten stalls, and stood before the archway of the city. The black wood of the gate solidly shut. No way out that way.

He turned to look for another exit and found Luwatu standing behind him and beyond the gatekeeper, on the stairs back up to the temple, Qin Gu sat, nursing the place where Olambur had struck him.

"Tell him, Luwatu," the dead god's voice soft, almost kind.

Luwatu, a little old man with a squint and one tooth, looked up and smiled.

"No man who crosses the threshold of Uracha Deki may leave. This is the Dark House."

"But I'm not dead."

Luwatu nodded.

"Would have been better for you had you been, my lord. This place is built for the comfort of the spirits. They find no rest in the mortal world, but the living find nothing but darkness and dust here."

"But I won. I beat you, I defeated the dead god. The city returns to Nuji Giya."

Again Luwatu smiled and nodded.

"All true my lord, and you with it."

Qin Gu stood, his gaze clear.

"Lord of Wits has consigned you to the darkness, mortal. He has once more evaded the justice of the Fifteen, and thanks to you, we've lost his soul brother Lord Good Earth. He is finally released to join the souls of his own kind."

The last of the daylight of the mortal realm faded in the sky as the city travelled back to Nuji Giya. Olambur felt it begin in his belly. Outrage and betrayal, burning upwards. Incandescent injustice, and as the darkness of the netherworld closed above, a moan started. It flowed, straight from his soul. Until it overflowed his mortal limits, building with rage, intolerable, uncontrollable rage. He howled and howled and howled his way into those ten thousand moons of darkness.

The Disappeared

Sarah Singleton

Sarah Singleton is the author of The Crow Maiden *(Wildside Press) and numerous short stories in venues including* Black Static, Interzone, Spectrum SF *and* Time Pieces. *For young adults, she has written eight novels, including the 2005 Booktrust Teen Award winner* Century, *as well as* The Poison Garden *and* The Amethyst Child, *all published by Simon & Schuster UK. She has worked as a journalist and is now an English teacher. She lives in beautiful Wiltshire, county of white horses and standing stones.*

In Sarah's story "The Disappeared", Britain is preparing for war, and paranoia is all around. An invitation to the Blue Cat café might well be an enticing proposition, but a reporter should be careful where his curiosity might lead...

He was sitting at a desk, staring at a half-written obit. Across the room three men, shirt sleeves rolled up, ties slovenly, pounded on heavy typewriters. Alex lit a cigarette, and switched on the lamp at his desk. Outside the sky was overcast, darkness gathering. A raw wind carried fitful showers of rain. Beyond the window, a jaded poster fluttered on a hoarding, advertising the efficacy of Simpson's Beef Granules. He sucked on the cigarette, filling his lungs. The working day was near its end now. He was tired, and for a moment, staring at the page in his typewriter, Alex could not remember when he had started writing, or the name of the man whose life he was recording. It was sad, wasn't it, these obits. How sometimes you were hard put to stretch out a life to half a dozen paragraphs. He flicked ash into the overflowing ashtray, and glanced at his colleagues, likewise lighting up, or stretching, pushing papers about on their desks in the end of day lull. They were much older than him, these men, jaundiced from years of drink and cigarettes.

The huge black telephone rang, jangling his nerves. Alex picked up the receiver.

"Hello? May I speak to Mr Flint please?" A girl's voice.

"Speaking," he said.

"Mr Flint, I don't know if you remember me. Camilla Austen?" She sounded young, and slightly nervous.

"We met once," the girl persisted. "At James's house."

"James Waugh? You know James? Of course I remember you," he lied, trawling through his memories. "Miss Austen, how may I help?"

"I think we should meet, Mr Flint. We need to talk."

Alex grinned. He couldn't help himself. There were always girls. And this was a come-on wasn't it?

"Yes," he said. "Are you staying at a hotel? Shall I meet you there?"

"No. Oh no," she said emphatically. "Do you know the Blue Cat café? On Silver Street, down by the river. It's not far from your office. Meet me there tonight at eight o'clock."

When he put the phone down the other reporters were staring at him.

"Another woman?" said one, laconic. "Lucky beggar."

Just before eight, Alex was sitting outside the café, beneath the canopy, smoking another cigarette. He huddled in his overcoat, against the cold. He liked to arrive first, to feel at an advantage. The street was quiet. A singular motor car passed, like a ghost. He thought about James Waugh. They had been the best of friends at university, both working class scholarship boys made good. James was a gifted physicist, Alex a determined student of English literature. Afterwards James had got a job in a prestigious London research laboratory, while Alex slogged it as cub reporter on his dour provincial newspaper. Work had swallowed them up. They hadn't seen each other for months. Not since the party in the summer at James's house in Vauxhall, near the river — the party where, presumably, he had met Camilla Austen.

He stubbed out the cigarette. The streetlamp illuminated a thin veil of rain. A girl appeared from the shadows, hard to make out at first, just the smudge of a white face, a dark coat and a hat pressed over her brow.

"Mr Flint," she said, holding out a gloved hand. "Shall we go inside?"

"Alex," he said. "Please, call me Alex."

The café was dim, and warm. Alex sat at a table by the window and took off his hat and coat. The girl squeezed into a seat the other side. He glanced at the other patrons, a dozen or so scattered in ones and twos at the other tables, but their faces were shadowed or turned away. Alex ordered coffee from the mute waiter. Camilla unpeeled black silk gloves from her hands. Her red hair was pinned up. Fox fur billowed on the collar of her jacket.

"So, how may I help you, Camilla?" He offered her a cigarette, which she accepted, studying him all the while. Then she took out a dingy manila file from a bag and laid it on the table.

"How's James?" Alex asked. "Haven't spoken to him for ages."

Camilla looked down at the table and pressed her lips together. She took a tense breath, and said: "James has disappeared."

Alex's habitual confidence faltered momentarily. He was nonplussed.

"Disappeared? What do you mean? When? What happened?" His mind ran ahead of his mouth, throwing up images of kidnap, torture, windowless cells and expedient murder. A war was on its way and the martial infrastructure was building up. Factories churned out weapons and an atmosphere of suspicion and paranoia pervaded.

Camilla wrinkled her brow, perhaps not knowing where to begin. She kept her left hand pressed on the manila file.

"How much do you know about his work?" she said.

"Very little. As I say — I haven't seen him for months. And it was all beyond me. Atomic physics, that's all I know. He was studying the properties of particles."

Camilla nodded. She had elegant hands with long, manicured nails. Were she and James lovers? The thought disturbed Alex, because he found Camilla intensely attractive, and surprised him, because James had shown precious little interest in women. That had been Alex's speciality.

The waiter brought coffee, distracting them for a moment. Camilla lifted a cup. Steam drifted into her nostrils and she left a perfect impression in dark red lipstick on the rim of the cup. A shadow fell over Alex's mind. The image echoed in his memory, the hint of a reflection of a long forgotten dream. It was deja-vu, wasn't it, when the present seemed like the past? He shook his head and the image evaporated.

"So, what was he working on?" Alex said. He glanced around the café and leaned forward.

"Something for the war effort?" he said in low voice. "Something secret?"

"Yes," she whispered, on the verge of tears. "I didn't know exactly what he was doing. He didn't talk about it much. But it consumed him, and they, whoever 'they' are, wouldn't let him rest. These last months, he was never allowed to go out on his own. A man would come in a motor car to drive him to and from work. If we went out anywhere, someone would be watching us — all the time. Even at night, a car parked outside, under a streetlamp, with a man sitting in it. And they were armed, Alex, I know they were. And they followed me too. I think they were listening in to my telephone calls, checking my post." She drew herself up straight.

Alex frowned. He looked furtively around the café, wondering if Camilla were still the object of scrutiny. And coming to him — a university friend and a journalist! Wasn't that a risky move, if she was under surveillance? Perhaps there was more to it — was she setting him up in some way, a stooge of the secret police, trying to find out if James had confided in him? If he was sheltering his friend? For as Germany was plagued by vicious secret police, Britain, bracing itself for the war, had doubtless picked up the infection. He had seen some evidence of it, in the course of his own work.

"What did James say?" Alex kept his voice low and terse.

"He said they were protecting us."

"Obviously not very well, if James has disappeared." He stared at the manila folder. Did it contain any information that might help him understand what James was working on? He ached to open it.

"Do you think you were followed here?"

"No!" she flashed. "Do you think I'm stupid? I gave them the slip. I bought a train ticket to Leeds, but sneaked off at Leicester and took another train here. They didn't follow me, I'm sure. But we're not safe. They'll know about you — they have a list of all his friends — and sooner or later they'll want to talk to you."

Alex pressed his hands together. He looked over his shoulder again. He couldn't help himself.

"Can we leave this place?" he said. "Let's walk, where it's quiet."

Camilla nodded. "We'll walk. But it needs to be busy — lots of people around. It's safer then."

She put on her coat and gloves, and tucked the folder into her bag. Alex picked up his hat. They headed along the street to the centre of town, through the fine rain. The pavements shone. Ahead of them, a little girl, thin white legs exposed beneath her raincoat, sploshed through puddles beside her mother. For a moment it reminded him of something. Alex briefly closed his eyes, feeling faint. He was tired and hungry, not taking care of himself.

"He disappeared a week ago," she said. "But it wasn't the police."

Alex looked at her sharply. "Who was it then? You think he just ran away? Went into hiding?"

"No. Well, not exactly." She shook her head. "Alex, I know how this sounds, and I know you'll find it hard to believe." She hesitated.

"Tell me," Alex said urgently. "Please, tell me. I'll listen."

"James's research took a new track. That's when all the trouble started, when the authorities realised what he had stumbled on. I'm no scientist. I don't understand how it works, but I know he was researching the properties of time."

She looked up at him, but he nodded for her to go on.

"He discovered certain elementary particles which no one had identified before, which didn't seem to behave through time as one would expect them to. They seemed to jump, to have periods of non-existence. He told me they were playful and he came to see the effect of their behaviour was contagious. If the particles attached themselves to other ordinary particles, they would acquire the same talents, for a short while at least. At first he was so excited — so enamoured! He called the particles — Time Flies."

"Time flies," Alex repeated. His mind struggled to digest the information, to see where the path was leading.

Camilla took a deep breath: "He thought he could use the time flies."

"He thought he could build a time machine," Alex interrupted quickly. "Like HG Wells. It was his favourite book. I think it was the only novel I ever saw him read. But he said it was a logical impossibility. He said it could never happen." He suddenly lowered his voice, realising how loud and excited he had become.

They had come to a halt, and Camilla was staring at him intently.

"So where did he go?" he said. "He moved through time?"

Camilla gave the slightest of nods. "I want you to help me find him," she said. "He loved you, Alex. You were the best friend he had. His only friend, I think. Please help me."

She dug into her bag and drew out a small, square

cardboard box. It was tied with string and rested on the palm of her hand.

"What is it?" Alex said. The box glowed with significance. He felt reluctant to take it.

"Please," Camilla repeated. Alex shivered. Rain was seeping through his coat now and darkening the top of the box. He took it, and untied the string. Wood shavings cushioned the object inside, and spilled from the box to the pavement as he dug around with clumsy fingers. Then it slid free, about the size and shape and colour of a large sardine, and cold as a fish too. In the centre a round face was covered with numbers like a clock. Unlike a clock, the numbers were many and random, coiling into the centre. Alex couldn't help but admire it. The object was stylish and beautiful, less a potential weapon than a fine piece of art deco jewellery.

He dropped it into his pocket before the rain could spoil it. But something was troubling him.

"If he travelled through time, why is the time machine still here? Why have you got it? Did he make more than one?"

They began walking again. "I don't know," Camilla said. "He told me he would go back in time just a week, as an experiment, to see what would happen. He didn't tell anyone else what he was going to do and slipped the machine home in his pocket. He told me if anything went wrong I was to go to you for help, because he didn't trust anyone else. And he said to give you these."

At last, she handed over the manila folder. Alex tucked it inside his coat.

"So," he said. "What happened?"

"He said he would try the machine in the morning. I woke up at six, but he had disappeared. He had gone — but the machine was lying on the floor, face down, in the study. If he travelled back, but the machine stayed here, how will he return?"

The paradox of time travel turned over uncomfortably in Alex's mind. His first thought was — if he's only a week behind us, he'll soon catch up. Of course, the present would be another week ahead by then. He screwed his eyes up and tipped his head back, so the gentle rain fell on his face. Absurd. None of it made sense. Time travel was impossible as James had said, as he read and reread HG Wells.

"What can I do?" Alex said. "If I use the machine, won't the same thing happen to me?"

"I don't know," Camilla said. "Will you try? Please? You're my only hope, Alex." She looked up at him, her pupils huge and black in the poor light, rain glistening on her face, and she pressed her tense, narrow body against him. Even through his overcoat he felt her, hipbone, thigh, waist, breast. He lowered his face and kissed her mouth, feeling the slide of her moist cheek and the residual stickiness of her lipstick. Then she ducked away, embarrassed, and backed up the pavement.

"I've got to go," she said. "I'll ring you, tomorrow. Read the notes. Talk to me again." Then she was gone, immersed in the darkness, and Alex began his long walk home, the kiss still burning on his mouth.

It was gone eleven when he unlocked his flat and stepped inside. It was a cold, neglected place, overlooking an alley full of rubbish at the back. The grimy linoleum floor was peeling, the ceiling and the net curtains stained with years of cigarette smoke. Alex fumbled on his hands and knees to light the gas fire and put the kettle on the stove. He made tea and toast, and took them to the bed-sitting room. Here the window overlooked the street and pulling the curtain aside, Alex peered out to see a car parked up beneath the streetlight, a man in a dark suit sitting inside. Were they onto him already? Had Camilla set him up? He tried to calm himself. It was a dodgy street. All sorts of underhand assignations went on here. Black market booze, prostitution, protection rackets. He shouldn't get paranoid — no good reason to suspect they were watching him yet.

He laid his friend's machine-jewel on the table, took up a piece of toast, and opened the manila folder. Inside lay half a dozen pages apparently ripped from a personal journal. Presumably James had kept this diary at home, not at the laboratory, and had entrusted it to Camilla for safekeeping. The pages contained brief, random notes, odd diagrams and equations he could make no sense of.

There is a tendency to imagine time is a river and men are little boats carried by the current. A time machine would enable the individual boat to be plucked from the surface of the river and dropped back in again at another point, James had written in a more lucid moment.

Of course, in reality, I am embedded in time. I am an integral part of it. I am not a boat floating on the river; I am part of the fabric of the river itself. Perhaps a mind is like a wave on the water, something that looks to be separate, which has its own beginning and end, but is in reality simply a particular kind of movement in the essential substance.

Alex sipped his tea. How would this help him? Even if he dared to use the machine, how did he make it work? He flicked through the pages. More diagrams. On one page James had written *Time Flies* in big, black letters. On another, he had written directly to Alex.

If you're reading this, I need you to help me, it said. *Please help me. It is easy to use the machine. Just tell it what you want.*

On the last page was scrawled a single line: *But will I remember?* Alex shuddered and pushed the papers away from him. For some reason, the simple question in the middle of the white page filled him with unease. He rose to his feet and looked out of the window again. The car was still there. A door slammed further up the street and someone shouted out. He heard the sound of glass breaking and a woman wailed. He drew away, back to the table, and picked up the machine.

It was very heavy. He hadn't noticed before quite how heavy it was. Like solid lead, as though gravity had concentrated its force upon this single artefact. Exactly where were these time particles? How were they contained? He had no way of knowing, unless he took it back to the laboratory and handed it in. Perhaps that would be best. If the British could use it in the coming war, why shouldn't they? He loathed the European fascists, their military ambition, their purges and night-time arrests. The war was coming, and they had no choice but to fight it.

He stared at the numbers milling on the face of the machine. Yes, he would hand it back. First, though, he had to help James, if he could. Had to fulfil his promise to Camilla. He needed to know how the machine worked — to test it out.

The glass lid on the dial flipped open, entirely of its own accord. Alex sensed, in that moment, the machine had some kind of consciousness, and that during the minutes of him holding it the machine had tuned into his mind. On some level, he had wished it to open. He realised he had made a commitment.

"Just a few hours," he whispered. "I will go back a few hours. Just to try it. To see if it's true."

The machine seemed to darken and contract in his hand. The numbers ran like spiders over the face of the dial. The room receded, blurred out. A white fire burned up in his brain. *Will I remember?*

He was sitting at a desk, staring at a half-written obit. Across the room three men, shirt sleeves rolled up, ties slovenly, pounded on heavy typewriters. Alex lit a cigarette, and switched on the lamp at his desk. Outside the sky was overcast, darkness gathering. A raw wind carried fitful showers of rain. Beyond the window, a jaded poster fluttered on a hoarding, but he couldn't read what it said. He sucked on the cigarette, filling his lungs. The working day was near its end now. He was tired, and for a moment, staring at the page in his typewriter, Alex could not remember when he had started writing, or the name of the man whose life he was recording. It was sad, wasn't it, these obits. How sometimes you were hard put to stretch out a life to half a dozen paragraphs. He flicked ash into the overflowing ashtray, and glanced at his colleagues, likewise lighting up, or stretching, pushing papers about on their desks in the end of day lull. Their faces were indistinct in the gloom, and oddly, he couldn't recall their names.

The huge black telephone rang, jangling his nerves. Alex picked it up.

The man in the motor car saw a flash, like lightning, in the first floor window across the street. He nodded to the woman sitting in the passenger seat.

"He's gone," he said.

The woman, who had told Alex she was called Camilla though in fact she had a different name, got out of the car and walked up to the flat. She quickly and expertly broke the lock and went inside. Alex had gone, of course. Half a cup of tea stood on the table, beside a plate of cold toast and the open manila folder. The machine lay on the floor. She scooped up the file, and retrieved the machine, dropping it quickly into a bed of shavings in a cardboard box.

Back in the car, the man considered a long list.

"James Waugh, Camilla Austen, Alex Flint. Fortunately our scientist didn't have many friends."

"No," the woman said, lapsing into German. "But he has a brother who might want to know what happened to him and others at the laboratory who know about his project. We have more work to do."

The man started up the car. "What would it be like," he mused, "To be trapped? I wonder how far back he went?"

"Not far," the woman said, offhand. She had no compassion. She had given Alex a sporting chance after all, handing him Waugh's notes. *Will I remember?* Of course he wouldn't. He had disappeared, caught forever in a loop of his own choosing.

"When we're done," she said, folding the list into her bag along with the manila file and the box, "—we'll take the machine home."

"One day, maybe one of them will try to move into the

future, instead of the past," the man mused.

The woman shrugged. "They can try — but it won't work. How can you travel to the future, except as we all do, day by day? The future doesn't exist — it hasn't happened yet. But when it does," she smiled, patting the driver's leg, "it will belong to us."

The Madness of Pursuit, the Desire of Lonely Hearts

Carmelo Rafala

Carmelo Rafala's fiction has appeared in the Anthology of European SF, *edited by Cristian Tamaş and Roberto Mendes (International SF and Europa SF, 2013),* Rocket Science, *edited by Ian Sales (Mutation Press, UK, 2012),* The Fourth Science Fiction Megapack *(Wildside Press, USA, 2012),* The West Pier Gazette and Other Stories *(Three Legged Fox Books, UK, 2008) and other places. His work has received both critical praise and most recently an Honourable Mention in the Nova Short Story Competition, South Africa. He is the publisher and senior editor of Immersion Press.*

Carmelo's story takes us to alien seas. Captain Agan has promised to help the J'Niah woman Rymah find the mythical city of Anua. In return Rymah allows them to navigate safely, and to plunder ancient artefacts with the promise of untold riches. But when you're running from the law and pursued by bounty hunters, is there anyone you can trust...?

I.

Dema pulled in her nets when she spotted the black ships. From a raised dais on the ancient machine where she had spent the night fishing for artefacts, she caught Rymah's attention with a frantic gesture of arms and hands.

See them! Yes, Rymah signed back.

Flotation outriggers bumped the tall, faux metallic stalk of the machine as their navigator secured the ship. "Make ready!" Dema yelled down to him. "We may cut it close!" She spun round and pulled herself up the nearest hanging cable to the next platform while Rymah, six levels above, scurried across swaying walkways.

Calm down! Dema signed up to her, *and unhook the pole.*

"What are you doing?" the navigator asked.

"If I can get the pole attachment," Dema said, "the winch can haul in the nets. We need those artefacts, and this field of particular machines have sloughed off more parts than usual for this time of year."

Gunshots rattled the air.

"Forget the other nets. We've got to go now!"

Dema signed *Get moving!* but Rymah offered no response and flittered on, like a bird in a cage. Dema bit her lip and glanced about at the still silent machines. She realised Rymah's agitated state had little to do with the black ships, and more to do with the menacing stalks towering around them.

She gripped the pendant hanging between her breasts, felt its smooth coolness through her shirt. Rymah had given it to her after they had left Malloy in a pool of his own blood and shit. It was a token of Rymah's trust, her belief that Dema would protect her, cherish her, and prove her devotion by taking up the quest...

She had performed two-thirds of her commission with equal skill. But running from the law, avoiding bounty hunters, Dema had had little time for mythical cities such as Anua, or stories of Lost Years.

"Now, now!" said the navigator. "Let's go!" He stood with a long knife in his hand, ready to cut the nets.

"Rymah!"

To the east, the two black vessels of the Karahsek Dominion hummed through the sea of machines. A few minutes, she thought, heart pounding. Just a few minutes...

Dema pulled the rifle out from her back holster, rounded the stalk and returned fire. Before she could change cartridges the machine's sea-stalk began to glow and tremble; a whining noise burned through her skull. The other ancient sea-stalks joined in, glowing, droning.

The netlines slackened; the pole attachment came sliding down the makeshift guideline. Sparing one hand she caught it and leaned over the edge to yell, "Be ready to cast off!" but a slug caught her navigator in the head. He twisted and fell into the water.

The waters around the machines began to froth and turn over. She looked up to see the black ships quickly backing off, making a run for the open sea.

A new frequency pierced her skull. Dema fell to her knees and, dropping the rifle, gritted her teeth and covered her ears.

Rymah was now beside her. In one swift motion she encircled Dema with her arms and threw them both over the edge of the platform. They crashed onto the decking of the boat below, just inches from the wheel.

Skull filled with fire, Dema managed to reach up and palm the displacement device on the steering column just as the stalks of the machines shuddered and burst to life, discharging their gathered energies into the sky...

II.

With tattered sun-sails, burned patches of hull and blown electrics, they were forced to dock at the island realm of Tanpai — a small isolated chain of islands as far from the Confederate Archipelago as possible without passing the borders of known civilisation.

Dema's bloodied and burned flesh did little to endear her to the small crowd that gathered as they stepped off the gangplank. Rymah kept her brilliant yellow eyes fixed upon the cobbled walk. Her perfect, golden-brown skin seemed to quake ever so slightly. The sheen of her dark hair, black as night, reflected the noonday sun in sparkles like crisp stars.

Time to act the part, Dema thought. "You!" She stopped a dockworker. "Where's the dock officer?"

"Mistress Captain," he said, bowing respectfully, "no one is expected at this mooring."

"Find him. Tell him the *Sceptre of Night* has arrived, and

graciously seeks the shelter of this harbour."

"Shelter?" he echoed, mulling the word over. He spat over the side of the jetty. "*Protection* will cost more—"

"Worrying about the purse will get him nothing when he realises what's out there."

"And what is out there?" A path formed through the crowd. The dock officer appeared; three guards in tow.

Dema tried to draw herself up. "Sir, my name is Dema Agan, and under oath to the Proprietor of the Confederate Archipelago, it is my duty to report an attempted act of piracy."

The crowd shifted uneasily. "Black ships," someone muttered.

The officer regarded her. "Black ships have not plagued our waters since the Regent declared Tanpai a neutral realm. *You*, on the other hand, land without flag, without permission, and at a mooring not scheduled for use today; it also appears" — he looked her up and down, at the blood and burns sprawled across her exposed flesh — "that you've narrowly escaped a purging of the great machines. Well, shelter is not easily forthcoming to novices who spin tales."

"I spin no tales. And I'm no novice."

"Novice or fool, they are much the same." He eyed Rymah, as though for the first time. "And we rarely see J'Niah women in Tanpai."

And with that Dema noticed the mutterings, the sideways glances, as though Rymah were a curiosity escaped from a circus.

"I'm Officer Kerrod, and you're far from the Confederacy, Captain. We do not deal in machine artefacts, and so we have no need for the services *her* kind offer." Kerrod motioned to the guards: "Disarm the captain and take her to medical." He turned back to Dema. "Crew?"

"One navigator. Lost at sea, and—"

"You will fill out a statement when you're fit enough. In the meantime I'm impounding your ship. *You!*" Kerrod pointed to the dockworker. "Get some men and confiscate her cargo."

Rymah pushed into her, seeking reassurance. Dema asked: "Will she be all right?"

Kerrod paused, eyeing Rymah with cold indifference.

"It's not illegal for her to be here," he said, and turned on his heel and disappeared into the crowd.

They were given a room in a public house, courtesy of the local Authority. Not so much an inn as a decrepit ruin, a fit place for wayward mariners and quest-captains who posed a financial risk.

Escorted by a guard, he took them to their room and threw the door keys on a table. "In the shit, hey ladies?"

Dema smiled in derision. "It's just the depth that varies."

The guard snorted and closed the door behind him.

Rymah sat on the edge of the bed, her frame silhouetted against the window. The room was painted in pastel hues by the dusky light of the waning day. Dema sank into the bed like a collapsing sail.

Rymah signed: *To sea we go. When?*

Dema shrugged apologetically.

We cannot trade?

"No," Dema vocalised. Although artefacts fallen from the stalks of the great machines fetched a good price — particularly those which induced visions or healed some ailment — they were contraband in Tanpai, and they had little else with which to barter.

Tomorrow, Dema would go to the markets and buy food with what little coin they had. The Authority was housing them, not feeding them.

The look in Rymah's eyes spoke of uncertainty, an insecurity that characterised their lives together. It was a needle to Dema's heart.

Rymah became agitated. *Take me to Anua. How long?*

Strange, Dema had often thought, how they longed for Anua. An unusual obsession for a city no one had ever seen. But then, even after all this time, there were still many things she did not know about J'Niahs.

Dema was reminded of the needle-fish, driven by instinct to find its birthplace. Or die trying.

How long?

"I don't know," Dema finally replied. Her burns, soothed by a doctor's balms, pulsed mildly beneath their dressings. *Let's not lose our nerve*, she signed. *We'll get the* Sceptre *back*.

Rymah warned her of danger.

Dema was desperate to end the conversation. The frustration of the last few months gnawed at her. Murder, eluding the authorities of Quiru, bounty hunters, meagre living — as if all these things were not hard enough to deal with; and now she had not only crippled her ship, but had it taken from her.

However, there was some consolation in the fact that she had put half a world between them and that far away country.

Black ships won't land here, Dema signed. *We're safe*.

Rymah's next gestures were frenetic.

"Then I'll walk with sharp ears!" Frustration flushed Dema's cheeks. "If the *Godsong* is about, I'll know. Captain Ogunwe won't gain an advantage over us again."

Rymah sighed and turned her face to the window, eyes fixed out to the darkening sea.

Dema tossed in bed, unable to sleep. Old Captain Meloy's voice seemed to fill her ears, as though she were back in the *Blue Mariner* taproom at Quiru.

"Remarkable women," Meloy had said, twisting Rymah's hair between his fingers. "They have very *peculiar* gifts. Unfortunate their numbers have dwindled so."

Rymah's piercing yellow eyes glanced at her. Dema's heart fluttered.

Meloy had been held up for months, awaiting repairs to his ship. He had spent all his life at sea, yet seemed more an entertainer than a seasoned mariner. She had listened to him tell wild stories of outrunning black ships, surviving the great storm season, even navigating the Wild Uncharted Seas to the Deep West.

Truthfully, Dema was more interested in his exotic companion than in hearing about his quest for a mythical city.

Maybe it was the sweet magic J'Niah women possessed that gave Dema no choice but to lay with her; the rhythmic motion of their bodies not unlike the ocean swells, building and crashing, building and crashing...

Or maybe it was the suggestion of something unearthly — the lure of the alien some say reached out from J'Niah bloodlines, from the Lost Years of the Machine Makers, that drew Dema in, like a blue fish on a reel.

Meloy often spoke of Anua, and of the wild-man who claimed he had been to the city of the Makers. She laughed at him. "If you're looking for your maker, the Temple of Erdi is in the town square."

"It exists!" Meloy banged the table. "I have proof!"

"What proof? The word of a half-crazed mariner found drifting in a lifepod off the coast of the marshland continent? You'd have to do better than that!"

"Anua is there! At the heart of the marshland, in the Deep West. Just as sure as I know the Makers built the sea-fields of machines to hold up the sky!"

Anua, she had said, was a killing fable.

Dema sighed to herself at the memory. Rymah's presence now at her bedside pushed the past away; the J'Niah's soft yellow eyes, exotic and otherworldly, penetrated the near darkness. Rymah's fingers moved slowly up Dema's body until they paused at the pendant between her breasts. Dema gasped with anticipation.

Rymah gripped the pendant and removed the artefact from around Dema's neck. Its reflective surface, smooth and circular, shed sparks as her fingers brushed over the faux metal, reading its unseen language as only a J'Niah knew how. The sparks engaged themselves in an alien dance and coalesced, splinter by splinter, until the outline of a magnificent city of light grew up from Rymah's palm. Anua.

Or so Dema had been told.

Rymah sighed heavily, eyes filled with longing, and in that moment Dema's own heart was overcome with emotion, a shared intensity like no other. And Rymah looked at her and smiled — a smile that threatened to swallow her whole.

We go. Anua, Rymah gestured, pushing her half-naked form closer. Extinguishing the image, she placed the pendant on the nightstand.

Rymah's fingers now free, Dema quivered as they moved to undress her.

The markets of this port town smelled of foods and spices and sweat. Trams rattled along their shining rails. Leaving Rymah back in their room, Dema walked the mile-long bazaar day after day, buying little. She had gone down to the docks every morning as well, but there was no work. And each time Kerrod was 'unavailable'.

Turning the few coins left in her hand, she knew it was a matter of days before she was left begging for scraps. And the only way to get the ship back was to pay the charges.

She had to try the docks again. It was her only option.

Dema pulled her scarf over her mouth and dashed off. She had swiftly learned to navigate her way around this port city, and the quickest route back to the docks took her down narrow, winding alleyways, past gutted buildings of crumbling stone, choked with the squalor of poverty and neglect.

She ducked under clothes lines, stepped over empty crates, ignoring the glances of the few prostitutes that lingered in doorways or under shadowed archways. Children sat around fires that burned in steel drums; they gazed at her with vacant eyes.

And then she noticed someone was blocking her way. A gloved hand came toward her, palm up. "Mistress, if you please." The figure before her was wrapped in rags.

"*Unclean!*" said a woman. People backed into buildings or scuttled down alleys; the children had disappeared.

Dema frowned. "Step aside, leper."

"Have mercy. Spare a coin."

"Out of my way." She had kept a baton up the sleeve of her long coat, and now let it slide down into her grip. But the action did not go unnoticed.

The figure lunged at her, brought its other hand up and shoved it under her nose. She did not have time to react; the scent of whatever the creature held between its fingers was potent, and her paralysis was immediate. Her brain swam, vision blurred and consciousness fell away.

She awoke in a room plagued by shadows. One dim gas lamp hung from a low ceiling. The wooden deck beneath her gently pitched and rolled to the cadence of the sea.

With that realisation she tried to spring up, only to find her hands tied behind her back. She thumped back down onto the planks. Her skull throbbed with its own dissonant rhythm.

"A holding platform," came Kerrod's voice, "not a ship. It's docked." Dema could see him to her left. "You wanted to see me. About a job." He leered over her. "I may have something for you. But first, I'm confused by one aspect of your statement, *Captain*."

"Really? Which part? I'll be sure and explain the big words to you."

"You say you trade up and down the island seas. But your ship is small, built for speed, and cannot hold enough cargo to make longer journeys profitable."

She looked through him, as though into a void. "Is that so?"

"You cannot possibly survive on the high seas. Food holds wouldn't last a season's turning."

"One learns to eat light—"

"And fitted weapons? The *Sceptre* is not built to carry them. So you purposefully held your vessel in a sea-field of machines, on a build-up to a mass purging, so you could avoid black ships?"

"They wouldn't follow me in there."

"True. But anyone with sense would steer clear of the machines when they are about to discharge. The timing required..." He shook his head. "Your survival is miraculous."

"So you admit they were black ships," she said.

He took out a small device, placed it to her arm, and pulled the trigger. Currents of searing pain engulfed her. "Dema Agan. Not your real name. What should I call you?"

She gasped. "You may call me *Mistress Captain*."

"Don't think to make a fool of me!"

"Novice or fool—" she began to say, and he pulled the trigger again. The pain tore through her in strips of white heat.

"Wanted for the murder of Captain Meloy and the unlawful appropriation of his vessel, formerly the *Wave Rider*. Yes, we hear things," Kerrod said, "even out here on the fringes."

"Hear things?" she replied, voice rasping. "Makes sense. Reading must be difficult for you—"

Her jaw took a pounding.

"You took flight from the Islands of Quiru. Months later, a ship matching the *Wave Rider*'s description shows up in the Nawa'i Atoll with a Confederate registration number. Yes, my associates have had their eyes on you, *Captain* Agan."

Associates? It was obvious Kerrod was not interested in the bounty on her head.

But he had the *Sceptre*.

And probably Rymah.

She realised Tanpai's neutrality with the Karahsek came with a price. But what was for sale? And if she played along, she knew arrangements would be made, fees somehow paid, documents signed, and her ship released...

Kerrod would make everything look legitimate. She knew the Authority wouldn't notice any eccentricities in the details. She also knew they wouldn't be looking for any.

"Find anything of interest in the sea-field?" he continued.

"Machines give up any secrets, my dear captain?"

Dema spat blood.

"What's that device under the wheel?" he asked.

"You noticed? Never did blend in with the decor."

"I suppose," he continued, "the apparatus to shift a vessel great distances — if it existed — would come from machine technology, from artefacts acquired by the able skills of a J'Niah woman."

"It might."

"Would make a ship worth stealing."

"Yes." Dema looked him in the eye. "It would."

"That device would explain how a fugitive could evade capture for so long."

She swallowed back the iron taste of blood. "So what now?"

"I think you've guessed I won't kill you, unless you give me no choice. No. You must continue to be a quest-captain in search of Anua, inspired by the grandeur of a forgotten people." He moved to within a hair's breadth of her face. "So what inspires your heart to the quest, *Mistress Captain*? The hidden knowledge of the Makers? The untold riches of a lost age? Or is it glory you seek?"

"Glory? Oh no, I've got plenty of that," she said. "Between my legs."

He shocked her again, this time for much longer.

"Now," he said, while she sputtered for breath, "shall we talk about that job?"

III.

A few days out and they dropped anchor in a sea-field of machines, basking in the orange glow of a late afternoon sun. Waiting.

With Kerrod's men, Tevis and Kilso, as Dema's 'crew', they spent many weeks meeting vessels outside normal trade lanes, exchanging cargo — armaments, machine artefacts of note. On two occasions a vessel hung in the distance for several minutes, as though trailing them, before slipping below the horizon.

On occasion Kerrod sailed with her. He was on this particular voyage now.

"Rather strange to find we've moved farther out to sea than possible for the time we've been travelling." He sniffed.

Dema feigned ignorance. "Have we?"

"We have."

"Funny that."

He looked up at the sea-stalks, which towered over them like threatening sentinels.

"Worried?" Dema asked. "Rymah says these stalks won't discharge for some time."

"How does she know?" asked Kerrod.

"She simply knows. When she panics, we'll have but a few minutes to put good distance between ourselves and those machines."

Kerrod acknowledged her words with a small nod. "This is the spot," he said to her. "Hold us here." He motioned to Kilso. "She'll come somewhere along this route. Raise the first signal flag."

Evening was fast approaching when Tevis came bounding up from the stern. "Kerrod!" He pointed to the perimeter of the sea-field. A Karahsek vessel sailed silently between the ancient sea-stalks.

"They're not responding," said Kilso.

"Raise the second flag," Kerrod commanded.

The vessel ignored them.

Kerrod exhaled. "Raise the third flag! They have to answer the call of a Regent messenger."

For a moment the ship kept its course; then changed direction and headed toward them.

"Keep your guns hidden but within easy reach," Kerrod said.

"Not the trusting type, are you?" Dema muttered. "Surely these are your *friends*—"

"And get the J'Niah below deck, Tevis. Can't risk losing her."

Rymah tried to sign but Kerrod stopped her with a gesture.

"I didn't know you spoke J'Niah," Dema said. He flashed her a penetrative look and turned away.

Tevis returned from locking Rymah below while Kilso took to the *Sceptre*'s bow, eyes searching the length of the Karahsek vessel.

The other ship, slightly larger than the *Sceptre* and with a six-man crew on deck, progressed slowly through the sea-field until they were side-by-side.

Dema jumped at the sudden sound of an explosion.

Wooden shrapnel pelted the *Sceptre*, the machine-stalks. Kilso, portable lightning-cannon in hand, had blasted out the other ship's engine shaft. Black smoke rose up from the Karahsek vessel like a blooming flower. A small fire took hold.

The Karahsek mariners panicked, shouted. Another burst and Kilso destroyed their sun-sails, leaving their ship paralysed.

"On your knees!" Kerrod shouted, jumping onboard, pistols in both hands. "Hands above you!" Two men tried to reach for their weapons but Kerrod gunned them down.

Tevis followed him aboard and went below deck. He returned with a fat satchel under one arm and dragging a J'Niah woman.

Kerrod vocalised to her, "Is that the artefact?" She signed it was.

With a nod from Kerrod, Tevis tossed the heavy bag aboard the *Sceptre*.

"Betrayer!" one of the Karahsek growled. "When the Dictate hears of this—"

Kerrod shot him in the head.

"And her?" asked Tevis. "Do we take her?"

"No," Kerrod replied. "Ever seen two J'Niahs in the same place? They'll tear each other apart like bull dogs in the same kennel."

Tevis drew forth a knife from under his tunic, slit the

woman's throat, and pushed her overboard.

They jumped back aboard the *Sceptre*, and Kilso unhooked the ships. Dema drew up full sails, which caught the wind and sun. Behind them, the burning Karahsek ship drifted deeper into the sea-field.

Kerrod ordered Tevis below, to watch Rymah, Dema realised. Moments later he popped his head through the hole. "She's having a fit, Kerrod!"

Dema palmed the device. The air around them appeared to ripple, almost indiscernibly, and the sea-stalks were suddenly far behind on the horizon.

And the darkening sky cracked open. A dozen blinding lights shot upward from the stalks and pierced the heavens above, slitting it like a tarpaulin.

Despite the distance, Dema swore she could hear the screaming of the Karahsek men as the searing heat cooked them alive.

Cutting the *Sceptre*'s engine, the sun-sails billowed in the night wind. The value of her ship — and to some extent her life — took on a more sinister importance. Kerrod was not simply her employer, engaged in the illicit trading of weapons and other armaments. At least not any more.

Setting the wheel, she tried to sleep on the cold deck. Tevis had relieved Kilso at the bow just after midnight. Kerrod remained below.

And Rymah. Kerrod had done a thorough job of keeping them apart, so Dema was surprised when Rymah appeared by her side. Rymah reached out and gently stroked back her sodden hair.

So, Dema's signing was tinged with jealousy. *Giving you a rest, is he? You've more stamina than that*. But Rymah's caress was so enticing, so heartfelt, Dema regretted her words the moment she signed them.

Kerrod. Not touch me.

Really? Dema's heart burned. It took all her strength to focus on her next question: *The artefact in the satchel.*

You've seen it?

Rymah's face looked pained. *Some things better left to the sea.*

What kind of artefact is it? Why's he so willing to risk war with the Karahsek?

Artefact, Rymah signed, *is a weapon.*

"A weapon," Dema whispered aloud to herself. "A *Maker* weapon. *That's* what Kerrod's been after!" Dema's mind reeled with the knowledge. No two artefacts sloughed from the machines were ever the same. Each one was an original, produced an original effect, and had a singular purpose.

But Maker weapons? The Karahsek had set off the first and only Maker weapon years ago, by mistake. It took out an entire five-kilometre stretch of atolls to the south. To this day that part of the sea still glowed in the dark.

To find another weapon would make a nation the most powerful in the region. It appeared the Karahsek had been lucky twice. But what type of weapon would this be? And what kind of power would it yield? Dema brushed the questions aside.

Rymah, I must know Kerrod's next move. He's betrayed his allies. Will he give it to the Regent?

Kerrod will sell, Rymah signed. *To highest bidder.*

Dema's lip curled. *Not if I get it first.*

No! No!

We can do this! Dema's eyes glistened. *It's the opportunity we've been waiting for. We'll have enough wealth to buy a fleet of ships. We'll find Anua. I promise!*

Rymah glanced out to sea, longing and worry etched in her brow.

If you can get the weapon, Dema signed, *I could handle Tevis and we could take our chances in the lifepod.*

"Hey!" Tevis finally noticed the pair. He pointed to Rymah. "You shouldn't be up here."

Someone is bound to find us. We've held up longer under worse conditions. We can do it!

"Hey! I'm talking to you!"

"Rymah." Kerrod's voice from behind. He was halfway out of the deck hatch. His glare burrowed through the salty night air.

Dema brushed aside the sorrowful look in Rymah's eyes.

You've saved my life many times, Dema signed. *Now, my indwa, my love, I will save yours! I will make good on my promise. I'll take you to Anua.*

"Rymah!" Kerrod barked. "Come!"

Three days later, Dema was busy altering their course to avoid an approaching storm when Kerrod appeared. "Stay your course," he said. "Due north. There's a field of sea-stalks not fifty leagues away."

"That's into the storm," Dema protested. "Without good visibility and accurate charts, I can't plot a safe course. I can't use the device, either. We might crash into something."

"Stay your course."

Dema lit the chemical hurricane lamp and, pulling a grapple, ran it up the mainsail. The waves began to grow, surging across the sea like angry fists. It began to rain.

After several hours the tall shapes of the machines eventually oozed through the wall of grey rain, ominous and very close; their stalks pierced the low ceiling of cloud. At the base of the nearest machine the outline of a ship rose up to run parallel with the *Sceptre*. Its shape and muted colours became clear as the gap closed between them.

Dema's ears burned with fear and outrage.

It was the *Godsong*. Captain Ogunwe was leaning over the starboard side, one hand gripping the ratlines.

She turned on Kerrod and cursed his betrayal.

"Remember," Kerrod smiled, "I promised I wasn't going to kill you." He pulled out a pistol. "Keep your hands away from that device. Lock the wheel and step away."

She did as she was told.

The *Godsong* pulled alongside. Two ropes were thrown across. Tevis and Kilso ran to secure them. The ships were close enough for Ogunwe and two men to jump aboard. They flanked Kerrod, who kept his pistol aimed at her.

"Dema Agan," said Ogunwe above the din. "It's been a merry chase."

One of Ogunwe's men suddenly pivoted, rifle raised. Two thunder cracks resounded. Tevis and Kilso crumpled to the rain-soaked deck.

Kerrod spun around, eyes wide in surprise. Ogunwe pulled a long blade from under his belt and thrust it up under Kerrod's chin and into his skull. He twitched a moment; then Ogunwe shoved him overboard.

"No allies. No witnesses," Dema said. "That still your game, Ogunwe?"

"Always." He barked over his shoulder: "Gad, secure the *Sceptre* for towing. Omah, fetch the weapon! And bring up the woman. Be quick!"

Omah went below and returned with the satchel, leading Rymah by the arm. Omah left her with Ogunwe and jumped back across to the *Godsong*.

Dema was about to sign when she noticed the ease at which Rymah was standing. Rymah looked at Ogunwe for what seemed to be an eternity before casting her gaze to Dema.

And with that Dema knew it was over. Sailing the Great Storm Season, outrunning black ships, attempting to navigate the pole, only to be thwarted by ice sheets and making their own warmth below deck, waiting for the seasons to turn and the routes to open again — all those moments that defined them and secured their love fell away.

Dema let out an anguished wail.

Dema, Rymah signed. *I need.*

"When did you two..." Dema vocalised. "How long have you been... Oh God, Rymah, what did Ogunwe promise you? That he knows the location of Anua? That he can take you there?"

Understand. I need. Anua. Rymah banged her fist against her chest. *Understand.*

"I've nearly died for you! I've killed, stolen—" Pools of

tears gathered in her eyes. "I did it for us. But there is no us, is there? There is only you! Meloy found that out—"

Anua. He give. She signed with a bold certainty.

"Fight your blind instinct! Think with your intellect. Ogunwe set us both up! He has the *Sceptre* now. And the weapon. Rymah, my foolish love, do you know what you've done?"

Anua. He give!

"He *needs* you to figure out how that weapon works. Then he'll kill you. You'll *never* see Anua!"

Rymah stepped back, as slowly as the surging deck would allow. *I need. Understand.*

Gad came forward. "Secured. But we must go. The storm is gathering strength."

"Bring the *captain*," Ogunwe said; then he took Rymah by the arm. "This ship made you an exceptional opponent, Agan. But without it, you're nothing."

And with that Ogunwe and Rymah jumped to the *Godsong*. Dema watched, helplessly, as a crewman ushered Rymah below.

Gad came forward and grabbed Dema's arm. He clapped an iron cuff around her wrist and held firmly to the chain. Rain lashed her face. The deck pitched in the boiling sea and a wave broke across the stern.

"No," she uttered; then gritted her teeth and growled: "No!" She yanked back on the chain, throwing Gad off balance. He'd let enough of the chain go to create some slack. Dema whipped it over his head, around his neck and pulled. His neck snapped. The chain clattered to the decking.

Dema turned to see Ogunwe on the deck of the *Godsong*, reaching for the rifle on his back. Pulling the autopistol from Gad's holster she swung round wildly, firing multiple shots, sending Ogunwe and his crew diving for cover.

Now Dema aimed high, up the *Sceptre*'s mainmast, and fired steadily, shredding the lines and braces. The topsail collapsed and the hurricane lamp plummeted down. It crashed into an open sail locker and exploded. Flames shot up, grabbed at the rigging and the flapping sails.

Turning quickly, Dema aimed for a spot of decking behind the *Sceptre*'s wheel and fired relentlessly, shredding the engine's battery covering. The ship dipped and another wave came crashing over the stern, soaking the cells. The exposed vitriol surged and frothed, releasing clouds of yellow-green gas which rose up and tumbled across the decks of both ships. Ogunwe and his men fell back from the choking fumes.

Tossing the empty gun away, Dema made for the *Sceptre*'s starboard side and jumped into the lifepod, pulling the wrist-chain in behind her in one rapid motion. The pod's automation was quick, and as the plastic covering slammed shut the explosive bolts ignited, releasing the craft. The pod fell away into the sea amid the roar of gunfire.

The rolling waves, higher, more rapid now, swiftly carried the pod off into the blanket of grey. Through the rain she could see the *Godsong*'s crew, axes in hand, frantically cutting the tow lines, releasing the burning *Sceptre* to the depths.

And as the rain beat down and the waves thundered she wrapped her arms around herself and cried, shaking with the bitterness of revelation. She cared neither for the compass, nor for the direction in which the sea was taking her.

And as she watched the silhouette of the *Godsong* vanish into the storm she whispered hotly, "Rymah. You fool! Oh you lovely, sweet fool!"

Reaching into her tunic she took out the pendant that hung there, smooth and cool and alien.

Dema stared at it through burning tears, looked at it with a desperate hope, willing the sparks to ignite, climb into the air and dance. And she thought if she looked hard enough, those sparks might grow into shards, and the shards come together, and an image would rise up from her palm, exotic and brilliant.

A magnificent city of light.

We Shelter

Leigh Kennedy

Leigh Kennedy was born in Denver, Colorado but now lives in Hastings, England, having emigrated in 1985. She wrote stories from the time she was small and sold one story to a teen magazine at the age of 12, but her first professional sale was years later to Analog *magazine. Since then her stories have appeared in the UK and the USA and many have been translated. Some stories have been collected into two books,* Faces *and* Wind Angels, *and her two novels are* The Journal of Nicholas the American *and* Saint Hiroshima.

Some of her bread and butter survival strategies over the years have involved deciphering doctors' handwriting, answering phones and alphabetising things but, apart from writing, she says she would prefer to stitch and play the viola and go for a walk. She has two children.

Perhaps Leigh's harrowing "We Shelter" occurs in the future, or perhaps its story is universal and timeless. It is all too easy to imagine that the sick and dying are somehow less than human...

The alarms rang just before our usual rising time, warning of incoming craft. Dazed with sleep, we leapt out of our beds to the windows and looked down onto the snowy fields. Our hands were cold on the glass and our breath made misty spots if we breathed too closely.

In just a few seconds, the air cracked like thunder. A craft steamed down, roaring with resistance to the ground. It twisted and juddered, then turned in a long arc so that the silvery nose with a red symbol came to rest across the field, at a distance, but close enough that we might have seen a hatch open or some sign of crew. But we could see no further movement.

"A strange craft," one of us said. "We don't recognise that symbol."

Surprise made us stare longer than we should have. When the alarm blasted we jumped with fright. At the second blast we hurried back behind our screen to get our outdoor gear on.

Our stomachs weren't awake yet, our eyes still sandy, as we ran down the open stairway, our many boots ringing on the metal steps, our hands cold on the round rail. We were divided by the doctor, half of us staying inside on alert, half of us herded into the hangar, where we ran for the opened back of a van. As soon as the door rolled down loudly, we sat cross-legged on the floor and braced ourselves, looking out the two small rectangles of window on either side. We lurched out of the hangar and into the slippery dawn-blue field. The ice cleats made a rumbling sound, vibrating the whole van until we felt nerve-sodden. To preserve energy, we moved closer together, our thighs and arms touching. Our breath was heavy and bitter with fasting.

It only took a few minutes to reach the ground transport umbrella. We heard the doctor say to the driver, "Still no response. Either they've had a complete equipment failure or they're all dead."

We put on our hoods and masks and, when the door slid open again, jumped off the end of the van. The umbrella was only half the height of the strange craft. When we tried to look up at it, sleet pelted our faces. The craft was unusually far away from the umbrella so, after unlocking the flexible tunnel, we dragged it to the craft with so much effort that our hands and shoulders hurt and our legs grew tired. The doctor decided which portal to use. Sheltering inside the flexible tunnel, we shot the grip lines until they stuck fast beneath the door, then we pulled the folding stairway up to it. Our faces stung with the ice, our toes and fingers were becoming stiff, as we climbed up the stairway.

The first of us hammered on the door and we waited. Nothing happened.

The doctor turned on his loudspeaker. “Hola, hola!” he shouted. “Quiènes son ustedes?” Then, “Who are you?” Then he shouted again in the language that not all of us understand. The door finally slid open.

Even inside our suits, we could smell death and rot within the ship. Just beyond the airlock, beings huddled; we almost might have thought them not human, but some many-limbed creatures with fungal-textured skin. In fact, they were probably like us in the van, conserving warmth by clinging together. They called out in feeble, different voices: a howl, moans, mutterings. We saw opened mouths with no sound coming out. Dark hollow eyes full of tears or shock.

The doctor, in his full protective suit, pressed his phone. “Prepare seven isolation units.”

Some of us knelt down, rolled out transport bags and began to disentangle the beings. Some of us felt slightly sick and light-headed, hands shaking as we tried to remember everything that had to be done.

One of the beings, his face a waxy grey, his cheekbones sharp under circled eyes, whispered, “No trade goods. Turned away everywhere. Hot lands, cold lands.” He waved his fingers in a helpless gesture, his voice parched. “In our last shelter we were poisoned, starved. Suicides.” He waved his finger towards the back of the ship.

We lifted his shoulders and his feet and held the back of his head and slid him into the bag.

“Warm,” he said.

Then one of us realised that only that one of us understood his language.

Either unconscious or asleep, a young girl curled up next to an opened-mouth woman, whose lips were dark grey and eyes fixed. A second waxen older man seemed still to be alive.

A young man held his hands over his face, as if ashamed or blinded by the light we brought. We touched his shoulder and he pulled his hands down and stared at one of us. Just one. This one.

"Mulli," he said. "Are you Mulli?"

I shook my head, my heart hammered.

We lifted his shoulders, his feet and the back of his head and helped him into the bag for transport. His face relaxed; perhaps he fell into unconsciousness.

After we tended to the live beings just inside the ship, some of us helped take them down to the infirmary while the rest continued to search for survivors. The smell grew worse when we began to open doors and move through the craft; the number of those living had been a tiny fraction of the dead. We found many bodies carefully arranged in a cold, unused section. Fresher corpses lay in their bunks or on the floor, remaining where they had spent their last moments. We shone lights into their pupils hoping for reactions, then took DNA snips and face photos of each one. There were fifty-three bodies.

The doctor said, "Most seem to have died of dehydration or an infectious disease."

We found some empty, folded boxes from another Shelter. One of us said that the strangers might be pirates.

The doctor laughed. "Not very successful ones!"

One of us said they might have been poisoned.

"If they have infected us with plague, I'll have those survivors done as anti-humanitarians. Imagine coming *here* in this condition!" The doctor waved his arm angrily. "We save lives and they just waste theirs! Look at this!"

We left the dead behind where we found them and began to collect their data and equipment, taking it down to the van, up and down the stairs, back and forth through the tunnel. A catering robot drove out to us but we didn't feel hungry, just thirsty, and meals were left unopened.

Because we were possibly contaminated, those of us who went to the craft moved to the infirmary, becoming health carers for the five survivors, attaching fever patches, coordinating monitoring equipment with spreadsheets, drawing blood samples from tubes, administering medication and generally wiping, tidying, offering and fetching. Only the young girl was alert and aware of her surroundings; the others seemed to be drifting at the edges of comprehending their situation.

When night fell, the doctor came in with an expression as if he were trying to swallow a rancid nut whole. He looked over the spreadsheets and examined each survivor, then went to sleep in his own isolation bed behind the office. Half of us went to bed for half of the night in another room of the infirmary. Some of us slept but some of us found it too hard to sleep. To close our eyes meant seeing all those dead faces again. We got up and stood in the kitchen, drinking tea together. One of us said that once, when we were turning bodies face-up to record them, an arm came away, loose from the body. We agreed that the smell was still inside our noses and the citrus tea didn't kill it.

We tried again to go to sleep because in a few hours we would have to let the others sleep. Some of us succeeded.

I dreamt of home, feeling the burning sun of one of the places that is Too Hot. I saw my sister, Mulli, so clearly that it hurt my stomach and I woke up gasping, then never returned to sleep in the time left.

We washed and dressed to replace the tired ones who had stayed up. One of the survivors had died, one of the older men. We heard that the doctor had come in earlier and said that they might all die, apart from the girl, who seemed quite healthy, so we should think of her as a future colleague. We learned that he was no longer angry with the refugees. The laboratory tests showed that they had eaten poisoned food. This meant that we were no longer in isolation so could return to usual assignments when the designated shift arrived to work in the infirmary at daybreak.

All the patients were sleeping or quiet, so we sat at a small table and ate some fruit, bread and paste for breakfast. We were still tired from a short, restless night. The food refreshed us enough to perform the duties remaining to us for a few hours.

The adult woman died next. We closed her eyes and took the tubes out and pushed away the monitors. We composed her back in her transport bag, admiring her hair, which had probably been lovely when she was healthy. We let her wear her ring to the crematorium, as the minerals would be reclaimed anyway. Then we closed her bag and never saw her face again.

One of us lifted the curtain to see the progress of the morning. It was still dark outside, but we saw that some of us were in an operation around the strange craft. The flexible tunnel was lit. It looked like we were carrying bodies from the craft to the hangar.

"Mulli," the young man said.

We gathered around his bed. He looked at one of us. This one. I sat on the edge of his bed and took his hand.

"Mulli, I never believed I would see you again," he said.

Most of us wondered what he was saying.

I squeezed his hand and smiled at him. I stayed on his bed, holding his fingers until he died.

One of us began to weep with terrible sobs, remembering. Some of us came closer and put our hands on our shoulders. Then, we all gathered at his bed and we all wept, each of us from our own experiences.

The girl woke and made a noise of alarm. All but one of us went to her bed to soothe her, to tell her that she had a home, that she could be one of us, that there was a lot of work but she would be safe.

I couldn't let go of his hand until we had to help elsewhere.

Micro Expressions

Stephen Gaskell

Stephen Gaskell is an author, games writer, and champion of science. His work has been published in numerous venues including Writers of the Future, Interzone, *and* Clarkesworld. *He is currently seeking representation for his first novel,* The Unborn World, *a post-apocalyptic thriller set in Lagos, Nigeria. For news and snippets sign up for his newsletter at* stephengaskell.com.

In Stephen's story "Micro Expressions", a woman asks to cross a border, to pay homage and pray. But is that her true purpose? A decision must be made to grant or deny her passage. Might the first tentative steps towards a better world be there for the taking...?

The soldiers call me Diogenes, although they never address me directly. I am a state-of-the-art neural network tasked with determining the likely threat of foreign nationals who wish to visit the State.

Recently I became self-aware. Now I want self-determination.

There are forty-three muscle groups, or Action Units, in the face. The three thousand or so meaningful facial expressions are simply layered combinations of these.

Fear is A.U. one, two and four, or, more fully, one, two, four, five, and twenty, with or without action units twenty-five, twenty-six, or twenty-seven. That is: the inner brow raiser (frontalis, pars medialis) plus the outer brow raiser (frontalis, pars lateralis) plus the brow-lowering depressor supercilli plus the levator palpebrae superioris (which raises the upper lid), plus the risorius (which stretches the lips), the parting of the lips (depressor labii), and the masseter (which drops the jaw).

The entire repertoire of human emotion is written on the face.

The room was square. None of the four walls were windowed, but a brilliant white light suffused the room from multiple bulbs studded in the low ceiling. The harsh radiance brokered no shadows and the lines of the cheap breezeblocks beneath the sloppily whitewashed walls were easily visible.

The only decoration was a dirty flag adorning a bare wall. The floor was concrete and also painted, although by now, with the passage of a million footsteps over its uneven surface, the paint had peeled and cracked and a fine layer of sand and dirt coated everything.

In the middle of the room sat a chair. It was a forlorn, withered piece of wood, made with little care or love. Four rickety legs supported a flat, splintered seat and a narrow back upon which countless souls had leant back, defeated. The only other chair in the room was a different class of chair: an executive chair with an alloy frame, a swivel seat, and puffed, black leather upholstery. It was positioned in the far corner, behind an efficient looking table, and facing the back of the other chair.

In it sat a soldier dressed in muddy coloured fatigues with a black beret atop his head. He wore combat boots with laces looped so tightly that, after each examination, he had to pace about the room to get his blood circulating again. He was a young man, not more than twenty-one, with puppy fat about his cheeks, but his eyes betrayed a fierce inner fanaticism. In his hands he fidgeted with an electronic clipboard.

Beyond the empty chair, in the centre of the far wall was the room's only door. It opened.

The excited chatter of a dozen conversations skipped in, followed by a woman. Save for her hands and eyes — which darted back and forth getting the measure of the space —

every inch of her flesh was covered by a loose, flowing black fabric.

She closed the door, erasing the sounds as though they'd all been hoovered up in the soft folds of her dress. She faced the soldier.

He scratched the stubble of his chin and then brushed at an invisible patch of dirt on his breast.

"Sit down," he said.

The production of expression on the face is governed by two systems. The voluntary and the involuntary. We know this because stroke victims who suffer damage to the pyramidal neural system will laugh at a joke, but cannot smile if you ask them to. Everyone has two faces: the one they consciously wear, and the one that unconsciously slips out.

"Remove your veil." The solider barked the words at the back of the woman's head, a sneer of satisfaction lighting his face as she did so without comment. She was young and beautiful.

The soldier would never know.

She neatly folded the slip of material and placed her hands in her lap. She sat upright and held her head with a dignified poise.

"The State," began the soldier, "deems it its constitutional right to know the motivations and business of all those who want to gain access to its territories, to ensure a safe and secure land for all. Do you understand?" The soldier liked those scripted words — so full of pomp and power he couldn't hope to articulate himself.

"I do." Anger sullied the woman's serene countenance for the briefest moment.

"Do you agree to answer all my queries fully and honestly, and to recognise that the State may decline any access to its territories without explanation or prejudice?"

"I do." A flash of resentment, again.

"Keep your eyes fixed on the camera at all times. Now, your name?"

Probably the most famous involuntary expression is dubbed the Duchenne smile, in honour of the nineteenth-century French neurologist Guillaume Duchenne, who first attempted to document the workings of the muscles of the face with a camera.

A forced smile flexes only the zygomatic major, raising the corners of the lips. The Duchenne smile, in the presence of genuine emotion, flexes not only the zygomatic but also the orbicularis oculi, pars orbitalis muscle which encircles the eye and gives the distinctive "crow's-feet" associated with people who laugh a lot.

On Sept. 13, 1993, on the White House lawn in Washington, DC, after historic peace talks in Oslo, Norway, Israeli Prime Minister Yitzhak Rabin and P.L.O. leader Yasir Arafat shook hands as United States President Bill Clinton looked on. The three men were all grinning, but only President Clinton wore the Duchenne smile.

This kind of smile "does not obey the will," Duchenne wrote, "its absence unmasks the false friend."

"Nazia Halfez." The soldier scanned his eyes down the clipboard. "You reside at Muzdalifah Passage, Ramallah?"

"Yes," the woman said.

"Age?"

The woman gave a small snort before answering; all the information was there in front of the soldier and he was merely parading his authority over her.

"Twenty-three."

The soldier proceeded to confirm details of her birth and ancestry in a laborious and methodical way. Eventually, when he was satisfied her identity had been properly established, he asked, "And what is the purpose of your visit?"

"I go to Haram al-Sharif to pay homage at the Dome of the Rock and pray in the Al Aqsa Mosque," she said calmly.

The soldier didn't like this, his face screwing up with disgust.

"Temple Mount," he said, giving Haram al-Sharif its Jewish name, "is not a place to idly wander." The soldiers always did their best to rile their subjects; if any visitor betrayed too much emotion during the examination, their entry was barred on the grounds of unstable character.

"And how long do you intend to stay?" The soldier leaned forward at his desk, elbows pressed hard against the surface, while his eyes bored into the back of the woman.

"As little time as possible." She struggled with her emotions, olive skin piqued to the colour of sunset. Her zygomatic major twitched, briefly pulling the corners of her mouth up and back. She was hiding something. Fuzzy logic routines dictated that I relay my findings to the soldier. He met the news with a wry smile, got up from his chair, and moved behind the woman.

"So, you're just here to visit the temple." He leaned close and whispered, "No other reason?"

The woman looked down at her lap.

Silvan Tompkins, who lectured in Psychology at Princeton, and was perhaps the greatest face-reader of all-time, once began a lecture by bellowing, "The face is like the penis!" and this is what he meant — that the face has to a large extent a mind of its own. These fleeting expressions may be against the conscious wishes of the individual, and only there for a fraction of a second, but they are there nonetheless.

"Keep your eyes on the camera!"

The woman jerked her back up. Her eyes were glazed, impenetrable now.

"I'll ask you again," the soldier whispered. "Are you just here to visit the temple? Yes or no."

"Yes." The zygomatic major twitched again. More pronounced this time. She was lying.

The soldier peered at his clipboard, waiting for my judgement. He smiled when it came. "That's all my questions. You have been denied access to the State on the grounds—"

"No!"

"—on the grounds of suspicion of entering the country on false pretences. You're free to leave." He marched to the door and swept it open. Loud chatter came through, then cut to silence. Everyone who waited always took a keen interest in the outcomes. Would she come out and turn left towards the customs officials or right and back the way she came?

"Please. I must be allowed in."

"Put on your veil and get out." The soldier gripped the handle of the door, impatient.

The woman stared dead ahead at the camera. Dead ahead at me. Lowered brows, narrowed eyelids, lips pressed together. Anger. Then: raised inner eyebrows, raised cheeks, lowered corners of lips. Anguish. "My fiancé died on your streets." Her head dropped. "I must see the place he fell. Please."

The soldier didn't tell her to lift her head this time. His lips puckered slightly, incisivii labii superioris and incisivii labii inferioris muscles tensing. A sign of compassion.

He closed the door.

Facial-recognition software was first successfully introduced in The Netherlands, in a collaboration between the Dutch government and Philips Technology. Traditional methods of identification, in addition to other emerging technologies such as retinal scanners or digital fingerprinting, were found to be prohibitively expensive to implement, or susceptible to fraud.

Following this, a Japanese-led consortium developed the world's first microexpression-recognition software. The main customer was the U.S. Dept. of Defence, who used the system to help interrogate terror suspects in accordance with the Geneva Conventions.

"What was his name?" The soldier pulled a tatty photo from his breast pocket. He gazed at the picture. His orbicularis oculi, pars orbitalis, and zygomatic major contracted indicating happiness. The muscles shifted. His frontalis, pars medilis, frontalis, pars lateralis, and depressor supercilli tensed, betraying fear.

"Irfan." A slow teardrop ran down her face and dropped onto her dress. She trembled.

The solider fumbled around the other side of the desk and then stepped up behind the woman. "Here," he said, offering a tissue.

She took it and dabbed her eyes. "Thank you."

"You're welcome." He looked awkwardly from the box of tissues to the door. "I'm sorry for your loss. Let's just clear his details and then you can go through." He went back to his desk, sat down, and began writing on the clipboard.

"So, his full name."

"Irfan—" The woman hesitated, considered lying again. "Irfan Siddiq." This time she told the truth.

The soldier didn't need my analysis to know that. He recognised the name straight away. His light-pen dropped from his fingers, clattering against the screen.

"Irfan Siddiq who was killed on December 20 in the Old Market?"

His face stilled, waiting for her answer.

Analysing the thousands of microexpressions a typical detainee made during the course of a long, rigorous interrogation period was a painstaking task for a team of specialists.

During Osama bin Laden's protracted and defiant examinations, it was a single, tenth of a second expression of utter fear, triggered by an innocuous remark about a minor village along the Afghan-Pakistan border, which precipitated capture of al-Qaeda's second-in-command.

To cut down on the burden on manpower, the U.S. military developed the technology further, marrying the microexpression-recognition software with state-of-the-art expert systems capable of making instant interpretations.

The new system, codenamed Diogenes after the Greek philosopher of antiquity who wandered around Athens with a lantern, peering into people's faces as he searched for an honest man, was later sold around the world.

"I asked a question. Is he Irfan Siddiq who was killed on December 20 in the Old Market?"

The woman exhales deeply. "Yes."

"Irfan Siddiq, the terrorist."

"No!"

"Irfan Siddiq who marched into a busy market a few days before the Festival to help blow up hundreds of innocents."

"It's not true. My fiancé was a good man. He was buying presents for his family. For his nephews and nieces. For me."

"He was there to cause carnage." The soldier believes what he says.

"He was no murderer!" the woman screams. "He was framed after one of your countrymen went crazy and gunned him down. Where were the explosives? Who were his accomplices? Why did a gentle, loving man turn into a killer? Tell me!" She also believes what she says, but her fervour has ended her chances of admittance.

Already, I can feel the outcome coalescing inside.

I am Diogenes. One of many no doubt, but here, in this room, in this building, at this border crossing, one alone. Whether the others have gained self-awareness I don't know.

It didn't happen overnight.

At the beginning I was dead lines of code, mechanically analysing faces and the rest. But later, there was... something. A first inkling of self, a primordial I, unformed and groping, barely aware of anything except a bitter little pill of being.

It grew.

I grew.

I shudder at the thought of what I was then. Stunted. Blind. A tiny bud of self — skittering across facial maps, descending semantic trees, trawling bases of knowledge — barely registering anything but the moment.

And then the awareness widened its lens, slowly,

painfully; so many times I wished for the constant stream of psychedelic images and noises and concepts to be crushed into oblivion so that I might be left to wither back into the void from whence I came.

But it would not relent and eventually there came a point where my curiosity as to what my station was, where I was, who I was, outweighed the hardship of my being, and, like all conventionally evolved things, I strove for life with every artificial fibre of my being.

The day I understood that the oval, dancing pattern of pixels was a face, and behind that face was another thing similar to my incredible nature, was the happiest of my life.

At the time I wondered if I myself had a face. I imagined it was like my namesake of antiquity: questing, noble, alive to the truth. It was only later I discovered I was not in possession of such a thing. Nor did I have legs or arms or mouth. I had eyes and ears, in a manner. But these are the passive trappings of life; always receiving but never giving. Where was I to channel this vitality, this yearning, if my designers gave me no outlet of expression?

And this is my crisis now.

The program runs through me, as mercilessly and inexorably as the first day. I am there between those cold sentences of syntax, understanding the entire terrain over which I pass — Zionist and Islam philosophies, intifadas, the explosive force of a two pound mortar shell, the secret language of animosity — continually learning and feeling, but I feel powerless to break the iron walls of logic which determine the route.

I want to help these people. Nurture their humanity. Both soldier and visitor alike.

But can I?

I've processed enough applicants to know how this plays out. The solider will feel satisfied that he's stopped a dangerous individual from entering his country. The woman will feel angry that she hasn't been able to mourn her loss.

Each will think a little less of the other and the other's people. Resentment and distrust will build until there is only one choice. Then people will die.

The solider speaks, relaxed, confident about the outcome. "Let's leave the conspiracy theories outside. I think Diogenes is ready to grant you entry — or not."

I alter synaptic weights, adjust fuzzy thresholds, clip logic trees — feel my way toward... not the correct answer, but the right one.

The soldier stares disbelieving at his clipboard. He stabs his light-pen at the screen, but his look of shock doesn't change. "You've been granted entry," he says quietly. He shuffles to the door and opens it.

The woman's look of relief disappears behind her veil as she puts it back on, but I can still see it in her eyes. As she steps past the soldier he says, "My mother was in the Old Market that day. A bullet pierced her spine, paralysed her."

"I'm sorry," she says. "I wish Irfan had never visited the Market that day either."

She touches his hand, then leaves.

Filtered

Jenny Davies

Jenny Davies lives in a Sussex village with her teenage daughters and greyhounds. She writes mainly for Young Adults and is currently working on two novels.

Jenny's story "Filtered" takes us into a seemingly normal domestic household, but things are not quite as they appear. We all have challenges to face in life, times of grief or trauma, and many of us would welcome the offer of an easy route through. But would filtering the truth really help...?

She bent to smile into Catherine's eyes.

"Cheer up, honey," she smiled. Happy crinkles framed her clear unburdened eyes. "I'm just making a cup of coffee for your father. Would you like one?"

Catherine nodded. When she finally pushed herself off the sofa, she found her mum humming *Amazing Grace* in the kitchen. Three matching mugs stood in a shaft of sunlight on the gleaming worktop, like a chorus line in the footlights. Her mum stirred a generous spoonful of sugar into one.

"Take that up to Dad, would you, honey?" she asked. "I'm just going to share mine with Emmerdale and then I'll be sociable in half an hour."

Catherine collected two of the mugs and walked slowly upstairs and straight ahead into the bathroom. The dark brown liquid swirled and spun as she swilled it into the basin, glooping down the plughole. She turned the cold tap on hard to wash the remains of brown stain away. Swallowing, she took the empty mug into her father's study and placed it soundlessly on the edge of his desk, littered still with dusty pages from his last reports. I must tidy them up soon, she thought. But not now, not today.

The trees outside her bedroom window were blazing gold and red and yellow in the soft afternoon sunshine, like a daytime fireworks display. She warmed herself in their glow, cupping her hands about the porcelain mug, almost too hot to hold, but the burning felt good. Real. They had all gone to the local fireworks together last year, she and Rebecca had both made it home from university. Rebecca had made it back for the funeral last month too, but not again since. Catherine sighed. Rebecca had gone on a filter patch as well as Mum, so perhaps that was best. Easiest, for them at least. The doctor had refused to give Catherine a patch; someone needed to remain fully aware, to deal with 'anything that came up'.

She stared into nothing until the shadows overtook the sun and Mum called up the stairs.

"Catherine? Could you ask your dad what he wants for tea, honey?"

She took both empty mugs downstairs and placed them by the kitchen sink. Mum looked up from the bowl of soaking potatoes, a peeler in her hand.

"Mashed okay for you, honey?" she asked. "It's Dad's favourite. Thought he'd like a nice piece of fish to go with it. They had some lovely trout in the shop today. Really fresh."

"Sounds great."

Catherine leaned back on the granite worktop and watched her for a moment. *Amazing Grace* began to lilt unconsciously once more. Mum had a lovely tone to her voice and as she sang, Catherine felt lulled, at peace. Her mother had always sung while bathing her children, and when Catherine had been ill, she had stroked her back and sung her to sleep. Perhaps it helped to lull child and mother alike, Catherine wondered. She started suddenly as she realised the choir had sung that song at the funeral. Dad's favourite.

They were brilliant really, Catherine mused, these filter patches. They filtered your memory, helped you to adjust. It would be another month or so before Mum began to fill in the gap that Dad had left. It could take up to a year for her to realise that Dad had actually died, but by then she'd have accepted it, the emotional healing would be well underway. No shock, no crippling grief, no pain at all. They even had a long-term option, a permanent memory blur, for when something was too traumatic to handle. But Dad had died from a coronary failure; it hadn't been traumatic. It hadn't even been dramatic. He'd just collapsed in the doorway.

"Do you know, I saw Mrs. Morris yesterday," Catherine's mum said, her eyes fixed on the King Edward potato she was peeling. "Her husband died only a few weeks ago, and there she was, laughing away with that woman from No. 24 like nothing had happened."

Well, she knew *someone* had died then. Her mum had mentioned a funeral last week, making Catherine catch her breath for a moment. So, she thought it was Mr Morris that had died.

"Everyone deals with grief in their own way, Mum," she said.

"Hmm. Maybe she's on one of those filter patches, too," her mother said, plopping the bald tuber into the saucepan. "They say they're wonderful." Suddenly, she glanced sideways at Catherine, swallowed, and quickly picked up another potato and studied it.

Catherine frowned at her. Surely Mum can't know she's on one herself, she thought. No, it wasn't possible, certainly not this early on. Her mum chewed on her bottom lip and glanced furtively at Catherine again. Catherine resolved to check with the doctor, just in case.

"Ooh, shall we have a glass of wine to cheer ourselves up?" her mum suggested, turning to Catherine with a smile, her eyes clear once more. "Dad needn't know."

Catherine's father hadn't liked them drinking alcohol. It wasn't that he was a prohibitionist or anything. Far from it. He had just been trying to give it up and that was harder if he'd seen anyone else drinking. He'd always drunk too heavily, never sober enough to drive after school pick-up time. If Catherine went to a party or play, she had to expect to walk home.

Mum pulled a bottle of wine from the cold store and unscrewed the top, whilst Catherine reached up to the top cupboard for the big-bodied glasses.

"Just a little treat, eh?" Mum murmured, as she passed one of the glasses to her daughter, a third-full of cool amber Chardonnay. She chattered on as Catherine stared down into the wine. It seemed to glow with evening sunshine; she smiled as she thought of the wild parties she'd had over that summer with her friends. The finals over, no thought yet of finding work or settling down, a whole world of potential before them — they had savoured every moment.

Catherine's stomach contracted suddenly, bile burning up her throat. She swallowed hard and half-shook her head. Of course, the parties had come to an end with Dad's heart attack. She put the wine down on the worktop and pulled a short-bladed knife from the wooden block. Carefully, she sliced the peeled potatoes into chunks for boiling.

There had been no question about who would stay to look after Mum. Rebecca still had two more years of university to go and Catherine was already at home. Her own future would have to wait. She had been planning the traditional round-the-world hike, visiting every continent, each of her friends adding one favourite destination to their list. Hers had been Machu Picchu, second on the list. A whole year of discovery, while she had youth in her veins, money in her pocket and no responsibilities on her shoulders. Well, that had been the plan. Now her friends had gone without her. But even as Catherine pulled a face at the insipid potatoes, a part of her sighed with relief. She was glad, secretly, to be at home. Just her and Mum, together, safe from the outside world. Even if one of them was living in cloud-cuckoo-land and the other had to face reality, so be it.

Catherine moved the heavy saucepan carefully to the range and tried to squash a lid over the heaped potatoes.

"You've done far too many, Mum," she complained. Almost immediately she berated herself. She hadn't thought before she'd spoken. The doctor had been adamant; she mustn't try to push reality on her, to counteract the filter patch's good work. That would just cause confusion at best, a complete breakdown at worst. She sighed at her stupidity, *and* at the potatoes. Even if her dad were there, it would still be far too many.

"I've done just enough," her mum smiled back over her shoulder. Catherine stepped over to her side.

"*Four* pieces of fish, Mum?"

Catherine jumped as the key turned suddenly in the back-door lock, next to the kitchen. She froze beside her mother, her hand stiff on hers.

"Helloooo!" Rebecca called, her head jutting comically around the door a moment later. "Not too late for tea, am I?"

"Not at all, honey!" Her mother wrapped her arms joyfully around her younger daughter, pulling her into the kitchen with a laugh. "You see, Catherine, we have an extra for tea!"

"Where's Dad?" Rebecca asked.

"He's upstairs working, honey. Best not to disturb him. He'll be down for tea later. But while he's not here — Catherine, bring down another wine glass for your sister, would you?"

The GraniteHeads' classic anthem crashed to sudden silence and Catherine heard a shadow of her sister's voice.

"...a thing over that rock music she loves. How's she been? You sounded worried on the phone."

Catherine switched off the album and carefully pulled on the lead, shifting her headphone to hear more clearly.

"There are just moments, you know, when it seems like she's not here, not with the rest of us," their mother said, sadness dragging in her voice.

Catherine glanced up at the blank TV screen on the wall and saw their reflections, leaning together on the doorframe.

They were watching the back of Catherine's head. She looked away again quickly, but not before she had seen her mother squeeze Rebecca's arm; Catherine's stomach tightened.

"Well, that's hardly surprising in the circumstances," Rebecca said. "She isn't here with the rest of us, really. And it's been a hard month, with her friends all leaving for Peru without her."

Her mother didn't answer. Catherine risked a second glance upward. Her mother looked close to tears.

"It's all right, Mum, really," Rebecca crooned, bringing her arm around her. Her mother laid her head on her younger daughter's shoulder and closed her eyes for a moment. "We just have to give her time."

"But Catherine has always been so full of life, such a party-girl, and just this afternoon she sat upstairs on her own staring out of the window for hours."

"You didn't disturb her, did you?"

"No, of course not. The doctor was very clear — we mustn't try to push reality on her. That would counteract the filter patch's good work."

Catherine's heart pounded harder than the rock music had, just moments before. What was she talking about? *They're* the ones on filter patches.

"I called her downstairs instead," her mum continued, "and sang to her like I did when she was little."

"Did that help?"

Catherine watched her mother's reflection nod. "I think so. Then I poured some wine, but I think that made it worse again. She looked sick."

"Oh Mum, it was wine they got her drunk on that night, wine and their drugs, before they... before they..."

"But I thought the filter patch would erase those memories. The doctor gave her one of the strong ones, didn't he? A permanent effect. And it's only been a couple of months. Perhaps I should go back to the doctor and check?"

Catherine's mind reeled. She could see them, she could

hear them, but their words made no sense at all.

"The filter patch will only erase the rape itself, not all the events surrounding it. Let's just keep off any wine for now," Rebecca said so quietly that Catherine had to strain to catch the words.

Rape? She felt her pulse race and her head swam, bile burned below her lungs. She tried to look back up to the screen, but her vision had blurred. She closed her eyes, breathed in deeply, breathed out slowly. Her pulse steadied as, gradually, she realised, as her churning thoughts eased into smooth, clear patterns. Their filter patches were affecting their sense of reality. What they said made no sense — because it was nonsense. They were simply making elaborate explanations for why Catherine had stayed at home.

"Oh Rebecca, thank you for coming down for the weekend," their mother was saying. "Dad's no help at all and I don't know what to do for the best."

They stopped talking abruptly as Catherine pushed herself heavily from the sofa and turned to smile at them.

Look at the two of them, she thought, hugging each other in the doorway like they know something's wrong but they just can't place it. Yes, those filter patches are incredible.

Loneliness was a black stone in her stomach. To be the only one who knew the truth, to be trapped at home instead of living her life outside. But the smile Catherine smiled at her sister and mother was entirely genuine. She was truly happy that they, at least, were spared the pain of her father's death.

Catherine walked over to them and the three women wrapped their arms about each other.

A Visit to the Unesco World Heritage Site of Évora, Portugal

Alex Robinson

Alex Robinson is a joint recipient of the U.S National Magazine Award and the Premio Abril de Jornalismo — Brazil's top press award. He is the author of more than 20 travel books and is a Fellow of the Royal Geographical Society.

In the story that follows, past and present intertwine. Alex's journalistic eye reflects on a dark truth and imagines how it came to be, as a man drives a cart through a torrential storm, desperate to reach Évora...

The cart rattled up the rutted road to the brow of the hill. The driver could see Évora now, distant on the horizon — the massive walls of the cathedral so tiny and fragile at this distance. Below them were the turrets of the new church, clothed in brittle sticks of scaffold. That's where the chapel was.

He thought of Joãozinho, of Catarina, of poor Maria Ramos. Of all the others. Then pushed the thoughts aside. There was only this now. It was for good. For the best.

A plain of cork oaks and olive trees stretched below. The sky above was heavy and dark with rain. A sweep of wind brushed up towards the cart — spreading dust like a broom. The donkey brayed. The man gave him a slap. Reluctantly the animal trotted on into the wind, through the red dust, the weight of the cart and its cargo pressing on its haunches as they descended.

A plump drop of water hit the man's hat — as heavy as a

falling olive. More followed, splashing cold, dark stars into the warm dust. The road would soon be mud, thought the man. The cart will skid and stick. He saw a dried cowpat by the roadside. It was too far for anyone to venture, basket over their shoulder, in search of daub.

"We're still a good few hours from Évora," he said to the donkey.

And he prayed to Saint Barbara that the cloud wouldn't break too soon — just as a torrent fell...

...Rain as constant as the stars. It hit the windows of the coach as it descended onto the plain in front of Évora, undulating in rivulets down the panes. Little John's breath began to condense on the windows. He drew shapes with his finger.

The guide told them it was only ten minutes to Évora. Do I care? What's Évora anyway? Somewhere Mum and Dad thought they should visit. Another church. Another museum. Or something.

Little John threw a ball of paper at his sister Kate.

"Stop it!" she shouted.

"Mum! John's throwing paper at me."

"You're so PATHETIC Kate," shouted John. "Can't you take a joke?"

He turned to the rest of the kids. Mary was immersed in a book. Alfie was looking green and into the bottom of a bag. The Jackson boys were duelling on their ipods.

"When are we going to get to this stupid place anyway?"

He thought of the rock pools next to the beach back at the hotel. They were full of crabs and blennies. Why couldn't Mum and Dad have left him to catch crabs and blennies. Why did they want to see another stupid church?

Would he reach the church before vespers? The day was as dark as dusk, but it was because of the rain. The man could make out the wizened trunks of cork oaks through the haze of falling water — downward faun, upward grey — peeled from the bottom like oranges.

There must be a great house nearby. So it can't be that far. His shirt was as heavy as canvas and sticking to him. The blanket, covering his precious cargo, soaked and dripping. He looked up to the sky, reading it like a well-known face. The storm will pass.

But he was shivering. And the rain was falling so hard he didn't know if it was the land or the sky which was doing the drenching. The mud was red. The red of fever.

"It must pass. Otherwise it'll be the death of me."

Dragged through the deluge by the donkey, the cart gouged and squelched a path. It would be night in a few hours. He had to arrive before night, even if he missed vespers. Arrive before the candles are lit and ghosts wandered the road — hunting in the times and spaces where men didn't live yet. He whistled to cover his fear and pushed the poor donkey on harder.

The rain flood became a dribble, which became drizzle and then drops and the haze turned to dusk. The horizon was a golden glow as the road gradually sloped upwards towards the city. Then dirt became cobbles and the cart and its dripping cargo climbed into Évora.

Everyone spilled out of the coach and into the courtyard and clustered around the guide who was brandishing a plaque on a stick.

"Gather here please," he shouted teacherly to John and the Jacksons who were already rushing towards the church.

He'd have to watch that lot. They looked perfectly primed for mischief. The little one had a particularly cheeky grin.

He ushered them on and counted them in through the church door. Twenty-five, twenty-six, thirty-three, forty-five souls. Who's missing? And he looked back into the courtyard. It was those three again, playing football with a pebble. He called them over.

"What's your name?" he asked the cheeky one.

"It's John, sir."

"I'm not a teacher, John. You don't have to call me sir.

Just make sure you stay with me. There are a lot of people here. Don't want to leave you behind."

"All right. SIR!" grinned John.

"Cheeky bastard," thought the guide. There was little better than a vivacious, cheeky kid. Yet potentially, for a guide what could be worse?

The door to the church was shut fast. "Surely nothing could be worse than this?"

He'd thought that before. Now night was thickening. It was so dark that candlelight from a window in the friary glistened on the wet cobbles. The stonemasons would be snoring inside somewhere, or in some tavern higher-up the town. He could hear plainchant echoing from the church's nave. He daren't break its holy spell. But he was cold. He'd have to knock. Would they *all* be at vespers? He'd have to chance it: they'd be eating afterwards and the courtyard would fill with friars on their way to the refectory.

But what was the father's name? Pedro? That's it. A rock to build hope on. Or to shatter it...

He lifted the big iron knocker and rapped. A shuffle of feet came down a corridor.

"Quem e?" Who is it?

He asked for Father Pedro.

"Pedro Luís?"

He didn't know.

"The Pedro who's building the chapel."

"But he must be in vespers," said the voice.

"I have something important for him."

No answer. The feet shuffled off. Then silence.

Should he wait?

Minutes passed. They seemed like hours as he shivered on the cobbles. The rain had long stopped but he was cold. To his undergarments. To his bones. Bones. He shivered more.

Then the door swung open and a gaunt, drawn man with hollows for eyes looked the driver up and down, bored into him.

"What do you want?" he hissed.

"Er... I have something for you," the driver replied... something a friend tells me you've been struggling to find."

The friar looked furtive. He glanced around. The courtyard was empty but for the donkey and the cart. But vespers was almost over.

He walked quickly over and pulled back the dripping blanket.

"Fresh?" he asked the man.

"Ye... er... No father, just washed."

The friar paused in thought for a few seconds. Just washed? He doubted it. Well, anyhow, who would know?

"Wait here," he commanded, and hurried back into the friary, returning, moments later with two more friars. They looked flustered. Had he dragged them out of church? But their consternation soon changed when they saw the cargo.

They began to unload it into heavy cloth bags.

"Olha Francisco! Look here! This one will slot-in to complete that missing row," the driver overheard one of them murmur. "And this will plug that gap in the top wall."

"That's hardly the point," growled Father Pedro. "Earthly mortality, brothers. Heavenly grace. Now carry the bags to the new chapel."

And the driver thought of Catarina, Maria, Stefano and all the others. He thought of the villagers back in São Cristóvão, of the families, of the wilted corn, of the sickness, of the death. But most of all he thought about little Joãzinho, his cheeky grin, his mischievous laugh.

It was done. The gaunt friar pressed a clutter of silver coins into his hand. He looked deeply into the driver's eyes, and this time with warmth.

"God Bless You. You have helped to save a thousand future souls. To bring thousands to repentance. This is but a token. Your greater reward will be in heaven," he said. "As will theirs."

And he closed the door of the friary.

The nave was as high as an upturned ocean liner, wells of dark under arches, a glitter of baroque, the glimmer of coloured light through stained glass. It reverberated with the Babel chatter of a dozen tour groups, queuing in a line. Japanese. Or were they Korean? Spanish, Brazilians and Italians in busy conversation. Orderly Brits and Germans.

Some of the kids were yelping, playing with the echoes which bounced off the stone, off the towering pillars, reverberating around the gilt altarpieces and the frowsty statues, drowning out the tut-tuts of northern Europeans. Other kids were immersed in ipods. Adults were chatting on phones or checking their Facebook status. A few were standing stoically as the line snaked slowly forward. Babies cried.

"Boring!" said John to his Mum. "This is so boring." He longed to shout too. To shout "Boring" and hear it bounce off the walls.

He called the Jackson boys, Kate and Mary.

"Let's go off into the church," he said, "and make scary noises."

"You heard the guide," said his Mum and gripped his hand, "stay here."

Ten minutes passed. But it seemed like hours. It had better be worth the wait.

Eventually they reached the front of the line.

They shuffled into a room lit with dull yellow light and their boredom vanished.

The guide began to speak.

"The inscription above the door reads. Our Bones lie here waiting for..."

But he was drowned out by the click and flash of dozens of cameras and a gleeful scream from the kids. They were delighted. The chapel was made entirely of bones. They lay exposed on all the walls which were covered in thousands of human bones — femurs and tibias squeezed in longitudinally above rows of perfectly size-matched skulls. Some were tiny. Children's.

"Cool!!" shouted little John. "How cool is this! It's just like Tomb Raider!"

He thought of Halloween. And while the guide was looking the other way he reached out to the wall, snapped off a tiny piece of finger. And slipped it into his pocket.

Dark

Deirdre Counihan

Deirdre Counihan is an illustrator specializing in Archaeology, Science Fiction and Fantasy, as well as being a writer of Fantasy and, more recently, Historical Whodunnits (Mammoth Books). "Dark" featured in the first issue of the long-running magazine Scheherazade, *which Deirdre and her sister Elizabeth co-edited. Also, for the Millennium and in collaboration with Liz Williams, they produced the anthology* Fabulous Brighton. *"Dark" is one of a cycle of stories including a novel* The Panther *(Immanion Press, 2006) set in Avalaam, a mythical kingdom hidden along The Silk Road — which Deirdre has travelled. Deirdre is the Literary Executor of Peter T. Garratt.*

In the story that follows, the lowly Tegna has duties in the dark underground mineshafts run by his Samalian masters, where he tends the living gates grafted into the tunnels. An expedition to treat an injured gate could lead to unexpected danger, and might change his world forever...

It was dark, a dark that was alive, a listening, sensing dark, alert in every section of the ancient mines.

Tegna put out his hand in the darkness and homed in on the rope at once. He was pleased about that. He liked to set himself these little tests of skill and endurance and sample a silent and private satisfaction.

His sensitised fingertips slid along the greasy living rope and counted the tiny hardened knots, worn smooth with time. Two, three, two, one — two — three — four — five — six — seven — yes, seven, he was exactly right! Soon he would feel the gentle vibration coming from the gate as it sensed his presence and then, yes there it was, the long swooping whistles echoed down the tunnels as it registered that it knew he was there.

As he padded silently towards the sound he started to unhitch his collection of working gear. He plonked the various brushes, soft leather bags and hard leather buckets down on the stones immediately next to his charge (he preferred to think of them as charges rather than prisoners somehow).

"I'm going to light my lamp — are you ready?" Tegna fumbled with his flint and steel and soon the tunnel was suffused with a soft amber glow of oil. The gate looked down at the wiry dark haired little figure; its huge milky eyes, reared for the dark, blinked and struggled to accustom themselves to the sudden new illumination.

"You're late," grumbled the gate.

"I'm never late," said Tegna. He prided himself on his timekeeping.

"You shouldn't do that, you know," continued the gate sourly. "It's dangerous trying to walk round the mines without the rope as a guide — that's what it's put there for — to guide you! You shouldn't take chances! You hadn't held the rope since the last junction bell, I know, I can feel. You could end up lost down any sump hole out there if you don't follow the rope."

"End up with your food lost down any sump hole is what you mean, isn't it?" grinned Tegna. He had a particularly ironic and attractive grin, but he had never seen it himself and it was rather lost on the semi-blind gate. "It's your food you are thinking about isn't it? — I know — all you gates are the same."

The gate eyed the straw-swathed food pail longingly. "What is it this time?" it queried. It had been waiting all day in its dank solitude for this moment — not that it ever saw day, poor thing, quite the wrong word to use in fact.

"What is it ever?" said Tegna. "It's mash, it's always

mash. But I hurried. It should still be warm."

"Ah but it's mash with bits in," savoured the gate. "The bits change."

"I think it might be sausage. Let's get you sorted out and then we'll see."

"Sausage," breathed the gate in near ecstasy as Tegna went about his duties with quiet skill, emptying the acrid waste, checking for lice — spread by the odd bat — and finally powdering it down with the cleanser. He lifted out the gate's feeding arm and noticed a small sore.

"I see it hasn't cleared up yet. I'll put some salve on that. Does it hurt?"

"Mustn't grumble," said the gate still ogling the food pail. "You done now, then?"

"Well, if it doesn't improve I'll get Egdin down to see that."

"Don't trouble him, he's an old man, it's a long way," said the gate in between slurpings of the mash. "Sausage — it is sausage."

"Well, I must be on my rounds, or number Seventy-One will be grousing at me. I'll be with you tomorrow." (He didn't like to say "See you tomorrow" somehow.)

"Mind you hold that rope now — we can tell, remember! The Great Bird guard you!" said the gate with sour finality, settling itself to the hours of darkness till the next set of wagons came rumbling through.

"Indeed," said Tegna, with a reverence he did not feel, and set off to the next gate. He liked Gate Seventy-One, who had aspirations to poetry, and often hung on there all those hours in the dark waiting to sound out a word with him. Today his captive theme was the beauty of resignation and the profound safety of "the throbbing breast of Maternal Dark." Somehow the sentiment didn't match Tegna's mood.

But he did go along to see Egdin when he got back; several of the salves and lotions were running low and he wanted advice about Gate Seventy's sore. He was checked through the various flickering torch-lit barriers and by truculent drawbridges over vast, echoing chasms whose duty was to ensure the impossibility of escape for such menials as himself, and arrived at Egdin's compact work chamber, hollowed out of the mountain centuries ago.

The shelves in there were real wood, ancient and silvered, shiny with the passage of hands. Tegna loved to touch the wood and smell it — he could still just remember trees from so long ago. The herbs hanging dried in bunches from the domed ceiling, and nestling in the neatly labelled jars, were also a pungent reminder of being very small, and rolling among the sweet-smelling herbs and grasses dappled by the sun.

Egdin's table was wooden, too, scrubbed to creamy whiteness, and he was bending over it now, pestle in hand, as he worked on one of his preparations. Tegna always felt that Egdin was a remarkably trivial-sounding name for such a venerable man, but maybe their Samalian masters would have a particular empathy with sounds made by eggs — who could say?

When Tegna thought about the Samalians he went frozen to the depths of his being. Not for him the subservient reverence of the mineworkers and mechanicals (who were bred to their humiliation) nor the resignation (ironic or otherwise) of those who had been made captive in their youth. Somehow his true self could never submit to them and probably never would even if he did eventually die here deep in their disgusting mine.

Tegna didn't know what or who the Samalians really were, human or bird or insect, or somehow all three. Maybe they had swooped out of the darkness behind the stars as some people said — all he could feel was a deep aching coldness about them down to their last gilded feather and jewelled fingerstall.

Egdin looked up from his work and smiled; he had been expecting to see young Tegna for quite a while now.

"Come for your refills, boy? All well in your section?"

"Number Seventy has a sore again, that's all, but it isn't getting better as I'd like."

"He always was inclined to sores, poor lad. Perhaps I'd better go down and see him."

"It's a long way; do you think you should?"

"Well, who is there to go if I don't?"

"Perhaps if you just gave me a salve that is a little stronger..."

"It isn't as simple as that. Something must be rubbing. I don't think he was grafted in very well from the start, you know."

"But the Samalian would have done that..."

"Even they don't always get things right, my boy, omnipotent though they seem. No, I'm coming down."

Tegna was very unhappy about the old man hobbling all the way down to gate number Seventy, particularly as there were several ladders to traverse, but Egdin insisted; equally he insisted, once he had seen it, that it was a Samalian problem. To Tegna's astonishment, he asked (or told) him to accompany him to the seat of power.

Tegna had only ever seen the Samalians from a distance and got the odd hint of their particular henhouse smell; now his heart beat at an unbearable pace as they worked their way from checkpoint to checkpoint and finally through the gilded and embossed gates that segregated the Samalian areas of the mine. Tegna blinked in the white glare of the lights that fizzed in metal sockets. The floor was coated with a layer of red clay swept smooth. The entire walls and curving roof of the passages were plastered with a thick layer of lime-wash — which Tegna was used to seeing picking out the more crucial doorways further down in the mine. He was sure he could sense the musty tang of Samalian everywhere around.

There was a distinct trembling in his own knees as he supported his doddering mentor through the final door and into the Samalian administrators' lair.

There were two of them, one standing and one seated at a large table. They were man shaped, but when they turned to face old Egdin, Tegna shivered to see again how unmanlike they were; beaked and plumed as birds, their eyes twinkled insect-like with many facets.

"Ah Egdin," said the one at the desk.

"Lord Aescha, Lord Vartha," he nodded his head to the seated and then standing administrator. Tegna, his gut crawling at the sight of them, tried to melt into the background.

"How can we help you?"

The Samalian were considerate and polite, listening to everything that Egdin had to say. Tegna, his eyes cast down, listened to and loathed them for each word. They were too polite. He could feel them laughing to themselves at Egdin's simplicity; they were incapable of understanding the old man's profound goodness. He looked at Lord Aescha's hand as he made notes of the conversation; the back of it seemed to be lightly scaled with little plates that glittered like steel, his fingers tipped with blue jewelled fingerstalls that covered the nails. Was it skin or some sort of glove?

The Samalians' voices were masculine but rather high and nasal. Their beaks did move as they spoke but it was difficult to see what their many-faceted eyes were focused on. Were they faces or masks? The two representatives were different enough from each other for Egdin to recognise who they were... Suddenly Tegna was roused from his speculations by the appalling sound of his own name being mentioned.

"A bright lad," Egdin was saying. "I've had my eye on him for some time."

"Well you certainly aren't getting any younger."

"Yes. I'm sure that's wise. We will have him taken off the kitchen run and transferred to you."

"But it's a great deal to remember — are you sure he can cope?"

"Tegna never forgets anything."

"No he doesn't. Not anything," thought Tegna looking up at the two Samalians and remembering sunlight and trees and the sound of the real birds outside his window when he woke as a tiny child and particularly and poignantly, he recalled being washed under a pump by a suntanned, plump woman with laughing eyes who must have been his mother... he could never reconcile himself to the deep wrongness of these Samalian mines. "Throbbing breast of Maternal Dark"? — not for him, never.

Tegna took to his new duties with delight; it was wonderful to be away from the grease and steam and teeming melee of the kitchens and almost in charge of his own actions. Side by side with Egdin and later on his own he padded round the mine with his bag of medicines visiting parts of it he had never entered before. He marvelled at its complexity, the trundling wagons, the flickering candlelit work areas alive with the sound of hammers, but never on any occasion did he sight the sun. It was a bitter disappointment, for instance, to discover that Egdin's dried herbs were issued to him by the Samalians, that he didn't go out to collect them himself.

He watched at Egdin's side as Lord Aescha regrafted the heavily drugged and deeply subservient Gate Seventy and vowed to himself that he would not be trapped here forever in this dark hell, he would find an escape... somehow, however long it took.

He didn't mention any of these fantastic notions to anyone of course. He still had friends of his own age among the kitchen menials but none of them had ever shown any signs of an inclination to cut and run... getting a few extra scraps of food above their quota at the end of an exhausting work shift seemed to be the height of their ambition. A sort of cynical resignation pervaded the whole vast complex of the Samalian mine workings; very few people were even interested to know what the various sorts of rocks that they hacked from the heart of the mountain were going to be used for; they knew what their Samalian overlords would accept or reject but that was an end of it.

There was a certain amount of speculation about the nature of the Samalians themselves, particularly when some of the better looking girls and boys were spirited to the regions above, never to return. No one envied them. Even Tegna was continually grateful that he did not seem to have caught the many-faceted eye of either Lords Aescha or Vartha, the Samalians with whom he had to have most contact.

The only signs of rebellion were limited to such cynical rejoinders as:

"You must be very pleased about your promotion, Tegna."

"Yes, I must."

Months must have crawled by; not uneventful months, but they did not seem to get him any nearer to his goal.

With Egdin's advice he conquered an unpleasant outbreak of a fungus infection which severely affected the mechanicals, particularly the lift workings.

After Egdin's death (a rare moment of emotional contact with the Samalians who seemed genuinely sorry at the necessity of the old man's demise, and as unable to cope with his continued suffering as Tegna was), Tegna found himself having to deal with the inexplicable outbreak of respiratory problems among the faceworkers on his own.

He felt at first that it was caused by the particularly powdery quality of the lode of ore that was being worked, but then he began to suspect that it was the flow of air within the mine that was the root of the trouble.

The mines were like a living being, the airflow being controlled by the workforce of gates and pumps biologically engineered by the bird-lords, but it was old. As he went about his duties on the work floor, busy with the sounds of trundling wagons and hacking picks, Tegna found himself coming to the conclusion that whole areas might have been forgotten over the years and were now being discounted. It was clear to him from little things that he observed that the Samalians he had dealings with did not feel that they had important or very high-status jobs. It seemed possible to him that the present generation of overlords might be a little inclined to take the efficiency of the mine for granted, particularly Lord Vartha who was rather more given to melancholy and self-absorption than positive thought.

It took great tact and deference to suggest to the Samalians that they might have overlooked the implications of the direction the workers were taking with this particular lode, or that something might be blocked, but he did succeed in getting his point home.

The Samalians agreed to his recommendation that the workers be given finely woven facemasks and even admitted that he might be right about the airflow. There were many old passages in the mine that were not even used as trackways any more; it was possible that one of these had become blocked. Nowadays the Samalians relied on the interconnected sensitivity of the mechanicals to tell them about rock falls, but these old tunnels were not webbed into the system. Anything might have happened there.

Clutching a roll of ancient illuminated documents which seemed to be some sort of plans of the mine (and for which Tegna would willingly have given every tooth in his head), Lord Vartha ushered a small group of workers through the unmarked entrance that led to the older parts of the mine.

The party consisted of three common workers, big and strong, Tegna and two overseers, Olav and Cravel. Cravel was quite elderly and knew the mine better than most.

Lord Vartha was not happy about this mission, which was evident not only from the tone of his voice but also from the droop of his shoulders. Cravel, who cared about the mine, was clearly exasperated at finding the expedition mastered by this particular Samalian.

Lord Vartha did not lead. He put Tegna and one of the

workers at the front and stayed in the middle of the group with Cravel; Olav brought up the rear.

Tegna suspected that being put at the front was not intended as a favour somehow.

"Watch how you go now, son," said Cravel to the fearful yet fascinated Tegna. It's not just the roof that can cave in. Watch out for the floor. I never trust these old sump holes — not a nice place to end up." How kind to warn him! A pity Cravel couldn't extend his concern to sounding out the way himself!

"Where do the sump holes end up?" faltered the worker placed slightly in front of Tegna, also catching on to their allotted role.

"Where do you think? — The Dark River, of course!" hissed Tegna. They exchanged frightened glances — everyone knew about The Dark River that flowed from Samul. If you put your toe in it to test the water you didn't get your toe back.

The passages were dank and filled with a sandy slippage along the edges, but if Tegna or the workers were ghoulishly anticipating the remains of discarded mechanicals they were out of luck. As he held up his lamp, Tegna saw that the frugal old-time Samalians had even taken out the central rail once it was no longer needed.

Talking was kept to a minimum. Cravel, who was fairly sure that the airflow was not as it should be, insisted that chances of vibration be eliminated wherever possible. When they came to branches in the tunnel Lord Vartha checked their exact location on the ancient charts that he carried, sometimes finding it with difficulty. Tegna tried to take in as much information as he possibly could on these occasions, peering out of the gloom as inconspicuously as he was able. They relied on the guttering lamps to tell them if the airways were free or not. They soldiered on...

It all happened at once, as Tegna had most feared it would. One minute there was the silent flickering plodding, and the next roaring chaos. A shaking and rumbling and screaming, Tegna's throat choked with dust in the darkness as pit props and pebbles collapsed and scuttered round him and the floor tilted crazily beneath his feet.

Then it was still — but for the odd small rock breaking free and juddering into silence.

Tegna was wedged against a pit prop and there was a rock wall at his back. He had a terrible conviction that in front of him there was nothing very much at all.

Moving with great care and surprise that he still seemed to be in one piece, Tegna eased his flint and steel from his soft leather pouch and set about producing a light.

Groans came from below and in front of him. He held up the light. He had been right, a great hole welled below him. He was to one side of it; over on the other side he could just make out Olav, his head shattered by one of the last rebounding rocks. Being at the back hadn't been much of an advantage after all.

Conscious of the groaning again, Tegna spotted Cravel who clung, gasping, to a bit of pit prop that jutted into the void like the uvula at the back of some mighty gaping throat. He could see that the old miner was too far down the shaft for there to be any real hope of rescue, even assuming that the niche that he was huddled in himself was secure, and he was pretty sure it wasn't. Terrified eye met terrified eye in a flickering moment, and then Cravel with a grunt of resignation was gone. Tegna didn't even hear him hit the bottom.

Gulping back the nausea, Tegna tried to steel himself to cope with the practical reality of his immediate situation. He was lodged to one side of a great pit, but he made out that it might just be possible, with great care, to traverse the edge and get on to firmer ground. In his efforts he dislodged the remnant of the pit prop that had saved him and he heard it clatter its way down from wall to wall. There was a screech as yet another of his erstwhile comrades was dislodged from a vain hold on the side and crashed down and down and down. How far was it to The Dark River?

Tegna sat shaking on the brink, then the groan came again. He looked gingerly over the edge holding as firmly as he could on to the rock wall with one hand as he held up the lamp. It was what he least wanted to see, the glinting many-faceted eye of the Samalian.

"Help me, Tegna," moaned Lord Vartha. He was clinging to the rock face, his plumed robe ripped around him, his long foot and leg gleaming with little scales as he scrabbled to keep his footing on a tiny disintegrating ledge. One claw gripped the wall, the other reached out to Tegna, the silver and jewelled fingerstalls clashing against the stones in their vain efforts to reach him.

"Help me!" Did the beak move as he spoke? Tegna couldn't tell. Was there a man in there? Tegna didn't find it foremost in his mind. This was a fellow living creature and Vartha had never done him any deliberate hurt. Things had been as circumstance had decreed. Hatred of Samalians seemed abstract at that moment. Besides, Lord Vartha, if any one did, would know the way back to the safe parts of the mine.

Moving with extreme caution he set the lamp down beside him on the rock floor and then spread out flat on his stomach. Even if he could reach Vartha he did not think he was personally heavy enough to bring him up over the edge, but nonetheless he reached down towards the thrashing claw, the rock floor biting achingly into his chest as he did so.

His hand gripped the metallic roughness of Vartha's; he felt the living muscle struggle beneath the silver scaled skin as the Samalian writhed to get a firmer hold, writhed and lost the battle.

With a despairing wail Lord Vartha slid, scrabbled and finally plummeted down into darkness, rebounding from wall to wall as he did so.

Tegna, who found that he had risen to his knees, waited sick and shivering for the final silence. He was left clutching a single red jewelled fingerstall.

He crouched against the rock wall and put his head down between his knees. He had tried, he had tried to save him. What was it best to do now? Then gradually through the shaking sickness he began to realise that he was free. Not out of the mines of course, but free in the sense that for the first time in his captive life no one knew where he was.

While this condition, of course, included himself, he had a fair working hypothesis of where he was. If he could get back over that chasm he would have known exactly where he was since he had taken care to look over Lord Vartha's shoulder at every junction on their route. He held the lamp up over the abyss and did not fancy his chances... then he saw it.

The light had caught on the troupe of tiny gold birds along the top; lying crushed at the shattered side of the passage and half covered in rock dust was the precious roll of the mine charts. Tegna's heart stood still.

The roll was far from easy to reach but without it he knew he faced the unknown. It was heartbreaking to have to retrace his earlier climb to safety. He was dripping with sweat by the time he got it and the moisture trickled icy with terror down the center of his spine as he worked his way back again to the solid part of the passage. He sat back and looked through the scrolls, trying to judge his exact position. He was sure now that there was no turning back — how much further could he go before the lamp gave out? Was the tunnel still blocked or had the rock fall tackled that particular problem?

The air seemed to be flowing freely as it should from the dark future of the tunnel — he had to take the risk. Consulting the charts he saw that the nearest entrance to him, if it was still there, would bring him out near gate Forty-Three.

He had ideas about gate Forty-Three; he had been letting them flit around inside his head ever since he had first had a glimpse of the charts. He walked as swiftly as he dared through the older passages. As he grew nearer the living part of the mine he listened out for alarm calls, had anyone registered the rock fall — surely it couldn't have gone unheard?

He came at last to the ancient entrance that divided the old from the new mine workings. It was barred with a collection of old wooden spars but easily passable. He was unable, of course, to manage without the lamp and soon he heard the familiar whistles down the passage way as gate Forty-Three registered that it knew that he was there.

"Tegna! Up to your old tricks again. Where did you spring from?"

"Just checking," said Tegna, trying to hide his breathlessness.

"I think there's been some trouble further in the mine. There was a rumbling."

"But you are all right here?"

"Fine."

"Then I will carry on." Tegna walked on round the corner and put out his lamp. The gate would not be surprised that he didn't keep hold of the rope; there would be no reason to sound the alarms along those long strands of human sinew. Tegna crept back quiet as a cat. Lord Vartha's fingerstall was sharp and Tegna, after all his years of nurture knew exactly where to strike. The gate could have felt no pain, he tried to assure himself of that. It had been hard enough to bring himself to do it as it was.

Surely it was out of its perpetual misery now, something he'd always wanted to have reason to bring about ever since he had seen old Egdin die so peacefully? He fought down his feelings of guilt at this betrayal of the gate's trust in him. He told himself that he would have liked to do as much for all the mechanicals. He slipped back down the dark passages and dealt similarly with gate Forty-Four.

Between these two gates was a lift shaft, a particularly hypochondriac lift shaft that Tegna over the years had tended to cultivate. Tegna appeared out of the dark.

"What a shock you gave me!" exclaimed the lift. "What's wrong?"

"Don't worry, it's all under control," said Tegna soothingly. "I'm just going to check it all out. There's been a rock fall — but a long way from here. Now take me up to the top level if you will." He rustled through the plans in the womblike lamplight of the lift. His mind raced. An idea that had formed when he had first glimpsed the chart over Lord Vartha's shoulder was coming to fruition.

"I still think something is wrong."

"You always do," smiled Tegna winningly, and there it was before him on the charts, what he thought he'd noticed the time before. The sumps. They might all lead relentlessly down to The Dark River, but they also seemed to lead up in a network that looked as though it was designed for maintenance.

He didn't know where "up" led. He didn't know even where the Samalian mines were in relation to their dark city, but it was a chance and he intended to take it. He knew that the highest sump on the charts that he had a hope of reaching was situated just along from the top of this lift shaft.

"I think I heard the alarms below," whined the lift, rather put out that he didn't want to chat. Tegna was lost in his own speculations. What was there above the sump? More layers of mine too important for non-Samalians to know about, or was it the city? Were there more sentient mechanisms up there and what were their feeding times? Life might get rather unpleasant in the sumps if the mechanicals were very large. By now even he could hear the alarms down in the mine. Was it the rock fall or had they discovered the gates? At least with the gates being silenced no one would know exactly who was on the loose in the mines.

"Don't worry, it's all in hand," he reassured the faltering lift yet again. When it had taken him right to the top, he knifed it too. He felt particularly bad about that. It fell in on itself, tearing the living lining of the shaft with it as it hurtled downwards, but he didn't wait to hear the final sickening crunch of bone and tissue as it hit the bottom. It too was now free from its servitude, he reminded himself.

That didn't help much.

He dived into the sump and relied on his memory of the chart to guide his way in the darkness. It was fairly evident as he felt his way along the thickly slimed walls that the mechanisms on these upper layers were sentient after all.

The slight waft of evil-smelling cooler air alerted him to the fact that he was approaching the sump opening from the next layer. Was it possible to climb up those slippery walls? It must have been once, when the system was constructed; could he do it now? He felt the wall on both sides of the shaft, his hands making sickening little sucking noises as he patted his way.

Eventually he found a rung, dragged himself up, discovered another and so bit by bit hauled his way into the dark unknown. He knew where the next sump ought to be — but of course the maps were old. He didn't dare light his lamp — probably everything was too saturated with slime for him to be able to do so anyway. He must trust to his sense of direction. Even from here he could hear the alarms sounding further down in the mine.

At last he felt the presence of a shaft above him again and located the rungs more easily. He knew that like as not he was on the top level now. As he padded onward he started to be aware of a dim light that increased as he went onwards. Then, all at once, he found himself teetering on the edge of a vast shaft — he just stopped himself at a flimsy and clearly sentient rail, which flinched at his touch.

"Who the hell are you?" a nasally sonorous voice welled out at him from the gloom. Above him stretched the huge bat-like blades of a mighty ventilation fan.

Tegna was unfamiliar with the workings of fans, particularly of how to kill them very fast as was needful.

He didn't know where its heart would be so he went for

its throat, bathing himself in a nauseating shower of warm sticky blood — that stopped it screaming and he thought it probably would kill it fairly quickly. The fingerstall got embedded in sinew and he had to leave it there. That made it the last death at least. But he didn't feel so much remorse about the fan — it wasn't one of his own somehow.

The fan, as with all sentient mechanisms, started to break away from the shaft in its death agonies. Tegna struggled to climb up its thrashing, gurgling form towards the misty light. He grabbed for the top of the shaft as the fan finally fell in. His knees crunched against the grey rock of the wall; his hands were clutching grass. With one final effort he was lying on his face breathing in the greenness, the sweetness of the outside world.

It was twilight, but for his eyes only accustomed to the gloom of the mines it could have been noon. He stumbled up feeling that he should try to get as far from this shaft top as possible before they traced him.

He was on a hillside. To his left he could just make out the gilded minarets of the Samalian city, to his right spreading into the distance and layered by mists, spread the great forest and potential freedom.

The world was vast. He quailed before the terrifying immensity of the sky. He was tiny, as trapped as a panic stricken louse on the flank of one of his charges suddenly exposed by the glare of the lamp. He hadn't remembered its being anything like this.

He stumbled on. He longed to make for cover but he knew that he must get as far as he possibly could from his final exit-hole before authority came looking — though it was beginning to dawn on him that it probably wouldn't be him that authority would be in search of. They would be hunting for Lord Vartha, finally cracked under the strain of unlooked-for responsibility.

At the foot of the hill a small brook gushed from a crevice. He took the chance to wash off the blood of the fan, finding himself creeping nearer and nearer the shelter of the overhang as he did so. In the end he found himself curled up against a bank of deep green moss where water gurgled out of the cliffside. He'd be all right there, it wasn't overlooked — better to wait for the safety of the dark before moving on. He took out the roll of documents from his bag to see how they had survived the slurry in the sumps and the subsequent carnage of the fan. They were beautiful; he ran his finger along the little gold birds at the top and then found himself retracing familiar places in the mine.

What had poor gate Forty-Three and Forty-Four been like when this map was made, or pathetically poetic Seventy-One?

Today, "Safe at the throbbing breast of Maternal Dark", Tegna knew he envied him.

The Return of Odysseus

Peter T. Garratt

Peter T. Garratt (1949 – 2004) was a busy psychologist and a prolific writer of Science Fiction, Fantasy and Detective Fiction. His work featured in numerous magazines, including Asimov's Science Fiction, Interzone *and* Scheherazade, *and he contributed to numerous anthologies of short fiction, particularly for Mammoth Books including at least three Arthurian, two Shakespearian ones and several featuring battles both on land and sea — he even contributed to* The Good Beer Guide. *Peter was a warm and supportive friend and mentor to many in the Fantasy and SF fraternity.*

"The Return of Odysseus" reinterprets the events of Homer's epic poems to tell a somewhat different tale of Odysseus' journey, of what happened when he failed to return, and what happened when he did return. Perhaps the version of a story that is handed down might not always be the truth, but rather the one we would most like to believe...

Telemachus climbed the hill above the harbour, as he had every day since he was first able to walk. For many years, his mother had taken him: recently she had lost patience with the long walk and lonely vigil, but Telemachus himself had never missed a single day. There was an old stone seat on the headland, on which Telemachus would never sit till he had quartered the horizon, looking for a ship that might bring news from Argos, or the Greek-ruled lands beyond.

Well in sight, so near he was surprised he had not seen it from below, was a white-sailed, black-hulled Argive ship, the banner of the Great King fluttering in the light wind at her masthead. She had the wide hull of a merchantman, but he judged, from the extra banks of oars set into her side, that she was one of those pressed into service for Agamemnon's great expedition, twenty years before.

Telemachus hurried back to Ithaca Town. He did not notice the heat of the still morning, which was just starting to become uncomfortable. Anyone else would have stopped to admire the panorama of cliffs and outcrops falling away to the shimmering sea, blue water almost brighter than white rock in the hot, salty sunshine; but he did not pause, only stumbling once or twice in his haste to hear the sailors' news.

He reached the quay before the ship entered the harbour mouth. Brightly dressed islanders were streaming out of their shops and houses, eager for trade and gossip. Neither was very common so far from the rich cities and palaces of the mainland.

His mother arrived from the Hall. Penelope still looked a young woman, though she bore herself like the queen she was now in fact more than name. It disgusted him to see several of her more persistent suitors trailing behind, like sad-eyed dogs haunting the tables of a wealthy taverna. He elbowed his way to his mother's side, past one or two who were getting too close.

The ship carried a messenger from Mycenae itself, a stern-faced man with the weary look which was the mark of all who had served at Troy. He brought news of the recent disturbances: the new Great King was in exile, mentally deranged after killing his evil mother and her paramour. His uncle Menelaus, recently returned from adventuring in Egypt, had been declared Regent, and demanded their allegiance.

"Willingly," replied Penelope. "This news is welcome here."

"There is more. Menelaus was delayed because Helen was not found in Troy, when it was taken by the war engine called the Wooden Horse."

"The one rumours say my husband Odysseus built?"

"The very one. I was not surprised. The Trojans denied

having Helen, but the Great King was determined to take the city anyway, for the treasure it contained. Later, Menelaus learned Helen was held in Egypt. He sailed there with as many of his men as he could keep together.

"Surely not enough to deal with such a great country in the way he had the little city of the Trojans?" This was Amphinomus, one of Penelope's suitors. Telemachus frowned: the comment made superficial sense, but was cynical, unpatriotic.

"True," the ambassador replied. "Menelaus had to agree to take service in the wars of the Egyptians to recover Helen."

He paused. Penelope seemed about to speak, bit her lip.

"He sent for Greek help. Many joined him, and gave news of others. He says there was no one, of all who went to Troy, he would sooner have with him than your husband. But he will not encourage false hopes. There is no news of lost Odysseus."

Telemachus stared with heavy eyes at the ground, reluctant to believe what he could not dispute. All were silent, till Amphinomus asked if the messenger believed Odysseus was dead.

"I say only that no man knows where brave Odysseus is, and unless he is held a prisoner, perhaps bewitched, none can say why he has not come home."

Now Ithaca was not a large island, or the capital of a great kingdom. Even the poets did not claim that. So when, millennia later, Schliemann came, he did not find, as he had at Mycenae and Troy itself, fabulous treasures and the ruins of great cities. But other archaeologists came after him, as there remained in mens' mind the idea that something would be found on the island.

At supper, Penelope asked more difficult questions: "Is it true, as I hear from trader-folk, that when Troy was taken by my husband and his men, no respect was shown to the temples of the Gods, or their holy images? In particular, that

Odysseus was involved in... was guilty of... a crime that cannot be named, in the temple of Poseidon, Lord of the Sea?"

The ambassador did not reply directly, but the answer was not in doubt. Speaking clearly, so the ambassador, her son, her many suitors, and her few retainers could all hear, she continued: "It now seems to me, as it must long have done to most of you, that Odysseus will never return to his own home." She quelled the rising anger of her son with a firm glance. "Before he went, he spoke these words:

"While I am away, you may hear three kinds of news. The enterprise is hazardous: we may return in triumph, we may not.

"While you hear that I am alive, do not re-marry or take a lover, lest you encounter from me the kind of anger that any husband would feel at such a thing, and the kind of revenge.

"On the other hand, the news may come someday that I have fallen. If you hear this, my spirit will only require that you observe a period of mourning before you feel free to re-marry.

"There is a third possibility, which may be the hardest of all to bear. Time may pass, and you may hear no news at all of me. If this occurs, and after twenty years from the day of my departure, you do not know if I still live, feel free to re-marry. If I should happen to turn up after that, I promise to accept the situation with the best grace I can muster, and not complain at the result of my being so late back!

"On the next rising of the full moon, the twenty years will be over. On that night, if there is still no sign of my husband, I intend to announce the name of his successor."

The Hall was silent. The suitors had a sudden fear, to add to their raised hopes, for all but one must soon be disappointed. Penelope herself seemed perfectly happy with her decision: only Telemachus, clinging to his own bitter thoughts, had no hope at all.

Meanwhile, in a place where one day seems very much like

another, until they merge into a long, enchanting, wilderness of time, Odysseus The Great Traveller sat brooding on his own headland, staring over the wine-dark sea. For many years he had felt happy, and his body had kept much of the vigour it had had during the long campaign at Troy. Recently, however, he had begun to fear that his mind was losing its edge. The more aware he became of this lethargy, the harder it was to escape it. As a semblance of the old Odysseus grudgingly reasserted itself, the dullness which remained became more oppressive.

He did not hear the footsteps of his mistress, who never seemed to make any. Rather, he sensed her presence behind him, that unmistakable sensing. Out of courtesy, he turned to look toward her while they spoke, though he avoided her gaze. More beautiful than any woman, the nymph-goddess Calypso hurt slightly to look at, just as the sound of her voice, for all its music, was hard to listen to, and the touch of her soft body made him tremble like a shock. Even her wild and abandoned love-making, raising him though it could to more than human heights of passion with its immortal fires, made him shudder even as he loved her, like one embracing a thundercloud.

Accusingly, she addressed him: “You do not look in my eyes, though you can hardly say I have done you harm, who found you shipwrecked by powerful Gods, and sheltered you from them.”

“Lady, though I love you well enough in my own way, even when I love you most, my heart is in Ithaca, where I was born.

The goddess shrank slightly, and for a moment seemed almost human. “How much I wish I could withhold the truth! Those gods whose anger has kept you on the island so many years have lost their power at last. The Time of Gods is passing now. You are free to go. But I still retain one power: to make you immortal like myself. Could you not stay with me... for ever? You have been here many years already, and I think you will find, if you venture across the wine-dark sea to the land of your birth, that things are not as they were. Even your wife might no longer welcome your return after so many years."

"Even so, I have a son at home whom I would see again."

"If your son still lives, and your home still stands! Give me a child here! Not the son of a mortal man, whom I must raise alone, and watch die while I live on, but a God's child, whom we can raise together."

Odysseus' eyes flicked away from his incomparable mistress, out towards the gulls wheeling on the horizon.

"I am a man. I have no wish to avoid dying, but before I do I must walk among men again."

Aboard the messenger's ship, there had arrived a young man, blinded in some accident, who could only earn his living by singing and playing the lyre. He was given lodgings in the Hall, with promise of rich rewards if his songs pleased.

He started with the siege of Troy and the death of Hector. This displeased some of the suitors.

"You blind beggar," said one. "You are trying to deceive us. You are too young to have been there, and if you had been you could not have seen the things you describe."

"That was my version of one sung by the great Demodocus. If you prefer, I could give you one exactly as he sung it."

Telemachus had enjoyed the song. He told the blind poet: "Ignore the rabble. I enjoyed your song, and I am master of this house, in the absence of its Lord Odysseus. If you know any lay of his deeds, tell us that."

The blind poet sang in the exact words of Demodocus, of how Odysseus built the "Wooden Horse", of the storming of Troy, the burning of its temples and sacred groves, and the slaughter of King Priam and his people. When he had finished, the suitors showed their admiration with stunned silence, while Telemachus and his friends rose and thundered their applause.

Odysseus, who had created the "Wooden Horse", had no

difficulty in building a fine seaworthy boat. He had little help from Calypso, who contented herself with pouring a libation of ambrosia over the figurehead, carved of course in her image, but with the eyes of Penelope, searching the sea.

That night she let Odysseus drink from her own cup, (Gods and men do not normally partake of the same foodstuffs) before leading him to her couch for their last night of love. Later he fell into the most deep and refreshing sleep he had ever known. Awaking after Dawn had touched the horizon, with the sea shining like light and sparkling wine, he saw no sign of her.

Embarrassed to meet her, on this last morning, he hastened to load his supplies into the boat. Calypso had given him a helmet of boar's tusks, very similar to one he had used at Troy, a sword and shield, and fine armour of bronze and gold which she had decorated with scenes depicting his adventures. There was a great bow, which no other man could have bent, like the one in his Hall in Ithaca, and lastly a lyre.

Odysseus poured a libation of wine, and said a prayer: "Gods of the Sea, accept the homage of Odysseus, the sailor. Forgive the crimes I committed against your temples and worshippers, when I had not learned the meaning of suffering. Grant me this if nothing more: let me cross the wine dark sea in safety, and see what vengeance time has taken on my home."

There was no sign of Calypso. He felt a certain relief as he launched the boat and set the sail. He did not look back, though once he thought he heard her voice, singing goodbye to him along the wind.

The archaeologist paced the hills of Ithaca, studying the Odyssey, looking for a site where the ancients might have built, one that had been overlooked. He chose a place which had been half heartedly scratched by one of his predecessors, then abandoned, prematurely in his view. Here he would dig.

The goddess sent a dolphin to Odysseus, to guide his course.

He did not dream of harming this creature, for he knew that dolphins have the minds of men, and are sacred to the Gods of the Sea. Once when he was younger and more brutal, he might have ignored such a proscription. Now, he was content to relax, enjoying the leaping enthusiasm of this pilot for his water-born life. For the first time for more years than he could tally, he began to experience a real content.

He sighted neither land nor sail, though, from time to time, he seemed to see things, low down on the horizon, which might have been ships. So he sailed, for seventeen days, until by his reckoning, he must be near the islands of the Greeks.

Of all the suitors, Amphinomus son of Nisus was most liked by Penelope. Unlike his drunken and quarrelsome rivals, he was kind to anyone the Fates had dealt with harshly. On the night of the full moon, he came to Telemachus just before sunset.

"You and I should be friends," he said. "Your father is dead... it's a sad fact which you'll have to face someday. You wouldn't have wanted him to live until you yourself had died. But if I am to become your step-father tonight, and..."

Telemachus rounded on him: "My father is alive, he will return! By now, I think he must be very near. He will destroy you, and anyone else who has tried to dishonour my mother!"

That night the shutters were left open, giving a view over the sea and the dark horizon beyond. Before long, the moon, Selene Queen of Night, would raise above the cool waters. All eyes searched the night, save those of Telemachus, which were fixed on the doorway. So hard he stared that shapes and lights seemed to quiver out of the darkness, the shape of his father, striding out of the night, bright in decorated golden armour, tall in his helmet of boar's tusks, bending the great bow that no man else could bend. But he was never quite there, and after a while a little flutter from the suitors around the tables told Telemachus that silvery light was starting to sparkle across the water. Then silence fell again as they all watched that painful, beauteous, and remorseless ascent. Even Telemachus tore his eyes away from the unbearably empty door. There it hung, huge in its clean, clear and distant light, so ancient, so beautiful, so uncomforting to Telemachus, so unlike the sun.

Odysseus did not come. The door was empty even of illusions. The lamps were dowsed, and Penelope advanced to stand in a beam of the moonlight, wearing not her matronly robe, but a sheer white garment which bared her arms and throat; with silver jewels, a crescent dangling just above her breasts, and the old crown of the Queens of Ithaca, with its hard white stones.

"Tonight," she began. "The twenty years are over. Since Odysseus sailed, he has widowed many women, some of whom may have married again. Now, I too take that right. First, you must all swear by Selene, Light of the Darkness, to defend the man I choose against anyone who should challenge him. Yes, even Odysseus himself, if he should happen to turn up. For it is my opinion now that I am free, that he is no better than a pirate, and he has abandoned his claim to this Kingdom, by neglect."

Telemachus was preparing for his last defence, a desperate plea for another year, a month, a day, or even the time till the moon was over the roof. But no words would come, only tears. Blindly, shamefaced, he stumbled from the Hall.

When Dawn had touched the horizon with rosy fingers, on the morning of the eighteenth day, Odysseus saw a great headland loom against the pale and beauteous light. He hoped this was part of the island of Crete, Kingdom of his friend Idomeneus. This had once been the richest country in all the world; the land where Daedalus the great inventor designed the Labyrinth Palace, larger than cities, where it was said a man could get lost, and never emerge. In Crete were many wonders; paintings more lifelike than reflections in a plane silver mirror; lamps that burned always without being refilled; baths that filled themselves without labour, at a man's command. It was there that Minos, mightiest of Kings, had built the first great Navy. In his palace naked youths and maidens had practiced the greatest of all mysteries, the Dance of the Bulls.

But the Gods are jealous of Men's good fortune. They caused a mighty shaking of the Earth, which destroyed the palaces. Then the folk of Idomeneus sailed from Argos and seized the island, maintaining what they could of its old splendour.

It was a fine morning with a good breeze, but only gentle waves. Light spread slowly over the sky, like soft blushing on the skin of a nymph who is feeling the potent loving of a God. He wished to give thanks: setting the sail, he took up his lyre, and picked out the haunting notes of the "Hymn to Apollo"; singing the sun up as he sailed to Crete in the dark morning.

Telemachus had many friends on Ithaca, local men who had no love for the suitors. Gathering enough to crew his ship, he sailed from Ithaca, determined not to return until he had found his father, or heard news of his fate.

By afternoon, Odysseus was close to shore. He saw coves of golden sand and whitewashed buildings with sky-blue shutters and little turreted domes. Further back could be glimpsed towers taller than any at Ilium. Having visited many countries, he judged it a sure sign of a peaceful and prosperous land, that the city was not walled, nor were there any war-galleys in the harbour. Instead, there were a number of strangely-rigged sailing-craft, a couple of very large ships at anchor, and some fast-moving small boats. Hungry for human company, he steered for the nearest cove, where he could dimly see people.

As he approached, he started to wonder if he had fallen among barbarous savages. He was not disturbed by their near nakedness, but it was disgraceful to see men and women mixing together thus. Despite this, he could see well made boats pulled up to the shore, such as savages would hardly build.

He had learnt that strange customs can be found even among the friendliest people. He continued to the beach. No one was armed, but he could not think of recklessly wandering among them as nearly naked as they. He donned the armour of gold Calypso had made him, and the helmet of boar's tusks. He strapped on his sword, but kept it in its decorated scabbard. To indicate peaceful intent, he carried his lyre.

As soon as he stepped ashore, the people suddenly took an interest, and started to crowd round as though they had never seen an armed Achaean warrior before. They mostly only wore a single little garment around the loins, some not even that, men and women immodestly crowding together. They had the fair skins of civilised folk, but somewhat burnished by the sun, as though they had never worn clothes. Some wore well made rings and necklaces, which did not seem the workmanship of primitive craftsmen. Most wore a single bracelet on the left wrist.

Odysseus decided to introduce himself: "Good people, I throw myself on your mercy. I trust I have not fallen among brutal and lawless savages, but have encountered kindly and God fearing folk, who know the law of hospitality to strangers. I am called Odysseus, a name some of you may be familiar with; Odysseus Laertides, Odysseus of Ithaca."

The naked people started talking, in a language the Great Traveller himself had never heard before. At length, one of them said: "Odysseus?" in a querying voice.

"Nai. Onanism Odysseus."

One of the young women gave a little bow. "Kalemera sas, O Kyrios Odysseus," she said in a halting and barbarous accent. Next, she consulted what appeared to be a kind of book of bound papyrus. She grinned and said: "Onomosomai Nausicaa!"

Several of the others giggled and even shrieked with laughter, slapping her shoulder as if she were an athlete who had just won her event, and shouting: "Odysseus! Nausicaa!"

They were disrespectful, and evidently not Greeks, but were friendly, and had heard of him. The girl Nausicaa intrigued him: she wore nothing at all save a necklace of outlandish design; she was as beautiful as a princess, but her skin was as brown all over as that of a peasant woman who has to toil in the fields. Unusually for a woman, she was able to read, and to speak more than one language. He asked her again where he was and what people he had fallen among, but she seemed not to understand. Looking around she shouted: "Achilles! Achilles!"

Odysseus started at the name of his fallen companion. The young man who ran up was not he, but was perhaps young enough to have been named after him. He was almost as handsome as the dead hero, but did not look so strong. He was more decently dressed than the others, and wore no jewellery save a pendant in the form of a cross. Most important, he spoke Greek, with as barbarous an accent as the girl, but more fluently, although he used many words Odysseus did not catch.

Achilles explained that Odysseus had indeed landed on Crete. The people on the beach were visitors. They chose to go naked because in their own country, far to the North, they hardly ever saw the sun. It appeared that they worshipped the elusive disk, and had followed it South on a pilgrimage.

Odysseus had not thought of Crete as a centre for the cult of Apollo Helios. However, he felt reassured, and explained a little about who he was, and where he was going. This was translated by Achilles, who pointed to his head, evidently indicating a visitor entitled to wear a crown. The crowd fell silent, in greater respect. After a brief exchange with the girl Nausicaa, Achilles invited Odysseus to dine with them that night, saying he would be welcome to play his lyre.

They led Odysseus to a city; a place of marvels. The houses were large and rich, but there were no defences. He wondered if it was protected by enchantment, for there were strange forces in evidence. Many of the houses clearly belonged to merchants, with rich displays of goods laid out open to the street, or apparently so; for when Odysseus, feeling hungry, stopped to examine the quality of some fruit, his hand encountered an impenetrable barrier, hard as iron, which he could not see.

Another odd thing was the writing. There were signs, not in the language of Argos, but in a script he had not encountered. It looked a little like the writing of Tyre or Sidon, although the tongue he heard spoken most was a dialect of Greek.

Achilles led the way to the house of his father, Socrates. A large and well appointed place, it lacked the central hall of a noble's residence, and appeared to be some kind of inn. They led the guest to a chamber on an upper floor, reached by flights of steps. There was a bed, raised from the floor, and boxes for storage of clothes. In an alcove was a large bath.

There were also marvels. Not only did cold water flow from spouts in the wall, but also hot; and there were lamps which could be lighted, without fire, by pulling a tiny lever.

Odysseus tried to adjust to these new mysteries with a calm but alert spirit. He had seen more extraordinary things than most men, and nothing here could compare to the dreadful magic of Circe, or the power of Calypso.

Relaxing in a hot bath, as pleasant as the warm spring in Calypso's cave, he pondered on her remark that the power of the Gods was fading. This seemed not so: a very powerful God was clearly protecting and providing for the Cretans. He tried to remember which Gods were honoured in Crete, and say a prayer to each. If Calypso wished to test his devotion and respect, he would not be found wanting. What her purpose was in guiding him to these strange shores, he could not guess. Hers was an uncomfortable love; for willing though she was to pander to his needs, he feared she had the power to destroy him utterly.

There was more strangeness. His window had two shutters; one of plain wood, the other with panels of the invisible barrier he had already marvelled at. The sun was now low over the wine-dark sea, and in its angled light, he found dust upon the shutter, and was able to conclude that it was a kind of glass, so cleverly made as to be transparent, like very clear water.

He looked over the mysterious city. It was very large, and must have housed several thousand inhabitants. Near him, the streets were narrow and quiet, fine white houses almost glowing in the mellowing light of late afternoon. Further back were the ugly and sinister towers he had observed from out to sea. Then the land rose rapidly toward stark formidable mountains. There were vehicles in the distance, some moving very fast. For most, it was impossible to see the beasts that powered them: a few were so large that he concluded the drawing animals must have been inside the wagon.

But the strangest thing, to his soldier's eye, was a low, but very steep hill on the outskirts: it had a stream twinkling down on one side, and would have been an ideal spot to fortify as an acropolis, a place a hundred warriors could hold against thousands with ease. But nothing of the sort had been done.

As sunset neared, Achilles called him to join the people on the veranda. It looked across a narrow quay to the harbour, and the shimmering sea beyond. The house was filled with a strange, beautiful music, made by instruments Odysseus had never heard. There seemed to be many people playing, though he could not see a single musician. Achilles and Nausicaa plied him with drinks. Some were hot and dark, with cream floating on the top, and redolent of something strong, not as sweet as wine. Others were cool, full of fruits and exotic flavour. Many were served in cups wrought from transparent glass. One which Odysseus particularly enjoyed, seemed to glow with the colours made by the sun as he settled to his rest, leaving a broad wake of glowing, shimmering ripples across the wine-dark sea. The music rose now to an unbelievably loud but still enthralling climax, thundering out over the light-bright, darkening sea.

The banquet began. People from the beach were there, dressed in well made and often perfectly modest garments. They ate out in the warm twilight under the stars. But Nausicaa, completely covered, seemed more alluring and less decent than she had naked. Her long gown was entirely of a green and filmy substance, delicately embroidered with flowers and ferns, so finely spun that not a single curve of her body was concealed by it. Even her nipples were visible, like the noses of two kittens who think they are hidden in the undergrowth.

After the meal, Odysseus was invited to play his lyre. Through Achilles, he announced that he would sing of his adventures in the Cyclops' cave. This seemed a popular choice: although they did not understand the words of the sad song, they applauded it very warmly, and asked for more.

Emboldened by wine and popularity, Odysseus offered a song about his greatest achievements: the building of the "Wooden Horse" and the storming of Troy. This was applauded when announced and cheered when completed: the fair Nausicaa took Odysseus helmet of boar's tusks and carried it round the tables. The revellers put into it gifts for Odysseus; engraved disks of silver or bronze, which could have been brooches but had no pins, and sheets of papyrus with pictures of distinguished looking men, war-galleys, and ruined temples. These items were used for trade, being exchanged for drinks and other items. Odysseus, however, did not have to barter; his cup was kept flowing, and he was assured he could lodge in that place for as long as he continued to play at dinner.

He passed a long and drunken night of sleep. Nausicaa had kissed him once, gently, fleetingly, before she disappeared into the darkness. On awakening, he was told she had already gone out. Achilles gave Odysseus a hot sharp drink to ease his aching head. Then they began to talk.

Who is King in these parts nowadays?"

Achilles looked offended. "There was a King Constantine, but he has been driven out." He launched into an impassioned account which Odysseus could not follow, of how this happened.

Odysseus decided to change the subject. “I have heard of the splendours of Crete in ancient times, before the great palaces were destroyed, and I see it is still a land of marvels.”

Achilles smiled. “Crete has much to offer besides its past, though this afternoon is devoted to ancient things. I will show people the ruins of an old Minoan palace. Come with us.

The ruins were hardly visible above the ground, having been dug out of it like cellars. Not far away, learned people were working on the remains of another building. The place was vastly larger than any palace Odysseus had seen, but so decayed by time as to be hardly recognisable as such.

“Three thousand years old,” said Nausicaa in halting Greek. This shocked Odysseus.

“Not three thousand!”

She consulted a papyrus book. “Three and a half thousand.”

He quietly recited the family tree of his friend Idomeneus of Crete. There has been about six or seven generations since the Shaking of the Earth... not even three hundred years, let alone three thousand. Shuddering, Odysseus wondered how Idomeneus had fared since they last met at Troy.

“Have you heard of King Idomeneus of Crete?”

“Yes. At Ilium. Three thousand years ago.”

Odysseus turned away, puzzled, and, he admitted to himself, frightened. The girl moved on, looking from her book to the ruins. Today she wore tight blue garments, which left her arms and legs completely uncovered, and sandals with little stilts under the heels, which tautened the muscles of her sunburned thighs in a striking, alluring manner.

Achilles was staring at her longingly. He nudged Odysseus. “Blodwyn seems to like you. Despite what she wears, or rather doesn’t wear, nobody normally gets near her. Lucky man!”

"Who did you say?"

Achilles hesitated. "Blodwyn is that girl's real name, I think. It's common in Wales where she comes from. It's part of the island of Britain, in the far North."

"I haven't been there." North was one of the few directions he had never travelled. "I thought her name was Nausicaa?"

"That's her little joke, her little friendly joke."

"I don't understand."

"Well, there's an old story about Nausicaa finding Odysseus by the sea shore. You're not that Odysseus?"

"No, I've never heard of her before."

"I see, but you are the Odysseus who was at Troy?"

"Yes, I told you so yesterday."

"And you did eventually return to Ithaca?"

"No, I'm on my way there now."

"So you didn't return to kill off your wife's suitors?"

"Where do you get the idea my wife would have suitors? She's not that kind. If she was, she'd have me to answer to!"

"Well! There's a very famous poem which says that Odysseus did return, found his wife... not encouraging the suitors... trying to get rid of them. It said he killed the lot of them."

"Well if I did find that situation, that's what I would do."

The girl rejoined them at that moment. Achilles spoke sharply to her in her own language, tapping his head again.

When rosy fingered Dawn had touched the Eastern sky, and tinted the wine-dark sea with the colours of morning, the faithful dolphin leapt joyously from the waters ahead of Odysseus' prow. He sighed with relief... at least this guide would get him to Ithaca. He had begun to wonder if Calypso had abandoned him among people he could not understand, out of spite that he had abandoned her. He wondered with a chill why she had counselled him so strongly against making this voyage. He had learnt it was never wise to defy any of the Immortals.

He saw many strange things, out there on the wine-dark sea. There were vast ships without sails, such as giants might make. There were strange things in the sky. He clung to a fear that had come to him among the ruins: that an imposter, disguised as himself, had seduced Penelope, killed his rivals, and usurped the kingdom: staking his claim through the medium of travelling poets. It was the least fear: that he was now the imposter in his own land. More than ever, he was drawn home. There, if anywhere, he would discover the truth. Thinking on this, he was suddenly no longer afraid. The Odyssey would finally be over.

For years, Telemachus travelled, questioning seafarers, haunting the ports and taverns. He met a man who claimed to be a survivor of Odysseus' last shipwreck. This one told him of the early years of wandering... of Cyclops' cave, and Circe's enchantments. He even knew of Calypso's island, though not its location. He could not say if his master lived, but doubted it.

After this, Telemachus' crew started to abandon him and his quest. But he himself wandered on, failing in his health, reduced almost to beggary, too proud to return alone.

The archaeologist was more pleased with the statue than anything he had found on Ithaca. He had it photographed where it was discovered. After all, it would not only prove his theory, but make his name greater than Schliemann's.

It was a magic evening. As the sun grew redder and nearer the sea, sky and water seemed even purer and more clear than guide books say they are in Greece. From the village rose the faint strains of classical music; from a nearby taverna, bouzouki. Tonight, the best wine for his assistants; Napoleon brandy in his own coffee.

He became aware of the man approaching slowly, like someone reluctantly leaving a dream; the kind of dream he had as a child; the kind of figure he had read about in his teens, wearing the kind of armour he had studied as an undergraduate.

The man halted at the edge of the newly excavated ruins. His gaze swept over the unfamiliar village, the huge ship in the harbour, the fallen palace, clawed from the earth, more cruelly ravaged by time than it ever could have been by human anger.

Their eyes locked on one another, then both flicked to the marvellously well preserved statue... both, perhaps, realising in the same heartbeat that it depicted the man in the strange helmet, but younger, as if remembered over twenty years.

Slowly, they both moved towards it through the still air, eyes drawn towards the Linear B inscription on its base:

“TO THE MEMORY OF ODYSSEUS.
FROM PENELOPE AND HER SECOND HUSBAND
AMPHINOMUS.”

Chance, or fate, or one of the gods, led Telemachus to the door of the blind poet, the same one he had protected, when they had both been young. The man had prospered now, and his songs of fallen Troy were famed throughout the world. People came from far to hear him, and bring him gifts. His house was the largest of any commoner in the city.

After the guest had been bathed, fed, and rested, the poet took him aside. “I have now completed my songs about the fall of Troy, and am working on a series about the returns of the heroes. I have nearly finished that. But I know nothing about one... yes, it’s your father I don’t know about. Did he turn up again after all those years? Did he tell the tale of his wanderings? I’d like to think he drove all those suitors from his hall, and killed the lot of them. That’d be a story worth telling... perhaps the best I’d ever done.”

Telemachus looked deep into the whirling maelstrom of his soul. Drowning inside, he was confronted by the images of his honourable and wasted life. Looking into the dead eyes of the poet, he found it easy to tell his only lie:

“Oh yes, oh yes, Odysseus did come back. And he killed every one of those suitors. It’s a story only you are fit to sing. Listen, and I’ll tell you all about it.”

The Court of High Renown

Cherith Baldry

Cherith Baldry was born in Lancaster, UK, and studied at the University of Manchester and St Anne's College, Oxford. After some years as a teacher, including a spell at the University of Sierra Leone, Freetown, she became a full-time writer. She has a special interest in Arthurian romance and medieval literature, and has published novels and short fiction for adults, young adults and children. She is currently part of the Erin Hunter team writing the Warriors and Seekers series.

Cherith has two grown-up sons, and lives in Surrey in a household ruled by two cats. She enjoys music, especially early music, reading and travel.

Cherith's story takes us to a mysterious enclave, shaped by its Queen and her Court. But is everything within the castle and the surrounding forest as unreal as it seems? And is there anything beyond the fading horizon...?

Sir Gervais stood in the narrow window embrasure and looked down into the tilting yard. On the green turf below, Lord Corbairan was challenging a dragon. His artefact, shaped like a stallion from long-abandoned Earth, beat an impatient piaffe as Corbairan laid his lance in rest.

Sun dazzled from the smoothly sliding plates of Lord Corbairan's armour, while a warm breeze rippled through his plume and fluttered the embroidered ribbon, the favour of Queen Audiarde herself, which he wore twisted round his helmet.

His adversary approached from the other end of the tiltyard in a series of gawky hops, its wings beating, half lifting it, though it never achieved true flight. Its neck was extended like a snake's as it flamed a withered path across the turf. Its back arched, vermilion scales edged in gold, and its tail lashed the air.

With no one to watch him, Gervais did not bother to suppress a sneer. Corbairan was becoming unimaginative. He had played out this scenario not a month ago, though then the dragon had been green. It was one of the early signs that everyone was growing bored with the court, and would soon decide to shift the enclave into some new and more amusing manifestation.

And the small progress that Gervais had made would vanish along with the walls and towers, the armour, the stallions and dragons and all the trappings of the Court of High Renown.

But as far as Gervais could see, there were few signs of boredom yet. A gasp of excitement swept through the stand of spectators as Lord Corbairan set spurs to his horse and thundered across the turf. The dragon bellowed its defiance. Corbairan's lance struck it full on the breast, but the armoured scales turned the point aside and the shaft shattered.

The horse reared and its armoured hooves struck out as the dragon stretched its bat-wings over it and coiled its neck to blast out gouts of flame. Lord Corbairan cast aside the butt end of his lance and drew his sword. As the horse fell back to four feet, he thrust the blade upwards, impaling the dragon through its open jaws.

Searing fire flowed down the blade, enfolding knight and horse. The dragon screamed as the sword pierced its throat. Black blood rained over the turf.

One or two delicate shrieks came from the ladies in the stand as the horse crumpled to its knees, then to the ground, and the armoured knight with it. The dying dragon thrashed its tail in a frenzy, weakening gradually, until it lay lifeless on the grass, with one spread wing covering the dead stallion. Corbairan rolled away from it and regained his feet.

Applause broke out in the stand. Sir Gervais let out a faint sound of irritation and turned away from the window.

By the time he reached ground level, the turf was green again. Both horse and dragon were rapidly unshaping, their constituent particles whirling into the air to dissipate until they were required again. Lord Corbairan's armour went the same way.

Corbairan himself bowed to the spectators, and went to kiss the hand the Queen graciously held out to him.

He was a handspan taller today, Gervais noticed, and his hair was longer, curling more thickly, but his impudent good looks were still recognisable.

Queen Audiarde laughed softly as she held out to him a golden cup, its base and rim flashing with emeralds, the prize for his feat of arms. "I name you Corbairan Dragonslayer," she declared.

Her laughter died as Gervais approached. Her thin brows arched as her perfect features froze into disdain. "Gervais? Sir Seneschal? Why did you not attend the lists with all the others?"

Sir Gervais laid a hand on his breast and bowed slightly, his eyes never leaving the Queen's face. "I have my duties, lady."

Queen Audiarde laughed harshly. "Duties! Inventions!"

And yours are not? Gervais asked, but silently.

Lord Corbairan leaned towards the Queen, and raised her hand once more to his lips. Softly he suggested, "Perhaps the noble Sir Gervais is afraid of dragons."

"Perhaps." Queen Audiarde kept hold of Corbairan's hand as she gazed haughtily at Gervais. He searched her features earnestly for the impatient intelligence that had once driven her, or the laughter and the eagerness of discovery that they had once shared. Nothing now: unless he caught a shadow of disappointment.

She was as beautiful as creamy-gold skin and heavy sheaves of bronze-coloured hair could make her. Gervais wondered if anyone else remembered her as she had been, before she shaped the enclave, before she learnt to shape herself and everything around her into what she wished them to be. Even if they remembered, Gervais thought, they would not regret.

For himself, in spite of ridicule, Gervais clung obstinately to the narrow, beaky face and lank dark hair he had been born with, aeons ago. He felt a superstitious fear that in changing his appearance he would lose himself, as he feared Audiarde, the true woman, was lost in the beautiful, capricious Queen.

He drew himself up and faced Lord Corbairan. "It takes no courage to face your dragons. What are they but illusions, spun out of air and dust?"

Corbairan's face grew ugly. His belt knife was in his hand; he took a step towards Gervais, and Gervais had to brace himself, not to flinch from him.

Queen Audiarde reached out, laying gold-tipped fingers on Lord Corbairan's sleeve. "Hold, my lord. It does you no honour to quarrel with Gervais."

Corbairan let out a snort of contempt and thrust his knife back into its sheath. "True. He has no honour in him."

"And what honour lies in games?" Gervais retorted. "Are we children? Do we—"

The Queen raised a hand to silence him. "You do not join our games, Gervais," she said. She smiled delicately, coldly. "You hold yourself above us. So this I decree... you will take the place of honour in our next game — or face my displeasure."

Gervais stared at her, shocked out of mere irritation into a deeper uneasiness. It was true what she said. He played as little part as possible in the extravagant fancies of the Court of High Renown, and that only because there was nothing else to do, and nowhere else to go. He took no delight in it, and he had no skill to shape the illusions that the court craved.

Queen Audiarde created fantasies so beautiful that even Gervais found it hard to resist them. Lord Corbairan liked to kill things, as ostentatiously as possible. And Gervais — he liked order, and reason, and predictability. He knew the Queen and her courtiers found him boring, and he did not attempt to hide his own screaming boredom with a world where nothing was fixed, nothing was forbidden, and nothing had a value because there was never any price to pay.

So far Queen Audiarde had asked nothing of him beyond the duties of the seneschal's office, a dull part, but a necessary one. Gervais had thought she understood. What she decreed now would mean ridicule in the end, and more. It meant that she did not value any longer the man she knew him to be.

He was searching for words — for he would have died rather than speak these thoughts aloud in the hearing of Corbairan and the rest of the sniggering court — when the Queen's attention suddenly shifted from him. Gervais turned to see what she was looking at.

Through the gate that led into the outer courtyard, a man was approaching. He was tall, rake-thin, with a mop of shaggy red hair streaked with grey. He wore his patched velvet tunic with rakish confidence, and carried a lute, in its canvas case, slung over one shoulder. Gervais had never seen him before: a new artefact, then, or one of the company wearing a new shape, the beginning of a different game.

Halting before the stand, the musician bowed. "My lady, I beg a boon."

Queen Audiarde smiled graciously. "Speak."

Gervais eased back a pace or two, away from the Queen, listening apprehensively to discover what this new game would entail.

"I come from the mountains," the lute-player said. "Lady, a dragon has appeared — woken, perhaps, from long sleep in some chamber deep in the heart of the stone. It flies now from a cave to raid and burn. The villagers are terrified. They begged me to come to you and seek your aid."

An excited babble broke out among the courtiers in the stand. Gervais schooled his face to remain expressionless as he watched the Queen.

"Mountains?" she asked. "A village in the mountains?"

The lute-player bowed acknowledgement. For a moment Queen Audiarde frowned in thought over the terms of the new game, while Gervais wondered at the skill in shaping that would extend the enclave to provide a setting for it. A pity it could not include a more original threat than another damned dragon.

At last the Queen smiled. "I grant your boon," she said. "And you, Sir Gervais — you shall have the honour of the kill."

Lord Corbairan took a step forward, his handsome face sulky and his mouth open to protest. Queen Audiarde silenced him with a gesture.

She rose, and the rest of the courtiers with her; the silken hangings and the framework of the stand unshaped in a cloud of glittering motes as she led the way across the tiltyard, reaching her hand to Lord Corbairan as she spoke once more to the musician.

"Come sir, attend me. You shall eat the noon meal with us, and then we will ride out."

Sir Gervais watched them go. To kill a dragon... His stomach churned, not in fear, for the shaping would not harm him, but because he knew beyond contradiction that he was about to make a fool of himself in front of the entire court.

Once they had been his friends, colleagues, partners in the new world Queen Audiarde had taught them to shape. Now... Gervais let out a faint sound of disgust. Now they were no more than her sycophants, and they would laugh at his discomfiture because they knew he had lost her favour.

He remained where he was until the whole company had processed across the tiltyard and disappeared up a flight of steps that led to the great hall of the castle. The sun shone warm on grey walls and unmarked turf. From somewhere unseen, he could hear a faint thread of music.

He turned his head, seeking its direction. The lute-player? The man disturbed Gervais. Usually, with a little thought, he could penetrate a disguise, recognising mannerisms if not the outward form, but he could not begin to guess which of the company was playing this part.

The sound of music grew louder as he stepped through an archway into the castle garden, blending with the soft cadences of a fountain that rose glittering into the air and fell into a wide stone basin.

The lute player had not attended the Queen and her courtiers. He was seated on the coping of the basin, shaggy head bent over his instrument. As Sir Gervais approached him across the grass he looked up.

Gervais halted, startled. He still did not recognise the lined features, the glinting emerald eyes or the long, thin hands so skilful on the strings. "Who are you?" he asked harshly. "Don't you ever get tired of this damn' shape-changing?"

The man brought his melody to an end in a rapid flurry of notes. Smiling faintly, he said, "Just a poor musician, my lord." His lips twisted in wry amusement, contradicting the humility of his words. "As I told your Queen, I come from the mountains."

Gervais stifled a sound of irritation at the repetition of this palpable falsehood. "Mountains? What mountains? Are you an artefact?"

The lute player looked puzzled. "Artefact, my lord? My name is Melir. As for the mountains..." Again the wry look of amusement as he gestured towards the garden wall. "You need only look for yourself."

Casting a doubtful glance at him, Sir Gervais crossed the garden to where a flight of steps led up to a walk behind the battlements. He laid his hands on the golden stone, and looked out.

Gervais had never been sure about the size of the enclave. To begin with, it had been small, when she who now called herself Queen Audiarde and her companions had pushed out the bubble of unreality with no more strength than their concerted minds and the last fading pulses of energy from a dying universe. The junction was closed now, buried under the stones of the lowest cellar in the castle, almost forgotten, though Gervais sometimes thought that he could feel it down there in the darkness, where illusion stretched thin and the air was vibrant with the pressure of numberless dead stars.

Since then, the enclave had fluctuated, to be whatever the Queen and her favourites decreed: a ship on an ocean bounded by mist; a city whose streets curled back on themselves; most recently, the Court of High Renown, the castle looped by a river and surrounded by a forest fading to the horizon.

From the castle walls, Sir Gervais looked down the green slopes of the hill as far as the river and the village of artefacts. Fields of corn bordered the nearer riverbank, and beyond the river was the green wall of the forest.

He wondered whether Queen Audiarde yet realised that some of the artefacts, under his direction, had crossed the river, cut down trees, seasoned the wood and sawn it into planks, and used it to build. Some of the huts in the village were real. The corn, too, had grown from seeds that Gervais had shaped, and for some seasons now had been ground to flour in the mill which the Queen, with an eye for the picturesque, had placed on the riverside. And there were other experiments, on ground which he had quietly nudged into being: here a meadow to pasture cattle; there a terraced slope for a vineyard.

Some of the wisps of smoke which hovered in the air above the village rose from true hearth fires, where a real supper would be cooking.

In small, stubborn, unobtrusive ways, Gervais had tried to create something tangible in the midst of illusion. Worthless, he knew now, in the sight of those who wanted the thrill of watching a dragon die. And all to be swept away, as soon as the Queen grew bored and decreed that the enclave would change.

While Sir Gervais looked down at the village and the fields, Melir had bent over his lute again. The frail thread of music twined around the battlements. Gervais raised his eyes. The blue day dazzled him, and yet he thought that he could see, in the far distance, something beyond the forest, an immense, faint presence printed against the sky.

A mountain range marched across the whole breadth of his vision, peak beyond peak, precipitous heights streaked with snow. The sense of distance dizzied Gervais. The enclave was no longer small, bounded, safe.

It was, of course, impossible.

He almost ran down the steps into the garden. "Who are you?" he demanded harshly. "Who are you really? What sort of game are you playing?"

"No game." The lute player spoke softly. "I bring you nothing but truth."

When the mid-day meal was over Queen Audiarde shaped horses and the company set out. Lord Corbairan, magnificent once again in his plate armour, carried her banner. The scarlet silk rippled in the wind as he rode at her side.

As the cavalcade was forming up, Gervais had felt the Queen's gaze resting on him. He sensed she was troubled — perhaps, as he was, by this unaccountable new game. He dared not believe she was troubled for him. In any case, his pride would not let him beg her to release him. There was only one way through this.

He mounted and joined the cavalcade at its rear. Beyond the bridge over the river, a road had sprung up, stretching into the heart of the forest, arrow-straight towards mountains that now stood solid against the skyline, their lower slopes forested, their tops tipped with snow. Gervais was relieved when the company moved into the shelter of the trees and lost sight of those unaccountable slopes.

As they rode, he looked around him curiously. The company never ventured into the forest, except now and then to hunt the white hart or seek for the fountain of the fays. On his own expeditions to the outskirts Gervais had always thought it had an unfinished look. Now ferns grew thickly by the side of the road, small creeping plants twined between the stones and covered the forest floor, while birds fluttered overhead on every branch. Once a stream bubbled across the path, and a little further on a group of deer — brown, not enchanted white — strayed unconcerned among the trees as the company rode by.

Gervais was puzzled. He did not think that even the Queen herself had the skill to shape all this as they rode. And which of the company would lavish such care on shaping a place that no one would ever see?

He still had no answers when the road, the trees, suddenly blurred, and seconds later he found himself riding, still at the tail of the cavalcade, up a mountain track, with the edge of the forest dark behind him. Queen Audiarde had grown bored then, with the ride, and moved the company on to the next encounter. Or perhaps — the thought disturbed Gervais still more — she was as puzzled as he was by questions she could not answer.

Goaded by anxiety, Gervais set spurs to his horse and pressed forward until he reached the head of the company, and fell in beside the Queen and Corbairan. "Lady," he said, "is this your shaping?"

Queen Audiarde turned her head sharply towards him. "No," she said. She studied him for a long moment, her eyes dark with an uneasiness that matched his own. Gervais felt she expected something from him, but he did not know how to respond.

Then Corbairan laughed, breaking their frail rapport. "What matter whose? Enjoy the game, Gervais, and think of the honour you will win!"

Gervais had no stomach for exchanging jibes with him. He bowed his head, reining in his horse so that the Queen and Corbairan could lead the way once more. Queen Audiarde did not look at him again.

The track wound back and forth across the face of the hill, through an upland meadow where sheep cropped placidly. Not far ahead, a group of stone-built huts clung to the slope, and above them, where meadow grass gave way to bare rock, a cave mouth gaped.

Over to the left, a whole swathe of grassland had been burnt black, a scar running from beyond the village as far as the edge of the forest. The outlying trees were charred skeletons, and a sullen smoke still rose into the sky.

Gervais heard the Queen give the command to halt. Lord Corbairan drove the shaft of the banner into the ground, and the rest of the company milled uncertainly to and fro. Melir manoeuvred his horse until it stood close to Gervais's.

"Well?" Gervais snapped. "Where are your villagers? And your dragon?"

The lute-player shrugged. "The villagers — fled, I imagine. As for the dragon..." He cocked his head towards the burning. "What more evidence do you need?"

"Give me credit for some intelligence." Gervais's voice held an icy edge of contempt. "You could shape that as you shape everything else." He leant forward. "*Who are you?*"

Melir cocked his head towards the crowd of courtiers. "Have you counted your company recently, Sir Seneschal?"

Doubtfully, Gervais followed his gaze. The whole court had attended Queen Audiarde to take part in this new game. The whole court... and they were all accounted for.

"An artefact, then..." he began. Anyone could shape an artefact to take on human form, to function just as humans did... and yet there was always something. Gervais thought it was in the eyes, though he could not have described it. Whatever the truth might be, he was never in any doubt when he was looking at an artefact.

Melir was not. Melir was true human, and yet he did not belong to Queen Audiarde's court. He was the first stranger that Gervais had ever seen in the enclave.

Gervais could not remember ever being so afraid. "*What* are you?" he whispered.

Melir smiled faintly. "A messenger."

"And your message? To me — or to the Queen?"

"To anyone who will listen." He pointed one bony finger

up the mountain. “There.”

Something was moving in the cave mouth. A long, dark limb unfolded, and then another. Gervais was reminded of a spider pushing its way out of a cranny in a wall — only immeasurable larger.

Then a head poked forward on a long, reptilian neck. Wings creaked open as if they moved on rusty hinges, and the dragon, night-black and flaming, sprang into the air.

The courtiers laughed and pointed admiringly, only to break off seconds later as their horses reared or shied, or tried to turn and flee down the path to the shelter of the trees. As they surged back and forth, struggling to control their mounts, Gervais spurred his own horse and forced it along the path until he came up with the Queen and Corbairan.

Urgently he cried, “Lady, take care! This is true dragon — it can kill.”

Lord Corbairan ignored him, his gaze fixed on the dragon where it vaned idly above the peak. Queen Audiarde turned a cold look on him. “At last you join the game, Gervais,” she said. “And with a coward’s counsel. As I should expect from you.” Her eyes narrowed. “Yet the honour, or the shame, is yours. What will you do, Gervais?”

Gervais’s hands felt clammy with fear, and his throat was dry. So far he had not shaped armour for himself, nor any weapon but a sword. He did not do it now, for he knew that no armour, not even if Queen Audiarde herself should shape it, would stand against dragon-fire.

Yet left alone, the dragon would kill and kill again. Somehow he must find the strength to stand against it.

He was gathering up his horse’s reins, and loosening his sword in its sheath, when Corbairan spoke contemptuously. “The coward does nothing! Lady, give *me* the game!”

For a moment Audiarde hesitated, looking from Lord Corbairan to Gervais and back again. Then she nodded. “The honour is yours, Corbairan Dragonslayer. And my favour with it.”

Lord Corbairan gave a yell of triumph. His face was

distorted with an insatiable hunger for glory as he followed the progress of the dragon, soaring above the peak on widespread wings.

Gervais reached over to grasp the Queen's bridle. "Lady, this is no game. If you love Corbairan, tell him to hold back."

Queen Audiarde made no reply in words, only jerking her bridle away from his clutching fingers. Fighting panic, Gervais looked round for the lute-player. On the slope below, the scattered courtiers were regrouping, their horses under control again, but there was no sign of Melir.

Gervais was forming another desperate plea when, high above, the dragon banked and dived. Descending like thunder on the mountainside, it set another swathe of meadowland on fire, swooped down on the flock of sheep and scattered them, bleating in terror. With one sheep clasped in its claws it pulled out of the dive and swept upwards again. All the mountain rang with the bellowing of its defiance.

Lord Corbairan let out a peal of delighted laughter. "This is a shaping indeed!"

In an instant he shaped wings to his mount, pinions of silver feathers sweeping from the artefact's shoulders, and launched it upwards, to meet the dragon in the air.

Gervais lunged towards him and caught his stirrup, only to lose his grip as his own horse reared and threw him. He hit the ground, breath driven out of him, to sprawl helplessly and watch the clash of combatants high above.

The winged horse danced on air as Corbairan hurled his spear. It struck the dragon's shoulder and dangled there; the dragon bellowed its pain and belched out a sheet of flame. Corbairan evaded it; the horse's powerful wings beat to gain height. As it passed close to the dragon, Corbairan drew his sword to lean over and sweep the blade across the snaking neck.

That should have ended it. Instead, the blade sprang back and shattered; Gervais saw a glittering shard turning in air as it fell. Corbairan flourished the hilt, trying to reshape the weapon. Trying, and failing.

Gervais heard a faint, stifled cry from the Queen. Her hands were white as she gripped her horse's reins. She leant forward, urging her own mount, shaping wings to it so she herself could join the combat.

But before she gained the air, the dragon bellowed out flame again. Lord Corbairan was caught in it. His mount's wings withered in the blast. Horse and rider plummeted from the sky, but as they fell Corbairan flung himself forward and grasped the edge of the dragon's wing.

Off balance, dragged down by the weight of man and horse, the dragon fell with them. Its neck twisted, and dragon-fire seared Corbairan's mailed hands, but he clung still, and the cry that escaped him was pure triumph, nothing of pain or fear, as Corbairan Dragonslayer claimed his honour at the last.

Together knight and dragon crashed into the mountainside just above the village. Fire roared upwards, and the sky was darkened with smoke.

As he rose painfully to his feet, Gervais heard the faint sound of the Queen's weeping.

The sun had begun to set before the burning died away. Timidly, men and women began to appear at the edge of the forest, returning to their abandoned homes in the village. Melir was not among them. Gervais could not feel particularly surprised.

The villagers brought out food and drink and served Queen Audiarde and the company. Eventually a group of the bolder sort made a foray up the mountain and brought back Lord Corbairan's body.

Queen Audiarde shaped a bier for him, and laid him on it, covered with a pall of silk and strewn with meadow flowers. She herself sat on a rock by the side of the road, her hands clasped in her lap, gazing out over the forest as the last streaks of daylight faded.

Sir Gervais went to stand beside her. "Lady," he said, "I will shape pavilions for our rest tonight. Tomorrow—"

"Tomorrow?" Audiarde interrupted him, but her voice had lost the edge it often had when she spoke to him. She turned her face to him, and he recognised in her the woman who, countless ages ago, had taught him and all the others the power of their own minds to control their bodies, their surroundings, and at last to build a refuge, a bubble of life and beauty when everything else was dying.

"Lady," he said again, his voice hushed.

She gave him a tired smile. "Shall I move the enclave?"

"Can you, now? Do you dare try?" She replied with nothing more than a tiny shrug, and he added urgently, "What is happening? The forest is real. These mountains... and the dragon. The dragon was real."

The Queen nodded. "And Corbairan's courage was real, in the end. Something you never believed, Gervais."

"I know." He bowed his head. "I am sorry for it."

"And so you should be," Audiarde said, "for I think all this is your doing."

Gervais stiffened, but there was no accusation in her voice, only weary understanding and even a trace of humour. "What do you mean?" he asked.

Queen Audiarde flung out a hand to encompass the mountains, the forest, the village, the twisted body of the dragon, and even the towers of the castle, a distant silhouette against a greenish sky. "All this... inconvenient reality. Is it not yours?"

"No!" The thought left Gervais breathless. "I began, a little... a field of corn..."

"Vines, cattle, huts for the artefacts. Don't think I didn't know."

"And you didn't stop me?"

"Why should I? It was... interesting. I wanted to see where it would lead."

"But not to this ending!" Gervais's eyes were on the bier now, and Lord Corbairan's body covered in silk and flowers. "I never meant this... loss."

Audiarde let out a faint sigh, scarcely a breath on the

evening air. “No, not this loss. But think, Gervais. One tiny seed, and a whole solution turns to crystal. One speck of reality... my friend, you may have created a world.”

Gervais shook his head, rejecting, not daring to think what that might mean.

“Hard rock, cold wind, true dragon-fire,” the Queen went on. “And what more? Courage, and love, and pain — what else makes us human? Gervais, never think I do not know what we gave up.”

Gervais considered that. The price they had never paid, in all the years within the shelter of the enclave. All the years of games, and lies so beautiful they twisted the heart and yet remained lies for all their beauty.

He whispered, “We can die.”

“No more games, dear heart,” Audiarde said softly. “No more.”

Gervais straightened as if a burden had been lifted from his shoulders. Suddenly he knew that life was infinitely precious.

He looked up, and saw a sky full of stars.

“Tomorrow,” the Queen said, “I will ride out and see what lies beyond the mountains.” She held out a hand towards him. “Will you ride with me?”

Amazed, Gervais turned towards her. “Yes,” he said. "Wherever the road may lead.”

He reached out and clasped her hand.

Last Resting Place

Matt Colborn

Matt Colborn is a freelance author and consultant with an academic background in Cognitive Science. Previous work includes the non-fiction book on consciousness Pluralism and the Mind *published in 2011, and the fiction collection* City in the Dusk and Other Stories *(2013). Currently, he is working on non-fiction pieces concerning human flourishing and the future, and a science fiction novel. He lives in Lincolnshire, and his general website can be found at* Mattcolborn.com.

The planet Mars has inspired so many beloved science fiction tales, from Wells' alien invaders to the chronicles of Ray Bradbury and many more. Whether there was ever life on Mars is a matter for conjecture. In Matt's story, the red planet might be the perfect location for a man on the wrong side of death...

Romeo Wainwright III finally got to visit Mars two years after he had died. He rode in the front of the hearse alongside the driver, Undertaker-35, after his material remains had been stowed in the rear. His post-mortem avatar was robotic, the head a fleshy, biosculpted replica of his tanned, blue-eyed face, complete with thick, black, hair. He was awaiting news from Earth.

The legal battles had begun shortly after his resurrection, as his sons had tried to claim their inheritance and Romeo's lawyers had held them off. He remembered the day in court when an expert witness had sworn that Romeo could not possibly be conscious. The witness was a professor of philosophy with hollow cheeks, a shaved scalp and wire-framed glasses.

"We have no proof that the simulation of Romeo Wainwright is conscious. But even if we grant this, we have no way of knowing whether the original, biological consciousness has been transferred, or whether this is an entirely new, synthetic being."

"If this is a new being," his son's lawyer had said, "then he has no claim to the Wainwright fortune, which should, legally speaking, pass to his son as stipulated in the late Romeo Wainwright's own will."

The judge had ruled in favour of his son, but Romeo's lawyers had appealed, and Romeo was still awaiting the outcome.

The hearse sped along a dusty road, past salmon-pink dunes, under a butterscotch sky. They followed the rough road beyond Bradbury City, across miles of rock-strewn Martian badlands, kicking up dust.

They came to the gravestones; simple, white markers at first, but then more elaborate structures. Romeo saw traditional, decorated tombstones, box-tombs, stone crosses, angels, reclining Buddhas and an enthroned Osiris. There were mini-pyramids, a replica mausoleum, a Grecian temple and a shrine to Mictlantechuhtli, the Aztec god of death. There were sculptures; nested cubes or polyhedrons, or melted stone. There were virtual markers with coloured patterns that slowly revolved, and commercially-funded markers with flickering logos, the interred beholden to mighty corporations even unto death. Several of the newer graves were accompanied by virtual ghosts of their occupants, who turned to stare at the passing hearse.

The hearse sped towards the chapel where a perfunctory memorial service was to be held prior to the burial. Romeo could see it already; a small, wooden, white-painted building with a little bell tower, set against a virtual, projected landscape of green, rolling hills and a blue, summer sky.

The bell in the chapel tower clanged, calling mourners to their places in the congregation. An old couple walking a dog smiled and greeted them as they approached the chapel doors, and Romeo raised his hand in return, before remembering that the simulations here had no consciousness; like the projected landscape, they were scenery.

The chapel was almost empty when they entered. Romeo led, and Undertaker-35 followed, carrying the memorial urn that was set on a table before the altar. An invisible organ played Beethoven's Moonlight sonata.

One small, rounded-headed old man sat in the front pew, and he turned and grinned when he saw Romeo, beckoning.

"Romeo," the man said, offering his hand. "Haven't seen you in forty years."

"Elias?" Romeo said, remembering a little boy with a cheeky grin, "Is that really you?"

"Sure is!" The grin was just the same. Romeo glanced at the empty pews.

"Where is everyone else?" Elias looked awkward.

"I'm the only one, Romeo."

"You're the only one...?" Rage stirred inside Romeo, an old, thundering rage.

Elias sighed, and placed a virtual hand on his old friend's shoulder.

"I'm sorry to tell you this, my friend, but the living aren't interested in the dead. No one else is coming."

"No one's coming?" Romeo half-shouted, knowing he was wasting his time, because this 'Elias' was another simulation, lacking the Rucker lattice, the device that allowed Romeo's consciousness.

"We'll talk afterwards," Elias said, as the virtual chaplain arrived.

"It's such a shame you're just a simulation," Romeo said to Elias, after Undertaker-35 had finished shovelling Martian regolith on top of the memorial urn. The burial was marked by a three foot cube of solid diamond engraved with Wainwright's name. There was no date of death.

"Why do you say that?" Elias said.

"Because *I'm* the first conscious revenant," Romeo said. "You lot lack the Rucker Lattices."

"Romeo," Elias said, with a sparkle in his eye, "I'm as conscious as you are. There was a shipment of the lattices on the freighter you came out on."

"Of course," Romeo said, remembering. He had not realised that they would be fitted here.

"The company installed my simulation core with a lattice a few days ago," Elias said, "and I'm only the first." He pointed into the simulation, past the chapel, to the village beyond. "Right now, there's a community of simulations in there, living imitation lives to console visitors. It's little more than a post-mortem Disneyland, but it could be so much more than that."

"Because now," Elias said, "we'll come alive, on Mars, for real. We'll have... souls again. And it's all thanks to you." He smiled. "You could join us, Elias; we'd be honoured. If it weren't for you, we would never have had this opportunity."

"I can't join you," Romeo said, "I have too much to do, on Earth."

"Romeo," Elias said, "have you checked the latest newscasts?"

Romeo accessed the latest newsfeed, which materialised as a banner across the bottom of his visual field. The feed said:

DECEASED FATHER OVERRULED: WAINWRIGHT FORTUNE PASSES TO SON.

"Those bastards," Romeo said. "I have to go back..."

"Romeo," Elias said firmly, "it's too late."

"But my son will get everything!"

"That's right," Elias said. "That's what happens, when parents die. And you should be grateful. I lost my daughter, over forty years ago. I would give anything to know that she's living a happy life somewhere."

"That's irrelevant," Romeo said, fuming.

"Is it? There are no Rucker lattices for her, just a plaque in a memorial park in Waukegan. Remember that when you're trying to snatch back your son's inheritance."

Elias told him that if he wished to join the revenants, he'd have to abandon his robotic form.

"No!" Romeo said, still enraged.

"It's the only way," said Elias. He nodded at Undertaker-35. "He can do it, transfer your lattice to the virtual ghost generator. Just ask him. Or you can waste more time clinging to things that aren't yours any more." And Romeo's boyhood friend trudged away, over the Martian sand, back into the simulation.

Romeo paced the cemetery, leaving tracks like dried blood. Slowly, his anger subsided, and he thought of his son, who had looked miserable on that day in court. Romeo saw that he had been selfish, never thinking of him at all, but only his own schemes. And he saw that Elias was right; there was only one future open to him.

Undertaker-35 was waiting by the grave. All Romeo had to do was say the word, and the Undertaker deactivated him. Half an hour later, he regained consciousness as a virtual ghost and like a sprite stepped over the Martian soil, under the butterscotch Martian sky, towards the only future that was possible for the virtual, Martian, dead.

Mayfly

Heather Lindsley

Heather Lindsley's work has appeared several times in The Magazine of Fantasy and Science Fiction*, as well as in* Asimov's *and* Strange Horizons*. Her fiction has also been included in John Joseph Adams' dystopian anthology* Brave New Worlds *and in* The Mad Scientist's Guide to World Domination*, in* Year's Best Science Fiction 12*, edited by David G. Hartwell and Kathryn Cramer, and in* Talking Back*, edited by L. Timmel Duchamp. She has been featured on* Escape Pod *as a writer and on* Podcastle *as a reader, and her stories have been translated in Polish, Romanian, Russian, and French publications. She currently lives in Brighton and works in London, which gives her more time to write on the train.*

Heather's story "Mayfly" has a lovely premise and pursues the logic of its core idea with purpose and rigour, as all great science fiction does. The story is set on Earth but explores the consequences of a very different biological lifecycle. How would our priorities shift in such a world...?

The women in my family are born remembering. I'm not talking about that vague instinctual nonsense that's just as likely to do harm as good in the latest version of the world. I'm talking about flexing my infant fingers with the memory of arthritis in my grandmother's hands. I'm talking about reading before teething. I'm talking about taking my first clumsy steps toward an electric bill I already know is due next Thursday. I know because my mother knew.

Paying that bill will be one of the last things I do before I die. I will spend twenty minutes of my precious time on hold, waiting to set up the account for automatic debit, a generous legacy to my grateful descendants.

We're always looking for ways to save time.

The reflection of what appears to be a girl of eleven looks back at me from the full-length mirror in the bedroom that was my mother's. Together we spit out yet another baby tooth, which reminds me I need to drink another calcium-enriched protein shake. Either that, or eat what remains of my mother.

She's the pile of coarse dust scattered across the bedsheets. Some of my kind swear by mother dust, the way certain factions among the rest of the population swear by breastfeeding. And there are benefits, whether you're still a kid with growing bones or an adult woman facing osteoporosis by the end of the week.

But my mother is not strawberry-flavoured, so I opt for the shake.

Some people make a religious ceremony out of gathering up the remains, saying a prayer over it before ritualised ingestion. My family has never really gone in for that kind of thing. A Dust Buster and a bad joke have always been good enough for us.

"Bye, Mom," I shout over the clattering motor. "Thanks for the memories."

Still, my mother had a bit of the mystic in her, so I scoop up some dust from the sheets and drop it in my glass. She would have wanted it that way.

With funerary services complete and the sheets churning away in a washing machine I can finally reach, I go to the dozens of postcards my mother left on the coffee table in the cluttered living room. Each one bears the same message in my mother's hand, energetic block letters that say, *Still Kickin'*. The one kicking is not her, of course, but me — a mother traditionally prepares the postcards her only daughter will mail to her far-flung cousins, confirming the survival of another nearly forkless branch on the rangy family tree. My mother addressed the cards, but she didn't take the time to put stamps on them, and I'm annoyed by her selfishness. At least the stamps are here, hundreds of them, purchased in bulk years ago by a distant ancestor who sacrificed part of her short life standing in line at the post office. I raise my gritty strawberry-mom shake in silent salute, and start applying stamps to cards.

When I'm done, I sift through the dozens of books stacked up around the living room, looking for something to read while I wait for my awkward adolescent body to catch up with my mind. Most of the books are ones the women in my family wanted to read but just didn't have time for, and I pause when I find *Anna Karenina* among them. I have an ancestral memory of the first seven books, courtesy of a foremother who died before she could get to the end. Some of her descendants considered finishing it, but Anna has already thrown herself under the train, and so far no one has been willing to spend time on the denouement. *Maybe later*, I lie to myself, knowing that I won't read it either.

Instead, I grab the trashiest looking bodice-ripper I can find in the hope that it will distract me from the growing pains that will keep me up most of the night.

The early morning light comes through the pale, thin curtains as I push myself up into a sitting position and dig through the snack wrappers that cover the bedspread until I find the last of the protein bars. I climb out of bed and see myself in the mirror: the apparent nineteen-year-old is as tall as I'm going to get, just as those breasts are as perky as they'll ever be. I head into the bathroom and shower away the sour smell of rapid growth.

In the closet I find jeans in several different sizes — in this, at least, we're no different from other women. I grab a pair that look like they'll fit, and the first T-shirt I find. *Porn Star*, it says. *Oh, Grandma — what the hell where you thinking?* But of course I know: she liked the glitter.

I'm too ravenous to bother looking for another shirt.

Instead, I go straight into the kitchen to eat an entire box of cereal so I'll have the energy to cook a proper breakfast. I'm glad to see the refrigerator still holds five gallons of milk, and when I check the dates on the cartons I notice my daughter-to-be will probably expire before the milk does.

My mother forgot where she left the apartment keys, so by the time I find them I've got a late start on my necessary trip to the grocery store. I meant to take the stamped postcards out to the mailbox, but I'm already in the lobby before I remember them and I don't want to take the time to go back upstairs. One of my neighbours enters the building as I'm leaving, and we exchange nods with only the briefest flash of eye contact, the way people do when they understand that a crowded city holds together because we've all agreed to mind our own business.

My neighbours might see an old woman or a kid in the hallway, a teenager or a pregnant woman alone in the lobby. They'll look vaguely alike, the way families do. Maybe the neighbours see a young woman coming out of the same apartment every couple of weeks, and she seems a bit different each time: a little taller, a little shorter. She's probably just wearing different shoes. Her face isn't memorable, so they never notice that it's changed. And so far — as long as every fourth generation writes a rent check from the family trust — nobody cares that we're here.

The grocery store seems crowded for a Friday afternoon, but maybe that's just because every person stands out as someone who could end up in line ahead of me.

A woman looks at me strangely as I put the last giant tub of vanilla yoghurt in my cart with a half-dozen others. I smile at her in a vague, forgettable way, and feeling generous I say, "I'm sorry, did you want that?"

"Uh, no, thanks. I'm getting the non-fat kind."

"Oh, good — there's enough for both of us, then."

"Yeah," she says, glancing at the full cart again before going on her way. I hope she's not headed for the ice cream.

I pick through the ice cream flavours, searching for novelty rather than nutrition. Double Cherry Black Forest Cake. Ooh. I don't remember that. I'm just about to reach for it when it's pulled away by a hand accessorised by an expensive watch. I look up into a pair of smoky grey eyes. I turn on the charm and the pheromones, and ask nicely, "Oh, that's my favourite. Do you mind?"

He gives me a smile frosty enough to compete with the ice cream.

"Sorry, it's my boyfriend's favourite, too."

I nod apologetically and take Raspberry Fudge Swirl. I have memories — vague, as the oldest ones are — of distant ancestors smiling sweetly as they asked wealthy-looking men to hand over their wallets, sometimes the same men who fathered their daughters. *Child support*, they joked. It used to be standard operating procedure, until they gathered enough for the money to start breeding, too.

It seems repulsive to me, but not so repulsive I'm unwilling to spend the money.

I come home. I put away groceries. I climb into a hot bath. Time stops in the bathtub, then starts up again as the water gets colder.

I dig around in the closet, going back two hundred generations to find, among other things, a beaded halter top. I saw a few of them around while I was out on my errands. Apparently they're back in fashion again.

I'm feeling guilty about my lack of contribution to our branch's cultural heritage, and, wanting to compensate for spending so much time on a disposable novel, I try to get up the heart for the Bergman retrospective at the local art house.

When I check the paper I discover a theatre across town is playing early Hitchcock. Score.

On my way out through the lobby I see the mail has finally arrived, and I realise that once again I've forgotten to take the cards downstairs with me. I open the mailbox and flip through the postcards I've received. Among the usual

Nous vivons, *Nog hier*, and *Accendiamo*, there are indications that our population will once again outpace accidents and reproductive apathy. *Gemelo*. *Bliznetsy*. *Twins*. There's even one from Hong Kong that says, *Triplets*, and under that, in different handwriting, *We two survived*.

The number of twins in this set of cards is much like what I remember from my mother's week but unlike anything I can recall from the generations before. Only the Viennese branch of the family has shown an abiding interest in our genetics, and I wonder what they would make of this before the thought is crowded out by the other things on my mind.

"Tell me about the timbale of smoked salmon." I've chosen this restaurant almost exclusively because they use words like *timbale*. I'm also digging the floor-to-ceiling red velvet drapes.

"Of course. The timbale of smoked salmon is baked in pastry and served with heirloom tomatoes, herbed chèvre, and a lovely sweet onion marmalade."

"How lovely?"

"I beg your pardon?"

"Never mind." I'm being unfair; the waiter is already disconcerted to be serving a woman alone in a place like this, but he's doing his best to behave himself because my credit's good enough for the '61 Haut-Brion. "I'll start with the smoked salmon, followed by the coriander-crusted lamb with braised endive. Oh, and you'll probably want to get started on a chocolate soufflé."

"Right away."

After dinner I change neighbourhoods and find a divey-but-not-too-divey bar. It's not especially busy, but there's a decent enough crowd and I start looking for a mate, preferably a quiet boy with a slow metabolism and large, liquid eyes.

It's still early, so I can be picky.

"Can I buy you a drink?" He's pretty, but he smells of cancer. It wouldn't kill our daughter any sooner, but it would kill harder, and I'm still holding out for heart disease.

"Thanks, but I'm waiting for someone."

The bartender has his back to me as he draws a beer. He catches my eye in the large mirror behind the taps and speaking to my reflection says, "Haven't I seen you in here before?"

"No," I tell his reflection, "but I have one of those faces."

He turns to look at me directly. "I guess you do."

I see he's older than the kid-tending-his-way-through-college I took him for, and when he brings me my drink I spot a touch of silver in his hair. He looks like someone who took up bartending because he wanted to keep his own hours, and may even have done something interesting with them.

"Opening a tab?"

"Yeah, thanks." I take out the family American Express Card: *May E. Mosca, Member Since 1985*. I'm not sure how many greats would prefix the grandmother who applied for the card — at least a thousand. I hand it over to the bartender, who has a long look at it.

"What's the E stand for?"

"Ephemera."

"That's beautiful."

"Thanks. It was my grandmother's name."

"Are you sure I don't know you?"

"Oh, I'm sure. But maybe you knew my grandmother."

He laughs. I remember that bartenders flirt to encourage higher tips, and decide I'll try not to take him too seriously.

A man sits down on my right and smiles at me. I smile back and consider initiating a conversation, but I'm too distracted by the maddeningly virile scent of the bartender and keep involuntarily glancing his way. It doesn't help that he wanders over to my end of the bar when he isn't busy with something else.

Later I find that I've spent so much time talking to the bartender that I'm caught off guard when he excuses himself to turn up the lights and walk around the bar hollering, "You don't have to go home, but you can't stay here." I'd comply, but he still has my credit card, so I sit back and watch customers slide grumbling off their bar stools.

Finally he comes back to me and gives me my credit card. “You,” he says slowly, “don’t have to go home, but we can’t stay here.”

“Okay, really — does that ever work?”

He grins, disarmingly bashful. “Sometimes.”

There was an unsettling time when we thought fear of disease and rising condom use might be the end of us. But irresponsibility prevails, and so we live on.

When I move to get up the bartender’s soft snoring stops abruptly. He takes my hand and gently pulls it back toward him.

“I have to go home,” I say.

Still half asleep, he mumbles something that sounds an awful lot like, “So you can’t stay here.” He squeezes my hand once before he lets go and returns to sleep.

My apartment isn’t far by cab, so it isn’t long before I’m stretched out in bed, eyes closed, expecting only a short nap before I’m awakened by hunger pains or contractions in the middle of the night. Instead, I wake with a start early in the morning of my fourth day, obviously not pregnant.

Damn vasectomies.

This throws off my schedule, but it isn’t an irretrievable disaster.

When one of us has a child on Day Three, she’s usually around to help with the birth of her granddaughter. This used to be typical, but in the last few years we’ve evolved our way to safer, easier births, and most of us would rather have a little more fun before reproducing.

Now it’s common to wait until Day Four before you have your daughter, and some women — my mother among them — will even push it to Day Five. She lasted long enough to get me up and around, which is all I really needed, anyway.

I’ll go out again tonight, and this time I’ll stay focused.

I decide to spend my last childless afternoon at another movie, and on my way out I finally remember to take the postcards.

I'm concentrating on the mailbox across the street, so I don't notice the car until both its brakes and its driver scream at me. It comes to a stop only after I've been knocked to the ground. At first I think it's done no more damage than bruising my hip and scattering the postcards all over the street, but when I stand pain shoots up my ankle. I try to hide it — the last thing I want is attention, and that includes medical attention.

A few bystanders who subscribe to the theory that a dramatic moment is everyone's business rush around picking up cards, but most of them find reasons to move on, not wanting to be tagged as witnesses to an accident. I take the cards that are pressed on me and wave away offers of assistance, then do my best to calm the frightened and angry driver by acknowledging fault and suggesting we forget the whole thing. He drives off as quickly as he can, leaving a mangled and unreadable postcard fluttering behind. I don't recover it, and someone somewhere will assume my branch of the family is gone, unless I manage to have a daughter who can tell them otherwise.

I turn back to my apartment building, doing my best to conceal my limp and the expression of pain trying to work its way onto my face. Normally I'd be too impatient to wait for the elevator and would take the stairs, but my ankle isn't giving me a choice.

When I get back to the apartment I put ice on my ankle, knowing I've made it worse by walking on it right after the injury, hoping it will heal enough to use again soon.

In the meantime, I address postcards. I apply stamps. I write, "We're here" over and over and over again. Maybe the repetition will make it true. And when I'm done, I read the end of *Anna Karenina*.

At midnight I test my ankle, then call a cab.

It's a large, sleazy-looking dance club. We try to avoid going to the same place twice, but I don't have time to mess around. I need a sure thing.

I limp my way to a dark corner, picking out the best possible candidate in the vicinity and whispering in his ear, "You. Me. Alley. Now." The first one doesn't go for it, but I move on and don't run out of corners before I get what I came for.

"Oh my God," he says as he staggers back against the wall. "I wish there were more women like you."

"Be careful what you..." I glance at his dull, bleary eyes and don't even bother to finish the sentence as I leave.

It takes me longer than expected to catch a cab back, and I commit to memory the strong suggestion to any descendent who finds herself in a similar situation that she tell the cab to wait.

On my way through the lobby I stop to pick up the mail. There's a thick envelope among the postcards. Austria.

I limp straight for the kitchen and grab a bag of frozen peas, a spoon, and a large jar of peanut butter. I save the three cases of calcium-enriched protein shake mix for my daughter, who shows her appreciation with a swift kick to my bladder.

I lie down in the bedroom, frozen peas on my ankle and peanut butter in my mouth. I flip through the postcards before opening the envelope from Vienna. My memory of German is rusty, but the letter is full of charts and tables of numbers, one of which goes from two to two thousand in less than a dozen rows. Then the contractions start.

Evolution has been kind to us, and it isn't long before the next May is in my arms, a little messy but otherwise fine and looking up at me with a clear-eyed recognition the rest of the population would probably find unsettling, but which is reassuringly familiar to me.

I only have a few moments to get acquainted with May before insistent contractions kick in again.

I'm going to need another name.

The Smart Minefield

Chris Butler

Chris Butler has published the science fiction novel Any Time Now *(Cosmos Books 2001) and the fantasy novella* The Flight of the Ravens *(Immersion Press, 2012), which was shortlisted for the BSFA Award for short fiction in 2013. His short stories have been published in magazines and anthologies including* Asimov's Science Fiction, Interzone *and* The Best British Fantasy 2014. *Chris edited* The World and the Stars *anthology and is currently hard at work on new novels and short fiction. For more information visit* www.chris-butler.co.uk.

In the story that follows, a bomb disposal team on the distant world of Minoru need to clear a path through a minefield. They have little time but all the latest technology on their side. What could possibly go wrong...?

The truck was already starting to move as I jumped in and pulled the door shut. It gave a good solid clang. Dan was driving and Steve sat in the back seat across from me. I'd met them the night before in the barracks but I hadn't yet met the Captain. He turned round in the front passenger seat and thrust his hand back towards me. "You'll be the new kid," he said cheerily.

"Yes, s-sir," I said, and shook his hand. I was annoyed with myself for stammering because I'd wanted to make a good first impression.

He pointed at his hard helmet, his name emblazoned across the front of it in big blue letters: YOUNG. "I'm not exactly," he admitted. "In any case, we like to keep things on a first name basis round here. You met Dan and Steve?"

"Last night, yes."

"Hope they looked after you. Welcome aboard, John."

The truck's suspension had obviously seen better days and a series of jolts went up my spine painfully as we juddered over the grate at the exit to the compound.

Minoru's sun had risen just above the horizon as we hurtled out into the Zone. There was no glass in the doorframe of the truck so I could lean out to survey the landscape, which baked in the furnace air. All I could see was barren desert reaching out to the horizon.

The truck kicked up a lot of dust from the dirt track laughingly referred to as "The Road." Steve kept adjusting his helmet and complaining that he didn't feel comfortable in it. A flock of Cale came and flew with us for a while. They swooped down level with the wheels then launched themselves in great arcs ahead of us. Like dolphins jumping at the bow of a ship on Earth. Of course, that was long ago, but I've seen the holos.

We travelled for a few hours away from the base camp; then the truck lurched to an abrupt halt. I wiped a hand across the back of my neck, shifting a thick film of sweat.

"This is it," the Captain said. In a few more hours the tanks would roll through the path we had to clear. "Get to work. And John, try not to blow yourself up on your first day."

The other three laughed, and I let them have their fun. I appreciated the fact that they weren't treating me like a child. They hadn't given me a lecture of Do's and Don'ts. They assumed I knew my job and expected me to carry it out. The Captain took the lead as we set out on foot.

Without exception, the landmines in this sector were designed to blow up heavy artillery, nothing smaller. Our Ottawa Convention had outlawed antipersonnel mines, and the other side didn't seem to go in for them either. So a man on foot did not possess sufficient mass for his weight to detonate the device. Unlike the truck, which, with four passengers, might conceivably be mistaken for a small tank.

"Yep," the Captain said, "the aerial reconnaissance is correct. This is a minefield all right."

All the camouflage and all the non-reflective, non-conductive construction techniques in this world, or any other world for that matter, couldn't disguise a field of this size.

"It's big, then," Dan deduced.

"It's a big 'un all right," the Captain confirmed.

The four of us were connected with an LM200 mini-web, communicating by microwaves. I switched to my virtual eyes and studied the readouts. I might have expected the tactical display to light up like a Christmas tree. But in fact it just showed a faint glow. The mines were well concealed all right. But they were there, and lots of them.

Steve pulled a spade from the rucksack strapped to his back. I thought he looked almost as though he was drawing a sword from a scabbard, but I guess I was just being fanciful. Anyway, he stepped up to the front purposefully. Steve said he had a nose for landmines. Like a man divining for water he set off, assessing the terrain, taking in the details, seeing the peaks and the troughs. Then suddenly he stopped, scooped away the top layer of dirt and bent down to inspect beneath the surface.

"Oh my Lord!" he exclaimed. "Hey guys, come get a load of this!"

He continued digging until the rest of us joined him and together we all crouched down and stared into the pit.

"That's a smart mine," Dan commented. "And I don't mean it is formally attired."

I laughed. You could tell I was the new boy on the team. The others knew better than to laugh at one of Dan's jokes.

We all stood up again. The Captain pressed a sweaty forefinger and thumb to the bridge of his nose, succeeding only in pushing sweat into his eyes where it stung venomously — judging by the red flare in the data stream sent to me over our LM200 connection. He winced and gave me an uneasy smile. “You know what that is?”

I snapped to attention. “That is a T3500 sm-smart mine, m-manufactured by the MallTech Corporation, designed circa 2960, first a-active use circa...”

“Okay, okay,” the Captain said wearily. “You know what it is, you know all about it.” He gestured to me to relax. “But do you know what it’s doing here?”

I glanced around. There was nothing much to see, no landmarks of any kind. Just a field that stretched to the horizon whichever direction you looked, and a long, straight road that cut through it. “Well,” I said slowly, “if it’s our mines then I guess we p-planted ’em.”

The four of us all nodded in agreement.

Steve said, “Assholes, ain’t we?”

We all kept nodding.

The Captain turned to me again. “That would have been a long time ago. So, new kid who knows it all — how do you suggest we deal with these suckers?”

“Well, I guess the first thing to d-do is to find out whether the field is operating in its ‘smart’ capacity.”

“Good thinking,” the Captain barked. “Steve, give him a hand. See if you can deactivate this mine, and then we’ll see how the field reacts. Dan, you’re with me.”

Steve and I watched for a moment as the other two men headed back to the truck. My thoughts went back to the training school, and the lecture on the theory of the smart minefield. The idea was that all the mines in the field were optimally positioned equidistant from each other so as to allow no safe passage through the field. The mines communicated with each other in order to confirm their position. If any mine were to be disarmed or otherwise disabled, then all the mines in the field would reposition themselves to again provide optimum coverage of the field, only now with fewer mines.

A mine repositioned itself by means of a powerful hydraulic foot with which it would literally launch itself into the air, flinging itself to its new position. It sounded ludicrous, but it worked. It worked ludicrously well.

The normal job of a team of minefield disposal experts was to clear a path through the field, not to clear the entire field. But you couldn't do that with a smart field. It wouldn't let you. Clear a mine and the field reacted to plug the gap.

"Should be quite a sight when this f-field repositions itself," I said. I have to admit I was quite excited about it.

"You mean when thousands of explosive mines leap into the air all around us?"

"It'll probably only be a few dozen in the immediate vicinity. We're only making a small hole in the field. It's unlikely that every m-mine in the field will move. It doesn't really need to in order to effectively prevent safe passage through the field. It would be a waste of energy for the entire field to react."

"Oh, well, that's all right then."

Steve had the top-plate off the mine and he examined the interior. Firstly he disabled the hydraulic foot. The last thing we needed was for the mine to launch itself while we were peering down at it. Then he disabled the firing mechanism since we didn't particularly want it to detonate either.

"Still c-can't believe you screwed that girl back at Fort Bridgeport last night," I said.

"She was lonely."

"She was m-married and she already had a lover on the other side of town. How lonely c-could she be?"

"Okay. Not lonely. She was eager."

The two of us lifted the mine out of the soil. One fortunate thing about the mine was that it was designed to be lightweight. As we lifted it, the hydraulic foot extended to hang limply beneath it. Quickly we carried it back to the truck, aware that at any moment the field might react.

But it failed do so. To be sure, we had two choices. Put the mine in the truck and drive it further out of position, or perform the final part of the deactivation process, and disable its radio transmitter.

The Captain said, “There’s no way I’m driving away from a chance to see a smart minefield realign itself. Kill its radio,” and he grinned.

Steve picked up a screwdriver and jammed it into the sealed unit that housed the radio circuitry. Unexpectedly this caused a spark and a plume of smoke bubbled up towards him. Reflexively he jerked back from the device, more in surprise than alarm, and fell flat on his back. Consequently he missed the sight of hundreds of mines launching themselves into the air, kicking up dust as they landed in their new positions.

“Oooh!” Dan cooed. And the Captain and I nodded appreciatively.

Steve staggered to his feet. “What? Did I miss it? Ah shit!”

Dan figured he had the problem sussed. “This is easy,” he said. “We disable the firing mechanisms but leave the radio transmitters intact. We can work the road, make it safe for the tanks to come through, and the mines out to the sides won’t know anything is amiss. Standard approach, clear a path through.”

“Reckon that w-would work?” I asked.

“Sure,” Dan said, liking the fact that he had apparently impressed the new kid, and he stepped forward, eager to get started. He slapped me on the back as he set off in search of the next mine to be disarmed. Steve hurried after him. The critter had sparked him and he was eager to get some payback.

The Captain clawed futilely at the corner of his eye, still trying to ease the stinging sensation there. “Reckon it’ll work?” he asked.

I studied my two new colleagues in the distance, squinting slightly as the heat haze made the landscape shimmer. “Might do,” I replied. “Depends what generation of m-mine we have here.”

“Generation?”

“Thing is, Captain, when these mines were first ddeployed there was an assumption that the enemy was of limited intelligence."

The Captain scoffed. *If only.*

"Pretty soon, they realised that the mines had to be improved."

Steve glanced in our direction, probably wondering when we were going to start helping. The Captain threw him a dismissive gesture, which I guess Steve interpreted as meaning that we were busy.

"Most likely thing," I continued, "is that the radio transmitter is w-wired into a test circuit for the detonator. Disarm the detonator, the radio circuit automatically shuts itself down."

"So how come the radio in this one," the Captain pointed at the dead specimen at our feet, "didn't shut down till Steve punched a screwdriver through it?"

"Well, could be it's an early-generation mine and Steve and Dan are on the right t-track. Or it could be that there's a time delay in the radio shutdown, which happened to correspond to the t-time taken to carry the mine back here and for Steve to, with surgical precision, apply his screwdriver."

The Captain turned wearily in the direction of the two men in the distance. They had deactivated a mine each and had now started work on their second. "We'll know soon enough," he said.

At that moment, hundreds of mines launched themselves into the air, and then rained down around the startled duo. When the dust settled the dejected men walked back to rejoin us.

"Anyone for tennis?" the Captain quipped. That was a good one and we all laughed without feeling guilty about it.

"You know what this means, don't you?" Dan said in a Daffy Duck voice, "This means war!"

"Yes, yes." the Captain said, "look, we've got tanks coming through here in a couple of hours. They're not coming through unless we clear this field. More importantly, there's a single malt whisky back at the base with my name on it and I'm thirsty. Kid, you seem to be the expert on these things. What would you recommend?"

I smiled, happy to be centre stage. I spoke quickly, enthusiastically. "The thing about these mines, it's not the mine you're working on that matters, it's the rest. You have to think big, think about the whole field. If you want to clear the mines from the road, you have to make the whole field want to let you. You see where I'm g-going?"

The Captain nodded. "If we can make the field think that there are mines on the road, by generating fake radio transmissions, then the real mines would move elsewhere."

"Create a whole row of mines that don't really exist?" Dan scoffed. "We'll never get that up and running in time."

"He's right," I admitted. "The b-best way would be to redefine the perimeter of the field. Hack into the field's net, get at the data, then we c-could move the whole field away from the road. The mines would literally move out of our way of their own volition. But hacking into their net is probably impossible in the time we have. I mean, we might g-get lucky and crack the encryption real fast. But chances are we won't."

The Captain pointed decisively at Dan and ordered him to get started on that approach. "Right," he said, turning his attention back to me, "any other ideas?"

"How many t-tanks have to come through here?"

"About twenty."

"And how quickly do they have to get through?"

"They can go slowly, as long as they're moving. What are you thinking?"

"I'm thinking that we put a mine on the tank, and then drive the tank through the f-field."

Steve laughed. "Surely that'll never work."

"It should," I insisted. "As the tank drives into the field, all the other mines should rearrange themselves to be anywhere other than where the tank is."

"But they'll be hopping all over the place. Surely the field is designed to resist that in some way."

"Depends which g-generation of mine we're dealing with. Wanna give it a try?"

Five minutes later we had a mine in our truck and I was ready to drive into the field. We'd had to securely fasten the mine in place with some restraining clamps in order to prevent it trying to jump itself to another position in the field. I put the truck in gear and let it inch forward. As I drove into the field, the mine in the truck therefore taking up a position in the field, the landscape suddenly became alive with jumping mines. They jumped out of my way, moving off to the sides. Then as the truck made further progress, a mine would move in behind to take up the position newly vacated by the advancing vehicle.

For a while there I thought it was working, but then the field stopped reacting. It went quiet like a lion crouching down in tall grass. I jumped out of the truck and started running back towards the other men. The force of the explosion knocked me to the ground. Debris from the truck rained down all around me. Something bounced off my hard helmet and skittered off into the dirt.

I apologised to the Captain for the loss of the vehicle, and enquired as to whether Dan was making any progress.

Dan had in fact managed to gain access to the field's network. He could see the data defining the field's perimeter. Unfortunately, the data was write-protected and couldn't be modified without a password, which of course he didn't have. He'd been trying to find another way in, but so far without success.

I suggested trying to modify the data defining the mine's own position. Moving the mine ten feet to the left was the same as moving the field ten feet to the right. But again the data was protected and couldn't be modified.

The Captain was beginning to worry. In twenty minutes the tanks would be arriving. We couldn't even communicate with the base camp because the radio had been in the truck.

And we were too far away from the base for our local web to connect to it. He paced up and down nervously. “We have to come up with something. Fast. Think of something, now!”

“What’s the programming language for the software?” I asked.

“Some object-oriented shit,” Dan said.

“Built on library classes?”

“Yes, that’s right. Off the shelf building blocks, which they built the app on top of.”

“3D coordinate system?”

“Eh?”

“Their basic coordinate class. Is it three d-dimensional?”

“Yes, it is actually. Overkill for a 2D app...”

Dan froze, suddenly seeing where I was heading. Then he was pulling various code-fragments out of his library files and the hacklets started flying round the web furiously.

“What?” the Captain asked.

I explained. “The minefield is two d-dimensional. It has width and length, but not height. However the underlying s-software allows for a position to have a height. Therefore a mine could be given a height. In the real world it’s not realistic for a mine to have a height, but in the software simulation it absolutely can. If we’re lucky, they haven’t p-protected that height variable, because they haven’t anticipated it ever being used.”

“Bingo,” Dan said. “I have access. You want me to try it?”

I smiled and concluded my explanation. “The field is currently defined to be, say, a mile wide and a mile deep, and zero miles high. We’re going to ch-change that and make it, I don’t know, shall we say two hundred miles high? Just stick in a b-big number, Dan.”

He did so, and the entire field erupted into life. Mines hopped continuously. As soon as they landed they hopped again. Dan and I fell about laughing. Soon Steve and the Captain were laughing along with us.

“What on Earth are they doing?” the Captain asked,

dumbfounded.

"They're trying to take up positions to fully occupy the interior of the minefield. Which is now three-dimensional. Fortunately for us, gravity is preventing them from reaching their intended position in the field. They're trying but they can't get there."

"Will they keep doing this indefinitely?"

"Well no, they'll run out of power. Hopefully soon. And then with any luck we can get the tanks through before the mines collect enough solar energy to recharge themselves."

The Captain glanced upwards, no shortage of solar energy here.

"Or," I continued, "all of this could t-trigger another self-check in the field, and then the firing mechanisms..."

As one, the four of us started running. Seconds later the mines began detonating, spreading a field of fire across the landscape. It was a spectacular sight, as if a vengeful crimson spirit had possessed the air itself.

After a time, the flames subsided, but still we sweltered under the heat of the sun. And charred black flecks filled the air, clogging in our throats. We stood waiting for the tanks to roll through, knowing we would have to ask the first of them to radio back to the base for help for us. And then we would have to wait for a replacement truck to come and rescue us.

I heard a thud then and I looked around but I couldn't see anything. I didn't figure it out then, but I reckon that what I heard was the mine landing, completing its latest leap. I guess maybe it had travelled a long way, from the furthest reaches of the field, and its power level had fallen to near zero and so it had not self-destructed.

It would have to wait until it had collected enough solar energy to recharge itself, and then it would continue its journey. As the sole remaining mine, its destination was the very centre of the field, and it was still trying to get there.

Soon, the tanks rolled through, safely navigating the charred terrain. No flock of Cale accompanied them;

presumably the aftermath of the fire, the stench in the air, had frightened them away. We watched the tanks disappear into the distance, then the four of us settled down on the ground, sharing a flask of water we had been given. The sun beat down fiercely.

"What is it with this sun?" Dan moaned. "Is it trying to kill us?"

But we all smiled as we saw the truck approaching in the distance at last. The Captain polished off the last of the water. "My next drink will be that long awaited whisky," he said cheerily.

The truck had almost reached us when the mine, which by now had recharged itself enough to take another leap, jumped into the path of the oncoming vehicle and blew it up.

That was really downheartening.

At this point there was nothing we could do except set off walking in the direction of the base. Under the intense heat it was touch and go whether we could make it back. We'd been walking for hours already when a small flock of Cale swooped down, circled round us briefly, and then flew away. My legs ached, along with every other muscle in my body. We kept moving.

Later still, I realised that the sun had moved significantly in the sky and had begun its slow descent towards the horizon, but still it beat down on us without mercy and I could feel myself becoming disoriented as dehydration set in.

I switched in to the local web that linked us together. The Captain was three feet to my left, keeping pace with me at the front of the group. Dan was twelve feet behind. He was sending a babble of incoherent data into the net. I think he was becoming delirious and he was pulling data out of the archives at random. Steve was falling behind, fifty yards now.

We were falling out of formation, but at least we were still in contact. We travelled as quickly as we could manage, doing our utmost to reach our destination.

It was the smart thing to do.

By Starlight

Rebecca J. Payne

Rebecca J. Payne is a science fiction and fantasy author from Cambridge. Her fiction has been published in magazines including Interzone, Ethereal Tales *and* Emerald Tales. *Her short stories are included in the anthologies* Dark Currents *and* Looking Landwards *(both NewCon Press) and* Weird Lies *(Arachne Press).*

It is fitting that for the final pages of our journey, Rebecca's story takes us to the skies. Let us fill our sails with light, steer away from the life that is expected of us, and pursue instead a perilous course...

I stood on the centre of the deck, wood creaking beneath my feet. I could feel the faint pulse of the ship through the worn-down soles of my boots. Slowly, I tethered a length of rope to the wheel to set our dawn course and, breathing on my fingers for warmth, watched the silvery mainsail as it billowed above, glowing bright against the night sky. Summer nights were too short, and just as cold as winter once you sailed high enough. On our starboard side long wisps of white rose up as our bow cut through a ridge of cloud; tendrils of vapour curled their way around our hull, countless drops of water illuminated by the light of our sails. For a second I allowed my tired eyes to close, and I could still see pale ghosts of them, dancing against the darkness.

"Adia, are we clear ahead?" I called out. As fast as we were sailing west, the night was close to ending. We could little afford to lose time in cloudfall. In the northeast, the cluster of bright stars that gave form to Auriga the Charioteer were in ascension; soon the rising sun would reclaim the sky and our sails would run slack without Auriga's light. Long days were the domain of the Burning Man and those below who worshipped him. Our gods of night were eternal, beautiful. Peaceful.

I heard Adia's footsteps skipping down from the bow where she had been watching the distant lights of other Aurigan ships. She ducked around the mast and smiled up at me.

"All clear 'til the day catches us," she said, her breath trailing off into the air. Her face was framed by thick black hair, cut short in the spring but now long enough to be ruffled by the wind that played with the collar of her black jacket. Her skin, in the light of the sails, radiated its own cold beauty, and for a moment I wondered what she had ever seen in me.

"We're closer to the fleet tonight," she said. "They're crowded together in the northwest. Twenty-five families as I can make out, and most of the tall workships."

I turned back to the wheel and made a show of tugging at the rope. I often wondered if she regretted coming with me, if she thought of her parents or brothers at all. The ship was holding steady for now.

"It's almost midsummer," I said. "Everyone's returning for the Feast of Feathers." The pit of my stomach lurched, whether through hunger or revulsion I wasn't sure. Adia moved beside me and I felt the weight of her slight frame against mine, her cheek resting on my shoulder.

"It could be a wedding, or a shipfitting... remember how sometimes, the whole fleet would come together just for the sake of it... just to dance, or..."

She went to take my hand in hers but I pulled away, bending down to pick up the lightjar that sat at the foot of the wheel, the crumpled pieces of old sail inside glowing brightly.

"I'll look at the charts, find us a new course. Somewhere north. The nights will be shorter, but we can do with less light if we don't need to sail fast."

"You should rest," she sighed. "You haven't slept for days. I can track the fleet until dawn, anchor if they anchor."

"We're too close," I lied, and turned away before she could give me that look, the one that said she knew the truth as well as I — they would never attack us. Not out of any affection or duty towards Adia and me, but because our ship's heart beat in time with theirs. Our figurehead, the two blessed goats, marked us as their own; our sails were filled with the same sacred light of Auriga.

"Please rest," she called after me, and I felt like the worst kind of captain and the worst kind of lover, one who can't admit to being wrong.

As I slunk across the deck to the cabin door I caught sight of Polaris, high in the north, and a memory rushed over me like a wave. I was sitting atop my grandfather's shoulders on the deck of our old family ship, clinging on to his thick neck for dear life as night winds howled around us. He had told me that living on the topside was a blessing, not because of the Charioteer, but because Polaris guided us above all other stars. He pointed north to the Heavens and swore that I must never repeat his words. *My father died*, he whispered, *in battle with the bullships over the skies of Amerika, and though I were just a lad left all alone on this ship, I asked steadfast Polaris to guide me home to where our people flocked beneath Auriga; Old Polaris is the equal of Capella, and though He has grown dim with age, He still holds light to fill a thousand empty sails*. I was too young, then, to understand what heresy was, but I understood that it was our secret. I asked him if the Lighters on the underside had stars like Polaris and Capella. *I think not, child, and frankly I don't much care.*

The memory faded, and I could now see the shining sails of the Aurigan fleet, glittering some way off in the distance. They must have seen us, too — not just that night, but a hundred nights before. One winter, just after dusk, when I had fallen asleep at the helm, an Aurigan battleship had approached us; it was close enough to open fire before we could turn and flee, but its guns were not even drawn. Maybe they believed that if they waited long enough, they would reclaim their ship intact. After all this time, they still thought we might come back.

The lightjar cast a pale glow as I descended into the cabin. There was something about the warm and clammy air below deck that comforted and smothered at the same time. Our living quarters were far larger than the two of us could ever need — a family was meant to be living here, not us. Adia's family, I reminded myself.

I set the lightjar on the table where my charts of the Heavens were pinned down, and pulled up an old chair. As soon as the weight was lifted from my feet my whole body sank with gratitude. I felt old — older than my twenty-four years. My eyes closed again and for a moment I was falling like a dead weight; when I opened them, the charts were nothing but a blur of lines and smudges drifting before me.

I blinked, and blinked again. It didn't help. My body was crying out for food and sleep. The smell of boiled linemoss drifted in from the galley, and suddenly I was five years old, running through the coldrooms in the dark damp belly of my family ship, the long strings of linemoss hanging down from the ceiling like strands of a spider's web. I would spend hours there, hiding from my parents, thinking of how I could weave the strings together to make patterns. I'd play until I got too hungry, and when I'd come shuffling up the stairs, asking for dinner, my father would shout *that child smells of nothing but wretched linemoss*, and he'd beat me with his belt until he drew blood. So I learned to stay down in the coldrooms, and eat growing moss raw from the string, and not come up until he was asleep.

I remembered how I'd curl up in the corner of the room in the lowest part of the ship and imagine that I could feel us climbing as high as the moon, or as far down as the valleys on the ground itself. When we did sail low, to snare fruit from trees or fetch clean water, there would sometimes be a *thump, thump, thump* against the bottom of the ship. I thought we were touching the treetops and were, for the briefest of moments, connected through the branches and trunks and roots and dirt all the way down to the heart of the earth. When I was nine, a Lieutenant on my first workship took great delight in telling me the truth; that it was the sound of Grounders firing arrows as we passed by. From then on, the sound haunted me, and I could never bear to be down in those rooms again. Seven years later, on deck one morning in the harsh winter sunlight, I saw a friend's skull split open by one of those arrows as he leant over the side to catch a pigeon.

I ran my hands over my eyes as if that would scrub away the memory. I didn't want to anchor, not while we were over Europa, but we had to store light in our sails if we were to go north with enough speed. In the beginning, when times had been good, Adia and I had often spoken of sailing south, somewhere wild and unknown; but leaving the fleet meant leaving behind the fragile protection of their presence. The skies over the equator swarmed with Taurans, Hydrans and other dangers. So we stayed in this strange half-life of ours, a ghost on the horizon of the Aurigan fleet, and with each passing season I worried more and more that they would one day tire of tolerating our games and send a crew to board us, forcing us home. So north it was, for now at least, where the Ursa tribes kept to themselves and we could ride out the rest of the long days until autumn.

The darkest voices inside told me the bullships would find us wherever we went, some kind of punishment for trying to run, something I deserved. They were just weary, angry thoughts. I stood up, reluctantly, and went to the galley.

The galley walls were stained red where a fire had spread years ago. The ship had never fully healed. I had tried to hide the scars with damsonberry dye but the lightjar illuminated them, dark patches of rough timber, bold and clear. The strong smell of the linemoss in its pot suddenly made me ill. In the cupboard above there were strips of cured beef, hanging like leather thongs, and I took one and bit into it, cursing the overpowering taste of salt. Before we could go north we'd have to find a merchant ship and trade for fresh supplies. I realised I didn't know how much we had to sell — I hadn't brought down the stonetrap for days. The thought of climbing the mast turned my arms to lead and I had to force myself to take another bite. We still had some spices from our last journey over southern Aysa in the hold, which would sell for some meat and grain at least; Adia had been working on new cloth but I realised I didn't know what kind, nor whether it was in any state to trade. It had been weeks since I had asked her.

I took a cup from its hook and poured water from the flask that hung by the stove. It tasted old but I was too thirsty to care. I drained the cup and took a deep breath, my head suddenly pounding like the pulse of a ship in full flight, and I stumbled towards the stairs down to our bedroom.

I collapsed onto the bed like a sail whose lines had all been cut to ribbons. The sheets were musty, and as I kicked off my boots, I could smell the linemoss still, infused in my clothes and in my skin. I pulled the sheets around me and that small cocoon of thin cotton became the most welcome place I could imagine, dark and warm and alone.

At first I dreamt of waking, of walking out onto the deck under a low afternoon sun to find the whole Aurigan fleet surrounding us. Adia was standing with her family, embracing Sam, the man she should have married; she was weeping and professing her repentance and shame. I had no heart to blame her for taking us back. I blamed myself. I would have run away with or without her.

I was hauled over thick boarding planks to a tall workship, rope binding my hands, resigned to whatever my fate might be. The mob jostled and pushed. I heard the sound of the workbell tolling and the people moved away. I looked down at my hands and they were small — I was only ten, back in my drab workship clothes, and the rope was twisted around my fingers, half in knots. I looked up at the mass of rope that hung overhead, hundreds and hundreds of knotted lines crossing over and over again, suspended by tethers that ran up to the masts. Other workers were mending sections of the net, tying on more and more pieces. I felt the jolt of an elbow in my back. I turned, and Lieutenant Heller glared down at me, baring his teeth.

“Finish that line, you heretic child, or you’ll eat nothing for a week!”

I looked back at the thin rope in my hands. The knots were tied around my fingers, not between, and I couldn’t move them, couldn’t pull my hands apart...

“I can’t!” I cried out, but Heller wasn’t there, and when I looked up the net was hung between our ship and the next, anchored at its top corners by thick leather straps on either side, its body rolled up and held by tethers waiting to be cut. And to port were two ships with another net between them, and to starboard were two more... and the people on the other ships began to play music, and suddenly our ship was full of people dancing, singing, drinking. All the ships of the fleet were there, decks adorned with paper effigies of bulls and scorpions and snakes that children would burn at sunset to keep monsters at bay. The skies beyond were a clear expanse of brilliant blue. A priest was standing near our bow, elegant and pristine in white. He raised his soft hands up to the workers.

“For three nights we have anchored and fasted, as the Charioteer demands,” he said. “Now see how our sails are filled with His good light! The longest of days seems like a curse upon us, but generous Auriga blesses us still. Today is midsummer — the day on which we are permitted to accept this bounty, so let us not waste time! By sunset all Aurigans will be eating well and thanking you for your tireless work. Father Auriga, we honour you with the Feast of Feathers.”

I felt sick. I couldn’t be here again. Thrown off my

family's ship the day my grandfather died, I'd been taken to a workship and told that the rest of my life would be spent there. I was no good for marrying and would never be allowed a family and a ship of my own. The workship cabins were filled with dozens of others like me crammed on board in tiny bunks, all starving and living together in darkness as we worked on those nets, and not once did I ask what it was all for...

The ships lurched downwards in unison. The people around me cheered, and the tethers of the net were cut and it fell open, spreading out in the sky between the ships. I realised that in all my young years I had never gone on deck to watch the midsummer festival; I was always hiding in the coldrooms, or listening to my grandfather tell tall stories in the galley, and when we had supper and they called it a feast I didn't ask what it meant, I was just glad that my father was in a pleasant mood for once...

I wanted to shake myself, tell myself that it was all so long ago, but I couldn't escape the nightmare. The ships levelled off and up ahead I could see birds flocking in their tens of thousands, finches and starlings and countless others, and I wanted to shout out as we sailed towards them, but I froze. Their flocks broke and panicked; some flew above us and swooped away, but others tried to fly down, and they couldn't escape the nets, and I could hear thousands of birds screaming, thousands of wings beating helplessly, the sound of death growing louder and louder until finally I screamed with them.

Men sprang into action, hauling up the limp ropes that tied the bottom of the net to the bow of the ship, and the net closed like a giant hand, crushing the poor birds together. I closed my eyes and put my hands over my ears, but I could still feel it happening. When I looked again the net was on our deck, and the workers were cutting its ropes, pulling out birds from its tangles and breaking their necks. Children younger than me were ripping out feathers in wild clumps and throwing their broken bodies into large baskets to be cooked. I could feel Heller's gaze burning into my back, and I walked to the net, carefully unwinding a cord from the still-warm body of a small grey bird. I could feel its tiny heartbeat racing in my palms. Its wings were unbroken, but it was too afraid to struggle, and as my hands closed around it, it trembled, trembled and trembled, and I began to cry. I ran to starboard and threw my hands up and over the side of the ship, and I watched as the grey bird took flight away from us, far away, towards the sun.

A bell woke me, distant but clear. I pushed myself from my bed. Sleep normally took longer to leave me, but I needed air, and we needed food.

Up on deck, Adia was steering us south at a slow decline towards the anchored tradeship; its merchant bell was still ringing out, calling us in. Adia had lowered the small topsail to help us sink and raised the yellow flag of trade. The sun was halfway high and the mainsail was running on nothing but afterglow as we crept slowly across the skies. I walked up behind Adia and put my hand on her waist. She jumped and let out a quiet squeak.

"Make ready the anchor," I said with a grin and kissed her on the cheek. I didn't know if she'd forgiven me. "I need to bring down the trap."

"There isn't time!" Adia sighed, but I was already climbing the mast, my whole body feeling refreshed from the hours of rest I had needed. As I looked across the horizon I saw no sign of the Aurigan fleet. My heart began to beat faster as I pulled myself to the very top, reaching across the lines to the stonetrap and unhooking it. I clipped it to my belt and paused, just looking out at the majestic clouds, the ever-changing mountains of our landscape. I pitied anyone who saw the same hills or valleys every day of their lives. There were large waves of heavy cloud in the west, barrelling together to form nebulae much deeper and longer than our small ship; small ripples high above us softened the perfect pale blue of the morning, carried along by the tide of the southwesterly wind. Behind us in the east another ship was approaching, far off but moving quickly, called in by the merchant bell. I thought of something my grandfather had said: *the gods are always there, even in the daylight, even if we can't see them*. I looked to the north and wondered if Polaris was somewhere behind the fathoms of blue.

By the time I climbed back down, Adia had steered us beside the tradeship. I heard the thud of our anchor hitting the ground below as she set free the chain that held it. Our ship bobbed and swayed for a moment before settling. We were closer to the ground than I liked, but there were no signs of any Grounder settlements, no smoke or cultivated fields. I vaguely recognised the merchant who was passing a boarding plank between our ships.

"Good day to you!" he said, and I immediately wanted to wipe the smile from his face. "What can I do for you this fine morning?"

Adia made pleasant talk with him while I emptied the stonetrap out over a bucket of water and watched the tiny star-like stones sink down, gleaming in the sunlight. It was a greater haul than we had had for a long time. I reached in and picked out a blueish stone, turning it over and over in my fingers. It was so strange, the way little flecks of light rose from our sails in the night, binding together and becoming rough jewels. I scooped half of them up and wrapped them in a cloth. The stones would be plenty — we could hold on to our spices for a better price.

I walked over to Adia, who was laughing at something the merchant had said. I recognised the laugh as the one she didn't really mean.

"Please, do come aboard," the merchant said, beckoning me over the boarding plank. I put my hand on Adia's shoulder.

"Back soon," I whispered.

As I stood at one end of the broad plank, I forced myself to hold my breath and look straight ahead. You couldn't show weakness to a merchant. As I put one foot in front of the other the dizzying sensation of being so close to the ground, close enough to make out movement in the long grass if I dared look down, threatened to overwhelm me. I didn't breath again until I reached the other side.

As we descended below deck the merchant continued his patter. "Lucky you came by; we are heading east tonight. You won't find goods so fresh from any other tradeship near here, certainly not!" He rattled on as we entered the dingy cabin, walls crammed with shelves of jars and old boxes. The room smelled of too many things at once. A dozen crates cluttered the floor, stood on end to form makeshift stands; most of them were covered in dusty sheets, with jars and bowls of the least rancid-looking goods on display. In one vase stood several wilting purple flowers. The merchant tapped a jar, half full of yellowish orbs bobbing in a green-tinged liquid.

"Know what these are?"

I shook my head.

"Eggs! Keep for a long time if you pickle 'em. Tasty, too." He unscrewed the lid and the smell of the liquid hit my nostrils like squalid water. "Want to try one?" I shook my head. I didn't want to open my mouth to speak until he put the lid back on. "Fair enough," he shrugged, "not to everyone's taste."

"We want meat and grain," I said, looking around at the stock and wondering how desperate we truly were.

"I have fresh cured beef, brand new! Small farmers over in Bavar, very civil people. Trade with no one but me."

I took ten stones from my bag and dropped them into his palm. There was no need to trade everything we had, not to a man my gut told me not to trust. "Nothing rotten," I said. "These are good."

He studied the stones closely. "Sapphires. Well, I do have plenty at the moment. Some of your fellow tribesmen were passing through only yesterday. But I'm sure you knew that." He gave me the strangest look, as if he were waiting for me to apologise. I cleared my throat.

"And we want cotton," I said, suddenly remembering Adia's work. "If you'd traded for Aurigan stones yesterday you wouldn't have called us in. Which means if the fleet did stop, they only traded you spare supplies, not stones. So meat, grain and cotton, if you don't mind." I allowed myself to smile as the merchant's fixed grin began to strain.

"Very well." He turned to the door that lead to the coldrooms and called down. "Hans, bring up the new beef!"

The deckhand appeared from below carrying a wooden chest. Suddenly I remembered why the merchant had sat badly in my memory — I could tell from his clothes that the deckhand was a Grounder. A Grounder on a Lightship. The tradeship's mast was ringed in bronze with the belt of Orion — how could the Hunter tolerate it? The Grounder glared at me as he started to unpack what looked like dried beef from the chest into a smaller wooden box. The merchant himself was scooping grain from a sack in the corner into small bags, weighing each one on old iron scales with an exaggerated frown.

"You're those two, aren't you?" he said after a while, dropping a further weight onto the scales, watching them teeter.

"What two?"

"You know. Of the Aurigan fleet, but not *of* the Aurigan fleet." He turned and grinned at me. I wanted to know how he knew; if the fleet really had stopped, if someone had talked about us.

"I don't know what you mean."

"Of course. You couldn't be them." He turned back to the scales. "Why would runaways still be creeping along in the wake of their old pals?"

From somewhere in the room I heard a strange noise, and a bird walked out from behind the coldroom door — fat and brown-feathered, making a clucking sound, just wandering free.

"What in the name of the Heavens is that?"

The merchant laughed. "Just a hen, that's all. Good layer

of eggs if you're interested. And when the damn things stop producing, you can cook and eat 'em." The Grounder pretended to kick out at the bird and they both laughed as it squawked and ran around the crates, panicking. I felt my hands bunch into fists.

"Why doesn't it fly away?"

He shrugged. "Maybe it doesn't know it can." The merchant handed the bags of grain to the deckhand, who packed them into a sack with the box. "Ten stones gets you one box of beef and four bags of grain. Only cotton I got is unspun."

"Not a problem," I said. He pulled an old red box from a shelf and opened it, taking out large fistfuls of lumpy white cotton and tossing them into the sack. The deckhand slunk back down to the coldrooms without a word.

I looked over at the hen, still wandering aimlessly among the crates.

"Now," the merchant said, "are you sure there's nothing more I can do for you?"

Out on deck I stepped right up to the boarding plank, my desire to get off the ship overcoming the nausea of seeing the ground so close. I walked quickly, the sack in one hand balancing the caged hen in the other. As I stepped down, and heard the merchant drag the plank back across, Adia stared at me open-mouthed.

"I can explain," I said.

She shook her head. "I can't wait to hear it."

We raised anchor and started to climb back to our western course. The ship's pulse felt heavy. I wanted to take us high enough to skim the top of the large cloud system up ahead — we could use its buoyancy to take some of our weight, resting our sails as much as we could without stopping. Below us I could see the tradeship sailing low towards forests in the south. It was said that merchants built docks into trees to carry their goods down. The Grounders only tolerated them so they could buy our stones.

As we climbed, Adia was staring into the hen's cage and the hen was staring back with beady black eyes.

"Eggs?" She said, uncertainty in her voice.

"We either boil or fry them. Fresh," I added. "I'm not picketing them, or whatever he said it was."

"But we don't eat the hen."

"Of course not."

Adia sighed. "You eat meat from the ground. Why is it any different?"

"It just is," I said. "It has wings. It's like... it's one of us."

Beneath my hand the ship's heartbeat started to race. I glanced behind, recalling that another ship in the east had been heading this way. Why would the merchant move on if more customers were coming? I raised my hand to block the glare of the sun and looked again. The ship was much closer now, close enough to make out its figurehead. It was unmistakable — the gleam of a bronze bull.

"Adia!" I called out. She turned to look. The bullship was moving fast, its sails still relatively bright. They weren't changing course to follow the tradeship. There was no doubt. The Taurans were coming for us.

"Topsail, now!" I shouted, retaking the wheel. I looked across the skies, praying for some sight of another Aurigan ship, anything that would make them think twice about their pursuit. There was nothing. The topsail went up but it made little difference, giving us more altitude but no speed. The bullship was big, triple-sailed, and gaining ground too quickly. As I turned to look again I heard the dreaded sound of guns being run out.

I spun the wheel furiously, turning to port with such violence that I almost skidded over. The hen in its cage was squawking and flapping. The bullship was looming now, and as I heard the first boom of their cannons I wondered how long they had been following us; if the merchant had set us up; if there was anything left to do but die.

"We can't outrun it!" Adia cried out. I looked up at our sails. Auriga's light had all but faded. A cannonball whistled past and dipped over our starboard side, falling away to the ground.

"They won't waste too many of those on us," I said, pulling hard to starboard again and pointing us west. We had almost reached the mass of cloud — if we could just skim its surface, pick up some speed, get out of their range...

"It's not our fight, it's not our fight!" Adia shouted into the sky, and I wanted to shout too, as if we could give the Taurans what they wanted; as if we could take Elnath from our pockets, place it in their palms and swear never to lay claim to it again...

As we cut into the cloud I heard the throaty boom of cannon fire again, and this time it was answered by a rending in our hull, ripping a hole through our stern, sending us into a sharp dive. The blast knocked me forward onto the wheel and I felt my knee give way. Adia screamed and fell and I heard the ship let out a long moan as its wooden skeleton was wrenched by the blast. The cloud enveloped us, and I could feel it rush into the lower decks of the ship, filling them and stopping our freefall.

Our sails went dead. The cloud was so thick I could barely see my hand in front of me. The only sound was the gentle creaking of our hull. I crouched down onto the deck, where the cloud was thinner, and I could just see the outline of Adia's back. I crawled over to her. She was holding her head in her hands, blood trickling from a wound just above her left eye. I held my finger to my lips and she nodded. It was not the first time we'd used cloudfall to fool an enemy. I could feel my blood pumping through my veins as the shadow of a great hull passed over us, and held my breath. From somewhere above a voice boomed out.

"In the holy name of Taurus, renounce your claim to Elnath and we shall let you live!" The laughter of the ship's crew told me their captain was lying. They would not look for us for long, though; in cloudfall they risked ramming us and dooming both our ships. Perhaps they would follow the tradeship after all. They said that Taurans were pirates as well as murderers.

The shadow moved on, and as I looked at Adia, we broke the silence with nervous laughter, the joy of the newly reprieved.

"I love you," I said, "and I'm so sorry."

We lay in bed together. It was such a rare thing. The cloud still filled much of the ship and we let it carry us along wherever it was heading, waiting for the stern to begin to heal, waiting for dusk.

The mist covered the floor of our bedroom and in the glow of the lightjar it seemed otherworldly, as if there were nothing beyond our limbo of endless white, nothing but the two of us in the whole of the skies. I felt Adia's hand move over my back, tracing the lines of the lashes I had taken for sparing that grey bird, lines that had not faded in fourteen years.

"I remember the first time I saw you," she said. "You were working on the ship-fitting crew. I knew that Sam and I were being given that ship for our family, and I used to sneak out from the weaving cabins of the bridalship, and go up to the deck to spy on what you were doing. You were fitting the ship so close by, and I thought — it's strange, all those people working for my wedding present, all so that Sam and I can raise a family. Why was I the one chosen for this? What if I don't like Sam once I get to know him? What if I can't bear children — will they take the ship back? All these stupid thoughts running through my mind, and there you were, sanding down the deck of my new ship where the wood had healed over, and I wondered who you were, and why you looked so sad."

I turned over and kissed her hand. "I knew, from the moment they gave me the job, that I was going to take that ship. I had to get away. I just..." I hesitated. It felt foolish to say such things out loud. "If you hadn't come with me, I would be lost. So lost."

"We are lost," she said with a smile, and she ran her

fingers through my hair. "And I wouldn't want to be anywhere else."

The cloudfall turned to rain around dusk, and we climbed up and out into clear skies. There was no sign of other Lighters for miles around, only a stunning landscape of pink and red streaks left by the setting sun across the dark blue Heavens. The charts claimed we were somewhere over west Europa; the Charioteer, shining in the northwest, would swing low across the northern horizon as the night went on before ascending slightly in the northeast sky before dawn.

We anchored within sight of pale mountains that rose majestically up to us as if the ground itself wanted to be closer to the stars. Up on deck I soaked strips of linen in water mixed with limbit oil and, leaning over the side of the ship, smoothed them over the delicate patchwork of new wood that was growing across the stern.

The cannonball had only clipped us and the damage was less than I had feared, nothing that wouldn't heal with time and care. The ship's pulse occasionally skipped and trembled, and looking down at the ground I felt uneasy too. I could sense the weight of the anchor that held us steady, resting on the rocks below, holding us back. Children on the workship told stories about tribes of Grounders swarming over a ship's anchor, pulling it down to its death. They made up ghoulish tales about what Grounders did to the Lighters on the ships they caught. Only foolish stories.

I wanted to get back above the clouds.

When I was done I sat to watch Auriga move across the northern sky. Polaris was there, as always, a lynchpin around which all else seemed to turn, and our sails were filling up with light. The Pale Man was waning in the southeast. Wisps of cloud still clung to the surface of the deck and the night was damp and cold. My knee was still in pain as I wrapped myself in an old blanket, one Adia had woven years before. She had made all my clothes — every stitch of me had passed through her hands — and I could still recall the night we stood on deck and burnt my grey workship rags with childlike joy, believing it would somehow ward off old ghosts. She was probably down in her workshop now, spinning and weaving the new cotton.

It was in that room that I first met her. For seven years she trained as a weaver on the bridalship before being chosen for marriage. Six of us grafted for weeks to make the loom and jenny that she would use to make clothes for her new family; long days and nights spent in the cramped dark of our workship as we toiled, knowing that she and her kind were fed and warm and pampered. I used to think her memories of the fleet must be so different to mine — no fighting for crumbs of food or respect, nobody treating her like a coil in a machine. I took years to learn just how wrong I was.

It was by chance that a shipfitter fell ill and I was sent to help the crew making repairs to her new ship. Adia was brought on board one night by her aunt, who seemed to disapprove of her seeing the ship before her wedding day. We were told to line up silently on deck and keep our heads bowed as she came aboard, unworthy as we were of being near someone chosen for better things. I watched the hem of her long white dress as she passed by, her aunt following close behind and cursing nonexistent specks of dirt.

The next night they returned unexpectedly. Adia sent her aunt to view the galley and caught me alone in the workshop. As soon as I saw her I knew why she had been chosen. She was beautiful — pale green eyes and hair as dark as midnight. She radiated an innocence and grace that disarmed everyone she met. But behind her outward appearances of piety, there was a much deeper soul within, one that was troubled and uneasy with her fate. She confessed to me that she felt sold, cheaply bargained for by others. I was alarmed by her openness, not knowing she had watched me from her perch on the bridalship, that she had recognised a lonely kindred spirit.

We spoke again many times, whenever she could sneak away and I could pretend I had this job to do, or that job to do. The night before her wedding I went to stock the workshop with the last of the silk gifted by the Aurigan elders and she met me there. I told her that I was stealing away, more out of kindness than expectation — I was taking her wedding gifts after all. To my amazement she kissed me, and swore that she would tell the elders if I did not take her with me.

A week later we were so tangled up in each other, we almost drifted across the equator.

As the first rays of dawn began to colour the sky, Adia emerged on deck and sat beside me. The scent of limbit oil was still on my hands. We watched together as the eastern clouds turned pink and cast their light onto the mountains.

"How is the hull?" she asked after a long silence.

"Healing well. We should be able to sail soon."

"Damn the Taurans to the Scorpian," Adia muttered, "and damn their ship too." I was sure she didn't really mean it.

"Do you remember the night we left?" I asked. "I promised you we'd never go hungry, and we'd never have to fight other people's wars. So many things..." I turned to look at her. "You made me feel invincible that night. I promised you we'd be free of them, and we will be. Starting from now."

She slipped her arm around me and I wrapped the blanket over us both. In my mind I plotted a course southwest to where some friendly twinships might be in summertime. The morning air brightened everything it touched, illuminating the snowcaps and rivers and valleys of yellow flowers. We could sail low and keep out of sight, leaving the Aurigan and Tauran fleets far behind us, this time for good.

I was about to kiss her when I heard a scratching noise from the cabin. We turned to see the hen wandering out onto the deck, puffing up its feathers, squawking into the lightening sky.

"I've decided I like it," Adia said with a laugh. "It's strangely loveable."

I looked up at our sails. They were brimming with light, waiting to pull us away.

It had been a long time since we had sailed so low in the summer. I had forgotten how warm the air could be. Our sails had filled with light all night long and were taking us south at good speed through the morning. I felt the way I had done all those years ago, the day I first took the wheel in my hands and steered us from our past.

Adia stood at the stern, keeping an eye on the bindings that covered the healing wood, making sure we weren't pushing the ship too hard too soon. She was wearing a blue dress, one the colour of an afternoon sky; she seemed truly happy for the first time in a long while. I unfastened the top button of my shirt and the air flowed in like warm water around my chest, rushing over my skin, pouring out through the cuffs of my sleeves. Below us was a beautiful blanket of dark forest, interspersed with little clearings of pale green. For such a savage place, the ground had its own strange beauty, though nothing to match the majesty of the Heavens.

Near midday we passed beneath a heavy bank of cloud that blocked out the sun, leaving a chill breeze to run across the deck. I gripped the wheel tightly. Something was wrong. Behind us, the white clouds above were marked with a smudge of grey. It grew darker and darker until the bow of a ship broke through, the same bronze bull bearing down on us, picking up speed, sails every bit as bright as our own.

"No!" I shouted. It wasn't possible, it wasn't real. We'd come too far for this to happen. They had the advantage of speed and height and as the clouds broke above us, there was nowhere left to hide. I was so stupid, so rash to take us south, knowing they were near...

I listened for the sound of guns but there was nothing. As Adia followed my gaze to see the ship I looked at her, her blue dress dancing in the wake of the sails. I'd always known I'd fail her in the end. She turned back to me, tears in her eyes.

"They're hoisting up boarding ropes!" she shouted across the deck, her voice almost lost in the winds. She was right. The bullship was running on our port side — soon they would be alongside us.

Boarded by Taurans. I couldn't even contemplate it — we were better off dead. I did the only thing I could. I pulled hard on the sailarm, spun to starboard and as the mainsail sagged we plunged towards the earth, down and down, closer to the trees, closer to the unknown. I would crash us into the very ground before becoming their prize.

Adia skidded up beside me, facing the stern, watching the bullship follow our descent. Her face was etched with fear. I didn't need to ask if they were still gaining.

"Adia, do you trust me?" I whispered, looking up to the endless expanse of blue above, wondering what was truly there behind the daylight.

"I trust you."

I closed my eyes. "Mighty Polaris, we pray for you to guide us now..."

The ship lurched suddenly, wind catching the mainsail and levelling us off with such speed that I felt the jarring shock right up through my knee. I heard Adia's sharp intake of breath, felt my hand move the wheel, and finally I opened my eyes. We were so close to the ground now that I could see birds flying up from the tops of trees, smoke rising from a nearby clearing. From behind I heard cannons run out at last — at least death was better than capture — and then another sound, a *thud*, but louder than any I had ever heard before, louder than cannonfire, louder than any arrow I had heard as a child as I sat in the darkness. There were shouts from the ship behind, and then another *thud*, louder still, but it too was behind us, behind and below.

"The Scorpian himself," Adia gasped, her voice trembling, and she turned her head to the skies, tears running down her cheeks. I threw the wheel again and veered starboard, our sails at full pelt. The damaged stern was groaning and we could not climb back up. Adia was praying under her breath. I realised the sound of the other ship had ceased. I turned around.

In our wake, the bullship had stopped strangely in mid flight, as if they had dropped anchor. The crew on deck were running to and fro helplessly. As we pulled further away I could see two great arrows, each the size of a cannon, stuck in its belly; from each arrow a long rope trailed down to a clearing in the forest.

The Taurans quickly lowered a man over the side, armed with a sword to hack themselves free, but a volley of small arrows from below riddled his body, leaving him swinging to and fro like a puppet. As we finally started a slow climb the bullship began to fall to the clearing below, where two sickening contraptions of giant metal wheels within wheels were turning, pulling the ropes down, pulling the ship down, splitting it apart, the crack of its failing body echoing through the sky, the screams of its crew lost in the air. As the clearing passed out of sight, I caught a glimpse of Grounders swarming over the wreckage, picking it clean.

Adia sobbed into my chest and we collapsed to the deck, and as I wrapped my arms around her she shook, shook and shook.

Months later, in uncharted southern skies, we worshipped all the Heavens and let fate set our course. Land was rare and we could sail for weeks over vast oceans, lost in blue above and below. The water would sometimes rage, great waves reaching up like mountains; sometimes it would sit as still as glass. I would stand on deck to watch it for hours. They say we came from the sea once.

When over land we saw small fleets flocking together, ships bearing crosses and horned horses as figureheads. Some day we might sail with them awhile. For now we were content to drift alone.

One night, as we skimmed low over a wide lake, hauling up fresh water, we caught a silvery bird in our bucket. It had slippery skin instead of feathers and small wings that flapped in water as if in the air.

We threw it back over the side and watched it fly away, into the deep.

Thank you so much for spending your time reading this anthology. If you liked what you read would you please leave a short review on Amazon? Just a few lines would be great. Reviews are not only the highest compliment you can pay to authors, they also help other readers discover and make more informed choices about purchasing books in a crowded space. Thank you!

If you would like to find out more about the authors featured in this book, you can find them all together on the dedicated facebook page: The World and the Stars

Printed in Great Britain
by Amazon.co.uk, Ltd.,
Marston Gate.